DREAMS

Lucinda Hare

Book Five of the Dragonsdome Chronicles

lucinda@dragonsdome.co.uk

http://www.dragonsdome.co.uk/

http://thedragonwhispererdiaries.blogspot.co.uk/

Published by Thistleburr Publishing

www.thirstleburr.co.uk

Dark Dragon Dreams
Thistleburr Publishing, ISBN: 978-0-9574718-7-0

The Dragonsdome Chronicles

The Dragon Whisperer
Flight to Dragon Isle
Dragon Lords Rising
The Stealth Dragon Services

* * *

The Fifth Dimension

The Sorcerers Glen

* * *

Catastrophe ~ A Scottish Wildcat's Tail
*
Haggis ~ A Blind Cat's Tail
*
Falling for Autumn: Child & Adult Colouring Book
Seadragon Songs of the Sea: Child & Adult Colouring Book

Praise for *The Dragonsdome Chronicles*

My 15 year old son picked up the first book in this series and was hooked over a year ago. He got me to read it and I was hooked too. *Amazon review*

I hold my hands up. I am a 62 year old woman who loves dragons. I have just finished all 4 books in this series in less than a week. What a ride I was taken on. This is not a children's book. It is quite frankly a superb fantasy adventure for all ages and the film rights need to be snapped up. All I can say is 'Thank you, Lucinda'. You have made an old woman feel young again even if just in my imagination. *Amazon review*

I'm not sure whether I'll be able to convey with words what I felt reading The Dragon Whisperer and Flight To Dragon Isle. The books were so irresistibly wonderful that I've read them back to back one after the other in a couple of days. I felt like I was ten again and that the universe was just a big adventure waiting to be discovered. *Caroline, from Goodreads*

I think The Dragon Whisperer is the best book I have ever read. (I have read a lot of books – in our house we have about twelve thousand) I think the way the words are written sounds like magic. *Rachel, aged 14*

'One of the most captivating new books to be published for 8+ for some time . . . It made me laugh, cry and remember exactly what's so special about the time when you or your child live in hope of finding a dragon of your own.'

Amanda Craig The Sunday Times

I am the voice of the voiceless;
Through me the dumb shall speak;
Till the deaf world's ear be made to hear
The cry of the wordless weak.
From street, from cage, and from kennel,
From jungle and stall, the wail
Of my tortured kin proclaims the sin
Of the mighty against the frail.
The same Force formed the sparrow
That fashioned man, the king;
The God of the Whole gave a spark of soul
To furred and to feathered thing.
And I am my brother's keeper,
And I will fight his fight,
And speak the word for beast and bird,
Till the world shall set things right.

By Ella Wheeler Wilcox

Main Characters

People
The King ~ the Earl Rufus DeWinter
The Queen ~ Caitlin
Dragon Whisperer ~ Quenelda

Major Cawdor ~ Warden of the Wall

The WarLock King ~ Hugo Mandrake
The Black Prince ~ Darcy

Dragon Master & BoneCracker Commando ~ Tangnost BearHugger

Ice Bear BoneCaster ~ Drumondir

The Queen's Constable ~ Sir Gharad Mowbray
Imperial Navigator & Scout ~ Root

Lady-in-Waiting ~ Armelia
Imperial Pilot ~ Bracus
Guild Mistress ~ Lady Mountjoy, Winifred Needlespin
Knight & Esquire to the King ~ Quester

Dragons
Two Gulps Too Many ~ Quenelda's sabretooth battle-dragon
Chasing the Stars ~ Armelia's & Root's gentle dragon
Stormcracker Thundercloud III ~ the King's Imperial battledragon

Artwork by Phoenix Wilson from Yorkshire

CHAPTER ONE
The Dragon Whisperer

The common people were openly calling the King's daughter a Dragon Whisperer. Crowds followed Quenelda around the Black Isle wherever she went, throwing thistles at her feet, amazed by the black scales which clothed her like a second skin save for hands and head, reaching out to touch a legend come to life. Some of the braver children even offered gifts to Two Gulps barrelling along behind her; worn out shoes, run over pigeons, burnt oat bannocks, rusty cauldrons; pretty much anything they themselves couldn't eat or make use of.

Now the Seven Kingdoms had a Dragon Whisperer they were going to win the war. Their Dragon Whisperer would defeat the WarLock King. She would capture the hated Black Prince. She could talk to all dragons, who did her bidding. She could do anything.

On Dragon Isle, soldiers saluted her because she had taken part, along with Bracus, Root and her sabretooth, Two Gulps, in Operation Brimstone to free Root's enslaved people and recapture the vital mines from the WarLock King. The SDS's first counter strike had brought hope to so many, and meant Quenelda was now the first girl in living memory to be a Dragon Lord, just as Root was the first gnome to be a Dragon Lord, serving as a navigator on Imperial Blacks. But Root had noted, as Quenelda strode around Dragon Isle and the Court in worn boots and leggings, not many called her Princess. They wouldn't dare. If his friend was becoming a young woman, no one could honestly say she was becoming a young lady, despite their friend Armelia's efforts!

The young Dragon Whisperer in question, from whom everyone expected so much, entered the HeartRock at dawn, drawn to its pure beckoning song that was now as familiar as breathing, looking for answers. Her world, the familiar world of Dragonsdome and the Sorcerers Glen, had changed forever when the ancient hegemony of the SDS had been shattered by treachery. The betrayal that had begun with the battle of the Westering Isles, where an entire generation had been annihilated by forbidden maelstrom sorcery, had created a world far deadlier than any known since the forming of the First Alliance with the dragons.

So now everyone expected so much from their young Dragon Whisperer, yet Quenelda was still unsure of herself. Her memories and knowledge were not those of a young woman with barely fifteen winters; her powers as yet unknown, and untested. Childhood ineptitude with magic of any kind had led to bullying by other young nobles' daughters and her half-brother Darcy. That memory, like her unsure grasp of magic, had lingered. And everything was changing too fast. Sometimes Quenelda just wanted to be like Root and Armelia, and not be trapped by a legend and others' expectations.

Crossing the narrow span that linked the HeartRock to Dragon Isle, past the elite dragon-helmed guards who had guarded it night and day for centuries beyond count, the young Dragon Whisperer paused at the rock carvings that girdled this ancient sanctuary, tracing its story with her hands. Son of the Morning Star, the first Dragon Whisperer, had been raised by dragons, weaned by an

Imperial, more dragon than prince. She was raised in the mortal world of men, more princess than dragon. Both born with the same gift, for the same purpose, but could she live up to her promise?

Tangnost, legendary dwarf Dragon Master, and almost a second father to her when the Earl Rufus DeWinter, the SDS Commander, had been fighting, had taught her all he knew of dragons, their well-being and training, and she was swiftly learning what it took to lead and command others. Drumondir, the Ice Bear BoneCaster was teaching her patience, and training her how to understand and use her burgeoning gifts wisely. But it was to the HeartRock she now came in the hope of learning what it was to be a Dragon Whisperer, to understand what her purpose ultimately was. For she lived in a world at war, and the maelstrom was rising.

Quenelda sat on the huge DragonBone Throne which towered about her. As before, the golden bones warmed to her touch and she opened her mind to the HeartRock and the slumbering Matriarch curled deep within the One Earth. A change in temperature told her she was no longer on Dragon Isle, was no longer in her body. Instead she looked down on the One Earth itself from an unimaginable height. Frost crackled on her body, turning black armour to white. The silence was immense as solar winds buffeted her armour, raising beautiful colours that danced in the sky. She spun joyfully outwards into the dark blue dome scattered with stars and unearthly nebulas, revelling in the unfettered freedom of flight before finally turning homewards towards the One Earth, a blue and white orb hanging in the midnight dome of space.

The Seven Sea Kingdoms laid out far below were a white winter-scape bound by an unnatural winter, reluctant to lose its grip; the sea frozen as far south as the Sorcerers Glen. The Old Wall was barely visible, buried beneath endless blizzards. It was such a beautiful world, but something was wrong, she could sense it through the bones of the mountains, the song of the sea, the whisper of the trees; at the heart of the Seven Kingdoms something dark hid itself, and like a creeping cancer it was spreading, masked by a cold malevolent mind. The SDS had yet to learn when and where Hugo Mandrake, the WarLock King would next strike, but strike he would. Folding her wings, Quenelda dropped, blinking her nictitating membranes that protected smouldering sulphurous eyes from the killing cold of space.

Down, down, so swiftly down to the Old Wall, she followed its snaking course from the Cairngorm Mountains in the east ever westward past scores of watch-towers and forts built on limestone crags, to where a great new fortress stood, home to her father's IX ThunderStorm Stealth Battlegroup: home to eight thousand dragons, fifteen thousand troops and as many pilots and navigators; and all those cooks, chandlers and smiths, bakers and brewers who serviced them. With vast Imperial roosts embedded in the cliffs, this great fortress would be a stepping stone towards attacking Roarkinch, the WarLock's fortress island far to the frozen north.

Frost dragon patrols pushed north from the Wall beneath her as she flew unseen towards the Howling Glen, where Imperials of the XIII StormBreaker Regiment were warming up on the dragon pads, taking advantage of the rare break in the weather to exercise their mighty Imperial Black stealth battledragons, and hunt for food. Smoke billowed from forges and thousands of fires as troops and dragons were engaged in winter training ground exercises in the glen, in their white armour. Gliding west, she soared over the liberated Brimstone Mountains to where the Highland dwarf clans, under the watchful eye of Malachite of the Red Squirrel Clan, were readying to ship stockpiles of brimstone from the Hidden Cove harbour aboard great sledges, each pulled by a team of sixteen harnessed frost dragons. Guild merchant galleons trapped fast in the ice would be of no use for moons.

Banking with powerful strokes of her immense wings, the dragon that was Quenelda swept eastwards and northwards over the endless ice shelf, but even her keen reptilian eyes failed to spot the Snow fortress, home to the fledgling XV Blizzard Regiment. Perfectly camouflaged, along with thousands of frost roosts, it was carved deep down into the ice. Only frost dragon and ice bear patrols betrayed the SDS presence out here in the endless frozen wastes.

The Dragon Lords were rising again, but so was the dark power of the maelstrom, an ancient predatory power; a deadly foe, once vanquished, now returned. Suddenly the regal isolation of the Matriarch was too much, the scale of the threats impossible, and Quenelda reached out to those she loved, those who meant the world to her.

She found Tangnost hard at work on the frozen Inner

Sea, training Imperial crews, BoneCrackers, Marines and scouts for cold weather combat insertion and extraction, and airborne support for Marines and Commandos on the ice. Men and dragons were suffering in the cold that froze unguarded skin to metal. Tangnost taught them how to stop their swords freezing in their scabbards, how to dig snow holes to survive a blizzard, how to use their dragons to melt snow and cook hot food. But how had Quenelda not noticed the Dragon Master was growing so old? Silvered hair was turning white in places, and his wounded leg pained him. She felt a protective surge of love towards the gruff, one-eyed dwarf who had guarded her from the moment of her birth. She tried to reach out to him, but her thoughts were a cold wind that brushed his face, a sigh he barely heard.

Swiftly she discovered Root in the Royal stables at Crannock Castle with Armelia...grooming Chasing the Stars, polishing her scales and spoiling her with honey tablets, their faces animated with their shared love for the mare. The Queen's lady-in-waiting was dressed in figure-hugging magenta flying leathers sporting two sparkly wand sheaths and a blue helmet with pink fluffy pompoms! Outside on the cobbles, slowly being covered by powdered snow, Quenelda's fledgling sabretooth dragon, Two Gulps, was snoring loudly, four legs in the air, hot breath raising a billowing fog. From the size of his stomach and the few cracked bones and bits of horn stuck in his teeth, it looked like he had eaten an entire cow!

Searching the Black Isle, Quenelda next found her mother, the Queen, accompanied by her elderly Constable, Sir Gharad Mowbray, adoptive father to Root. They were visiting Grand Master Rumspell of the Sorcerers Guild, discussing the repair of the City's crumbling defences and the recruitment and training of the new City Watch and Guild Guard, giving work to the thousands of refugees who now clogged the City's streets begging for food and shelter.

Leaving the Black Isle, Quenelda turned towards Dragon Isle to the west of the sea loch, searching for those she loved who served in the SDS; to where her friend Quester lay tossing and turning in his bunk trying to hide his fear; afraid of the dreams of murder, mayhem, and battlemagic that stole his sleep. Afraid of the memories that still thronged his waking hours.

Down in the Situation Room deep beneath the Battle Academy of Dragon Isle, her father the King and his Strike Commanders were planning the war against the WarLock King. Already they were drawing up plans for Operation White Out, the greatest battle games ever held: a live-fire exercise where regiments were pitched against each other, drawing everything they had learnt together before the coming campaign season after the thaw. But for the first time since the Mage Wars, they would be fighting their own kith and kin who had sworn fealty to the WarLock King and the Abyss, setting son against father, family against family.

In the great halls of the Academy above, the Guardian, Magnus Fitzgerald, his elite Faculty Guard, Deans and Professors were debating tactics and strategy, how to apply their research to aerial and winter warfare, devising new weaponry, already testing their new battle spheres for Command and Control (CAC).

Drumondir, the Ice Bear BoneCaster who had returned with Quenelda from the north, was exploring the ruins of Dragonsdome, searching the Keep and its Library for texts about the Mage Wars and Maelstrom magic, about the Elders and the first SeaDragon Lords. She looked up and smiled, as if sensing her pupil's presence.

And then the visions faded and Quenelda was back in the HeartRock seated upon the DragonBone Throne, but still her open eyes did not see the four stone Companions arrayed about her, or the constellations of stars flickering in the darkness. Instead the tawny eyes of Quenelda DeWinter looked back through time; learning, discovering, questing, remembering all that a Dragon Whisperer was. Touching the lives of her royal ancestors, great and small: the kings and queens, battlemages and warriors she had once been over ten thousand lifetimes. Absorbing the fading memories of all those who had gone before; memories now fading into antiquity. Closing her eyes, Quenelda listened to their voices and their stories.

CHAPTER TWO
The Hammer Blow Will Fall

The Night Hall of the Dark Citadel was packed, loud and hot, despite the killing cold outside. Four fires and countless branches of candles made it feel like a brooding midsummer storm about to break, and not midwinter. The WarLock King's table was laden. Darcy wondered at the wine and fruits from the far south that accompanied the game and fish. As fine a table as Dragonsdome or the Palace had ever hosted: none would go hungry this midwinter. Grain had been stolen from byre and barn. Oats the north had a-plenty. The troops, well, soup, porridge, roast walrus, turnips, black rye-bread and oat beer were their lot.

But those Lords and high-ranking guildsman who had taken a gamble bringing their families and their future to Roarkinch, this isolated frozen island so far to the north of their comfortable homes and estates, had to be reassured they had taken the correct choice. Not that any would dare cross the WarLock King should they be having second thoughts. Much of the tapestries and gold, dragons and food captured by Darcy's Knights of Chaos were given by his father as a reward for loyalty, with more promised.

The WarLock stood, goblet in hand, torches turning the shards of his black crown to gold. 'Our Kingdom thrives! Soon there will be rich rewards of lands and lordships to the south for those who fight well.' That raised a cheer from the younger landless knights. 'The Abyss is rising, and the SDS will fall!'

'The Abyss is rising!' They drained their goblets, and did not see their peril.

CHAPTER THREE
We Take the War to Him

Change was in the air, along with rumours. The Situation Room deep within Dragon Isle was packed. The Guardian was a late arrival, joining his Deans of Faculty with a half dozen of his best scholars. On the other side of the large stone table inset with battle runes, Strike Commanders from all seven regiments mingled with senior officers from the King's own ThunderStorm Strategic Command and the newly promoted Warden of the Old Wall, Major Cawdor. The intense buzz of speculation fell silent as the guards outside grounded their spears and opened the doors to admit the King, attended by Quester and followed by his daughter and Tangnost. The Princess Quenelda was scaled in black like a second skin, with graceful wings that swept down to the ground

The King didn't waste any time. With a word, a three-dimensional image of the WarLock's island fortress arose from the table, contours outlined in ice blue.

'This year we are not holding the time honoured Dragathon: pitching regiment against regiment in an endurance race. This year our military are going to execute a simulated attack on Roarkinch, the WarLock's heartland. We will launch a coordinated land, sea and air attack on an island fortress on a scale never imagined in a live-fire exercise. Then,' he grinned wolfishly, 'we are going to take the war to Hugo!'

Clenched fists drummed armour and table, and a muted growl of approval greeted that news.

'This is Roarkinch, a supposedly deserted volcanic island in the frozen north-west, masked by the power of the Abyss. Only my daughter could see it for what it truly is. We have also based our information upon a young navigator's journals, the same young man who navigated Stormcracker into the unknown north to find me. Oakley reported a permanent ice shelf to the west, north and east here, but to the south the ice was broken by magma flowing from the volcano. The sea here is thick with icebergs. This warmer water carries them southwards during the thaw all the way down to the Isle of Midges.' He turned to his daughter. 'Goose?'

Quenelda stepped forwards, trying to quash her jangling nerves, throwing a nervous smile at her friend Guy, Jakart DeBessart's young son, and her imperial pilot. Her first battle council! She had dreamt of this moment for as long as she could remember. Soon she would be fighting at her father's side. She did not want to fail him, or her family and friends. But could she live up to their high expectations? The King's daughter took a deep breath, and drew on her nascent skills and borrowed knowledge.

A few barely perceptible hand gestures and suddenly the island before the gathering began to take form and shape. Sheer black volcanic cliffs rose up to a frozen land of hot springs and geysers, a harsh world with a smoking volcano to the south and a towering black citadel to the north. 'I don't remember the details,' she apologised. 'The power his camouflage matrix radiated was immense: it made me feel sick. The sea below was alive with hobgoblins and razorbacks. The island is crowded with

troops and dragons. Within, there a
coombs beyond count. And there was
Abyss. I could not penetrate the cloak cast a

Her sombre words led to a short silence as
military minds in the Stealth Dragon Services, the
considered the enormity of their task and its implication

'What is the scale of the island?' Jakart De Bessart, Strike Commander of the III FirstBorn, asked.

Quenelda frowned. 'It's difficult to say. We flew down its eastern flank in heavy snow, and Storm was tired. At least the length of the Sorcerers Glen. And the cliffs of the Citadel were high, higher than Dragon Isle. It disappeared into the clouds.'

'How can he shroud an entire island?' Guy had not heard this part of his friend's tale. 'How is it even possible?'

'If the scale is true, it's vast,' the Guardian judged. 'And so are his armies.'

'This great citadel, how could he have built it so far north and survive?' one of his Deans of Faculty asked. 'You say it is dark half the year, and blizzards across the arctic waste never relent?'

'Dark sorcery,' the King said flatly. 'He draws on power beyond imagining. His Citadel is built, knit and guarded by the subterfuge of the Abyss. We are fighting blind. We must find some texts from the Mage Wars, so we know what we face. We cannot be caught as we were on the Westering Isles with no means of defence.'

'Records such as we have found suggest the Maelstrom drives those who wield it to madness,' the Guardian mused. 'Perhaps it will affect his judgment. He

…arch for that flaw.'

…me such dark power?' an …gan, asked. 'How can we …s?'

…ting this and more at this …aised calm blue eyes. 'They …Conjuring Halls since Mid-…

A Dean of … ded. 'We have designed the battlespheres already being tested here on Dragon Isle, and by Your Grace's Thunderstorm Battlegroup CAC. Working with the Pyromancers Guild, we have developed a dragon-fire mine that will explode on contact underwater. If it works, if we can devise a way to safely transport them on special ships, it will eliminate the WarLock's vaunted hobgoblin banners.'

The Guardian nodded. 'Developing battlemagic and weapons for our assault on Roarkinch is the Battle Academy's sole research task.'

'Indeed,' agreed the King. 'And ours is to devise a strategy and perfect our tactics over the next three or four moons to take an island fortress. We must train men and dragons both to fight in extreme cold. Every soldier and dragon is undertaking winter survival training as we speak.

'The III FirstBorn and the XX ShadowWraiths will defend Dragon Isle,' he glanced at the Guardian and Jakart.

'Agreed? The IX WinterKnights and the XVIII SeaReavers supported by the newly formed XV will attack. My IX Airborne Battlegroup will be held in reserve, to judge where they are most needed, where we fall short of our objectives.'

'From now until the corn planting moons,' the Guardian's gaze marked his officers out. 'Dragon Isle will practise counter air, ground and sea defence, using airborne early warning and control.'

'And Strategic Air Command will test your theoretical attack strategies and joint battlefield airspace control in the field,' the King finished. 'Using our new battle-spheres.' He nodded, satisfied.

'So, it is agreed then?' The King looked around the Inner Council with unseeing eyes, his heightened dragon senses since his bonding with Stormcracker telling him effortlessly where each officer sat or stood, and how they responded to his words. 'We take the fight to Hugo on his island holdfast?'

Heads nodded about the table.

'Brief your senior officers only. Everyone must think we are still training for the Dragathon, that we fight in the snow because we must, and not because it's a key component of our strategy. There are most certainly spies within the glen and Black Isle.

'I want us ready in time for the spring thaw to sail and march north to attack Roarkinch with a pre-emptive strike! On Wings of Vengeance,' he saluted.

'On Wings of Vengeance!'

CHAPTER FOUR
Infested

Knuckle, the WarLock's one-time Dragon Master scratched irritably. Despite the bitter cold, the prison inmates were infested with lice and fleas, and even worse, some scale mites, clinging on to those barely clinging on to life. The rats had long since been eaten and cockroaches were not to everyone's taste. He looked up at the barred window. Who would have thought such old prisons were built into the cliffs? The only way out was down, a long, long way down to the frozen loch and certain death. At least he wasn't in those dark hell holes below the water.

A flickering light drew near, and the sound of voices. The clink of metal and the key turned in an outer lock. Feeding time.... Turnip gruel and oatcakes, then they would be shackled and out to work on the city defences. He could watch the SDS all day long on their wretched dragons, constantly out on exercise, honing their air-to-air combat skills. Training to defeat his master in battle. But the WarLock King would be coming for them and their precious dragons long before they were ready.

A guard placed a cauldron down, still hot for once. The new turnkey shoved filled wooden bowls through the bars. Knuckle waited in line.

'Sssst.... ssst...' A hand beckoned him. The hooded turnkey knuckled his forehead. 'Boss,' he whispered.

'Gaffer!'

'We've gathered in the Down in One...all the lads we could find who escaped.'

'How many?'

'Sixteen, but we can buy more. Many is looking for work, no questions asked. We'll join the Watch, boss. Free you soon, as soon as chance allows.'

CHAPTER FIVE
Ummm....

'You're organising a what?' Quenelda scowled

'We thought it would be a fun way to show the....err...the more err, exclusive,' Armelia ploughed on gamely, 'and *expensive* end of my ranges......and it's to raise funds to equip and train the new Guild Guard and City Watch. Five thousand gold dragons a table.'

'What?!'

'Your mother is to be patron to both causes. Say you'll come! Quenelda? Pleeease,' Armelia wheedled. 'It'll be fun.'

Remembering her last visit to Foresight & Hindsight's Exclusive Emporium, Quenelda was not at all convinced it would be fun, but she owed Armelia her friendship. And she knew how her mother very much wanted to become involved in protecting her Kingdoms like her daughter and husband. 'Yes,' she said with a resigned sigh. 'I'll come, but I'm not putting any of your...creations on.'

'Oh,' Armelia wilted. She had been saving that request for later. 'I know you won't wear pink...or sequins, but I have two new ranges. Inspired by *you*. I was going to call one the Dragon Whisperer range. And...and I think you would like the t...' she trailed off seeing Quenelda's face. 'Would you at least look...and I was...'

Quenelda sighed after a long pause. 'You were?' she waved a hand in front of Armelia's glakit expression.

'Talking to Tangnost...you know when I first learnt to fly, no one at Court knew dragons...understood them.

They still think that dragons are 'just animals', the way I did,' she admitted. 'Just to be used....and I thought, well, this might change opinions.'

'What would?' Quenelda was interested despite herself.

Armelia told her friend.

Quenelda looked at her with grudging admiration. Armelia was becoming most adventurous. It would most certainly change opinions. It might even cause a stampede!

'Err...' Armelia began hopefully. 'Um, does this mean you'll agree?'

Quenelda's eyes narrowed suspiciously. 'Have you even talked to F&H about...?'

'Ummm...' Armelia's nose wrinkled. 'Not in so many words. Not in detail as such. I thought if you agreed, they were more likely to say yes.'

Quenelda doubted it, but the prospect of Samantha Spellgood's horrified face would be worth it.

'Yes,' she said cheerfully. 'I'll do it.'

CHAPTER SIX
The Black Prince

The thick dirty smoke was choking, hugging the frozen ground as Simon DeMontfort ran up his Imperial's wing, away from the cloying smell of death and into clean salt laden air blowing in from the sea. His house banner of a white griffon on red, and the emerald banner of the Knights of Chaos cracked and snapped behind his chair, once a source of pride, now a badge of shame. The fishermen's crudely built sod-roofed dwellings on the cliffs of the Isle of Midges were too damp to light, as the hail drummed down on armoured dragons like a racing heartbeat.

'Ma! Ma!' A child broke away from one of the ragged lines mounting Darcy's Imperial and ran screaming towards her mother.

Thump. Nothing but red mist settling on the churned snow as Darcy turned away laughing, his green eyes reckless.

Simon, one of Darcy's elite Knights of Chaos shivered in his armour and fought down growing disquiet. This was not war; this harvesting of the weak to meet the WarLock King's avaricious needs for his forges and war galley slaves. Their soldiers were quiet too, heads down as if they did not want to be recognised by the fearful shuffling, stumbling villagers. There was none of the usual banter after a successful engagement. They were ashamed. They, too, were afraid. He prayed the family he had pretended to kill remained hidden. Simon looked up to find Darcy's speculative gaze eyes upon him as the

Prince climbed to stand beside his friend.

'Their fathers and sons fight against us. Others will think twice when they return to an empty village, when they return to their loved ones waiting for them.' He laughed.

Simon shuddered at the horror of it. Walking down the lines, Darcy had selected a half dozen of the prettiest young girls who were dragged screaming to where he stood. Reaching out with a mailed gauntlet to touch their heads, there had been the smell of burnt flesh as motes of green sparked about them and his victims shuddered and convulsed, their fractured screams falling to sudden silence. They were left behind, mindless and broken, to be a burden on those who found them. To serve as a warning that none could fight the kiss of the Abyss.

Sickened, he turned away before the WarLock's son could see his revulsion. Darcy was always going to inherit the great Earldom of Dragonsdome. From childhood, Simon knew his star would rise with that of his childhood playmate, that he would one day stand at Darcy's side as household knight and Thane of Cawdor in his own right. Together they read the stories of knighthood and glory, practised long bells at the lists, went dragon racing and dreamed of glory. But that was before the cruel and jealous streak in Darcy reared its ugly head, before his younger sister, Quenelda, had shown her skill with dragons. Now there was a pale coldness to the WarLock's young son, an aura of dread that unmanned any who fought him, peasant or knight. It was that black sorcerous armour...crafted from the same metal that now bound their Imperials, and it reeked of the Abyss.

Now his friend was a Prince who would one day inherit a Kingdom, and Darcy had raised his childhood friend to Earl of Badenoch...and yet where was the glory in this? Fighting hobgoblins, his sword sang in his hand, he preferred that even to sorcery...more honourable to fight your opponent as an equal.

But Darcy? There was a fell madness in that damned armour which imbued their young Prince with a new strength and energy. It made Simon ill. Looking at the Knights of Chaos readying for take-off by razing the settlement with dragonfire, he couldn't repress a shiver. Darcy was growing fell like his Sire, and any who didn't fear the WarLock King was a fool.

CHAPTER SEVEN
Cooking Books

Battlegame training was about to begin when a message arrived from Drumondir. The BoneCaster was in the upper reaches of the High Cloud Library in the Academy, a place of ancient books that were disintegrating, set side-by-side with cutting-edge research from the four Academy Faculties. It was a peerless collection, added to almost daily. Grimoires and theses on navigation, aerial combat, weaponry, cloud formation, strategy and tactics, cauldrons, breeding vampires, dragon armour and a hundred thousand other subjects...and now, to Root's delight, maps of the far uncharted north based on his cartography and notes from their quest to find Quenelda's father, had been added to the map section, and were in constant demand.

Drumondir had been busy searching for records of the Green Dragon Lords as she had discovered they were called; those first sorcerers who bonded with the mighty seadragons. She wished they could return to explore and document the secrets of the ancient Sea Citadel where the King's life had been saved: his skin where it had been burnt by the maelstrom was now being hidden, armoured, by growing scales of green and blue. The Guardian had also given her leave to search for any undiscovered texts on the Mage Wars that might shine light on maelstrom magic. Drumondir hoped, too, to discover mention of the fabled Dragonsdome Chronicles, believed to hold the secrets of the One Earth. But today she had also been searching for something else far more mundane, and in that at least, she had been successful.

The bright scholarly robes of different faculties and schools mingled with apprentices and students as Quenelda and Root searched the first gallery for any sign of the Ice Bear BoneCaster. There they found her in a quiet annex, poring over an old book on a table. The message had invited them both to come as soon as they could.

'Is that a grimoire?' Root eagerly looked at the huge heavy book, its yellowed pages cracked with age.

'No, young Root,' Drumondir smiled, turning another page and raising a cloud of dust. 'A cooking book! I wondered, just wondered, if a plant with medicinal properties might have been over-looked when all other references to the Mage Wars had been destroyed.'

'A...cookbook...?' Root trailed off, not certain if he was being teased.

'Herbology, young Root! I think I have found the answer to your dragon's bane,' Drumondir bobbed her head and smiled with satisfaction, reminding Root yet again of a bird of prey.

'Oh?' Quenelda remembered how they had thought Two Gulps had been poisoned by the weed, rolling and frothing at the mouth, eyes crossing; later identified with the inexplicable name of dragon's bane.

'Have the foragers found more?' Root's people loved herb lore.

'Yes, it grows in profusion in a small sea loch near Stalker castle. A cutter docked yesterday with as much as they could safely harvest, along with many young shoots. The gardeners of the Herbology School are now planting it in in the Healer's Gardens, and your mother,' she smiled at Quenelda, 'asked for some for her palace garden. The Master Healer gave me some leaves so that I might test its properties.'

Drumondir placed the book carefully on a low lectern lit by more candles so that they might all see, and moved back a page or two. There, beautifully inscribed and illustrated, was the thorny dragon's bane plant, and a pressed leaf. Root sniffed, carefully turning the fragile leaf in his fingers to examine it: it smelt like foosty tea.

'I don't recognise that script from my studies.'

'It's Elvish from the Old Kingdom,' Quenelda unthinkingly answered his question before Drumondir could.

The BoneCaster calmly nodded her agreement as she lightly ran her finger along the graceful script. *Her knowledge is growing fast...she can remember more and more...does she hold all the knowledge of the First Age?* She pulled over a small map and unrolled it.

'The plant originates here in the east, in the Sixth Kingdom,' she continued. 'I spoke with the Eldritch, of your mother's personal Elven Guard. She says it grows profusely in the wild like a weed. The elves drink it as a tea, and to treat the wounded; it calms and refreshes like camomile does. But the fact that it can also fight the black death is known only to us. As is its other strange property.'

Root and Quenelda nodded; they knew all this.

'This cook book,' Drumondir lifted a second tome, 'describes a similar weed, that once dried, can also produce a calm meditative state if smoked. So, I added it to the drying racks of smoke weed...and then shredded it. Tangnost and I thought to try it. It might serve both to heal the body, and the spirit. We thought it might become standard issue for healers in the field for those who are injured.

'We were sitting up late in Tangnost's quarters next to the stables where one of the Windglen Widdershanks' hatchings was due, and lit up our pipes and-'

'And every dragon began behaving like Two Gulps?' Root's keen mind guessed.

Drumondir smiled. 'Just so! Not all, but most. They behaved as if drunk.'

'So that is why it's called dragon's bane,' Quenelda was amused and amazed. 'They become daft! Do y-'

'But!' Root interrupted excitedly, gripping her arm. 'My people use red thorn to keep out dire wolves and cave bears, to keep our warrens safe without hurting those who hunt. Why not the same with this? It could be used instead of a weapon!' He looked at Quenelda. 'A weapon that wouldn't hurt the dragons, but -'

'But might stop our enemies attacking,' Quenelda finished thoughtfully. 'Or disrupt them.'

'I don't think it would affect Imperials,' Drumondir cautioned. 'It might have to be carried in such large quantities as to be impractical.'

'But with the lesser dragons: sabretooths, vampires, spitting adders...frost dragons, chameleons...'

Quenelda grinned. 'It could cause chaos,' she was thinking out loud. 'It could be rolled into balls of hay or straw on a slinging rope, or fired from catapults. We'll have to try it out.'

Dusk was falling swiftly later that winter's afternoon as Root and Armelia approached the royal stables wrapped in warm hooded cloaks and lined boots. The lamp lighters were already out and about. Tomorrow, Root reported to Dragon Isle and would not be granted leave until the end of Operation White Out. The young gnome was describing what he had learnt about the weed, *dragon's bane*. Taking a small amount from Drumondir's smoking racks, Root had decided to treat their favourite dragon.

'Here,' Armelia tentatively offered a handful of the weed to Chasing the Stars, who bugled a welcome to two souls she loved more than any others. The mare sniffed, then eagerly chewed it, before blowing hotly on the young woman's hands, snuffling for more. They waited. And waited. Suddenly the dragon's eyes widened and crossed. She made a funny noise and began to drool. Then-

'Err, I think –' Root never got any further as he ducked. There was a short silence punctuated by the mare's happy gurgling.

Armelia tried to open her eyes. She turned towards Root with her hands outstretched as if sleepwalking. Goo dripped from her nose. Her mouth was opening and shutting, but she couldn't make a sound. Staggering to her feet, Chasing the Stars lent forward solicitously over the stall gate and began to lick her. With a squeal Armelia fell backwards into the straw. Root grabbed a handful of hay and tried to clean her face, but Armelia squealed and batted him away.

'Well,' said Root brightly as Chasing the Stars fell

with a thud, claws in the air, crooning happily. 'I think that went well! Don't you?'

CHAPTER EIGHT
Chain Gang

The impact jarred up Knuckles' arm, the pickaxe jumping in his freezing hands, rubbing against the rough callouses that had long since taken the place of blisters. It was freezing and the ground hard as rock as he swung again, chips of ice and rock stinging parts of his face not covered by a scarf. Children wrapped in rags giggled, pointing, threw snowballs. Ice smashed into Knuckles' neck. Turning swiftly, he raised the pickaxe and lunged, only to be jerked back by his chains. He slipped and landed heavily. Spitting blood, he climbed to his feet to find the tip of an arrow a scant hand's breadth away.

'Get digging,' the old man threatened. 'They're just young 'uns. Pick on someone your own size.'

Oh, I will, old man, I will. The City Watch was hiring the young and old it seemed. The sweepings from the gutter. He had watched them being trained to use a bow ~ the safest place would be right in front of them! Glancing up, he saw dragons putting down near the south gate, bearing the royal standard. Head down as a lash whipped out, reminding prisoners to kneel, he squinted against the brightness. The Queen again, in shining armour breastplate and helmet, with some ladies-in-waiting, surrounded by her Elven Household Flight on their feathered dragons. *What on the One Earth was she doing here?*

The work was backbreaking. Chain gangs, mostly prisoners taken in the war, the rest from jail, laboured with pickaxes and spades and leather or woven buckets from dawn to dusk, and well beyond into the long nights, all about the outer city walls. What in the name of the Abyss were they digging? A moat protected by earth-works? Fat lot of good that would do them if his Master arrived with his hobgoblin banners; and his Master would come for them all, it was only a question of 'when' not 'if'. The WarLock King's Dragon Master smiled as he bent to his task. It wasn't pleasant.

CHAPTER NINE
Hic!

Quenelda wobbled first one way and then the other. She grinned at Root before staggering sideways into a wall hanging. The heavy threadbare tapestry from a bygone age slipped from the pole. Quenelda folded as its weight pinned her down. Dust billowed, raising a cloud of moths. The House Mistress and a gaggle of maids abandoned their brushes and dustpans and ran to assist.

Quenelda gurgled up at them. 'That was a good flight!'

Knuckling watering eyes, Armelia snapped at the guards. 'Give us room...the Princess needs air!'

As the guards pushed back onlookers, a baffled Armelia considered her friend, who was giggling and wriggling around on the ground despite all efforts to get her on her feet.

Tangnost arrived at a run, lame leg dragging. 'What's happened?' He looked stricken. 'Has she been poisoned?'

'Oops' Root suddenly pulled a guilty face.

'Oops?' Tangnost repeated, suspiciously.

'Err, I think she's eaten the tablets for Two Gulps ...that Drumondir brought. That have dragon's bane in them. I left some with her for Two Gulps, so that we could learn how much is needed to make a sabretooth silly.'

'What? She's eaten dragon food?'

Everyone, Armelia, maids and Dragon Master looked accusingly at Root.

'Well,' he said defensively. 'what do you think she eats

when she's a dragon? It isn't the first time! It could have been a lot worse if you think about it! She's an Imperial after all!'

'Hic!'

Tangnost's eyebrows met in the middle as he caught Drumondir's twinkling eyes. To be truthful they hadn't given it any thought at all.

'Well,' he grudgingly smiled...., 'at least we know it works.'

'Hic!'

'Just so,' Drumondir said with a smile, 'Perhaps she should be taken to her chambers to sleep it off?'

Quenelda hiccupped and looked up happily as Tangnost lifted her effortlessly. 'WhereamI? Hic! Feel a bit woos hic-y!'

Tangnost turned. 'Armelia. I think someone should watch over her until she...she...' he looked hopelessly at Drumondir. 'Feels better. And it might be a good idea to see how long it takes before she is herself again.'

He turned on his boot. 'And keep those new honey tablets away from her.'

'Hic!'

CHAPTER TEN
The Wychwood Knight

Quester gazed nervously up at the stars, willing the dawn to arrive. The Great Ice Bear, there! The Dancing Dragon, the Demented Earwig almost above him. The North Star. In truth, the young man preferred not to sleep. Sleep brought unwelcome dreams. Sleep brought flashbacks and suffocating fear with it, and he woke soaked with sweat, trembling, hoping he hadn't cried out loud.

Quester instinctively reached down to rub his thigh and flex his left leg, marvelling again at how the wychwood was warm to the touch, how it bent at the knee. He wigged his bare toes. It was a strange feeling, or rather a lack of feeling; his wychwood leg was supple and light and he could will it to move unthinkingly now, and yet it felt like a stranger. And because of that crippling injury, when he faced down the hobgoblin WarLord Galtekerion, and lost his leg and nearly his life saving the King's, he had missed almost a whole year at the Battle Academy with his friends, Root and Quenelda; and Operation Brimstone, the mission to retake the precious ore mines and free the slaves who toiled there. And yet...and yet he feared to go back into combat. Closing his eyes, he saw that huge flint sword swinging round...heard the crunch, the explosion of white hot pain, the gushing blood and broken bone. He shivered.

Taking a deep breath of bracing air, Quester shook his head at his own foolish behaviour. He could walk when no one thought he ever would again, and was about to become a knight of the King's household; was to have the honour of being at the King's side as his esquire, since the King's own son now fought for the WarLock King. And he had seen such adventures, for the youngest son of a rebel household attained as traitors. He had flown north in the dead of winter with Tangnost, Quenelda and Root to find Quenelda's father, missing in action following the massacre on the Westering Isles. Few had survived the frozen wastes, or had survived a maelstrom, seen the wonders of a long forgotten SeaDragon citadel, and lived to tell the tale. The people were calling him a hero. Knighthood was the first step towards manhood. Was everything he could have dreamt of and more. So why was he so afraid?

Overnight, snow had climbed higher, burying the palace battlements in deep drifts. Heavy blankets smothered the roofs and crunched underfoot as the guards changed. Braziers attempted to throw back the cold creeping from the north.

Scores of sweepers had been out long before dawn, labouring to clear the palace pentangle for the knighthood ceremony, and already the crowds were gathering to see the youth who had nearly died for their King at the hands of their ancient enemy. Wood was getting scarce, so bonfires of peat and dried dragon dung were stacked on many streets, so the commoners could warm themselves about the fire pits.

Down below the castle, burrowed into the cliffs of the loch, they were preparing the ceremony in an ancient cave that Quester had not even known existed. Burning brands lit the pool and burnished its still surface to gold.

The flickering light revealed ancient paintings on its rugged walls that had caught Drumondir's quizzical eye, but she had much to do and would have to leave their study for another time.

After he was shrived, anointed by water, Quester would be led up to where a large audience of nobles and Courtiers were gathered, and of course crowds of commoners eagerly awaited the distraction of pageantry and power. He could hear their rough eager voices even here, had not expected so many to attend. The old and the new now stood side by side in this changed world, and so the honour of shriving him had fallen to the Ice Bear BoneCaster, Drumondir, to perform. She had been anxiously conferring with Sir Gharad, so that she understood perfectly what was required of her in this most solemn of ceremonies.

Squirrel, Root's gnome esquire, came to fetch Quester as the low winter sun crested the Dragon Spine Mountains, reverentially leading him down the worn steps to where Drumondir, solemn as an owl and dressed in ceremonial robes bright with wychwood beads, waited. Small charcoal braziers filled the cave with a delicious drowsy warmth and the smell of pine and rosemary. Quester owed much to the northern clan BoneCaster and returned her welcoming smile nervously. She had been working with the young man patiently, pushing him to begin exercising; after so many moons in bed he was still gaunt, and his muscles slack. He tired too easily, but finally he was putting on weight and able to begin light sparring with other esquires. It was no longer his body the BoneCaster was worried about, it was the young man's mind. Not all injuries could be seen in the light of day, or be hidden in the depths of night.

'Kneel.'

Quester went down on both knees, head bowed at the edge of the pool reflecting his nervous face back. Dipping a ladle into the lake, Drumondir poured water over his head. Quester hastily supressed an unmanly cry as some trickled down his back, raising yet more goose bumps.

'May this water wash away all that has gone before so that you come into the presence of...'

Quester welcomed the second ladle of water as the BoneCaster's words completed the ritual. Squirrel had fitted fleece boots, and was fastening a blessedly heavy warm cloak about his shoulders, when the Queen's Constable and Commander of the Queen's Castle Guard arrived to lead them up and out into the early dawn.

Sir Gharad led the youth across the slippery cobbles to where a pavilion had been erected, royal standards snapping in the rising breeze. Despite boots and cloak, Quester could feel the cold cut like a knife through his light robes as he took his place. Wychwood thrones stood with Imperials of the Household Guard arrayed behind in their silver armour, their mounts' breath smoking in the air, talons sparking on the cobbles. The crowds were held back by unicorns of the Light Household Cavalry that stamped restlessly in the cold.

Without moving his head, Quester searched for familiar faces. Swiftly he found Root and his sister Bracken who shyly waved, and then Quenelda who didn't stand on dignity and shouted out his name, waving both hands, just in case he couldn't see her!

Sir Gharad beckoned him forwards as they had rehearsed, to mount the five steps before the King and Queen.

'Kneel,' the King said softly, moving to the Queen's side.

There was only the faintest hesitation as the young man went down on one knee before King and Queen.

'Do you swear to serve the Crown and the One Earth: its peoples and creatures?'

'I willingly lift my staff in service to the realm. I raise my shield in defence of all who dwell therein. I am bound to my Imperial by oath and bond never to be broken, even in death. Light shall fight dark. Fire shall fight ice. Friend shall fight foe. Harmony shall be born of chaos. I so swear service so long as I shall live.'

'Then we name you our man, a knight of the Queen's Guard.' The King touched Quester's shoulders lightly with a sword. 'Arise, Sir Quester.'

The young knight stood to cheers from the crowd who were straining forwards to hear. He was an anointed knight! The Queen also stood, beckoning Quenelda forwards. Her daughter was holding a cushion.

'You have already won your spurs in battle saving my husband's life.' Squirrel had also been anxiously practising, making sure he did not do himself a mischief with the razor-sharp spurs. He swiftly fitted them about his young knight's boots.

Armelia moved shyly forwards. She wore a pale lilac dress stitched with water pearls, her hair loose beneath a soft hooded cloak. She looked beautiful. She was holding a folded cloth. Quester looked at her expectantly. Armelia looked at Quester. Quester raised his eyebrows.

'Psst!' Taking a step forward, Quenelda gave her friend a helpful nudge. Armelia had a habit of freezing when she was feeling a little stressed.

'Yes!' Armelia held her gift out to Quester. 'It's your banner. I stitched it myself.' She beamed.

'Thank you!' Quester was touched. He took the banner from the Queen's lady-in-waiting and shook it out.

'It's...ah...it's wonderful,' Quester quickly said. Needlework was clearly not one of Armelia's gifts. The wychwood tree looked as if it had been struck by lightning and the stitching was...well it was...'Lovely,' he smiled. 'It's lovely. I've never seen anything quite like it,' he added truthfully. 'Thank you.'

'Truly?' Armelia looked relieved. 'I have something more,' she turned. Quenelda had stepped forwards this time with a garment. It looked as though she was biting her cheeks in an effort not to laugh.

'I hand-stitched your surcoat, too.'

'My thanks, Lady,' Quester remembered the knightly values and bowed as he had practised dozens of times, raising a clap from the crowds.

It was even more elaborately embroidered and...*was that pink hearts growing on the wychwood tree?*

'Go on,' Armelia shyly encouraged him. 'Put it on.'

'Am I allowed to?' Quester looked hopefully at Tangnost to be rescued, but the Dragon Master brushed aside his question. 'Of course,' he said gruffly, giving the youth a warning frown. 'You must put it on.'

'My Lord, allow me,' Squirrel, was instantly again at Quester's side, he had all but adopted his master's young friend. 'If you can just bow your head, Sir?' He raised his eyebrows meaningfully. The young knight was tall, and Squirrel, like all his people, was a good deal shorter.

'Of course!' Quester belatedly bent down so the gnome could reach over his head. Standing, he shrugged into the surcoat, arms stretched out to allow Squirrel to tie the laces. It was deep sea green, with gold stitching, only it was truly terrible. It hung lopsided almost to his feet. He'd have to walk carefully, or he would fall flat on his knightly face.

'One final gift,' the King said, nodding at his Dragon Master who stepped down to lead a young colt forwards from the parting ranks of juvenile Imperials. 'For a young Dragon Lord.'

Quester's throat caught painfully as he took a deep gulp of freezing air. Barely daring to move, the newly minted knight turned on his heel into the intense golden-eyed scrutiny of a juvenile Imperial, barely weaned. Great nostrils sucked in his scent, lifting his hair and surcoat. Wide-eyed, Quester looked at Quenelda and Armelia, who were grinning and clapping, pleased they had managed to keep this rather large secret from him.

'Go on,' Tangnost said softly as he offered the tether. 'Name him. He's yours.'

Quester felt a moment of panic. His mouth was dry, and he felt tongue-tied. Frantically he cast about for a name that would honour his mount, bring honour to the SDS and the King and Queen. A Dragon Lord's mount needed a special name.

Powdered snow drifted lazily down. The juvenile gave him a friendly nudge, almost knocking the young man to his knees, enveloping him in a welcome cloud of warmth.

'*Wychwood Warrior...?*' it was almost a whisper, as those in the front of the crowds strained to hear.

Tangnost nodded gruff approval; it was different, but the name was a good choice for a new generation. 'Wychwood Warrior it is. You'll train him for battle, to cement your bond. I'll show you how, as often as we can fit it in between your regular training'

Quester wordlessly nodded his gratitude. All those who mattered in his life had played a part in making him a knight. 'I name him Wychwood Warrior,' he addressed the crowds. 'Wychwood Warrior.'

'The Wychwood Knight!' Someone shouted at the front. There was a ripple of laughter, but it was warm with approval, and then someone else repeated it. This boy, this young man had saved their King. Had miraculously learnt to walk again with a wychwood leg. Pure dead magic.

'The Wychwood Knight! The Wychwood Knight.'
The crowd took up the chant as Quester's sword was buckled on. 'The Wychwood Knight.'

Drumondir allowed a smile of approval to touch her lips. This was exactly what young Quester needed to help him heal. As the crowds surged forwards to lift the young knight above their shoulders and carry him about the pentangle, the Queen's Guard Unicorns stood back and formed up outside the palace gates. Tradition was ignored; let the young knight have his moment of celebration, and the common folk their fun.

CHAPTER ELEVEN

Dark Dragon Dreams: The Hunt Begins

Hunting... Hunting...

Quenelda turned restlessly, dreaming...of a creature out of nightmares. Deep out in the open ocean, in canyons where the darkness was absolute, the Warlock's dark dragon Queen glided slowly southwards like a phantom, eerily lit by the flickering green and purple of the Abyss. Down and down its deepest canyons she went, down into the inky black depths where the pressure would crush any ordinary creature like a soft bellied bug. How deep none truly knew save her. Down here, far removed from the sun, the Queen ghosted through vast underwater mountain ranges that had once towered so high they kissed the cold depths of space, and had drawn its cold power down with them here into the deeps.

Flashes of colour streamed from her tail like a thousand lamps, beckoning, bewitching, luring the curious and the careless to their doom. And always she was waiting...for when her master would call her from the ocean deeps to come and feed on a different kind of prey...those kindred who had cast her out so long ago. Hot blooded and sweet, oh, how sweet revenge would taste! As the smoky red sun dipped towards the horizon, the creature swam past the Isle of Midges into the Inner Sea. With mere flicks of her four huge paddle-shaped limbs, she powered her long body effortlessly through the dark waters.

*Hunting...Hunting...*her thoughts faded as she dived and Quenelda slept on.

CHAPTER TWELVE
Fire and Ice

'What's happening?' Root asked for the dozenth time, as Chasing the Stars put down in Glen Etive and Quenelda waved to them. 'What is she up to?'

Behind him, wrapped in a heavy cloak, boots and gloves and a thick lined flying suit and hood, Armelia shook her head. She was none the wiser. For three days Chasing the Stars had been stabled at the domestic roosts of Dragonsdome following an infestation of scale mites at the royal roosts, which had since spread to the Guild. Ghastly little things, Armelia shivered, and hard to eradicate according to Tangnost. She had seen some of the dragons out in the palace paddocks, bucking and rolling, snapping at their flanks, trying to rid themselves of thousands of blood sucking thumbnail-sized parasites that hid under their scales. Even worse was the sight of roost hands and grooms who were also running around scratching and screaming, trying to divest themselves of their unwanted visitors. Unfortunate victims, dragons and people both, had to be dragged to and totally doused in a foul-smelling cold bath that killed the mites! Although, Quenelda had mysteriously said she had a much better idea, whatever that meant, and frankly, so long as her precious Chasing the Stars didn't catch any, Armelia didn't want to ever encounter scale mites again!

Dragon Isle had banned all flights until the infestations were brought under control. The last thing they needed was an outbreak there; and so Quenelda and Root had been granted unexpected leave.

Powder snow was drifting down and the winter light was soft as they reached Glen Etive. The silence in the glen was immense save for a snow eagle calling high above. The sky of soft rose was turning from gold to the palest blue. The twin crescent moons were on the rise. It was beautiful, Armelia realised, as she dismounted in the breathless silence.

Quenelda came bouncing up whilst Two Gulps ate a couple of gorse bushes and snapped up a brace of ptarmigans who weren't quick enough to realise their danger.

'Exercises begin tomorrow. We won't have any leave for moons to come. I thought we could have some fun!'

Armelia looked about, trying to see what fun her friend had in mind. The snow where they stood was a stride deep at the foot of an icy slope which rose up sharply to an overhanging slab of ice, several hundred strides above them.

'Right watch this!' Quenelda grinned. 'We've been practising for the last couple of days!'

Leaping onto Two Gulps, she flew him up to the outcrop looking down on her two friends. *Fly!*

The sabretooth leapt, and with one powerful down stroke to soften his landing, he folded his wings, and flamed. It was so cold the melted snow instantly turned to ice, and Two Gulps shot down the slope.

'Yah!!!!' Quenelda shouted. 'Look at us gooooo!!' Root and Armelia dived out their way and Chasing the Stars took off as Two Gulps hurtled between them, before ploughing into a massive drift.

Armelia and Root cringed as Quenelda went head over heels.

'Well, bottoms up,' Root said cheerfully. 'We'd better go and dig them out!'

It was, Armelia thought, once she got over her fright at the sheer speed, the best fun she had had in a long time: young ladies at Court had not been permitted anything so vulgar as sledging ~ that was for the common folk. Chasing the Stars had finally got the hang of sliding like a toboggan, wings outstretched to keep her balance, and Quenelda had asked Two Gulps to create a long smooth area where they could reduce speed without having to end face down in a snowdrift. Hanging onto Root, speeding down the slope was exhilarating! Their cheeks were ruddy with the cold, and now they were hurling snowballs at each other as Two Gulps passed by.

Later, before they left, as dusk was coming down, they built a snow dragon. It was rather plump and had a crooked tail. Ptarmigan feathers were sticking out of its mouth.

CHAPTER THIRTEEN
The Forsaken

Stormcracker put down at dawn behind the Old Wall on the great dragon pads that rose ten-deep into the winter sky, now bearded with icicles that hung a full spear cast long. Following a break in the blizzards, the King had come to inspect his newly completed fortress, built on the ruins of the old.

Dusk was falling and still they had not finished the inspection, Housesteads was so vast. The air was charged; raw power that had once resided in every living thing had come alive at the touch of a Dragon Whisperer, Quenelda had drawn it up like sap in a tree. The very stone bones of the fortress were alive in the same way as the HeartRock. The land now had a living beating heart and the dormant power of all living things responded to her touch: earth, wind, fire and water. Quietly the King's daughter walked about the outer battlements, standing at the merlons beside catapults and trebuchets, and reached deep down into the earth and rock, drawing up their ancient power.

Once great castles had ringed the land, but the Mage Wars had left devastation and rubble in their wake and few had been rebuilt when the sorcerers returned after the Long Winter. Here at Housesteads, the walls were so thick men could walk within them three-deep, and great spiked battlements were flanked by dragon gates on all four points of the compass, which could pour dragon fire into the earthworks surrounding them. The barracks and roosts were sunk down into the bedrock in countless layers, a defensive maze designed to entrap an army. Quenelda was making use of her ancestors' memories.

'Lady,' the newly appointed Warden of the Wall took step beside his young guest. 'Well met. I have not seen you since the battle. You are well? And your...' he paused looking for an acceptable word. 'Your rather plump sabretooth. How is he?'

She smiled, welcoming the young Major whose bravery had helped her, and her father, escape the hobgoblin WarLock's clutches. 'Still rather plump,' she admitted with an ironic grin. 'But he has seen battle now in the Brimstones. He has shed his juvenile scales.'

The Major nodded and looked out over the fortress lit by thousands of braziers. 'Have we built to your expectations? The very fortress feels alive, like a living creature itself.'

Quenelda smiled at his perception; Major Cawdor was an exceptional and gifted young man. She knew her father looked on him as the son he should have had. His bravery and intuition had led to the gift of command of the Old Wall, despite his youth.

'These so called "Forsaken",' the King asked, as he stretched his legs on the slippery battlements, gloved hand lightly on Quester's shoulder, and his daughter back by his side as the braziers sparked and smoked with wet wood; 'who attacked last night and are throwing themselves at the Wall wearing black death masks. Who are they? Have we managed to take any prisoners?'

'Yes, Your Grace,' Cawdor said heavily in the sudden silence. 'We have taken prisoners, but at a cost, because they fight with such reckless abandonment, even when severely injured, or their weapons are taken. They,' he coughed, his voice husky, 'they – they are our people; missing troopers, downed pilots, though most are farmers, fisherfolk, woodsmen, dwarfs from the west and north ~ from most clans, although there are also trolls and even gnomes reported amongst the dead, who will have never raised more than a pitchfork. Their kin-'

'Gnomes?'

'They don't know themselves, Your Grace. They are driven to madness. Even children hardly old enough to lift a weapon fight like the damned.'

'Children?'

'What has he done to them?' Quester's face was a mask of horror as Quenelda stepped down into the barbican where corpses were piled a dozen deep, and knelt by one of the twisted bodies dressed in rags. She lifted the frozen mask, it fragmented at her touch. The face beneath was that of a young girl. Her frozen body petrified hard as stone. Her brown eyes staring up at the stars.

'It's the kiss of the Abyss,' Quenelda said into the heavy silence, an ancient fear rising in her memory.

'The kiss?'

'They are touched by the maelstrom, it has destroyed their minds.' Quenelda's voice was flat, her face hard. 'The walking dead, subject only to the WarLock's will. They are not the people they once were.' She reached out to close the eyes then withdrew her hand as if stung.

Cawdor leapt down the steps, sword unsheathed.

'What? What is wrong, Lady?'

'I...' Quenelda was breathing heavily, condensing the sparkling air about her. She looked as if she were about to be sick. 'They,' she panted. 'They still have a memory of who they once were!' She raised horrified eyes. 'A part of them remembers.'

'You mean that she is still alive?' Cawdor said, shocked. 'With those injuries?'

'Ye-'

The body twitched and sat up, bony arm flailing for Quenelda's throat. Cawdor leapt, but Two Gulps was swifter; flames wreathing both Dragon Whisperer and Forsaken in fire. The girl's body burned to ash.

'Then we do them a mercy to kill them,' the King said roughly with a muffled curse. 'Pass the word,' he ordered Cawdor. 'Kill them on sight. Take them down first'

'Go in peace across the bridge,' Quenelda said softly as the bitter wind lifted the ashes from her gloved hand. 'Join your loved ones. I swear we will end this.'

CHAPTER FOURTEEN
How Deelightful to See You

'Whey, Lady Armelia,' Samantha Spellgood curtsied to the young lady impeccably dressed in sublime layers of brocade and gold thread. 'How deelightful to see you,' she ushered Armelia up sweeping steps to the gallery. 'As you can see, an entire floor has been given over to your label. Your new exclusive accessories range, such as these pointed-toe boots with bells, are selling like hot cakes.

'Sparkly pink is much in vogue this spring....and these wands here...inlaid with gold and inbuilt spells, are hugely popular.'

'I have a new idea.'

Samantha Spellgood's smile was a tad stretched. 'A...new idea?' Hopefully it did not involve legs.

Unfortunately, it did, rather more than she imagined; two more in fact. Samantha Spellgood felt faint, but she couldn't sit if Lady Armelia was standing. Luckily her bone corset was stout.

'What exactly does Madam have in mind?' Samantha fanned herself. She was getting rather hot under the collar. And if Lady Armelia's ideas for an F&H's spring Fashion Day went ahead, it might get hotter yet.

'We may have to, err, widen the doors...you see, because of their size.'

'Their size?'

'And possibly the, the walk, would have to be forged...'

'Forged?'

'Well, err, Princess Quenelda's...err...'he's...a teeny-weeny bit overweight.'

'A teeny-weeny bit overweight?' Samantha echoed weakly.

'The Queen is pleased to send her very own carpenters, masons and smiths from the Palace. Who have... err...quite a lot of experience in the matter.'

To hell with protocol. Samantha Spellgood sat.

'Does Madam have any sketches for my ladies to begin work?'

Madam did. And in fact, her idea for leathers sewn in the colours and magical sigils of noble houses, their coats of arms was very clever. Hitherto only menfolk wore helms, surcoats, shields and standards denoting their houses. This would ingeniously allow noblewomen to declare their loyalties as well.

'Or of course, some may wish to be colour co-ordinated with their mount. As mine are.'

Samantha's mouth formed a polite O.

If you wish, the Royal Dragon Master, BearHugger, will accompany you to the royal roosts to see the colours for yourself.'

Samantha hastily indicated that would not be necessary.

'Err, and these are the designs for my second range.'

Samantha Spellgood stared at the sheaves of paper. Just when she thought it couldn't get any worse.

'As you can see...inspired by the Princess Quenelda *herself.* These designs shall be named for the Dragon Whisperer; the most exclusive range of all. And of course,' Armelia played her final card. 'The most expensive. The detailed appliqué might be a wee challenge, but the royal stables will provide the, err...necessary. And, the err, the Queen has said how deelighted she would be, if hers were to be pale blue and magenta like those you created for me, to match her mare. In fact, she insists upon hers being ready in time to wear it on the day.'

'She would? She will?'

'Oh, yes,' Armelia nodded happily. 'It will be quite *the* social event of the year! *Everyone* who is *anyone* will be waiting for a royal invitation! I was hoping that F&H would organise it all. That you yourself...?'

CHAPTER FIFTEEN
A Secret Weapon

Sir Gharad, the Queen's Constable, was overseeing reconstruction of the palace defences. Following the WarLock's failed coup, at the Queen's request, he had taken command of the newly formed elite Palace Guard, including four Imperials with their newly built roosts. The moat, like the city defences, was being deepened. A thousand ampoules of dragonfire were to be stored below ground in the nearby ice house once the Guild had completed the SDS requirements. Their secret weapon, sheaves of dragon's bane to be added to the thousand braziers about the battlements, were stored beneath the gatehouse turrets, and in the loft in the royal stables.

Following the WarLock's attempt to take the castle, largely thwarted by cook Agnes Dingleweed commanding her many relatives amongst the kitchen servants, everyone below stairs had been given two gold imperials as a mark of the royal gratitude. Agnes also received a pension for life. Most would never earn that coin in a lifetime of service. Since the kitchen staff seemed competent with pans, hams and rolling pins they were the first to be taught some simple swordplay to improve their technique. Agnes oversaw the household's training, reporting to the Queen whilst discussing the next week's menus.

Sir Gharad nodded to the Captain of the Watch. 'And our other little surprise?'

The Captain scratched beneath his helmet strap in reflex. Then under an armpit. Trying not to react Sir Gharad found himself scratching his head before firmly putting his arms by his sides, despite an irrational need to scratch under his armour.

'All…err…in old whisky barrels, my lord Constable. Ten barrels of the wee…bu- beasties,' he scratched under his helmet. 'Stacked in the side room over the gatehouse. Firmly hammered in.'

'Jolly good, Captain,' Sir Gharad moved on at a brisk pace. Up in the unoccupied guard room he undid his breastplate buckles and had a jolly good scratch.

CHAPTER SIXTEEN
The Game Begins

Darcy, Simon and his friends were in the baths when the summons to Council came.

'My Lord Prince, your father bids you come to the Night Tower.'

'What?' Darcy starred at him blearily, pushing away the hand of the young lady who had been lavishing her attentions upon him. 'Now? Tonight?' When he said he wished to learn strategy and tactics, he had not envisaged tonight! What was the hurry? He and his friends had been racing frost dragons out on the endless ice all day. It had been exhilarating! He had won! Darcy knew he was a poor flyer, but on the ground he was very good indeed.

'My Prince,' the Constable bowed low, fear snagging his throat. His young master's emerald eyes were becoming like his father's ~ pools of black flecked with green. 'As soon as...you are ready. Your elixir, my Prince, is in your chambers.'

The mailed guards saluted as Darcy made his drowsy way up the Night Tower and stood on the porting stone. Outside, the blizzard moaned and howled like a wild beast. It was cooler in the WarLock's Tower, but his father was lightly dressed as he greeted Darcy.

'Come, my son.' Darcy nodded to now familiar faces as his father's heavily dressed nobles and Captains bowed and murmured greetings to their Black Prince. Darcy then shifted attention to what they were studying: to the familiar contours, the two islands, the high crags on the map on the table.

'The Sorcerers Glen?' Darcy frowned. His head hurt from too much red wine and too little sleep. His father had planned to strike last year when the SDS and the Guild were in chaos. The Black Isle had been set on fire and the glen was overwhelmed by refugees seeking sanctuary from the war in the north. Betrayed by their Grand Master, the Guild was in total disarray, and the SDS had lost an entire generation at the battles of the Westering Isles and the Battle of the Line, and were leaderless. The Seven Kingdoms had been ripe for the picking: many Lords loyal to his father had not yet revealed their true intentions, still held positions of power at the heart of the Kingdoms.

But inexplicably, the hobgoblin warlord Galtekerion had disappeared, captured they now knew by the SDS at a battle on the Old Wall, when the missing SDS Commander had so nearly been killed, and when victory had been within their grasp. With their WarLord and his Chosen dead or captured, the hobgoblin tribes had once again fallen on each other. Without Galtekerion's hobgoblin banners, Dragon Isle was untouchable.

By now the SDS had had time to rally, to rebuild under the greatest soldier in the Seven Kingdoms; the King, the man whom Darcy had once thought his father. The Dragon Lords had survived repeated attacks on the Wall and even won back the Brimstones as winter closed in. Commoners were flocking to their banners, including women, if the ravens from Knuckle Quarnack were to be believed. The Dragon Lords were rising again.

'We are still going to attack the Sorcerers Glen?' he

asked cautiously.

'We are going to attack Dragon Isle.'

'We ar- What?' *A joke surely?* Darcy looked at the hard faces ringing the table but there were no smiles. 'I thought the Black Isle? Crannock Castle...to take the Queen? Force the Guild into submission. Besiege Dragon Isle. Starve them out.'

'No longer. We are going to strike the beating heart of the SDS,' his father answered dryly, amusement tinging his handsome face. 'Destroy or take Dragon Isle.'

Darcy tried to swallow the bile that rose in his throat. *Dragon Isle? No one has ever attacked Dragon Isle since the First Alliance. It is the most powerful place on the One Earth.*

No longer, my son...

Darcy's head snapped up to meet his father's eyes. 'When?' he coughed to cover the catch in his throat.

'My spies tell me they are once again holding their regimental race: their so called Dragathon. The races traditionally take place over six glens at the time of the corn planting moon when the thaw sets in. To test their new recruits, give them battle experience. Commoners. Peasants. Even gnomes have swelled their ranks! But the fools fight a new foe, and regimental honour and outdated tactics count for nothing.'

Derisive laughter rolled around the table. Peasants! As if they know how to fight...pitchforks...

'We will strike then.'

'But...Dread K-king,' Quester's father's lands were far to the south, the cold ate at him despite the heavy furs and the heat in the hall. 'We are still icebound this far north. Even in...the Inner Sea the icebergs block the shipping lanes and make them perilous after the thaw. We cannot move our army. Our dragons cannot fly save for the frosts, and your...' He faltered in the face of silence.

Darcy's father grinned wolfishly. 'My dark dragon Queen? We now have a creature from the realm of chaos who will break a path. Our ships have been sheathed in metal that slices through the ice. And we can harness our razorbacks to navigate our way south. They won't expect an attack until the thaw: we will take them by surprise.'

Darcy tried to assume the mien of his father's hard-bitten commanders. He was their Black Prince and future OverLord. His next words were measured, his voice steady. He tried to think of a sensible question that would not show him for a fool.

His eyes narrowed in contemplation. 'But why during the Dragathon?'

'They'll be busy fighting each other and widely dispersed in surrounding glens,' the Earl of Bothwell answered. Although he smiled, the Lord Jamie Hepburn's eyes were flint. 'It's a live-fire exercise, an endurance race that ends only when the dragonglass crown is lifted. So, they won't even realise to begin with that we are there until they truly begin to die.'

Darcy nodded, wanting to appear knowledgeable despite the fact he hadn't attended a single war council. 'They lost most of their Commanders at the Westering Isles...now they are just children led by old men. Ripe for falling. They are no soldiers.'

'They haven't lost their bite, boy. They retook the

Brimstones.'

Darcy bridled at the slur. *Boy!* 'A bunch of rag tag mercenaries led by a useless Dragon Master,' he snarled. 'They wouldn't have put up any fight!'

'Nonetheless,' his father gently chided him. 'If rumours are true, the so-called "Juveniles" were involved in that fight. A talon of novice sabretooths led by your one-time sister, their so called "dragon whisperer".'

Rough laughter echoed round the chamber.

'The fools pin their hopes on a legend.'

Darcy felt familiar fury rise in his throat. *Even here Quenelda cast a shadow over him.... taking the glory that should be his by right. It was unbearable that she had led a successful military operation!*

'My Lords, call your men to arms. Muster your resources. Those of you who hold lands to the north of the wall will add your strength to ours as we sail south. We have our strategy, now to our tactics. We have three moons and then we strike, thaw or no!

'Fear gives words wings.'

'Fear gives words wings.'

CHAPTER SEVENTEEN
DVEs and EFVs

The young Dragon Lords were eating with Armelia in the royal apartments on Dragon Isle when Root bounded in, brandishing a black training helmet inset with runes and strange optics.

'I have it!' he announced. 'We're going to be the first to trial it!' He grinned at them all. His face and ears were bright pink from the cold, and his winter flying suit looked sodden, but the young navigator didn't appear to notice.

Quenelda recognised the look and welcomed her friend with a weary smile and a raised eyebrow. 'A new helmet?' She was exhausted like all of them after three intensive weeks of winter training, and was looking forward to a hot bath and bed.

'Nooo!!!' Root was offended. 'Not just *any* helmet! It's got a runic HUD for DVEs. Designed by the Guardian's new Winter Strategy Group led by Professor Dimwrinkle! It's heads up and eyes out. It will give us greater situational awareness! And heat-seeking runes, so we can track enemy troops in nil visibility.'

There was a short silence. Root looked up into a polite sea of incomprehension. Quenelda's eyes had crossed. Armelia's smile clearly said she had no idea what he was talking about, but she was too polite to say so. Once Root began, it was hard to stop him, and Quenelda had never been good at the technicalities of battlemagic.

'DVE?' she prompted, bowing to the inevitable.

'Degraded Visibility Environments. For when it's

snowing....with this we can navigate in blizzards. Featureless terrain, like the ice shelf.'

'Ah,' that perked Quenelda's interest just as Bracus strode in with the same helmet, looking rather crestfallen that Root had beaten him to it. But he was determined to have his say.

'It interfaces with the EFVs,' the tall pilot announced. 'The enhanced flight vision sensors,' he ducked as Quenelda threw an apple at him.

'Root, let's go and test it? We could go now! It's a white-out outside. It's got a dual integrated aviator and navigator HUDs... '

'But you begin training again tomorrow!' Armelia protested. She had so been looking forward to this supper. Life wasn't dull at Court, it had never been busier, but she hadn't seen her friends in nearly a moon. Her appeal fell upon deaf ears.

'We can link directly with CoreCom guidance spheres as well!' Bracus was saying, as he and Root departed to test their new toy without a bite to eat. 'How about plotting approach vectors? We would....'

Quenelda and Armelia exchanged resigned glances and lifted their forks to their dinner.

'Quenelda, look!' Guy bounced in.

'Look! I've got the new helmet!' He announced. 'I - What? What have I done?' Guy asked plaintively as two apples bounced off his armour.

CHAPTER EIGHTEEN
Beat to Quarters

The northerly wind wailed around the craggy peaks of the Brimstones. The only things flying were the northern stroppy ice eagles who rode the wild winds. Far below, Malachite of the Red Squirrel clan watched the third brimstone convoy of the new year depart the wharves of the Old Chain Harbour, carrying desperately needed ore bound for the watch towers between the Brimstones and the Sentinels. Despite its merrily jingling bells and lanterns, the convoy was swiftly swallowed up by the blizzard, but that was good, because no dragons would be flying. Unusually by now, there was no sign of a thaw; in fact, the weather was deteriorating and the brimstone fleet of one hundred icebreaking galleons remained ice locked in the harbour. Endless blizzards had totally grounded Imperials, and a flight from the Howling Glen carrying nets had had to abandon their cargo or die. This convoy had to get through. Harnessed by ten frost dragons apiece, the fifty iron-shod Guild sledges were escorted by a BoneCracker platoon made up of Narwhals, and a talon of newly trained Ice Bears.

It took nerves of steel to deliver these winter convoys, crossing frozen lakes, rivers and sea during the worst winter months. Once they were safe from hobgoblins who hibernated, the dangers lay in thin ice, rock falls and avalanches. Now, they not only faced hobgoblins but fell sea creatures conjured by the warlock: razorbacks, bristling like hedgehogs, but a thousand-fold deadlier.

A half-moon later, a lull in the bad weather revealed the great watch towers of the Sentinels rising skywards, guardians of the Chain strung between them that kept hobgoblins from the Inner Sea and the countless crannogs and sea lochs it harboured. Skirmishers of the Ice Watch had nothing to report as they circled ahead. The ice was thicker than usual, so no danger from hobgoblins. There would be snow by nightfall again, their Captain judged, as he contemplated a hot dinner and his own hammock on the morrow.

Down the line frosts began to get skittish, some spinning on their hocks. The huge ice bears, usually so calm, were growling, setting the Captain's hackles on end. Animals were far more sensitive than humans, their instincts finely tuned. Their Captain squinted through his snow mask seeing nothing. Nonetheless...

'We shall beat to quarters!' His experience told him something was very wrong. 'Beat to quarters.' The bugle rang out, alerting the tail of the column. Whips curled and cracked. Rapidly the bears began galloping until the sledges formed circles, sledges in the middle, bears arrayed outwards in a circle protected by BoneCrackers. The frosts were strung out on point ready to give swift support.

The captain searched the ice for hobgoblin breathing holes but could see none.

Crack!

The ice beneath their feet trembled and buckled before settling. The frosts circled about the convoy in screaming confusion.

Crack!

There was a terrible grinding and groaning as vast shards of the ice rose up and up, cracks racing like black veins through the ice. Bubbles broke the smooth black surface beneath and heavy sledges slewed sideways, some overturning. A foul bestial stench enveloped the convoy. The frosts shrivelled and fell out of the sky. The bears bolted. Soldiers fell to all fours retching; curling up, they died.

'Fire flares,' the Captain croaked, hand on throat. 'Fire flares!'

Boom... Boom... Boom...red starbursts rose high overhead. The Watch Towers of the Sentinels should surely see and come to their aid?

'What in the abyss?' The Captain's deathly words hung in the air as all about the convoy yellowed points punctured the ice, slowly rising like a vast circle of standing stones. The bears still alive were up on their hind legs trying to break their traces. A few bolted. A sledge dropped through the ice and was gone with barely a wail.

The Captain swallowed, sword falling from his lifeless hand as yellowed fetid fangs breached foaming black water. *Teeth?* His heart slammed in his chest as he understood he would not see his wife and children again. Clambering on his overturned sledge he realised the creature must be impossibly large. Whatever it was, perhaps it could be hurt.

'Fire your brimstone! Fire your brimstone.' Grabbing a lantern, he raised frost stiffened covers and thrust the flame into the ore.

CHAPTER NINETEEN
Dark Dragon Dreams

Hunting…hunting…close, oh so close…

Feeding…such sweet morsels…such easy pickings… men and bears and dragons…so sweet…

Quenelda suddenly cried out as explosions burnt her mouth and gullet. She dived into the soothing cold darkness, alone with her rage… the nightmare faded, and she slept.

CHAPTER TWENTY
What a To-Do!!!!

Noble ladies were gathered in bright, gaudy flocks for afternoon tea at F&H's. It was surprising the floor could handle the combined weight of gold, precious gems and prejudice. Fierce competition lurked behind lace, honeyed words, and scones with clotted cream and jam. There was only one topic of conversation. After all, the entire entrance hall had been completely sealed. Endless bangs and the sound of sawing only added to the intrigue. F&H was holding its first Spring Fashion Show, and *everyone* who was *anyone* had been invited. Such excitement had not been seen in the galleries and halls of Court for many a year. Of course, no one would be so vulgar as to bring their vellum invitation beautifully written in gold ink, embellished with the royal seal ~ and some pink hearts!! But...one's seat meaningfully said it all.

'And what row are you on, my dear?'

'The gallery.'

A short silence.

'And yourself, Lady Bracegirdle?'

'The...' The slightest of hesitations. 'The third.'

'Ooh?' Eyebrows were meaningfully raised.

'Ai have a front row seat close to the Royal Box!'

A silent gnashing of teeth.

If looks could kill...dahling!

CHAPTER TWENTY-ONE
Do You not yet Understand?

Quenelda sat on the DragonBone Throne, quietly trying to find an inner calm and strength for what she was about to do. The SDS was training night and day, and yet they were fighting blind. None knew what the SDS would be facing next. No one understood the power of the Abyss.

She had not yet dared seek out Roarkinch, where the nights were long and daylight short. The island radiated a malice that masked a living pulse within, a hungry avaricious power that was growing, its tendrils creeping out in darkness to ensnare willing minds. With sudden realisation, she knew there was a dark thread reaching into the heart of the Seven Kingdoms, a hidden cancer that was growing here too. What did it mean? She had to discover their enemy's plans. She had to take a risk.

Gripping the smooth arms of the DragonBone Throne, seeking solace and inspiration from the Matriarch, Quenelda summoned her strength and moved out of her body. Out and out she quested, swiftly passing over the Old Wall ever northwards till she reached the harsh, treeless permafrost of the tundra. Rising higher and higher, she whispered until she hovered cautiously high above the ice shelf. Cold wards barred her gaze, dark matter that she could not penetrate. Foolish even to try. But even as she thankfully turned from that fearful, dangerous place a predatory mind suddenly snared her; she was held captive, found herself being pulled down towards that pulsing darkness.

Quenelda couldn't breathe. A crushing emptiness suffocated her...she was weakening, thrashing on the DragonBone Throne.

The young Dragon Whisperer struggled, panicking, as helpless as a moth in a spider's web. *So,* the voice mocked, *you think to test yourself against me? You are nothing, child, dabbling with powers you cannot understand or control. Plans are already in motion. You cannot run from me. Do you not yet understand?*

The WarLock's laugh rang out, breaching the walls of her sanctuary.

In fear and dismay at the WarLock's words, the young Dragon Whisperer suddenly realised the answer to all her questions. Her path was chosen for her, a path which would only end in battle with the maelstrom, given form by the WarLock. Chosen for her by others, whether she willed it or no. And it would only end in death.

The gleeful voice laughed cruelly. *Oh, yes, child. You are to be sacrificed by those who profess to love you...did you not know?* The air about Quenelda was coming alive, twisting darkly like ink in water, forming and reforming into arcane runes. *Come,* the voice turned gleeful...*come to me, child, share my dark dragon's dreams...*

'Quenelda!'

Some sixth sense had drawn Drumondir from the hospital, discordant notes jarring in her head that spoke of urgent danger in the HeartRock. She raced towards the darkness growing at the heart of Dragon Isle. Something was terribly wrong; there was an evil here that should not be, that had been searching for a way in. Now it had found one. *How?*

Taking in Quenelda's seizure at one glance, grabbing one freezing hand and closing her eyes, the BoneCaster became still as stone, and crossed what her people named the Bridge of Veils. Quenelda's terrifying, soul-sucking fear engulfed Drumondir. Heart pounding, she cast herself between the WarLock and Quenelda. Snatching the young woman in her talons the snowy eagle soared, up, up and away from danger into the whiteness, gripping Quenelda's limp body as if she would never let go.

You think your petty magics will keep her safe, BoneCaster? I am coming for her, for all of you...

'Drumondir? Drumondir?' Quenelda was beginning to panic. The BoneCaster lay on the floor, pale face slack. Her breathing was shallow and rapid. Quenelda dragged her against the throne, sitting her upright. Turning to fetch some water she was stopped in her tracks by a strange voice.

The Hold of the Empty Well has awoken. It was Drumondir who spoke, but the unfamiliar voice was not that of the BoneCaster. Her eyes were open but unseeing. *The Maelstrom is rising, and the Knight of Darkness has claimed the empty throne. The earth trembles and heaves beneath his feet. Stones crack. The air steams. Water boils. Sulphur burns.*

'Roarkinch', Quenelda breathed softly.

'Darkness and ice shall rule all under endless night when he comes. He will devour the stars and cast all into darkness.'

Quenelda shifted uneasily.

'The stone watchers await to be woken. The whisperer awakes, but whose call will she answer?'

'What...what does that mean?'

Drumondir groaned, eyelids fluttering, eyes coming into focus.

'Here,' Quenelda raised the beaker. 'Drink some water.'

Drumondir coughed. 'Child,' she lifted a hand to Quenelda's cheek, looking anxiously into the young woman's eyes. 'Are you hurt?'

'No,' Quenelda shook her head, ashamed, knowing the BoneCaster had saved her life. Her folly could have killed them both. Their foe was far beyond her fledgling powers; she was not yet ready to test herself. Quenelda sighed ruefully. She had a lot to learn.

Drumondir smiled weakly as she allowed Quenelda to help her to her feet. 'Yes, you do,' she said gently. 'And the first lesson is that you must not draw the maelstrom to you: he can kill you on the Bridge of Veils as easily as if he ran a sword through you. You would never have awoken. I have not yet taught you. It was well intentioned, child, but foolish.'

And then Quenelda told the BoneCaster what she had said. Drumondir frowned. 'Roarkinch makes sense. And we know the maelstrom brings death.' But the last part neither could make sense of. Disturbed, Drumondir cautioned her pupil with a kiss and suggested she return to training. She herself went in search of the Guardian. Perhaps his scholars could make sense of the riddle her words posed.

CHAPTER TWENTY-TWO
Roast Elk Wine and Icebergs

The fire cracked in the huge hearth, sending a flurry of sparks up the chimney as three old friends relaxed over roast elk and red wine in the Guardian's chambers, and debated as old friends do.

'We have a strategy and are honing our tactics, but we know nothing of Hugo's plans,' the King sighed. 'He suffered a setback for the first time when he lost control of the Brimstones, he didn't expect us to strike. Now he will know we are not so disorganised or so weak as he thought. I think we can be certain that he will strike again soon, and hard. We just don't know how or where.'

'We should be safe until the thaw,' Jakart judged, 'if this wretched weather is ever going to break. I swear winter is deepening its grip. I have never seen such large icebergs in the Inner Hebrides.'

'How is our Special Ops Winter Warfare regiment coming on?' The King accepted a mug of spiced dwarf cider, relaxing as its warmth coursed through him.

'We have five hundred crews training in advanced winter warfare. Veterans from the Ice Bears, Narwhals, White Foxes and the Winter Wolves are training them.' Jakart responded. 'We have sent only those born in the north and used to the cold.'

'And our fortress in the north?'

Magnus Fitzgerald stood to retrieve waxed papers from the table beneath engineer drawings. 'Your daughter's suggestion that it be built underground, carved out of the ice, like your new fortress on the wall, has challenged our engineers. They are struggling to heat barracks and halls, but nonetheless it will be operational by the time we strike. Ice can be carved more swiftly than stone.'

'That is good news,' Jakart said. 'We lost our specialist winter forces when the Night Stalkers fell so we- '

'He knew,' the King said flatly. 'Hugo *knew*, even back then, that they were cold weather troops, that they would be a specific threat to his citadel in Roarkinch. He was just making sure that if we ever found out, we would not have winter warfare capabilities to do anything about it. We just didn't see it for what it was, which is of course what he intended.'

'Of course!' The Guardian closed his eyes, they had been so blind. 'We thought he was eliminating any witness to his treachery. But he was eliminating a clear and present danger to his Night Citadel.'

'And we have barely two moons at the most before the thaw must surely set in. It is precious little time to relearn winter tactics for one regiment, let alone train all seven and your battlegroup with a handful of veterans.'

Jakart bent to throw another log on the fire when a guard knocked and stepped in.

'Your Grace. My Lord Guardian, Commander. Your Grace, your daughter is asking a-'

'Papa!' Quenelda, followed by Tangnost, burst in anyway, banging into the hapless guard in her haste, making him stumble further into the room and drop his halberd. He crossed his eyes as he picked it up. He would get into trouble.

'Lord Guardian! Jakart! Papa, I have an idea! Tangnost and I have been talking about it. He thought I should bring it to you straight away!'

The King smiled as he dismissed the red-faced guard. Quenelda had never been one for protocol.

'And what is your idea, Goose?'

Quenelda stepped forwards and unrolled a crude map of Roarkinch, hastily sketched, on the table, pinning it down with a flagon of wine and several heavy cut glass goblets. 'We need more light.'

Tangnost brought over a branch of candles.

'I've been thinking of when we flew north to find you. We can attack Roarkinch from the south too.'

'It's too far from land,' Jakart pointed out.

'Not if we use the icebergs as staging posts'.

'It's impossible,' the Guardian judged, blue eyes quizzical, prepared to be proven wrong. 'Only Imperials would have the range and the ability to inflict serious damage with ordnance and troops, and they are too heavy to land and take off from icebergs.'

'I know it's really dangerous! But we *know* it can be done,' Quenelda argued. 'Storm has done it twice. Papa, you know it's true. If we can do this, we can attack him from the south from open water. He will never expect that! I know I can do this. Let me try! The dragons will do it for me.'

'BearHugger?'

Tangnost pensively studied the table map where Quenelda had marked ten brigades of frosts and seven Imperial Squadrons spread over hundreds of leagues. 'It will be very dangerous, and we will lose many patrols in close logistic support the closer we get, in order to provision those remaining. We should expect casualties. Without Quenelda we couldn't even attempt it. Injuries to both dragons and crews would end it before we began. Imperials would never willingly land on an iceberg. But,' he inclined his head towards Quenelda. 'The WarLock will know this also. His defences to the south might just be his weakness. His blind spot.'

'As is Quenelda,' the King nodded. 'His arrogance will never allow him to believe in a Dragon Whisperer, let alone a young woman.'

Tangnost nodded. 'I think if Quenelda says she can train the dragons, then at the very least we should let her try. After all,' he bestowed a rare smile on the young woman now hopping up and down in excitement. 'This is why we have a Dragon Whisperer! To do the impossible!'

'And the flight crews? How are the trials going with our new helmet from the School of Snow & Ice Studies?' The Guardian queried Tangnost. 'Their success would be essential for such an operation.'

'Our handpicked squadron have been trialling them for nearly a moon. Debriefing is unanimous. Navigators say it means they can navigate and identify targets in all weather, even in a blizzard. The pilots can attack without lifting their staffs, simply by looking at their targets and the new battlerunes are flawless in execution. Ice formation could be dealt with by sabretooths.'

The King sighed and Quenelda knew she had won. 'Goose, I have no memory of that time after the battle, so I cannot help you, and Storm's leg would not hold up, he cannot do it a third time. But,' he glanced at his Dragon Master sensing his affirmation, 'I will give you Tangnost and Odin and you can pick the best dozen dragons and flight crews from the III and the Wall to show what you can do. If Tangnost is satisfied, then I will give you two thousand Imperials drawn from all seven regiments. But,' he warned, 'you have little time before Operation White Out.'

The King kissed his daughter on the forehead. 'Make it happen, Goose. But,' he cautioned. 'You cannot tell anyone why, and train on the Inner Sea with eyes above. This training is strictly on a need to know. Ouff!' He grunted, as Quenelda hugged him fiercely and ran from the room, to the amusement of the Guardian and Jakart.

'Look after her and the dragons, BearHugger,' the King sighed in fond exasperation. 'Temper her passion with judgement. And deploy frosts both as path finders to identify suitable icebergs and to serve as guards on take-off when our heavy Imperials are most vulnerable.'

His Dragon Master bowed and left.

CHAPTER TWENTY-THREE
Woman to the Fore

'Armelia, my dear!'

The Queen's favourite lady-in-waiting curtsied as she stepped into the solar. It looked a little strange being there in flying leathers, even if they were bright pink and sewn with sparkly hearts and a small magenta blue dragon. Armelia's boots had lots of bells, you could always tell when she was nearby ~ no creeping up unexpectedly behind you. Some laughed behind her back but sales of the ladies flying range at Foresight & Hindsight's were booming, and Armelia was becoming a wealthy young woman in her own right. And the Dragon Master's range was selling like hot cakes as aspiring young Dragon Lords spent their gold on the very latest gear designed by the legendary BearHugger.

'How is our favourite mare today?'

Armelia's expression softened. She loved Chasing the Stars, they both did. 'I exercised her this morning with Root on Two Gulps and Quenelda on...err...yes, with Quenelda.' Armelia reflected she still found it difficult to believe that her friend could turn into a dragon, well half dragon, and fly herself. It was strange to hold conversations in her head, too, but she and Root could hear their friend as if she were speaking normally.

'I have not seen her fly,' the Queen admitted of her daughter. 'Many times, I have seen her sheathed in black scales, even in the palace; but not winged or with a tail.'

'The tail is the hardest part to get used to,' Armelia nodded.

They shared a smile.

'When she is with her father and other officers, her black armour is not so different to theirs. Perhaps it's time I went flying with her also? Is it fun?'

Armelia wrinkled her nose doubtfully. 'Weeeell...she shows off a lot. Loops about us. Flies upside down. She dives so close that Chasing the Stars got a fright and nearly threw me! Two Gulps never does anything in a hurry, and she can fly so fast I think it irritates him. Root lost his temper and told her she was as pesky as midges! Just as I think I know about dragons, she shows me how little I have learnt!'

The Queen sighed. 'Perhaps, when she returns from training... I was hoping you might be free to join me today?'

'Where are we going?'

The Queen smiled a little wickedly, 'I thought we might arrive unannounced at Foresight & Hindsight's to see how our plans are coming along, then inspect the City defences. Everyone must become involved in this war or we will lose. I thought F&H could, ah, perhaps knit unmentionables[1] for the troops. My husband tells me the soldiers are suffering dreadfully in this cold. F&H have already taken the plunge with your flying suits and have made a great deal of money. Unmentionables might not be so glamorous, but they are, Drumondir tells me, essential to prevent frostbite.'

Armelia smiled with pleasure. As Fashion Day drew ever closer, so excitement in the City was growing; and

[1] Underclothes to you and me, but 'unmentionables' in Foresight and Hindsight's Exclusive Emporium.

whereas the idea of inspecting fortifications would have once horrified her ~ all that mud and ice, and crowds of revolting peasants held back by the soldiers ~ now she found the cold air exhilarating, and to her great amazement and delight, the unruly and decidedly unwashed crowds were warming to her, particularly since she had taken up a pickaxe herself to show willing. Although her feeble strike had bounced off the frozen dirt and knocked her out, dozens had rushed to her aid. Coming to, feeling ever so foolish and with a bump the size of an egg on her head, the Black Islanders had helped her to her feet, clapping and cheering. A dozen rough hands helping her out the ditch patted her back and tugged their foreheads in respect. Now, like Caitlin, she was cheered wherever she went.

'Our Great Ditch, as the common folk now call it, is well underway, the Queen continued. 'Thousands dig in return for food and drink and a roof of any kind. It is their homes and families who have been destroyed. Their loved ones who swell the ranks of the Forsaken. I know the Guild think it a foolish and expensive waste, but now as my daughter says, we must expect the unexpected. She has taken that as her motto.

The Pyromancers Guild has devoted itself solely to producing dragon fire for the moat and I believe ~ they are working with Dragon Isle ~ to...create a mine of dragon fire that can be sunk underwater to kill hobgoblins. What a fascinating age we live in! They have assured me our ampoules will be completed and laid in time for Operation White Out where one moat will be fired. The City Guard have now been organised into quarters,' the Queen continued, eyes wide with amazement. 'So many have joined; the elderly and the young, man, woman and child.'

Armelia nodded. 'Even gnomes are signing up, having seen what Root has achieved,' she said proudly. 'They work with the Healers, in the kitchens and the stables. Many are training to scout. They do not despise humble tasks'

'If they have half the aptitude of young Root,' the Queen smiled, 'then their gifts are priceless indeed.'

CHAPTER TWENTY-FOUR
Icebergs

Crystals of ice flurried across the endless expanse of the frozen Inner Sea where a small circle of red flares swirled and eddied, watched intently by a dozen Dragon Masters and Mistresses. An argument of brightly robed Faculty academics from the newly created Faculty of Winter Warfare and Tactics were eagerly watching through their telescopes. Their vector calculations were being put to the test. Their frost dragon mounts had drawn together in a group, constantly changing those on the outside so that they kept warm when any other living creature would die in such low temperatures. Thirty Imperials were also there in heavy winter harness, half of them airborne, banking in a wide circle above as the lead Imperial, Night Frost, piloted by Bracus with Root as navigator, swept in, stalled, filled her wings with air, and landed on the flare target in a spray of powdered snow. Talons scrabbling for purchase, she managed one step, two, and then one of her talons caught and she fell with a massive undignified thump face down, her ongoing momentum carrying her forwards for a hundred strides before the pile of snow finally brought her to a stop.

Hands on face, eye closed, Tangnost cursed with sheer frustration. *Not again!* This would not do, not at all. Already the best of their young flight crews had been practising for an intensive half-moon to land on an ever-decreasing circle. One juvenile was retired with a broken leg, and there were some half-dozen flight crew casualties. The rest had finally conquered the steadily decreasing approach vector and landing pad.

Tales that their King had survived by putting down on an iceberg after the battle of the Westering Isles, and that Quenelda, Root, Quester and Stormcracker had done so a second time whilst searching for the Earl, were widely known, but watching this woeful performance few would believe it possible, and if he hadn't been there himself, Tangnost was beginning to doubt it too. *Perhaps our tactics are too ambitious?* But there was no telling the size of icebergs in the far north about Roarkinch, and it would not do to get stuck out in the ocean far from their intended target and simply freeze to death.

'I think we need to adjust those talon sheaths,' Odin was already striding off to where Night Frost was struggling to her feet and shaking herself down, causing a chorus of protests from the commandos who had unbelted their harnesses. The snow settled. A few Bone-Crackers falling down the icy wings took a little longer, some ending face down in the drifts.

'Perhaps the points are too sharp?' Odin suggested. 'They are grabbing.'

'Perhaps we should ask Drumondir?' Tangnost countered, helping an embarrassed commando to stand the right way up and empty his helmet out. So far today there had been two knocked unconscious, and three broken arms, legs and ribs airlifted by attending harriers to the infirmary on Dragon Isle.

Root felt like his ribs had been crushed by the belts that held him in his wychwood chair. Already black and blue, he would be stiffer on the morrow unless he could have a soak in the baths beneath the sabretooth roosts.

The thought cheered him up.

'Root? Bracus? Are you alright?' Quenelda alighted on Night Frost's withers, her jet black wings furling then disappearing.

'I'm beginning to doubt we ever did this,' Root unconsciously echoed Tangnost's doubts as he grumpily took his helmet off and scrubbed a hand through his hair. 'If we can't land on flat ice, how are we ever going to manage on bobbing icebergs?'

'Well, we did land! And take off! I think everyone is tired.'

'We'll give it one more approach?' Bracus asked of his navigator. 'Affirmative,' Root nodded returning to his seat. 'But we are losing daylight.'

'One more attempt. B Wing, one last pass before darkfall. Command, we are going to make one more attempt with full payload.' The Imperial began to warm her wings.

Tangnost nodded, eyebrow raised questioningly to Odin and Dragon Mistress Greybeard. *Perhaps this time?* The cohort had been training with increasingly heavy combat loads. Now they were carrying a full contingent of sabretooths and air assault commandos, but they just couldn't manage take off. And they would have to begin all over again on icebergs without Root and Bracus. Night Frost had been deployed north of the wall on reconnaissance, and would be leaving with first light tomorrow.

'Slowly, slowly does it,' Night Frost put down at the very edge of their target. Bracus let her rest this time, a fine judgement given the cold. 'Warming up. Warming up.' Bracus let out a deep breath. 'Take off, take off, take off.' The huge wings swept down, One step. Up. Two steps. Down. Three steps and a leap and...then up, four, wings swept up, wings down and up. 'Command, we are airborne. Night Frost is airborne!'

Finally! The Dragon Masters and Mistresses punched fists with quiet satisfaction as cheers broke out. If the other dozen hit their target, and managed to take off too, then it was time to begin intensive training on icebergs.

'Delta Wing. Stand down for the day. Dark is already falling. Debriefing at 1800.'

CHAPTER TWENTY-FIVE
Dark Dragon Dreams

Hunting...Hunting...

It was late: the bells had tolled the witching hour. Root and Quenelda were about to return to their barrack bunks when the hairs suddenly prickled on Quenelda's head. The King's daughter sat bolt upright, the book on her lap falling to the floor. Her companions were sleeping where they sat about the dying fire; exhausted.

Hunting... Hunting...

Some inexplicable *other* was out there in the dark of the night sucking at her soul. Something vast. Cold. Deadly. Water gurgled. It was so dark down here. The scale on her palm throbbed dully and began to glow with a soft phosphorescent green. A creature was out there, perhaps part dragon, its presence clung to her thoughts like a shadow and it was drawing ever closer. A feeling of heavy dread settled on Quenelda, her eyelids began to shut as she swayed.

The maelstrom is rising....

'What?' Root blinked like an owl. Bracus was snoring loudly.

Quenelda looked at him blankly.

'You just said something. Well,' Root qualified, poking Bracus in the ribs so he could hear better, 'you said it, but it didn't sound like you.'

'What did I say?'

Root rolled his shoulders to relieve their aching. 'You said...' he looked worried, 'the maelstrom is rising.'

Quenelda stared. 'I've been having nightmares, I must

have been talking in my sleep,' she admitted, 'the same dream every time.'

Root was much more wide awake than he had planned. 'What kind of dreams?'

'That something... dark and dangerous is drawing near...'

Root swallowed. 'What sort of something? The War-Lock? He's dark and dangerous!'

Quenelda shook her head. 'Infinitely older...from the darkness before the First Age...'

'A dragon, then?'

She looked up at him. 'No... Yes...I don't know, Root. It's in the water...'

CHAPTER TWENTY-SIX
Up! Pull up, up, up!

'UP! UP! UP!' Tangnost cast his voice, that of a Bone-Cracker used to making his orders heard on a battlefield. 'UP! UP!' the Dragon Master repeated, hands on head in consternation as the huge belly of the Imperial barely cleared his position. 'Pull up! Too fast! Too fast!'

There was a horrendous noise as the Imperial banked, its wing tip talon cleaving through the iceberg, setting teeth on edge. There was a collective moment of horror as the Imperial pivoted sideways almost slamming into the berg before the pilot and dragon, clawing desperately, floundered, then began to gain height.

The Dragon Master let his breath out. That was too close a shave!

'Perhaps it simply cannot be done on icebergs this small, and what we did was exceptional. We were going to put down or die in the sea. And we may just have landed on the perfect iceberg. We have successfully put down on over a hundred in the Inner Sea, but the icebergs are getting smaller and smaller as the new moons approach.'

'But we *did* do it,' Quenelda smiled infuriatingly. 'Didn't we? It wasn't that large a berg.'

'Yes, but we- '

'We just need fire power, and Imperials have plenty of that do they not? They can carry brimstone for how many days in the field?'

'A quarter moon,' he answered testily. 'But you know that already.'

'Mount up!' She toggled her helmet. 'Lift off, Simon, let's find an iceberg!'

The ice frost 'path finders' as they were being called, proud of their new 'Dragon Whisperer' patch of a black imperial against an iceberg, had marked two of the largest bergs near the Sentinels. One had height, and a well which might be large enough to put safely down on, Tangnost agreed. *But taking off?*

Phoenix Firestorm folded her wings. Tangnost relaxed a notch. It was a perfectly executed drop in a slight swell, no one could deny, but that was the easy part.

'Hang on,' Quenelda warned.

'Hang on? What for?'

Climb...

Unseated, Tangnost hung onto his tether as, vast talons gripping the ice, Phoenix lifted herself onto a higher point. Tangnost looked at their vantage with confusion. There was no way the Imperial could run forwards. He frowned as Two Gulps took off and landed just to the fore of the Imperial.

Quenelda bit back a smile. This should surprise them. She and Two Gulps had been practising this little manoeuvre as often as they could. They had first tried it in Glen Etive on the ice pitch with Root and Armelia.... although they had ended up in snow drifts once or twice, they had finally got the hang of it, but it was, Quenelda thought with the optimism of the young, far more fun than tobogganing and surely wasn't impossible on an iceberg.

'Flame!' Tipping on the edge, Two Gulps obliged.

Soon the berg was slick with melting water which immediately refroze. Two Gulps slid over the edge, flaming as he went like a pendulum back and forwards, up and down till he came to rest in the saddle of his creation. With pedantic dignity he moved as far aside as possible before clambering up Phoenix's wing.

Tangnost stared in disbelief. An icy slope had formed.

'We're not going to...?' He left the thought hanging hopefully in the air.

'Oh, but yes,' Quenelda answered cheerfully. 'We are.'

Tangnost closed his open mouth, now full of snow crystals, and contemplated the lazy ocean swell that lay beyond the lip of the icy ramp. The greenstone ocean rose and fell. Rose and fell. Feeling queasy, he was grateful as Phoenix Firestorm began warming her wings before stretching them out as instructed.

Hold your wings furled as you drop, then open them to catch the air as you rise. Time your down stroke to the final moment and we shall climb.

She sensed the Imperial's hesitation.

*Sister, I shall show you how...*wings appeared as Quenelda scaled and leapt in one smooth motion ...she was hurtling down the ice as if she were a toboggan, down and down like she had with Two Gulps and then the lip rose up and...

'Oh, dear,' Root said, as the S&R harrier hauled Quenelda out the water in a net and unceremoniously dumped her back on the iceberg where Phoenix snuffled solicitously at her bedraggled teacher before drenching her in fire to dry her off.

Would you show me again, Dancing with Dragons?

Phoenix teased. *So, I may do that also...*

This was not going to be as easy as I thought. Perhaps less of a lip and she wouldn't have executed a triple somersault followed by a belly flop. At least her hard scales had cushioned her from the landing, and dragon fire from the bitter sea and certain death. There was a rising toll of the injured as the training became more dangerous and difficult, she had to get it right.

Phoenix stood perched on the rim of the drop, wings flailing. No, she couldn't. Tangnost tightened the straps that held him to her spinal plates. Yes, she could. No...

Then she changed her mind once again and with a horrifying lurch the Imperial suddenly dropped onto her chest. With a screech of scales on ice like a banshee wail they fell, happily drowning out Tangnost's scream. Down, down... unbelievably swiftly and those great wings beat downwards just as they hit the upward rise and then ...and then they were rising with a powerful crack of wings and away. Tangnost closed his mouth, opened his eye, and thanked Odin and Aegir, gods of the sea.

CHAPTER TWENTY-SEVEN
Who's Afraid of the Big Bad Dragon?

It was still dark and Samantha Spellgood was feeling quite discombobulated. Today was the day! Organising *the* Royal event of the year at F&H's Exclusive Emporium had been *such* an honour, but also an onerous responsibility as she told anyone prepared to listen! The golden invitations in the shape of a sabretooth ~ which were really a command when sent by the Queen ~ had to include a book on Guest Etiquette. But F&H had not, hitherto, had to take account of dragon etiquette, and on her way to greet their arrival at the trade entrance, Samantha heartily wished it could remain so.

Following at the heels of the Lady Armelia and the Princess Quenelda, the two dragons in question were introduced to Samantha as if they were real people! Certainly, the blue and magenta dragon that nosed the Lady Armelia gently looking for tablets, was beautiful. But the battledragon was positively frightening as it watched her with disturbing interest.

'Won't they...err,' she waved her hands about as if conducting an orchestra, while she searched for the right word. 'Make a mess?'

'Oh, not to worry. The City Diggers will be on hand to clear up if there are any little accidents.'

Samantha doubted that anything to do with these dragons could be described as 'little,' or that the City Diggers could even begin to clean F&H's expensive cream carpets. Horrific visions of clients being buried toe to tip thronged her mind. 'Perhaps they might be taken for a...walk before the show begins?' She ventured, hopefully.

Then the wretched golden dragon with the biggest fangs Samantha Spellgood had ever seen, took a shine to her feather fascinator, the very latest in vogue accessory which she had purchased for the fashion show today, despite its outrageous price tag. Perhaps she could pop it back in the Hat Department without anyone noticing its absence? She nodded to herself. Yes, that would do the trick. Two Gulps had other plans, he hadn't had much breakfast. Thinking it was a pheasant perched on Samantha Spellgood's head, he whisked it away with his huge tongue. One gulp and it was gone! It had taken smelling salts to bring Samantha round. She fluttered back into consciousness only to find the wretched creature was gazing at her intently, drooling, as if it fancied the rest of her for breakfast too!

She was not the only person whose nose was put out of joint by these unusual comings and goings. At F&H's grand entrance where the red carpet was already laid out and the royal standards flew, pouting patrons *without* invitations, were finding their way barred to the ground floor by Yeomen of the Queen's Guard. As they were politely and helpfully redirected, two dozen Juveniles arrived in their armour. Dropped off by an Imperial at the Guild, they had been given special leave by Tangnost, from training for the day. The excited troop were immediately whisked inside, to the outrage of those who hadn't been allowed in.

'Well! One doesn't expect see the lower classes in this establishment,' Lady Bumpberry complained to her companions, as they were ushered through the side entrance. 'Unless in F&H livery. Trolls and gnomes are useful for opening doors are they not?'

'Quait outrageous! Did you see how scruffy they were? They're letting in all sorts these days,' Lord Kerfuffle looked disapprovingly through his monocle. 'Ai shall complain.'

Alerted by a footman, Samantha and her staff arrived at a run ahead of Armelia to find two dozen heavily armoured and grimy troopers of the Juvenile III Brigade in her once pristine entrance hall, leaving a trail of dirty footprints and fallen seats. They were clustered about the tables eating the exquisite pastries and nibbles by the handful off the snowy white tablecloths.

'These...these special friends of yours are...?' Samantha left the question hanging in the air along with her eyebrows, which were about to take off.

'Are going to be wearing my designs,' Armelia said brightly. 'Yes. They are going to model my designs.'

Had they tried, on any other day the Juveniles and their families would have been denied even a reinforced boot toe over the threshold. Opening her mouth to berate one of them who was climbing onto the walkway and strutting along it, Samantha paused. Remembering the Lady Quenelda's first visit in similar attire, Armelia and the Queen's wishes expressed on their last visit, she humbly swallowed a life time of prejudice. They may all come from the Gutters, there may be gnomes, dwarves and trolls amongst them, but these young people were going to war. Had seen action in the Brimstones. One limped. Another had a scar across her face. A third's hand was burnt. Suddenly the reality of their sacrifice hit home.

Samantha coughed. 'I shall arrange for plenty food and drink to be brought to the changing rooms.' That produced a cheer! 'We have arranged fittings in the Gentlemen's and Ladies' changing rooms, and of course Shortcut Stoneman is waiting to do your hair once you are suitably attired.' *Perhaps he could wash their faces at the same time?*

It was not long until the doors would open. Armelia and Quenelda were leading Chasing the Stars and Two Gulps through their paces along the walkway, so they would know what to do. The orchestra had arrived and were in the musician's gallery trying to play what Armelia commissioned, but she had been a bit vague in the detail of it. What exactly did 'atmospheric' mean and what were two muckle great dragons doing in F&H's hallowed halls?

'And of course,' Quenelda added conversationally to Samantha. 'Two Gulps will be doing the smoke effects.'

'The...smoke effects? B-but, won't he set fire to the building?'

'Oh, no! Nothing as dramatic as that! Just enough to make them sit up in their seats.'

'Dahling! Oh, *do* sit still,' Shortcut Stoneman despairingly lifted comb and scissors from Quenelda's hair, bangles jingling in irritation. 'How am I going to finish if you keep bouncing about?'

Quenelda rolled her eyes. 'But I looked...alright anyway.'

Shortcut pressed the back of a hand to his brow in despair as his army of helpers looked shocked. 'Dahling! This is our moment of glory! The whole world is coming today! I'm trying to create perfection itself, not just "alright".'

Armelia groaned inwardly. The stress was getting to everyone. Quenelda was looking like thunder. Armelia was feeling nervous enough, uncertain if her ideas would work. Visions of F&H on fire and the Kingdom's nobility, hats on fire, fleeing Two Gulps, screaming as they ran, were hurriedly quashed with a shake of the head. Armelia didn't want her friend to change her mind. Without Quenelda there would be no dragons. And dragons were at the heart of her Spring Collection, and its purpose of changing hearts and minds.

'Aren't those scales awfully uncomfortable, dahling?' Shortcut's comments to Quenelda broke into her reverie. 'No wonder you can't sit still!'

The Queen's heralds were arrayed along the red carpet that swept up the steps to the elaborate gates of the Sovereign's Entrance to Foresight and Hindsight's Exclusive Emporium. The royal coach pulled by unicorns, accompanied by the Light Unicorn Household Cavalry, arrived to the cheers of the large, and largely unwashed crowds, who had gathered the length of the route from the palace.

Grooms in F&H tartan rushed to help the Queen and her Constable, Sir Gharad Mowbray, down the two steps from their open carriage. Pageantry and precise choreography were going to come together in F&H's first Spring Fashion Day to raise funds for the Queen's special projects. Guests had all already arrived as etiquette dictated, and were seated as they should be according to rank, save for a few who took another's more desirable seat, and refused bad temperedly to move. Glasses of champagne were drunk and refilled, and delectable nibbles nibbled. The orchestra played. And yet, where on the One Earth was the Queen? The quietly smiling Constable took his seat, ignoring all the glances, anticipating the surprise to come.

Speculation was silenced as the candelabras died down almost to darkness. There was a soft roll of drums and coloured motes spun and danced in the air as a fiddle took up. Soft blues and russets spinning and dancing, becoming denser, taking on the outline of two figures. Faster and faster the fiddle played. Smoke blew down the aisle: there was an indrawn breath of expectation which resulted in a lot of coughing. Something moved in the darkness.

Suddenly light shot out from about the room, crisscrossing over the walk-way. *Mages! Light magic!* There was an excited buzz of conversation, and then... A beautiful blue and magenta pedigree dragon stood revealed in the braided light, harnessed in the same colours, glossy scales gleaming, glittering like a thousand candles. There were gasps of admiration followed by a few squeaks of consternation as the gathered audience realised the dragon was not a prop, as Chasing the Stars turned towards the Constable to say 'hello'. Someone in the front row next to him fainted. Several others decided to follow her example until eyes were raised to the two helmeted riders wearing flying leathers in the Queen's colours of russet and blue, stitched with her sigils picked out in silver thread. Then, as the light slowly grew, the audience realised that the slim figures were young women. Dismounting gracefully, they walked to Chasing the Star's head, kissing her nose, one giving her a honey tablet. Then they removed their fantastical winged and spined helmets.

With a shock the audience finally understood, and stood to bow, or curtsey. Hair and faces glittering with diamonds and stardust, the Queen looked at Armelia and smiled triumphantly as clapping and cheering broke out. The elderly amongst the guests, who did not approve of feminine legs that weren't hidden by bloomers, five layers of petticoats and a dress, swallowed their outrage, muttered into their moustaches, and politely clapped as a succession of young men and women appeared in flying leathers in the colour and sigils of the twelve greatest noble houses in the Seven Kingdoms, to loud applause. There were some loud whispers and pointed comments when the audience realised there were gnomes and dwarves and several trolls; silenced as the Queen and the Lady Armelia pointedly moved to join hands with the troopers and take a bow. The fashion designer herself gave a graceful pirouette, which she had been practising for weeks, and led her dragon out. Then the lights died down again, and more champagne was served. There was another round of bowing and curtseying as the Queen shortly took her seat.

A kettle drum began beating, its deep sonorous notes rolling over the audience. Golden motes sparkled and spun in the air. Tiny coloured flames sprang up the length of the walk. In their flickering uncertain light, scales appeared. Flames sprang to life to reveal the scales belonged to young troopers, wearing figure hugging flying leathers, hand-stitched with nine thousand scales of gold or green, red or yellow, blue or white that rippled as they walked. Their matching wild fantastical hairstyles unmistakably the work of the royal hairdresser, Shortcut Stoneman himself. They knelt in a circle facing inwards. At their heart a young woman stood, black-scaled with delicate wings that swept to the floor. Black-scaled save for her hands and head. The audience realised it was the young woman who had inspired the entire collection. A Dragon Lord. A princess. Their Dragon Whisperer.

Armelia came forwards to stand by her friend, and beckoned Shortcut Stoneman, resplendent in kilt and so much jewellery it was surprising he could move at all, to join hands and take a bow. And then the lights went out to uncertain applause.

There was one last surprise in store for the unsuspecting audience. Once again smoke flurried along the walk, pouring off the sides...followed on this occasion by its owner causing consternation amongst those who were regretting their seats on the front rows. The click of talons was loud in the sudden brittle silence. There was a shriek. Everyone else opted to stay quiet and not stupidly attract attention to themselves. Because a gold and red battledragon had stepped out into the hall. No mistaking this, though few in the audience had ever seen one, let alone one so close you could look up its hairy nostrils. Two massive incisors and unbelievably sharp talons provided further clues for the mentally challenged. A battledragon with a rider in matching gold and red scales, riding bareback, so that the two had become one: One Kind. Stunning. Beautiful. And very frightening!

To gasps of horror, the Queen stepped up onto the dragon walk to stand by Two Gulps' head. Laying a hand on his muzzle she turned.

'My Lords and Ladies.' She beckoned the Juveniles forward to stand around her in their leathers and scales.

'May I present the young men and woman of the Juvenile Talon, III Heavy Brigade, commanded by my daughter, the Princes Quenelda, and her battledragon, Two Gulps Too Many, who all fought together with many other brave young people to free the Brimstones. These are the young people and dragons who hold the line against those who would bring our Kingdom down. These are the young people and dragons who die ~ for us. For me....and for you.

'My Lords and Ladies, our Dragon Whisperer fashion collection has been designed by the Lady Armelia to support our brave Guild Guard and City Watch! For we can no longer stand back and let others die in our name. We stand together, or we will most certainly fall.'

And one by one they stood. And one by one they applauded.

Samantha Spellgood wiped away a tear.

CHAPTER TWENTY-EIGHT
Frostbite!

'My people call it frostbite,' the Ice Bear BoneCaster completed her examination of the five score pallets in the Inner Hospice Hall, heated by the sabretooth roosts. 'Where the skin is swollen and red, wait one moon to see the depth of the damage, for they may yet heal; but those with blackened toes and fingers will need amputated, else it may putrefy and they will lose their legs or lives, as well as their fingers and toes.'

The military surgeon nodded. He was used to battle-field amputations.

'I will help as much as I can. My people have a balm to help healing, I will tell your apothecaries the reagents. And I have sent north for as many healers as can be spared by the clans.'

'What do we do, brother?' Odin was clearly worried as he watched the BoneCaster's progress. 'More casualties are arriving every day. And there are many accidents. It will only get worse the further north we travel.'

Eyebrows furrowed, Tangnost took a deep sigh as he watched a young troll about to face the knife. 'Drumondir's people and all the other ice clans survive in the far north without frostbite. We must learn from them.'

'Welcome, BoneCaster,' the Guardian nodded as Drumondir entered his study. 'Please sit. Our soldiers and dragons are suffering in the cold. Tangnost says you may have the answer?'

Drumondir bobbed her head. 'When Quenelda first saw the WarLock's lair, I foresaw the day may come when fighting might take place in the north, in my world. And the Sagas foretell of a great battle between ice and fire for the soul of the One Earth; Roarkinch is an island of fire and ice. I sent snow ravens to my people, who sent scouting parties north into the FrostMarches to seek the nomadic clans of the White Woolly Mammoth, the White Fox, the Dancing Wolves and all others who dwell there.'

'White mammoths, you say?' The Guardian's blue eyes brightened with keen interest. 'I thought they were gone from the One Earth long ago?'

'That is because the Clan wished us to believe so. Their mammoth were hunted to the verge of extinction by the end of the First Age. For centuries, the White Mammoths have guarded and nurtured their children apart from any other peoples, and their herds have prospered and grown numerous as the stars in the sky. They found a hidden world and dwell there in bone and felted igloos. For four moons, their land lies in total darkness beneath a sky of dancing colour they call Heaven's Waterfall.

'Before we even departed, our Chieftain and Clan Elders sent word of the WarLock's betrayal and his alliance with the hobgoblins to the northernmost clans. The Mammoth pledged they would harvest their children's under-wool, which can be felted to make under-garments to keep your Dragon Lords and soldiers warm. And your dragons. Their vanguard of four thousand mammoth head south as we speak, dragging great sledges of wool and felt. They will arrive in time for your military exercise, your Operation White Out, so that you can come to know them and where they may be best...deployed. A further ten thousand mammoths are being prepared for war and will be ready for your attack on Roarkinch, attacking from the north across the ice. They are a people for whom the cold and dark hold no fear.

'They hate the hobgoblins who killed their young and carved weapons from their bones and tusks. With chest armour a thunder of mammoths would destroy massed hobgoblins, much as your sabretooths can. But mammoths are larger, *far* larger. The WarLock will suspect nothing of their presence until he meets them in battle.'

'Hugo for once will be ill prepared,' the King nodded. 'We are grateful. Your clans and warriors have much to teach us.'

'Welcome news indeed,' the Guardian agreed. 'An age of wonders, BoneCaster.'

'With your permission, I will go to the Guild to talk with the Wool Gatherers, the Spinners, the Seamstresses there. Women and children will arrive with the Bears and Mammoths to show how this is done.'

'The Guild are bitter at their betrayal,' the King said. 'Anxious to redeem themselves.'

The III Strike Commander sighed. 'It is true, but be warned. The Grand Master lacks any appetite for conflict, matched only by his ample appetite for banquets!'

The Guardian allowed a wry smile. 'He was badly hurt, Jakart. You must forgive him that. Not many survive a WarLock's wrath and live to tell the tale! His meat must be cut small, his jaw has not set well.'

'Yet he parts reluctantly with his gold...despite it all.'

'The Guild have sat idle and comfortable far too long,' the King agreed. 'Leaving the war to others whilst filling their coffers with gold supplying the SDS; idleness and pomposity deliberately fostered by Hugo. He flattered Rumspell's vanity. He sought to disarm them, and he succeeded. But my wife and the Lady Armelia are about to change all that.' He grinned. 'The Guild won't know what hit them! Quenelda has truly let the cat amongst the pigeons, and feathers are flying. I have been told F&H have been persuaded to join their endeavours to raise and train a Guild Guard and City Watch. A huge success by all accounts.'

'I think Mistress Winifred Needlespin is your woman,' Jakart suggested. 'I was told she was running towards our battle rather than away when the tapestry and half a wall fell on her. Perhaps a simple right hook might have felled Hugo where I failed! I think you may find your match in her, Drumondir. Speak with her, rather than the Grand Master, and find out what the Guild can do. Speed is of the essence!'

Drumondir bobbed. 'Your Grace.'

CHAPTER TWENTY-NINE
We've Caught Them on the Ground...

'ETA?' Bracus asked.

Root checked Night Frost's position, hands playing lightly over his complex runic displays, 'ETA... with this rising wind...1800 bells. Back in time for supper, Bracus. Unless that blizzard catches us first!'

'I'm starving!' The huge pilot complained.

Root grinned. 'You nearly ate a whole cow for lunch! How can you possibly be hungry already?'

'How can you possibly *not* be hungry after eating a plate of nuts and berries? That's what squirrels eat!'

After an uneventful half-moon beyond the Howling Glen, their reconnaissance wing were escorting a medevac out of the Howling Glen to Dragon Isle; thirty-five wounded, two sabretooths and three harriers along with a platoon of the Boars Head Brigade returning to get some rest. The badly injured were already being treated by surgeons and scalesmiths on the Imperial, Dark Dawn, flying just ahead of them, with a half dozen of the lesser wounded with Night Frost. Four elderly Imperials carrying brimstone made up the wing. A routine resupply and withdrawal.

To the west an SDS patrol was also heading south to the Wall. The break in the weather meant the skies were busy with patrols and foraging parties, but already the predicted storm was bearing down on them from the north. The Department of Air had forecast correctly; they had a tight operating window to pick up the wounded from the Howling Glen and get back to the Sorcerers

Glen before blizzards made flying impossible again.

There had been no aerial combat for a moon, the weather was too bad and the days too short: dark was already falling. In the swiftly gathering gloom, Root could see the distant lights of the Old Wall strung out like a necklace across the Kingdoms, fifty leagues to the south. Home, a warm bed, food and friends! Root relaxed into his wychwood chair when distant flashes of light caught the navigator's attention, followed by the slower boom and pop of battlemagic.

He swiftly pressed his com runes.

'SDS patrol, forty klicks west engaging hostiles on the ground. Wait... Three hostiles getting airborne,' he confirmed, hands playing over his instruments. He toggled a coms channel to listen in; it was the edge of their range and already the blizzard was interfering...

'We've g... them on the ground, boys!'

Boom! Boom! Boom!

'We've caught them on the ground! Drop dead, drop dead, drop dead!'

'The Knights of Chaos, the... Knights... Combat drop.

The Knights of Chaos! Root's heart thumped.

'Weapons free. Weapons free. Shoot ... kill.'

'Twenty still on the ground!'

Pulses of light flashed as the SDS engaged. Cracks and screams came over the coms.

'Caught on the ground with no sentries ~ careless.' Root recognised the young Warden of the Wall's calm voice.'

'Let's assist,' Bracus swiftly decided as Phoenix Firestorm cloaked. 'Alpha Wing,' Bracus commanded, as snow began to fall. 'Continue your course. We will re-join you as soon as we can, over and out,' and already Night Frost was banking and climbing steeply to gain height. 'Root, we'll take on board the wounded and the villagers. Get them to the fortress and safety. Course?'

'Intercept vector: west three niner zero'

'West three niner zero, it is.' Bracus gave Night Frost her head and the Imperial disappeared in a thunderclap.

The blizzard and nightfall arrived ahead of them, battering the open moorland, obscuring everything. They were flying blind: Root could barely see ten strides ahead. The young navigator flipped down his new HUD and the world turned into a tactical three-dimensional grid display, his mount's thermal image overlaying it. Great care was still needed to navigate. Even with their newly developed helmet and wychwood displays, it would be all too easy to fly into the ground. But this meant their enemy would struggle to get away this time! Perhaps they could even capture the notorious Black Prince himself.

'Dragon's teeth!' Bracus cursed as two entangled Imperials spun past in a ball of flame, the tip of a wing talon ripping through their shields and scoring Night Frost's wing. Their Imperial screamed in pain. Root screamed as cartwheeling bodies, armour and weapons bounced off their shields before spinning into the outer darkness.

'Taking her up, Root,' Bracus's voice was shaky. 'We'll do a recon pass at four thousand strides. Tell me what's going on down there.'

Climbing steeply, Night Frost approached the battlefield, visible only as opaque flashes through the snow. Swiftly drawing in his battlesphere, Root bent to his displays trying to tease out the detail from the chaos. Strobing light lit up the chaotic darkness beneath as dragons flamed and sorcerer spells scorched through the heavy wet snow like comets.

Just ahead of Night Frost a cloaked SDS Imperial swept down for a combat landing to get more boots on the ground, briefly decloaking as BoneCrackers, sabretooths and men-at-arms spilled down the wing, and then the Imperial was away and cloaking in a wash of swirling snow, leaving the commandos advancing inwards behind their sabretooths, tightening the cordon about the Knights of Chaos.

'Firefight,' Root reported. 'Six hostiles still trapped on the ground and five engaged in low sky combat.' Root instantly fed the information to his pilot's integrated displays. 'The rest have fled or are down.'

Darcy's Knights were wielding their staffs with abandon, waves of sorcery rippling out in cascading circles, careless of casualties inflicted on their own soldiers or their captives. Beneath the endless staccato crack and boom of battlemagic, the air was violent with screams and curses and pleas of the wounded and dying.

Night Frost settled on a ridge on the Brimstones overlooking the battle. Bracus toggled his coms. 'Night Frost in support with medevac. Sending coordinates. Standing by to assist casualties'.

'Night Frost, this is White Leader,' Cawdor replied. 'Stand by.'

'Standing by.'

'Incoming! Incoming!' Bracus warned as a bolt streaked overhead, destroying a stand of rowan trees, its power almost spent.

An image caught Root's attention. Caught in the crossfire, one of the hostile dragon's wings was damaged. The Imperial tried to get airborne but failed; leg collapsing, it crashed down barely a thousand strides from their position.

'One hostile Imperial wounded. Outside the perimeter.' Root switched to his thermal imager. Prisoners were spilling to the ground regardless of the men-at-arms trying to stop them. 'Bracus, look!' He swung his helmet, runes targeting the villagers who were stumbling through the snow, hands bound, tripping, falling, crashing blindly through copses onto open moorland, oblivious to the cloaked dragon above them.

'Combat extraction. We're going in,' Bracus informed his navigator as Night Frost leapt forwards, huge wings spread until Bracus banked her about and she swung her huge hind legs forwards. Air spilling from her wings the mare landed, starboard wing extended, creating a small blizzard of her own with the massive downdraft. Thick ice cracked and broke beneath them as she sunk into the frozen bogs. 'Ready to decloak on your mark'.

'Run!' Root broke silence as a tongue of dragon flame licked out and the stragglers were silhouetted briefly then gone. 'Run!' Leaping from his chair he leapt over the Imperial's plated armour and ran down the mare's extended wing.

'Root, you're betraying our posit-' Bracus began, then closed his mouth. Damn protocol, they knew what would happen to those captured for the WarLock King. They couldn't sit back, and watch others do the fighting. 'Decloaking. Shields down! Get them on board, Root! Stat!'

They were on the ground now, visible and vulnerable.

'Here! Here, get on board!' Root then changed to his people's mother tongue. 'Here! Here, get on board!' and again in Dwarfish.

The stumbling figures halted, heads searched for his voice in the white out. Root quickly struck a flare that burnt hotly, driving back the snow.

A flash burnt a copse of trees next to the fleeing group, killing two of them. As they stumbled the other way, plumes of dirt and ice fountained into the air and more were gone. The knight was killing his prisoners before they reached safety!

'Run,' Root screamed. 'Run!'

'Incoming! incoming!' Bracus warned. 'Shields up. Cloaking.'

Light exploded overhead, darts rattling off their shields.

Furious, Bracus turned his head, and a twin burst of pulses streaked across to explode against the downed Imperial's shield. Bracus struck again and again, his battlemagic meeting fire from his enemy in a coruscating explosion that torched trees. The flames betrayed the fleeing villagers' position.

Explosions a hundred strides to starboard rained down tree splinters, followed rapidly by another much closer, as the enemy found his range. Straddling Night Frost's neck, light streaked from Bracus's staff to strike again and again against the hostile Imperial, to prevent it attacking, trying to buy time for Root.

'Root, get them up, stat.'

'I've got them! You're safe now. Y…'

The youngest, a girl, had nearly reached Root on the wing tip, hand outstretched, when a searing tongue of purple dragon-fire engulfed them all in a fiery embrace. The huge claw of a half-cloaked dragon suddenly came down rib-rattlingly close, the hind claw deliberately crushing everything underfoot as the Imperial's hind quarters bunched to lift off.

'Root?' Bracus screamed. 'Root? Are you alright?'

Armour smoking, stunned, Root was the only survivor as the downdraft of the Imperial knocked him off his feet and lifted the ashes of those who were living people barely a heartbeat before.

'A-affirmative,' he croaked, as he numbly climbed his Imperial's wing. 'He torched them, Bracus! They're all dead.'

'Oh Root, I'm sorry,' Bracus's voice was rough with emotion and raw anger. 'It's the Black Prince!' Root, too, had seen the flash of an emerald standard slashed with a striking adder when the Imperial took off. 'We're going for the kill. We can't waste this chance to take him down. We can't. He has no honour. He's a murderer. Wings up, we're going after him! He must be injured, he can't cloak fully.'

Already Night Frost's wings were rising, and she was running to get airborne as Root collapsed into his pilot's chair, trying to plot the trajectory of the enemy, passing it to his pilot. Plugging in the coordinates, Bracus gave

Night Frost a free rein.

'Command, we are in pursuit of a hostile believed to be the Black Prince, heading zero three five eight. He torched his prisoners. Night Frost in pursuit.'

'Acknowledged,' Cawdor was involved in his own battle on the ground.

Behind Bracus and Root, two cloaked Imperials perched on the Brimstone outcrops took off as Night Frost cloaked.

CHAPTER THIRTY
We have an Imperial down

Root said nothing, trying to wipe the sticky soot from his visor as he gained his seat. He was in turmoil as Night Frost swept upwards. He had lost his father and warren to the hobgoblins, and the remainder of his family save for a sister, in the brimstone mines; he knew what awaited those captured. Everyone had heard rumours of the Forsaken that spread fear and fury in equal measure. Like a slow fuse, anger had smouldered inside him since he was rescued during Operation Brimstone. That a knight sworn to serve would torch helpless villagers exploded like red hot rage inside as he fed coordinates to Bracus with shaking hands. 'He's making for the Brimstones. He'll be able to hide in the ravines.'

'No! We've got him!' His pilot exulted. 'He can't see where he's going. He's rapidly losing altitude, he'll be below us in a moment. He's going to put down until the weather breaks. He thinks we can't see anything, either!'

'Brace for impact. Drop dead. Drop dead.' The huge Imperial folded its wing and dropped like a stone into the swirling white darkness.

Root had watched Imperials of the III FirstBorn Air Attack Group practise on the dragon pads of Dragon Isle, their downwards velocity driving the pad to the ground, absorbing the impact. It was an unused relic from the Mage Wars, attempted only in times of dire need, until the WarLock and his Imperials began to kill SDS Imperials with increasing success.

'You can never train for the actual collision,' Root had

been told by Tangnost and other veterans. 'Your Imperial's weight and speed will break your target's back or neck, a swift death for the dragon. The impact on the ground, for those not already crushed, will kill the air crew and all that dragon carries in one fell swoop.' It was one of the few ways an Imperial could be killed outright.

That memory flashed through Root's mind as their descent was rapidly scrolling down on his eye imager, closer and closer to the hated rune.

'Brace for impact.'

Crack!

The sudden snap of wings and jolt took them all by surprise as they rapidly lost speed. Night Frost had stalled, her huge wings outspread and tilted to fill her wings, sweeping her backwards. Dragonfire blazed in a tongue of incandescent purple that washed over their enemy's shields. Finding a weakness, two dozen men-at-arms died before Darcy's Imperial was out of range.

Stunned, Root watched as their target, suddenly aware of its danger, began to flee over the open moor. Night Frost had lost speed and height and was struggling to rise when...

Boom...Boom! Pulses exploded in black puffs about them. Caught by surprise, Root flinched even as his hands were already dancing over his battlesphere. Boom! Boom! Boom! Further away this time.

'Shield integrity holding.' *Where had they come from? Who were they? They had cloaked again.*

'I can't find them, Bracus. There's at least three of them.'

'They're flying blind, Root. They can't see us, they were just trying to flush us out. They only hunt in packs, the cowards!'

'Dragon's teeth! They're putting down on top of us! Brace for imp-'

Heart beats later, Bracus jinked Night Frost to one side as an Imperial dropped through the air where they had been. Bones snapped: Night Frost screamed as her wing was damaged. They were spinning. Tumbling. Dragon blood sprayed Root's visor.

Bracus's voice was calm as he tried to pull his dragon up and slow their descent. 'Command, we are going down.'

Spinning. So fast. Too fast. Pinned to his chair, Root tried to read his runes, but they were blurred. Flame and smoke poured from Night Frost as her injured wing bones shattered against the ragged rock of the Brimstones.

'Night Frost is going down. Command, we are going down.'

'I can't bring her up! Eject! Eject!'

Stars streaked. Slammed back into his seat, barely able to move, Root struggled to press the rune on his chair.

'Ouff!' With an explosive blast of power, the young navigator was punched upwards through choking smoke and flashes of light. His ascent slowed and then he began to fall, buffeted by wind and hot air from the battle below.

'Bracus? Bracus? Eject!' Root screamed at his pilot. 'Bracus! Eject, Eject!' He couldn't see the Imperial any more, its flame had dwindled to a spark and was then swallowed by the night.

'Trying...trying to pull her up...save our men...' the whisper faded into silence.

Root slapped his webbing coms. 'Bracus? Bracus?' His voice broke. 'Where are you?' Was he the only survivor?

On the Old Wall, the Watch Tower following the battle unfold, responded. 'We have an Imperial down. An Imperial down. Night Frost is going down.' Next second their rune winked out. The second in this engagement.

'Last known coordinates – '

'Scramble S&R,' the officer of the watch ordered. *Not another Imperial?* 'Scramble...scramble... scramble .... Imperial down. We have an Imperial down. Night Frost is down. Wounded are inbound. Wounded are inbound. ETA a half bell.'

With a grunt of pain, Root landed awkwardly, his wychwood chair tangling in the snow-laden branches of a large oak. Pressing a rune, the wychwood instantly took on the aspect of a twisted branch that cocooned him. Huddling in its warmth and shelter, Root became invisible. He touched the rune on his helmet, as it quietly pulsed his location.

CHAPTER THIRTY-ONE

Why did our Imperials Refuse our Commands?

Daylight bled slowly into the white colourless world as Major Cawdor walked the battlefield, talking to the wounded waiting to be medevacked to the Old Wall; the rage of battle an ebbing tide that left him exhausted and shaken. Mud and blood pooled everywhere, trapped in the ice that had swiftly refrozen after the battle. The wreckage of the village engulfed by dragon fire still smoked, a pyre for the enemy dead and the luckless villagers who had been caught in the cauldron of battle. Elsewhere, the heat of dragonfire which had eaten down to the stone bones of the moorland, still glowed. The bodies of three enemy Imperials lay like black hillocks, bones broken open to the sky. One lay injured. One of their own lay amid its dead troopers and sabretooths; its navigator, head resting on that once fearsome great muzzle, knelt weeping, blind to his own injuries. Night Frost was MIA over the Brimstones. They had killed four of Darcy's knights, but the cost was high, and there were urgent questions to answer.

The dead were being laid out into ragged lines. Surviving villagers were numbly searching for their loved ones. Keening carried on the drifting air as husbands and wives, sons and daughters, friends were found. Most however would never be identified, charred beyond recognition. By evening the pyres would be lit at the top of the cliffs of the Old Wall to honour the SDS fallen. How could they fight an enemy who sacrificed their own foot soldiers and dragons with such reckless abandon?

Dirty snow and ash floated down, slowly obscuring the battlefield. The sulphurous smell of dragonfire and battlemagic clung to everything. An Imperial fresh from the Old Wall put down, healers already running down the spread wings. Those that could be saved would be airlifted out to the new infirmary deep below the Old Wall beside the sabretooth roosts. Those that remained would not live to see another sunset. The surgeons and healers were doing their best to ease their passing, packing their burns in snow. Some, in agony, had chosen a soldier's death rather than linger screaming.

'Casualties?'

The physician looked up, wiping sweat with a bloodied arm. 'Ninety dead, twice that injured.'

So many. Cawdor moved on to talk to the dying.

'Rangor. How are you?'

The pale-faced dwarf attempted a smile. 'Just a flesh wound. Will be right as rain, sir!' Cawdor smiled and grasped the offered arm before moving on down the line.

'We-we beat them, Sir, didn't we?' Cawdor held the young man's ice-cold hand, eyes raised as the medic shook his head. 'We killed some of them? We got the Black Prince?'

'Yes, we did, soldier.'

Cawdor stayed as the rising chest grew weaker. The boy smiled between ragged breaths. 'Tell my Ma I died bravely, Sir...tell them I love what I do...' The warm puff of breath faded. Cawdor reached out to gently close the boy's eyes and cursed.

'Lord Warden?' Cawdor looked up into his young esquire's anxious face. 'A courier has been sent to

Dragon Isle on our swiftest dragon, as you commanded.'

Why did our Imperials refuse our commands? Then we would have captured or killed the Knights of Chaos and ended this murder.

(Drawing kindly provided by Phoenix Wilson)

CHAPTER THIRTY-TWO
Gorrangochs

Darcy had been going hunting on the mainland when he saw his father talking to the Dragon Master in the royal roosts. His father beckoned him forwards.

'Why are so many dying?' the WarLock King repeated.

'I do not know, my Lord King,' the Dragon Master swallowed. 'It is too cold for them, they are not creatures of the north. Yes, they are warm here in the roosts, but they come back from battle or patrol with cracked talons, raw muzzles and brittle scales. Their eyes weep from the cold. Their talons turn black and rot. But,' the man hesitated. 'I think the...' he glanced warily at the King's son and took the plunge, 'I think the collars are killing them. They fight them to the point of madness and self-injury. I have heard tell some have flown into the ground.'

'Fight them?' Darcy sneered. 'They're just animals. How can dragons fight collars?'

The Dragon Master lowered his head to hide his anger, but the WarLock King's green eyes were now on his son, who had never had an affinity with that creature.

'Noble dragons have magic of their own, my son; how much has not been tested, but I think their magic wanes. Even so, clearly it will take more than collars to subdue their spirits, and we cannot afford to lose more. Imperials are slow to breed.'

Darcy nodded. He knew all this. 'So?'

'So,' his father said, 'although the collars compel them to obedience, if some have gone mad and others die of exhaustion fighting them, each loss is one too many. Without our Imperials, we cannot attack the Sorcerers Glen. My war Captains tell me this war will be won in the air, not on the ground.' He turned back to his Dragon Master.

'How many smiths have we lost in their forging?'

'Two, my King. And scores of roost hands and several dragon masters…all to the Black Death.'

'We cannot risk Faldir. Roost hands we have aplenty, they are of no concern. Dragon Masters, however,' he smiled thinly, 'are valuable, and a Master Smith most valuable of all. Bring our Imperials, one by one into the Deeping Well. Once they have tasted the kiss of the Abyss, the cold will no longer be a problem. Nor will we need collars. Go! Now!'

His Dragon Master gratefully fled.

'What will happen in the Deeping Well, Father?'

'They will become creatures of the night; of the dark and ice. They will become gorrangochs and serve our needs better.'

'Your dark dragon Queen is not enough to win the fight?'

'You fear her?'

'Who wouldn't?' Darcy retorted bluntly as he stepped down behind his father through one of the gatehouses. 'Even being close made me feel sick.'

'That will pass as your elixir makes you stronger; you will be able to wield the maelstrom as I do and not suffer the Black Death as the SDS call it. But my Queen can only be in one place, and the war is fought on many fronts. She may destroy Dragon Isle, but she is more vulnerable on land. She cannot win this war alone.'

As they descended towards the Deeping Well the young prince's breath turned to coils of mist in the frigid air. Ferny white tendrils patterned the smooth dark basalt as the temperature dropped even more. He shivered as his black armour crackled with frost and hoped his father thought it was due to the cold.

The cavern was immense. At its core a deeper pool of darkness flickered with green light. A soul sucking, heart stopping fear emanated outwards from its un-guessable depths. Darcy had fled this place once before. He stopped at the threshold, unable to go further a second time. Curses and cries rebounded through the tunnels as the first dozen Imperials were being led through the coombs by chains. They fought their bonds as if they knew their fate; it took a cabal of battlemages to drive them forwards, one at a time.

Taut violence filled the cavern. The Imperials were screaming, fighting. Magic flared as they resisted. Hands over his ears Darcy gritted his teeth. Unease stirred.... memories of a younger sister. *Of course, dragons speak. Can't you hear them?*

He could hear them now. Their fear was raw in any language. Screams and shouts were abruptly cut off as handlers died by the dozen, crushed by an Imperial turning to flee. Men at arms were abandoning their posts when coruscating green lightning-like fingers reached out to trap the Imperials and drag them into the hungry pulsing darkness. A young roost hand fell to his knees crying. This was murder.

Yet at the last heartbeat one raised its head defiantly, jerking the handlers from their feet, it smashed its head to one side. Bones broke: loud in the void as it collapsed. Thirty more chose that path despite the WarLock's fury. Over the days, one-by-one the noble Imperials were led in. Darcy did not dare see what emerged.

CHAPTER THIRTY-THREE
Dark Dragon Dreams

Quenelda was screaming. Heartrending cries that roused everyone from sleep.

'Child', Drumondir was the first to arrive. 'Child, what is wrong?'

'Dark dragon dreams. Dragons were...' Her head ached with the memory. 'Screaming, they were screaming. Being enslaved.'

'It was pitch black and freezing,' Quenelda was breathing heavily. 'The Imperials were already bound by the maelstrom, but they were fighting it. And then...and then...Oh, Drumondir! Thousands of them, tens of thousands were being dragged into darkness...into the Abyss...and then they were gone. I couldn't hear them anymore.'

Quenelda's anguished eyes met the BoneCaster's. 'They've gone! I can't hear them anymore.'

CHAPTER THIRTY-FOUR
Search & Rescue One

The twin sap moons were full, painting the towering Brimstones in a ghostly light; their ragged ridges and deep, dark ravines veined with precious ore gleaming like silver. Stars were scattered like dust, brilliant and bright. It was crystal clear and freezing. Without his wychwood cocoon, Root would have died the first night.

'Stay where you are, Sir,' a voice said softly. 'Don't move,' the pilot was looking at his thermal imager, showing the weak signature of the half dead. 'There are a dozen Forsaken nearby, sweeping across the moor, closing in on your position. We have two harriers coming in low and slow. Silent now.'

Softly reaching for his flying knife in his boot, Root tried not to breathe and betray himself. He was shaking with cold and fear and grief. His sheath was empty! His flying knife must have been lost when he ejected. He had no weapon.

A twig snapped just as the wychwood warmed and Root felt something quest into his hand like a root before hardening. Amazed, he brought it into the light. He was holding a slim wychwood dagger!

Crack. Questing from side to side almost like hunting dogs, walking brokenly, the ragged soldiers passed silently below. Save one. One figure in rusty mail and a half helm looked up to where the gnome hid in the scant foliage. Bruised gaunt hands reached up and the figure swiftly climbed leaving several rotting fingers falling to the ground. Shaking, Root waited and waited until the helmet came into view. He kicked out hard, his boot snapping the head back. The helmet toppled. The young man froze.

The skeletal creature was missing half its face; its remaining eye stared with mute appeal as it raised a sword.

'*Kill me...*' it breathed. It was a gnome, a young boy. *Kill me...* it was barely a breath. The rusted harvest scythe arced back to strike, and still Root couldn't move as horror and pity held him. Next heartbeat, the creature crumpled as two arrows took him in the chest. The boy tumbled from the tree, his bones cracking as the body hit lower branches. Above Root a net was lowered, and a welcoming arm reached to cinch him about the waist.

'As quick as you can, sir, there are hostile Imperials approaching from the north.'

CHAPTER THIRTY-FIVE
He's Alive

'He's alive, Quenelda. S & R picked him up at the foot of the Brimstones, he just came in with the wounded, and Simon flew him here once Drumondir had had a look at him.'

'He is alright? He's not badly hurt? Frostbite?'

'No. Suffering from cold, but his wychwood chair saved his life. But Bracus is m- Wait! Bracus is MIA-' Tangnost tried to warn her, but Quenelda was gone, racing to find her friend.

She knew where to find Root. She hurtled into the royal stables, but she was not prepared for his anguish. He was still armoured, still had his special HUD sight above his left eye. He was walking aimlessly in circles talking to himself.

'Root! Root, you're safe!' She tried to gather her friend in an embrace, hands coming away sticky with black soot...*dragonfire*! 'Root?' she took in his sooty face, the tear tracks. 'What's wrong? What's happened?'

'Bracus is dead,' he had run out of tears, but the words tumbled out in a torrent. 'He d-died because he wouldn't leave Night Frost and our men to die. We were hit, her wing was damaged. We went into a spin.' Anger and anguish twisted his face as Chasing the Stars anxiously nuzzled the navigator, her flat ears and tail between her hind legs revealing her distress. 'He ordered me to eject...and I did,' his face crumpled. 'I obeyed him. I'm alive and he's dead. I'm a coward!'

'No! You're not!' Quenelda denied it, as tears stung

her eyes. *Bracus? Dead? It's not possible! Night Frost as well?* 'How did you engage in a firefight? You're on medevac and reconnaissance.'

'Dark was falling and a blizzard was sweeping down from the north. We were returning to the Old Wall with wounded and with troops coming home for some rest. There was a patrol to the west. They'd caught the Knights of Chaos on the ground, taking prisoners, destroying another village. We flew to medevac casualties...but then,' his lower lip trembled, and he could barely speak. 'Some prisoners escaped, and we put down to save them...I'd – they'd – when an enemy broke through and was taking off. It flew Darcy's standard. He deliberately flamed them, they were a heartbeat away from safety, and he burnt them. It caught me but my armour protected me. But th-'

'No!' Wide-eyed, Quenelda's hands covered her mouth in shock. 'Darcy? How could he do such a thing? That's plain murder.'

'And Bracus...we went after him. Darcy's Imperial was wounded and couldn't cloak, or gain height, and they couldn't see anything. They thought they could hide, but we can find them now, even in a white-out. We swept in above them and dropped dead...we had him, but Night Frost wouldn't obey. She stalled. We almost hit them anyway, but Darcy realised his danger and we lost our advantage of height and surprise. And then two of his knights, they attacked us from behind. We tried...but we couldn't throw them, and Night Frost took several injuries.

'They all died!' Root turned in circles. 'Night Frost

wouldn't fight. She flamed, but we could have killed Darcy, got rid of him for good; instead he and his friends killed Bracus and everyone we carried.' Tears of bitterness and bewilderment streaked his dirty face. 'We had him, and Night Frost wouldn't go in for the kill. Why don't they fight for us, Quenelda?'

Seeing her friend's anguish, Quenelda shivered with an uneasy premonition as scales began to clothe her, as the growing inner dragon effortlessly shrugged off the young woman.

'How can *you* say that?' Quenelda's voice was changing, edged with anger. Her outline was becoming hazy...a shadow darkened the roosts. Her eyes blazed in the semi-darkness. 'You, of all people?' she accused. '*You* don't fight! Your people don't fight.

'Would you see Chasing the Stars fight? You don't even fight the hobgoblins when our dragons do. So why should dragons fight each other? Dropping dead would have meant killing Darcy's Imperial too. It might even have been Night Frost's mate. Did you think of that? Why should they kill their kindred? Just because we do? Do you want to force them?

'It's *our* war, Root ~ not theirs! I would rather die than force them to fight!' Quenelda fled, leaving her friend shocked.

CHAPTER THIRTY-SIX
SitRep

Outriders arrived before nightfall just as the braziers were being lit, heralding the approach of the King and the Guardian, guarded by the elite Faculty Guard. Two escorting Imperials landed on the parade ground with fresh troops and sabretooths to replace those killed. The young Warden of the Old Wall had not long returned from the battlefield, and hadn't had enough sleep.

There was the crack of wings and a huge downdraft as five Imperials, escorted by three wings of frosts, put down on the royal pads, driving them down deep into the heart of the underground fortress. The Imperials were flying the Royal Standard of a unicorn and the silver DeWinter's wolf's paw, and that of the Guardian: two swords crossed against a book. Already forewarned, the Warden had an escort ready.

Cawdor's face was still filthy from battle, but Quester recognised him.

'Lord Warden,' he saluted.

'Sir Quester,' Cawdor's white teeth gleamed against the soot. They clasped arms. 'It's an honour!'

'We all saved him that night.'

'I am glad to see you on your feet. They said you would never walk again.'

'Quenelda gave me a new leg.'

'We heard. The men marvelled at that. She is an unusual young woman!'

They grinned, that was certainly true!

A bugle sounded, and the lines of troops saluted.

Cawdor turned to greet his King and the Guardian with a salute.

The Operations Hall looked north from the limestone cliffs out over the Midge-Ridden Moor towards the mountains. It was the first time Quester had seen the newly built forward operational base of the SDS, the first time he had returned to the scene of his nightmare. He could not believe how much had changed in such a short time.

Curiosity and amazement vied with a fear that fluttered in his chest and made him sweat, despite the cold. He closed his eyes as memories flashed through his mind. The noise. The smell. Light searing across the darkness. The utter chaos of battle on the Wall as hobgoblins threatened to overwhelm their desperate departure last year on Stormcracker, finally to bring Quenelda's father back to safety.

Startled he felt a hand on his shoulder squeeze him gently, and looked up into the King's blind milky blue eyes. The King's nod was barely perceptible before he turned away. *He knows*, Quester realised, trying to still the shaking. *He understands.*

The King sat, Quester at his shoulder.

'Sit down, man,' the King said to Cawdor. 'Before you fall. We heard your report from the courier, but want to hear it in detail in your own words.'

The Guardian nodded to Cawdor. The young man was bruised and bandaged for injuries he probably did not remember taking. Exhaustion and something more was etched on his young face.

Cawdor gratefully sat as his esquires used fire irons to warm leather mugs of wine. He took a deep breath. 'There have been a dozen raids down the coastal fishing villages along the Ness in this last quarter-moon alone. Villages and boats burnt to the ground. Two days ago, they attacked Duskendale near Obban. The castle was destroyed, and nigh on ninety men, women and children taken, the rest dead. There are few sailors and fisherfolk left now. As usual we were too late. It's as if...' Cawdor paused, searching for the right words.

The Guardian's blue eyes narrowed. There was much here to worry about if their suspicions were true.

'I know it sounds fanciful, but it's as if he can control the weather. The Knights of Chaos are more cautious since they took casualties at the end of last year. They appear only as the weather breaks. By the time we arrive we find them gone, and we can't pursue because the weather closes in again with a vengeance. We know it's the Black Prince, because in every case there were a handful of survivors, if you can call them that, making at least one of our patrols stop.'

'Forsaken?'

'No,' Cawdor shook his head and winced as stiches tore and fresh blood seeped through the bandages on his neck. 'No, my Lord Guardian, but just as evil. The Black Prince leaves only children behind. Less than thirteen winters. Robbed of their minds as if they were babes or elders in their dotage. A burden to their kindred. They can't even feed themselves.'

The King closed his eyes. *What are you doing? You were my son, I raised you as my heir. So like your mother...feckless and fell...*

The Guardian quietly stood and walked to place a hand on his friend's shoulder. 'Your son or no,' he said softly. 'Darcy had everything, Rufus. And he chose to walk away, to embrace the Abyss. He is damned for what he has done to our people. Do not look to yourself to blame.'

Looking away from his King's grief, Cawdor bit his lower lip, wondering how he would feel if it were his son. But both boys were gentle and fun loving, safe here within their great fortress. That nudged his thoughts.

'My Lords, the soldiers are frightened that their families too will become the Forsaken, and many want to return to their stockades and villages to protect their kin. All men of fighting age are deployed in action. Recon suggests it's just the coastal fishing towns and villages up and down the coast that have been hit. They are isolated, few travel inland; so we did not see a pattern until this last moon.'

The King wondered. 'Mayhaps, but Hugo does nothing without a reason, so why do they raid the coast? There must be something more... A clue we are missing.'

Cawdor shook his head, exhausted. He was too tired to think.

'Send out Imperials, those elderly, lightly wounded, not engaged in combat,' the King ordered. 'Take your Boars Head brigades, they can penetrate the deep forests, and bring them all behind the Wall. Otherwise we will end up fighting them.'

He raised a hand to stay words of caution. 'I know, Magnus, we are already struggling to feed refugees, and

Hugo will know it. But our troops will fight the better knowing their families are safe behind the Wall. Is this not why we are here?' He turned back to Cawdor.

'You have yet to tell us how you caught our so called Black Prince and his knights?'

'I decided to deploy a score of ground attack Imperials to the old half-completed fort on the Isle of Midges. Under cover of night, we have been restoring the roosts and stockpiling brimstone. At the first sign of a break in the weather, we patrolled the Inner Hebrides, watching, waiting. We were lucky. They fired the village, and that drew us to them. We caught most on the ground and the others preparing to get airborne.

'We deployed five hundred BoneCrackers with a combat insertion, and as a dozen were getting airborne I ordered Drop Dead. I knew it would mean multiple casualties, but killing the Imperials and killing or capturing any of the Knights of Chaos would strike our enemy a heavy blow; mayhap, end their harvesting of the common folk. Perhaps we might even have captured the Black Prince. It should have succeeded. But...'

The King sat forward, hearing the tremor, the disbelief in the young officer's voice. This is what they had come for. 'They refused you?'

Startled Cawdor looked up. 'Yes, Your Grace! Our Imperials refused us. All of them. They dropped, but when they realised their targets were their own kind, they stalled. It took precious time to regain height and they killed one of ours close to the ground; a second went down over the Brimstones, one of your Imperials.' He paused, suddenly realising. 'You know of this already.' It wasn't a question.

The Guardian nodded. 'We have suspected it. But it has been impossible to verify ~ until now. In the heat of a firefight, amidst smoke and sorcery and the noise of battle, who can clearly see why one dragon dies and another lives?

'Battles, and they have been few this season, have always been to the north. It has hardly ever been practical to do anything other than retrieve our crew and troops. It is folly to wait to be ambushed.'

'We know his Imperials kill ours,' the Guardian said. 'We have yet to work out how or why. I fear we may not like the answer: Hugo cares nothing for the lives of his men or dragons.'

'My Lord King, they know our weakness now,' Cawdor was anxious. 'Only a fool could have failed to see our Imperials refuse. They should have died, and they know it; and by now the WarLock King will know it too.'

'Perhaps,' the King allowed. 'Perhaps they may question it, but I doubt in the firefight that ensued, my s– Darcy will be able to work out why. They may put it down to inexperience or injury. You were attacking before you ordered drop dead, and you were cloaked. Unlike us, they wouldn't have known you were even there, our battlemagic, thankfully, is beyond him.'

'Or they may think, correctly, that if we can, we will capture Imperials alive rather than kill them,' the Guardian suggested. 'They were worth their weight in gold before the battles of the Westering Isles and the Line. He knows how depleted our ranks are.'

'Our Imperials kill hobgoblins without mercy. They kill the Forsaken out of pity. They kill the WarLock's men from high mages to foot soldiers. I doubt anyone else knows of this one refusal. We clearly ask too much of our dragons, and we must devise other tactics.'

'There are many who will decry this if they hear of it, Rufus,' the Guardian warned. 'Who might say, with justification, that to win this war we need Imperials to kill enemy Imperials. Who will want to force them to our will, as Hugo clearly has done.'

'Which is why this must not be openly discussed. Should Hugo hear of this, he will throw all his Imperials at us in one fell swoop. If he has studied the Mage Wars, he knows this war will ultimately be won in the air. Only Marcher Lords have been given leave to fly Imperials, and they don't have the training to execute SDS manoeuvres like Drop Dead. Let us hope their one refusal passes unmarked.'

'And meantime,' the Guardian added, 'a cabal from the School of Aerial Strategy & Tactics are researching alternative tactics to disable enemy Imperials without injury.'

The King nodded. 'We must find new ways of winning this war, and find them fast. And then we *will* brief our flight crews. We talk of change. Well we must. And fast.'

CHAPTER THIRTY-SEVEN
Roarkinch

Smoke billowed from the forges, mingling with black volcanic clouds lit from within by lightning. *An island of ice and fire,* Darcy thought. A bubbling cauldron of contradictions. From his vantage on the lower slopes of the volcano, surrounded by his Lords and Captains, the WarLock sat on his gorrangoch overseeing the preparations, as slaves laboured and died night and day to launch his mighty Armada on time. Iron-shod icebreaker ships built on the mainland were joining daily, testing their seaworthiness on the journey to the island through pack ice and icebergs, bringing yet more men-at-arms, soldiers and knights. Great dragon carriers, six hundred strides long; nine-masted with twelve sails, towered above flat-bottomed, broad-beamed troop carriers, merchant galleons and brimstone ships.

Vast battle galleons, with fore and aft castles bristling with spikes and dragon pads, were anchored beside swift long-oared longships with hidden battering rams below the water line, and shields along their sides. The largest warships for his father and lords had staterooms and balconies, with hundreds of crew and servants.

Over three thousand ships in all were anchored about the south end of the island where the lava-heated waters were warm and the ice thin. Over a quarter of a million sailors, for the most part slaves, crewed them. Masts looked like a forest, sails like clouds trapped in their bows. Canvas and hulls were being painted; but for once white instead of black. This was an Armada designed to disappear on the freezing currents that would carry them and icebergs south.

I have never seen anything like this, Darcy thought in awe. *Fire and brimstone will rain down on them! The SDS don't stand a chance. They will fall before our banners. We must have felled all the forests in the entire north.*

Darcy looked behind, unable to take his eyes off the legions of gorrangochs that crowded the volcano's lower black slopes. It seemed they no longer needed brimstone nor warmth, unlike their riders and troops who shivered and shook as frost cracked at their feet. He swallowed, hoping he wasn't going to be sick again. Once proud Imperials were dark and twisted things, a parody of life. He had had his first row with his father after refusing to allow his Imperial to be taken into the Void, or those of his household knights. He was afraid of them, perhaps seeing in them a mirror of his father's dark dragon Queen. Collars were enough.

Behind those twisted creatures, encamped about sulphurous steaming pools, the largest army Darcy had ever imagined was slowly assembling. The soldiers drilled, besieging the old castle, firing catapults and trebuchets, practising sword play, whilst the frost dragons hunted for food to feed them.

Satisfied, the WarLock turned his gorrangoch towards the citadel. 'To Council, my Lords.'

'There is a cold current.' As the WarLock pointed to the map hanging in the air, a blue line appeared following the craggy western coastline down to the Isle of Midges. 'It will carry our Armada as it carries the icebergs. Already our frost dragons have drifted south on them, testing the current as the ice shelf breaks. They will do so again ahead of our arrival to keep us safe from discovery. Rumours are already spreading of our dark dragon Queen. Entire convoys are disappearing. Fear gives words wings.

'If the ice is too thick, Dread Lord?'

'My dark Queen will return from her hunting. She will easily break the ice; and if need be, we can harness razorbacks and gorrangochs both.'

'Harness dragons?'

'They are beasts of burden, my Lord,' the WarLock's eyes flared, 'and will be used as such. The SDS will protect their Imperials, hesitate to lose them: that is one of their many weaknesses we shall exploit. We will use dragons in any way we can to help us win this war. If necessary, like the hobgoblins, they will be sacrificed. We can breed more once the Seven Kingdoms are ours.'

'Dread Lord.' The WarLock's Battle Council was still debating as dark swiftly fell, there were so few hours of daylight this far north. 'We need more brimstone for our battledragons.' Heads nodded about the trestle table.

'Orkney has only enough for a few more moons.'

'Caithness less than one moon. Our sabretooths are barely flaming, are losing condition.'

Other nobles nodded about the room. None dared to mention that the Brimstones were now back in the hands of the SDS.

'My Imperials are dying this far north,' Quester's father was grim. 'My men too. They were not born to this cold. We need to move soon, Dread Lord before casualties become too high.'

'We have discovered Roarkinch is rich in the ore. We have huge stockpiles, already hundreds of ships' holds are full. No need to mine; our volcano spews endless brimstone ~ it lies in seams. Enough for a kingdom. As we speak your dragons are feeding in the volcano caves, and great ice sledges are ready to depart with you for your castles and lands.'

'My Lord King. We have no means to pull them in this cold.'

'The so called "Forsaken" will pull your sledges, my Lords. Do not fear, I will give you enough creatures to reach your castles and lands. You need not return them. But, in time you will not need brimstone for any but your lesser dragons. You have seen our gorrangochs today. My Imperials have been introduced to the Abyss to create something new, a creature that does not need brimstone, does not mind the cold, breeds swiftly.'

'How can they flame without brimstone?' a young knight asked.

'They do not flame. Their very breath is death. Theirs is the freezing cold of the night, not the fire of the sun! All my creatures draw their power from the Abyss.' *As do I.*

I am not the only one who is afraid, Darcy realised, recognising the uneasy shift of hardened soldiers around the table in the chink of armour and the creak of leather. *They are not afraid in battle, but they are afraid of the Abyss. Afraid of the freezing Darkness about to be unleashed.*

'Dragons, dark or no, are expendable. As are our hobgoblin allies, let them consume their strength and that of the SDS before we attack.'

Talk turned to the vast Armada anchored offshore.

'So, the hobgoblins gather and will swim south soon to the Inner Sea to await us.

'The hobgoblins can brave this ice? It's twenty strides thick.' Darcy would be happy to see them go. The sea about the island was alive with them. They were clustered so thickly that it seemed as if the bergs crawled with maggots. When a west wind blew, the island stank. 'Once they are out in the sea the volcano won't keep them warm.'

'They have been nurtured by the Abyss, born of both fire and ice. But you are correct, my son. Many thousands, hundreds of thousands will die before we reach the Sorcerers Glen, but there are millions of them, so we can bear high losses. There will be enough to drain Dragon Isle's wards, destroy its armies.'

First the hobgoblins and now the dragons were becoming creatures of the night, creatures of the cold... Perhaps, Darcy thought, he too was beginning to feel the alchemy of that cold sorcery. The elixir was foul, yet he felt a surge of power each time he drank; sometimes he felt wild with energy. He turned back to the conversation.

'How about The Chain, my Lord King?' One of his captains asked. 'Its very touch is said to spell death to hobgoblins. None have entered the Inner Sea let alone the loch since the First Alliance. History tells us it is a net cast by the Dragon Whisperer and his SeaDragon Lords that hangs between the Sentinels. Woven with wards.'

'The Chain?' The WarLock sneered his contempt... *I will break it.*

'My dark Queen will break it; the wards are ancient, decayed; the SeaDragon Lords who cast them long gone to their graves. The net may keep the hobgoblins at bay, but they will not keep my Queen out any more than their ancient wards will save their Dragon Isle from the Abyss. The banners will lie dormant until the attack begins. The loch is deep, and ice bound. Let their hunger grow as they wait.'

'Can hobgoblins and razorbacks truly be trusted, Dread Lord, to even understand your will and purpose? Hobgoblins are mindless savages, and their warlord untested. Razorbacks feral. Will they not betray our presence? If the SDS even suspect hobgoblins are in the loch they will summon every dragon and soldier to its defence and take away our advantage of surprise.'

The WarLock shook his head. 'Their seadragons are long gone. They will not know their enemy is even beneath them until it is too late. They cannot fight them until the banners rise from the sea. Hobgoblins and razorbacks will take the outer wards down, simply overwhelm their magic faster than their battlemages can mend them. If we are fortunate, they may even bring down the inner wards. There are secrets on that island I mean to make mine.'

The WarLock stepped out with Darcy.

'My son, I need you to press-gang more fisherfolk and sailors.

'There are few left, father. There are no more villages

to raid.'

'Then take peasants wherever you find them. It is a long journey south and my ships are hungry for more galley slaves and soldiers. We are already losing too many to the cold. Do not get caught on the ground a second time. Have your sport and leave the reaping to your soldiers. We can afford to lose them. But not you, my son.'

CHAPTER THIRTY-EIGHT
Fools

'The Guild were fools! Duped into this madness and now *we* all pay the price for their stupidity! It is *our* castles and keeps beyond the Wall who are fighting this war every day!' Lord Henry Percy's anger spilled over. 'It is *our* people who pay the price for war, not yours! In your rich robes you are growing fat while our people starve. Crops are ruined, our cattle stolen. Our people are taken, our soldiers killed. We are starving in the north. It's all your fault, old man! You're a damned fool!'

The atmosphere was heated in the Hall. The King and Queen were holding Court, attended by their Lords, Captains, courtiers and the Guild. Suffering huge losses, the Marcher Lords who held lands in the tundra were rebellious and looking for heads to roll.

The Grand Master stood to answer with the aid of a staff and an apprentice, chins wobbling with indignation. 'T-t-that is outrageous, my Lord Norfolk. How w-were we to know?'

'A WarLock in your midst and you noticed nothing?'

'You never saw him for one, either, My Lord! You a Mage! We are scholars and merchants here, not soldiers!'

'Yes, scholars, traders, merchants, so why didn't you think it odd that the Grand Master wanted an army?'

'You had lost the war! The SDS were defeated. The hobgoblins had united. You were not here, my Lord! Fear spreads like the plague.'

Arguments broke out.

'Silence! It has been forbidden since the First Alliance,'

the King rebuked coolly. 'And since the First Alliance, none save Dragon Lords have flown Imperials. And for good reason: and yet while we fought the hobgoblins at the Battle of the Line you saw fit to allow him to take and breed my pedigree Imperials from Dragonsdome, and raise an army! You were warned against such folly. No one man should hold such power!'

He turned his blind penetrating gaze onto Rumspell, who shrank back. 'And so, because we cannot fly in this endless winter our hand is forced, and we must give our Marcher Lords leave to fly Imperials also, so that they may defend their castles and people. Else we retreat behind the Wall. Everyone.'

That silenced them.

'Y-your Grace,' Rumspell quavered. 'Refugees already flood both City and glen. Our warehouses are emptying. They fish and steal to eat. They bring nothing but poverty and empty mouths to feed. Should we empty the north, we shall all starve.'

'As Hugo intends.' *He harvests men and crops...*

'We have heard rumours, my Lord King, that our Imperials will not fight his, my Lord King?' The Thane of Cawdor stood. 'Has the WarLock bewitched our Imperials. Perhaps his power is greater than any of us know.'

All eyes turned towards the throne.

'They *do* fight,' the King's voice brooked no argument as he stood so all could hear, repeating the same reassurance he had offered Calder. 'They kill the hobgoblins without mercy. They kill the Forsaken as a mercy. They kill his battlemages, destroy his armies and supply lines.' His blind gaze swept the Hall. 'None can gainsay this.'

It was true. There was a murmur of agreement.

The King motioned his Dragon Master forward. They had discussed this eventuality arising, and that moment had come. Lying would only make it worse. The future of the Seven Kingdoms may come to hinge on this one moment.

'But, unlike us,' Tangnost's growl fell into taut silence. The legendary BearHugger was highly respected by Lords and Courtiers alike. 'They will not kill their kin.'

'They will not -?' Norfolk scoffed. 'Will not? They are animals.'

The hall erupted.

'They are just animals!' The Thane of Glamis, a minor lordship, was worn out with worry. 'They don't have a choice but to obey us!'

There were laughs. 'Trained to kill. Only,' Norfolk dripped sarcasm, 'they are not killing.'

'Expensive animals,' another Lord cut in. 'Worth their weight in gold. The mightiest creatures on the One Earth, but just animals for all that.'

'Many still collar juveniles whilst training them.'

'Training collars are forbidden.'

'Collars are a legacy of the Mage Wars, and rightfully ended,' the King commented dryly. 'Perhaps they refused then, too. Perhaps they were coerced. It might explain why the seadragons are no longer. Mayhap we killed them.'

'Well, we can force them, too!'

'Open your eyes, man,' Tangnost said. 'They are dragons. With power and a voice of their own if you could but hear it!'

'How dare you!' Norfolk bridled. 'A commoner. I'll have you hung for your impudence.' *You will regret that BearHugger ... as will your King...*

'Enough!' The King's fury silenced the Court as he turned his milky gaze on Arundel and beckoned him forward. 'You will not threaten my Dragon Master,' the King's voice was soft but menacing, cast for Norfolk's ears only. 'For speaking the truth. Those days are past.'

'Do you still not understand our peril?' Magnus Fitzgerald stood in the grey armour of the Faculty Guard, and his cloak of all the colours of magic. 'There is only one enemy: the Abyss, and those who wield it. Our kingdoms are in peril. Our lives. Everything we hold dear will be swept aside in the storm that is coming. Our very *world* is in peril. The Mage Wars and the Long Winter that followed destroyed all land to the south of the Frost Spine Mountains. Are we going to repeat their folly? Where then would we flee?'

'My daughter can talk to dragons,' the King spoke. 'She is half dragonkind, none can deny it. If you have not seen her fly for yourself, my Lord Duke, many have. She can converse with them; and since she saved my life in the ancient Sea Citadel of the first Dragon Lords, so can I. At least, I can speak with my own battledragon. He affirms what we were beginning to suspect. Imperials will not kill their kin.'

'But His Imperials kill ours with impunity.' The Earl of Moray and Caithness had lost most of his lands and castles to the WarLock King. 'They kill ours!' He repeated. 'And tens of thousands of Imperials and

Dragon Lords killed each other in the Mage Wars!'

'Not willingly. The WarLock binds them to obedience with collars,' Cawdor stepped forwards between the tables, his young voice carrying clearly, demanding attention. 'Perhaps all were bound by the maelstrom in the Mage Wars.'

He has grown into his command... The King was pleased.

'Yes,' Cawdor turned so all Lords could hear his words. 'His Imperials *do* kill ours. We have lost seven on the Wall since midwinter, and another out of Dragon Isle in one engagement this quarter-moon. I have witnessed one such death for myself. Yet, at the same time the WarLock's Imperials kill themselves, as if seeking death is the only answer to the compulsion of the Abyss. Two of his dragons died along with one of ours, refusing to let go in the air, seeking death. Death and an end to their suffering. Death to end their grief that they should be forced to fight against their will.'

'How can you know this?' Norfolk was contemptuous. 'Perhaps they could not break free.'

Cawdor turned cool eyes towards the Earl, anguish and anger on his pale face, neck still bandaged. 'I was called by the watch at dusk yester week as our Imperials were being scrambled. A young Imperial bearing the banner of the Army of the North was flying for the Wall, but it was bucking and jinking in the air. It rolled and spun and flamed as if trying to rid itself of something. We saw troops falling to their deaths on the Midge-Ridden Moors and the flash of sorcery as those riding it attempted to bring it under control. They failed, and it landed badly near the wall, then turned on those who commanded it. Despite being bound by the maelstrom it killed both battlemages and the troops it bore. And then...' the young Warden's voice cracked, and he coughed.

'And,' he swallowed. 'And then we went to it, but it was clearly dying. Its scales were dull and brittle. Skin was flaking from ulcers. There were terrible weeping sores about its neck where a great collar hung, and its eyes were black, flecked with the green of the maelstrom.'

A gasp blew round the Hall.

'Our scalesmiths and healers, knowing they risked the black death, tried but could not free it. I stood beside that great head, hand on its muzzle as it strove to breathe and begged for mercy, and I swore an oath by all our Gods that we would free them from servitude, and then I ended its suffering.

'In that one heartbeat between life and death, when the soul flies, its eyes turned back to gold. I gave it peace, if only for a moment.' Tears ran down the defiant young man's face as he challenged the doubters.

Some, mostly the young knights, ladies and esquires, wept openly. Dour battle-hardened men in dinted armour hung their heads, ashamed, or coughed gruffly to clear their throats. As goosebumps whispered across her skin in eerie premonition, the Queen brushed hot tears of anger and was grateful her daughter and Armelia were elsewhere. Her husband's hand found hers and squeezed, as if he could read her thoughts. Others were not so kind.

'You believe this?' Norfolk scoffed. 'This arrant non-sense? They are mindless beasts.'

'Even the enslaved can revolt against their masters. Dragons have a language,' the King challenged his subjects. 'They love as we do.' *When did I come to realise they are no different from us save in their language?* 'They bond for life as we do with their mates, and grieve their loss deeply. They need food and air and warmth to survive as we do. They feel pain and fear and can suffer as we do. Are we all so blind we cannot see the suffering of others? Dragons are not "just animals". They are animals, but they are also our equal, deserving of our love and care. Of our respect.'

'Perhaps Hugo and his Lords are tainted by the maelstrom and do not see yet that his warped magic is killing their own Imperials,' the Guardian speculated. 'Even as he forces them to kill ours. He has made his first mistake, the flaw we look for. But it will be a hollow victory if we defeat the WarLock yet lose our dragons. We style ourselves Dragon Lords,' ice blue eyes swept the chamber. 'Let us truly become so. For what would our world be without dragons?'

That sobering thought fell into utter silence.

Norfolk had never known when to stop. 'If he is collaring his Imperials, then let us collar ours! Force them to fight.'

'We have just said Hugo is binding his Imperials to *obedience* using the dark power of the maelstrom, turning them to madness and death.' The King was relentless, his anger rising. 'Is that what you are suggesting, Lord Earl? No, we will not bind the dragons to our will, even if we could. We would become what we fight. But that knowledge is lost to us even if we willed it.'

Norfolk stood his ground. Not the time to mention his Constable had found a hiding hole deep in the bowels of Urquhart Castle. Old texts and diaries wrapped in waxed leather. There was dark sorcery there, writ large, the runes and their meaning unknown, but his mages were working upon it.

'That is all very well, my Lord King, but my castles and keeps need defended now. If you will not collar SDS imperials, give me leave to fit training collars on mine. I must protect my lands, my castles, my people. An Imperial can destroy an army in a heartbeat. Mine must fight.' *Who will know the difference betwixt the two?*

'I will think on it. Beware my Lords, for if the dragons turn on us we will be utterly lost, no matter what the WarLock does.'

The Court bowed as he left the Hall with his Queen. Bowing, Norfolk's hostile eyes watched them go. Conversation broke out as the Guardian sought out the Warden of the Wall as he was leaving.

'This one dragon's death that you spoke of,' the Guardian looked at Cawdor seeking his opinion, 'may give us the chance to study the maelstrom for the first time, to understand how the artefact is imbued with dark magic. You fly north tomorrow? Good. I will come with my Professors and Deans of the Night Faculty, along with our most skilled battlemages. We have no records, no artefacts, nothing to study, to learn from. This is our opportunity to learn how to shield ourselves from it, how to break it, how to fight it! Show me where the dragon and its collar lie.'

Cawdor nodded. 'As you command, Guardian. The collar corroded the dragon's body, ate into the bones and flesh and down into the frozen ground beneath. We set it about with a ward to contain its evil. I will gladly surrender it into your care.'

CHAPTER THIRTY-NINE
Collars

'Come on!' Root urged his friend as he ran towards the porting stone. Quenelda smiled, grateful that her outburst had not lost his friendship. It was as if an inner voice had spoken with her voice, and the power of it had left her shaken too. Root was still far too pale, and his grief for Bracus etched on his young face aged him. Squirrel had confided that his young master cried in the depths of the night for his lost friend. Quenelda feared Root felt himself to be a coward for surviving when his dragon and pilot died. She had been only too glad to agree that they go flying, she could cheer him up by flying rings about him on Two Gulps. And she needed to stretch her own wings, so to speak. She had had more sympathy for Two Gulps of late, now she had learnt how punishing flying could be.

Root smiled as Quenelda followed him. She also was too pale these days, working herself into the ground training Imperials and working with frost dragon pathfinders so that they could come upon the WarLock's men unawares. He was grateful his anger had not jeopardised their friendship, for he had been wrong to attack her for Bracus's death. That lay at Darcy's feet, like so many other deaths. He found his sleep disturbed by dreams of that night, time and time again, and now understood better when Quester had confided he too suffered endless flashbacks to that moment when a huge flint sword nearly took his life.

So Root, with Tangnost's permission, had persuaded

Quenelda from the HeartRock and her training, and they would now fly to collect Armelia and Chasing the Stars. It seemed an age since they had been in Glen Etive, having fun. Root felt the familiar blurring and sickness as the porting stone stopped, and yet it was Quenelda who staggered as she stepped off into the huge flight cavern.

'What is it? What's wrong?' Root reached out to grab her elbow as his friend nearly buckled. 'You've gone green. You've been training too hard!'

'My head... My head hurts.'

'Are you sure you want to go flying?'

Quenelda nodded vehemently, almost falling over again. 'I'm just tired,' she admitted. 'Those dark dragon dreams keep waking me.'

Root nodded, not entirely convinced, but he had really been looking forward to this afternoon off. Even now he could scarcely believe he was flying Two Gulps, admittedly a rather unusual sabretooth because of his weight, but also his nature. A very different battledragon to his sire, the highly strung and lethal Two Gulps & You're Gone, whom Quenelda still grieved for.

'Let's look at his new winter armour?' Root suggested, 'see if it's finished?' They peeled off towards the smith caves to the right of the flight cavern.

The forges were roaring hot. The clash of chains and the hammer rang out. Huge bars of raw iron were being fed into the crucible. But there was another forge in a cave open to the sea, apart from all the others, set about with wards. Root had never seen anyone work there before, but the forge was hot. Chains on pulleys swung from the ceiling, lifting a great round span of iron from a steaming seawater pit. They were surprised to find several battlemages at work embedding runes. They wore the badge of the triple tree against a stone tower.

'The Duke of Norfolk's knights.' As navigator, Root had to be able to identify coats of arms, friend and foe alike. Mistakes could be deadly.

'What?' Quenelda suddenly frowned, '… are *those*?'

'Collars, Lady,' the bellows boy replied.

'Collars?' Quenelda went deathly pale, her voice suddenly flat and hostile, drawing Root's startled gaze. 'Who for?'

'For the Earl's Imperials, Lady. I don't know why.'

Root blanched. He knew why. He hadn't meant this to happen! He opened his mouth to admit blame…

'So that they fight, Lady!' Behind them Norfolk's gaze was as cold as his voice. 'Like they're supposed to.'

'You are forbidden dark magic!'

Norfolk sneered. 'Who will stop me? You, Princess?'

'Yes!' Quenelda's inner dragon self, ancient beyond reckoning, gave voice to cold fury. *Dragon should not be fighting dragon… this betrays the Covenant. A blood price will be paid.*

The voice of sorcery unbound ghosted through the coombs, resonated in minds on the threshold of hearing, causing confusion and havoc. The power of the Matriarch's words blasted Dragon Masters and Battle-Mages where they stood. In Dragonsdome, engulfed by the touch of such baleful magic, Drumondir staggered and fell. Just as he fainted, Root saw a blurring of outline, and Quenelda's eyes blazing with the wrath of another world.

The ancient heart of Dragon Isle itself shook with her fury. In their roosts dragons reared up and cauldrons overturned or exploded. Chimneys and slates fell from the steep blue-gabled roofs of the Academy. Chains rattled. Dragon pads dropped to their anchors and the earthquake sent shock waves radiating out to rock the Sorcerers Glen, setting off a dozen avalanches, and launching a tidal wave that surged outwards, slamming into the battlegalleons and troop carriers that crowded the loch, before washing against the harbour walls of the Black Isle in a froth of foam. Dragons stalled and threw their riders before streaming westwards. High above the island, the afternoon suddenly darkened, and the air grew chill. Thunderclouds appeared from a clear sky, spitting lightning. Unnatural darkness fell. Far to the north, the WarLock King felt the unexpected unveiling of immense power, and wondered.

CHAPTER FORTY
She's Gone

The hot rasping tongue was persistent. Root opened his eyes to his worst nightmare, scant hand spans from his face. Wide nostrils smoked warmly. Thick creamy incisors that could kill a bull arced over him. And as for the bad breath, that didn't bear thinking about. His heart frantically fluttered in his chest and he nearly fainted before he realised it was Two Gulps who was anxiously nudging him, the juvenile's huge tongue almost pulling the groggy, soggy gnome to his feet. The sabretooth spread a wing to the ground in invitation and butted the youth on his backside to help him along. Rocks were still falling to the cavern floor as the last tremors died away.

'Two Gulps?' Root put out a hand to steady himself as he mounted, trying to clear his ringing head. Grateful for something solid to hang on to, he didn't even notice there was no saddle or bridle.

'What just happened, boy?' He looked about, trying to bring his eyes back into focus, and blinked in disbelief. Around him, others were struggling to their feet in utter confusion. Some were retching miserably, making Root gag himself. Many were trapped beneath the rubble. Chains were still swinging. Quenelda was nowhere to be seen ~ and neither were the dragons!

'Where are they? Where are all the dragons?'

That same question was on everyone's lips.

CHAPTER FORTY-ONE
Dragon Gyre

In that moment of rage, hot as the One Earth's heart, Quenelda had felt her life subdued by the HeartRock, by the soul of the Matriarch deep within the One Earth. Her inner mortal self surrendered to that ancient will, and she became dragonkind; one of the oldest of an ancient race who had birthed the One Earth and given life to all its creatures. As she opened her wings and swooped out from the flight cavern, she became the Matriarch in all her magnificent fury. Dreadful power coursed through her as her bones grew vast, her wings spread, and diamond hard scales clothed her. Her great tail lashed from side to side in fury as she spiralled upwards, sending a tower of the Academy crashing to the ground. With each beat of her immense wings Quenelda's own inner self faded further, and still the Imperial grew to unimaginable size.

How dare they? How dare they betray dragonkind? They are unworthy! Their gift shall be taken...

At the top of the Battle Academy, as the vast shadow finally passed, six battlemages co-ordinating and monitoring battlegame exercises across the glen swivelled in their battlespheres, trying to understand what was happening. An enormous spike of raw magic had flared, obliterating everything else. Down in the Situation Room where the Guardian and the King were evaluating regimental performances, they both staggered with blinding headaches.

Cringing as the tower shook and debris tumbled down

upon the roof of the Seadragon Tower, a dazed technician turned on his seat to the Officer of the Watch who was still getting to his feet. 'Unknown Imperial! Out of nowhere! It's huge!'

'What?' Frowning, the Officer of the Watch pressed some runes, but nothing was working. The magical fault that lay along the length of the glen had flared into incandescent radiance. 'What's happening? We're flying blind! No imperial can climb that fast. It's impossible. Where did it come from?' He swiftly moved to occupy a display as readings and glyphs rekindled, drawing in the runes, trying to analyse the detail. 'It's impossible,' he repeated to himself as he rotated, hands darting swiftly to confirm what his mind refused to accept. 'How many wings and squadrons do we have on exercise?'

'Six squadrons and fifty wings.'

'What are they doing? These readings don't make sense!'

'Multiple signals,' the goblin technician's long fingers were dancing over their displays. 'Incoming...incoming.'

'Affirmative,' a second confirmed. 'Multiple contacts converging on Dragon Isle.'

'Scramble everything we've got. We're under attack. Get them up there!'

The horn began, Wooo...Wooo...Wooo... 'Scramble ... scramble...scramble...'

Pilots and navigators of the Rapid Reaction Force swept down their chutes. Collecting their weapons on the run, Bone-Crackers stormed from their barracks down poles to their dragon pads. Only to find to find...empty roosts. Not a dragon in sight.

Jakart DeBessart punched a rune embedded in the stone table in the Situation Room and looked up to where a sphere appeared, showing Dragon Isle at its centre and thousands of dragons exiting the island from flight caverns and roosts, and thousands flying towards Dragon Isle, thousands! Too many to track individually. 'SitRep?'

'We... don't know Sir,' the Officer said truthfully. 'We've never seen anything like it. We are tracking an unidentified Imperial directly above us. It's huge and climbing rapidly, four thousand strides, five thousand. Also, multiple targets ~ spherical convergence on Dragon Isle. The sky is alive with dragons. Come and se-'

The door opened to admit Quester. The King's young esquire was out of breath. 'Your Grace, Guardian, you will want to see this for yourselves...'

'What on the One Earth is happening?'

'They've gone, my Lord King.' Quester's answer was tinged with fear. 'There are no dragons on Dragon Isle. They're all in the air.'

The King, the Guardian and their officers stepped off the Observatory porting stone to an amazing sight. Like swarms of bees, dragons were rising to join into a synchronised dance, growing larger by the heartbeat. Streaming, swooping and diving in perfect unison, a dazzling pulsating cloud drawing together like a dance only to come apart again. Breathtakingly beautiful. Heads lifted fearfully as thunder rumbled and the sky grew darker. The dragons began to join in one great rotating column of air that spiralled like a funnel.

'They are forming a gyre, Rufus,' the Guardian said

with reverence. 'Truly we live in an age of wonders.'

More and more students and academics were standing at windows and balconies, eyes wide with wonder or fear, or both; as yet more dragons streamed westward from the Black Isle. The thunderous drum of their wings over the loch sent spray high into the air. Growing groups of soldiers and Dragon Lords, roost hands and scholars, stood shoulder to shoulder as the gyre above them grew and grew.

The King with his attuned senses understood. 'They are angry with us, full of rage. There is a collective will at work here. Yet, they are also here...for my daughter! But I cannot sense her at all!'

In the dark cold of space, at the edge of consciousness, Quenelda's mortal spirit began to die and her body burn. Fear battered at her mind, the inner fluttering of a butterfly lost in the wrath of a dragon whose power was consuming her. Sensing the imminent death of her child, the Matriarch relented, released her grip. Like a dying spark in the darkness, Quenelda's spirit leapt forwards, grasping for life. The Imperial became both Quenelda and dragon again. Folding her wings, the Matriarch dropped, her size diminishing as she fell until she became wind and starlight.

B-boom...B-boom...boom...boom...the twin heart fell silent. Then the inner dragon was utterly gone and Quenelda's limp body was falling...falling...falling...into darkness.

CHAPTER FORTY-TWO
Where is She?

Thunder drummed from two-hundred-thousand wings, making Root cringe. Bursts of lightning flashed. His hair radiated out like thistledown. Thunder cracked, its sonorous boom deafening him. His head still felt thick as cotton wool, and an eardrum had burst when he lost consciousness, so now he was partly deaf and the blood trickled down his neck. Around the gyre, thousands of dragons were still swooping and diving as one, spinning, dipping...dancing. It was a glorious sight if it had not been so frightening.

'Where is she, boy? Where is she?' Root was mortally afraid as he clung to Two Gulps, who appeared to know what to do. His wings had grown, thankfully, and so had his power. Muscles bunched, the sabretooth strove for height towards the base of the gyre, but he was struggling in the turbulent air. It was a horrible bumpy ride to join the sabretooths concentrated about the base of the funnel. Suddenly, the dragon song fell silent.

'Quenelda? Quenelda? Come back. Come back. We love you.'

Barely conscious, barely aware, Quenelda fell as if in a dream, and each wing she touched slid gently away, from one to another to another, a thousand wings, ten thousand wings, each slowing her descent down and down and softly down. Imperials' black wings, the golden red of sabretooths...vampire black...snow white frost dragons...blue magenta widdershank wings. Soft... soft as powder snow she fell and then an open maw stayed her fall and, holding her gently between fearsome teeth, a lone golden dragon beneath the gyre, with a dazed and battered young gnome on his back, folded his wings.

'That's Two Gulps!' Quester's sharp eyes had seen the tiny red-gold speck that was dropping towards Dragon Isle like a stone.

In his haste to dismount, Root fell down Two Gulp's wing as the sabretooth stepped back from Quenelda's inert body. Roost hands and running soldiers stopped in their tracks as the angry sabretooth stood protectively over her, smoke pouring from his nostrils. Everyone could feel the sabretooth Two Gulp's quivering rage about to break like a storm.

'Healers,' Root shouted at them. 'We need healers!' For he could feel no pulse. Shoving people aside, oblivious to all but the young woman he had protected since birth, Tangnost arrived to find Root cradling Quenelda's limp body to his chest, her arms, head and hair hanging loosely to the ground. She was pale as snow. The familiar black scales on her brow and arms were gone, vanished.

'Nooo! Noooooooo!' The Dragon Master's heart thumped in his chest as he dropped to his knees, hands on his head in denial. 'What have we done?'

Chapter Forty-Three
Broken Link

The quarry was dark as Knuckle wiped the blade on his jerkin. Stepping over the murdered guards he smiled; it wasn't a pleasant smile. He rubbed his wrists, a blacksmith would have to remove the shackles. They would pay. Oh, yes, they would all pay.

Those dragons flying west had made it easy. No one was paying any attention, as citizen and Lord alike had stood open mouthed, watching carriages crash in mid-air. Riders had been thrown; hundreds of the Black Isle's citizens had taken an unexpected bath in the loch or crashed through timber-tiles roofs. It had given him the chance to break a chain link with the small knife he had been given in prison, then he just bided his time until dark fell. The streets were crowded to bursting, the City Watch occupied trying to keep order and stop looting, so he was able to slip away. His master had many friends on the Black Isle, and he needed gold for his plan to work.

CHAPTER FORTY-FOUR
Our Cause is Just

Dusk had fallen. The assembled officers in the Situation Room were fully armoured. The Academy scholars and Deans in their bright robes were debating scrolls and books. Retired Dragon Masters and Professors had been recalled in haste. They had gathered from all about Dragon Isle, the Black Isle, and some were returning from patrol or a mission, all reporting the strange phenomena they had seen and heard in their heads. SDS dragons were now returning to their roosts. Search & Rescue harriers were out rescuing pilots and riders thrown by their mounts.

Those caught up in the gyre were the source of envy and pity. Most were battered and deafened, but what a tale they had to tell! Scores had minor injuries, were deaf or had suffered broken limbs, hit by beating wings.

Consternation and bewilderment had led to no consensus. The King, just back from sitting with his daughter, was calling for silence when Drumondir begged an audience. They looked up as the pale BoneCaster entered, clearing a path for her to the King at the head of the table. Drumondir still felt sick, and her head was hammering despite valerian tea. The Black Isle had been in chaos when she left. Fear was running wild as few dragons had returned to their stables. She had finally managed to find an SDS dragon courier at the Guild who would take her to Dragon Isle once she said she had to see the King and Queen. *What had happened?* Her pupil's rage still hammered at her skull. *And the power of it! The wrath! The dragons had flown? Was this a foretelling of the future? Where is Quenelda? Whose call had she answered?*

'Sit,' the King could feel the tension in her tread, hear the catch of her breath. 'And tell us what just happened?'

Drumondir gratefully took a chair. 'My Lord King,' she swallowed, weighing her words carefully. 'We always assumed that a Dragon Whisperer would be on our side ...that our cause was just. No one considered what might happen if she were not.'

There was a shocked silence. Whatever they were expecting, it wasn't this. Heads turned towards the King for guidance.

'That was my *daughter*?' The King asked softly, failing to hide his shock.

'Yes, and no.' Drumondir nodded, just as the King's Dragon Master was admitted. Tangnost's weathered face was equally strained. 'I believe it was the inner dragon, not the girl. It was her voice that you heard, or through her, the voice of the Matriarch, and I believe the source of the earthquake was the HeartRock itself; it mirrored the Matriarch's anger. But as to why, I do not understand. Where is she?'

'My daughter is in a deep sleep, barely breathing.'

Drumondir took a deep sigh. 'I would fear now to wake the sleeping dragon within her, my Lord King. There is power in the HeartRock beyond our imagining. We have taken for granted that a Dragon Whisperer would protect us. But what if she turns on us instead?'

The King turned to his newly arrived Dragon Master. 'Can you tell us what happened?'

Tangnost nodded. 'Your Grace, I think so. She was down in the eastern flight cavern with Root to look at Two Gulps' new winter armour. They came across armourers casting collars. A cabal of Norfolk's battle-mages were forging strange spells of *compulsion* and *obedience* in the Old Mage Foundry: they are all dead, just ashes along with their collars. The crucible of the Matriarch's anger was more than any could withstand. A scroll was found next to where they stood, unharmed. I dared not touch it as the black runes written on it moved and changed, coiling like ink in water. A mage has suspended it in a bubble. I fear it is dark magic at work.

'Those who are recovering say your daughter began to change aspect; that the shadow of an Imperial towered about her, filling the cavern, but then they and everyone nearby fainted. When they came to, she was gone, along with Root and Two Gulps, and every single dragon in Dragon Isle. Many thrown by their dragons are being treated in the hospital, scores have died. All those here on Dragon Isle, in galleons, or on the ice are badly shaken.'

The King let out a deep breath. 'So are we all. This happened because that fool was collaring our Imperials?'

Tangnost nodded. 'I believe so, Your Grace. Root can tell us for certain, but he is at Quenelda's side, as is her sabretooth. They are both distraught.'

'But we know dragons fought each other in the Mage Wars and yet...' Jakart began. 'We have discussed this.'

'And yet we are still here?' The Guardian turned thoughtful eyes on the BoneCaster.

Drumondir's eyes flashed dangerously. 'There was not a Dragon Whisperer to champion them. There is now!

Perhaps all dragons in that war were compelled or enslaved by the maelstrom.'

'But other dragons fight,' Jakart persisted. 'They– '

'Are not noble dragons,' The King suddenly knew the answer to the riddle. 'Sabretooths, harriers, vampires ...spitting adders, dales... have no magic, so they have no choice. We have ever waged war commanding or compelling other creatures to obedience. Using them to destroy our enemies, no matter the cost to them.'

'Hobgoblins were both our enemies,' the Guardian pondered, nodding. 'So SeaDragons and Imperials, the last of the noble dragons, fought them willingly. Now they will not kill their own kind, and seadragons are no more.'

'If what we know of the lost Dragonsdome Chronicles speaks truly,' Drumondir said sadly, 'dragons died in their hundreds of thousands in the Long Winter and the Great Extinction that followed the Mage Wars. For centuries the land lay toxic.'

'Many breeds did not survive at all,' the Guardian agreed heavily. 'We were reckless with their lives. Their lands were destroyed, their roosts, their food was gone. Many, dragons and men, did not survive.'

Drumondir's eyes closed as her voice took on a sing-song cadence of the BoneCaster. *The Darkness comes once more, and the Maelstrom rises, bringing with it endless winter.*

The Guardian's eyes narrowed thoughtfully as Drumondir continued, seemingly unaware she had spoken. *She truly is a BoneCaster with the gift of foresight. Did she not say the Whisperer had more than one call to answer?*

'Quenelda has been born of the One Earth in direct lineage to Son of the Morning Star and the Matriarch's First Born to defend the One Earth, to honour all life as the Matriarch intended. Your daughter is here not just to protect us from the Abyss, but to protect the One Earth itself, and all the creatures that it nurtures. In our arrogance we have forgotten how to speak to animals, to honour them as teachers and companions, for in their language and their soul lies true magic. What if we too stray too far from the path? Will the Matriarch turn against us also? Our wondrous world will become ash and dust.'

CHAPTER FORTY-FIVE
Deep Sleep

Root sat holding Quenelda's hand. Her skin was smooth and white as veined marble, like the alabaster tombs he had once seen in the Palace crypt. Not a single scale remained after her flight to the stars save the one golden red scale of a sabretooth on the palm of her left hand. It seemed her inner dragon was gone, fled, had abandoned those who tried to shackle dragonkind, compelling them like the WarLock King to kill their own kindred, leaving behind a burnt-out husk of a young woman. Her single heartbeat was so slow and laboured that he kept leaning forward to listen, afraid she had gone to dance with the dragons. Had left them to face the WarLock King alone. Bracus was MIA, presumed dead. Now Quenelda was dying, and it was all his fault.

Tears dripped hotly on her cold skin. He looked back on his outburst with shame. He would not lift a sword, not even in mercy. Yet he had demanded that the mighty Imperials do what he wasn't prepared to. And yet...in his darkest mind he had wanted to kill Darcy with a hate that had kindled deep within his soul. He wanted to kill those who had taken the world of his childhood and broken it. Doubt and grief were etched into his face. How could one who revered life in its myriad facets want to kill those who took those lives so carelessly? *Because they will never change...*

'I used-' he tried again, desperate to explain to Drumondir, angrily wiping tears with the back of his hand, scrubbed it through his rumpled hair. 'I used to think dragons were animals. Never "just animals" like so many say, but animals. Somehow lesser than us.

'My people revere life in whatever form it takes, from an earwig to the mighty whales. Our warrens, our whole lives, were tied to the rhythms and forces of nature. We never kill to eat another's flesh or wear their skins. We live off the land according to the seasons. Only when a creature dies do we bless them and take their gifts of fur and bone and sinew. And yet, I – I still thought of dragons as animals that we could command.

'But,' Root's eyes brightened as he thought of Chasing the Stars; 'when I am with Quenelda, I can hear the dragons! Their thoughts become mine. They love, they are happy and sad, feel joy and grief, and fear. When I first met Chasing the Stars she could feel my fear. I could barely move,' he smiled ruefully. 'I thought dragons were just an assortment of teeth and talons and tails that could kill you. Chasing the Stars saw my knees knocking so hard she teased me, baring her teeth. I fainted!' He shook his head.

'I love her to bits now. Dragons bond for life and love their own, did you know? And yet we are forcing them to fight each other for us. I-I attacked Quenelda because Night Frost wouldn't fight, and Bracus died. I was angry with her! I told Tangnost. And because of it they began to forge collars to compel them. And I don't fight! I should be the one wearing the collar.'

'No, Root, you are wrong.' They had not seen Root's father standing at the door. The Queen's Constable, Sir Gharad, opened his arms to his son. 'Ah, Root, it's not your fault. I could have told you. The patrol whose fight you joined experienced the exact same thing. In fact, that is why the firefight was still raging when you arrived. Their Imperials refused to Drop Dead. It was Major Cawdor, our young Warden of the Wall who sent a courier south with the news. And the King forbade even training collars. Norfolk, in arrogance and ignorance, broke his orders, and awaits his penalty.

'It took great courage to approach a gyre…and love,' Sir Gharad knelt with a crack of old knees to look his son in the face. 'Don't grieve yet, for when she wakes she will need you as she never has before.' He kissed his son on the forehead. 'Now go and rest. I love you, and so does Quenelda.

'Then talk to your sister. She is anxious about you. You both have suffered too much grief in your young lifetimes. You will be recalled to operational duty tomorrow.'

'Do not give up hope so easily, young Root,' Drumondir cautioned. 'She has not flown yet. Nor do I think she will, else she would not have been returned to us. I look on that with hope. We shall all watch over her, talk to her. She needs to be drawn back into our world. She will return when she is ready.'

'Will y-'

'Of course, I shall send word,' Drumondir smiled. 'Now go! Do not fear, I shall not leave her. Nor will he,' she nodded to the large head that had broken through the dividing wall between the royal apartments.

That raised a small smile. Unwilling to let Quenelda out of his sight, Two Gulps had brought down six doors and half a ceiling following Quenelda's return to the smaller corridors and halls of the palace. No one had tried to stop the stricken juvenile. Those huge teeth and smoking nostrils meant that anyone sensible got out of the way, but the Queen had only smiled and bent her head to pat the juvenile's. 'You saved her. And you, young Root. I think your love saved her, yours and Two Gulps', when her spirit was about to leave, you called her back. Your love anchored her spirit to her body. She knows you are both here, I am sure of it.'

The candles had burnt down another bell before Quenelda's next visitor.

'How is my daughter, Drumondir?' The Queen didn't look like she had slept much either as she took a chair by her daughter's side. She had held Court today for the ordinary folk, judging petitions, seeing food and beer were distributed to the poor fleeing the atrocities north of the Wall. Her personal anxieties had to be placed aside. But she and the BoneCaster had fought and won the battle to keep her daughter at the palace. Root, Tangnost and the King feared that without the cradle of Dragon Isle, the young Dragon Whisperer might die. But Drumondir had been characteristically blunt. 'Her inner dragon has flown, and your daughter needs her family about her, to help her as her body heals. It is your daughter's life you need to save now.'

'What are you saying?' Tangnost was aghast. 'That she is no longer a dragon whisperer?'

Drumondir nodded. 'I believe so. When she wakes she will be an ordinary young woman, if indeed anyone can ever call her that.'

And so Quenelda lay there pale and cold as many came and went with a whispered word to offer their love. To offer small gifts. To give comfort to those who sat vigil as days turned into a quarter-moon and then to a half-moon.

CHAPTER FORTY-SIX
You Fool

Norfolk was dragged into the great hall by the Faculty Guard, blustering and cursing.

'You fool! You disobeyed me. The gods alone know how much damage you have done. My daughter lies in a coma. You may have lost us this war with your ignorance and disobedience. Take him to the Tower.'

'But....' Norfolk blustered. 'You cannot do this. I am of the blood!'

'Oh, but I can. Make no mistake, my Lord, not only is your life in peril, but all of ours. I will despatch five Imperials to bring all your folk behind the Wall, they do not need to suffer for your folly. Take him to the Tower.'

CHAPTER FORTY-SEVEN
Dark Dragon Dreams

Quenelda would never know how long she lay there; motionless, pale, barely breathing, lost to the worlds of dragons and men as stars wheeled overhead. Soft voices called…familiar voices.

Quenelda, please don't die…I love you…we love you…Two Gulps is lost without you…

Oh, my daughter, the speaker wept…*what have we done to you?*

Child, if you can hear us, come back to us…you are needed…loved…

Goose, they will never be bound against their will. I swear it.

But they were so far away…from another lifetime…

Quenelda dreamt, cradled within breathtakingly beautiful nebulae, where planets were birthed, and stars blazed and died, where the wheel of time meant nothing. Where dragons danced and shone like stars in the dark sky. Eons passed in the blink of an eye and she found herself standing on the One Earth. But this was an ancient world of fire and scorching winds, a smouldering volcanic cauldron of creation, being spun by the Matriarch who danced in the night sky. As it cooled it became a world of earth, wind, fire and water that gave birth to the eldest of the One Earth's dragons; her four children, the First Born.

As the world cooled and oceans formed, Quenelda swam in their greenstone depths, racing dolphins and diving with whales. Mountains of rock and ice rose and she rose with them, the sharp jagged plates of her spine reaching so high towards the dark void that they knew only snow and ice. In warmer regions great lush forests grew, trees beyond name and count, and she grew with them as one of many over the long centuries, becoming each creature, furred, feathered and winged that lived amongst them. Howling, she ran with the wolves, hibernated with the bears, grazed with the deer and scurried with mice, eating seeds and berries. Finally, mankind arose from the oceans in myriad form; and she knew their languages and history, their music, their dreams, and their fears.

Quenelda, the familiar voice persisted. *I'm sorry ~ this is all my fault. I was wrong. So wrong to be angry. Forgive me...*

And then from the outer darkness between the stars, from some dark glimmer of endless night, from a flaw deep within her world, darkness grew. A bottomless void of dark matter and energy; and this flaw gave birth to the hobgoblins, the enemy of all living creatures on the One Earth. A predator of the oceans that could also live on land.

*Quenelda, Quenelda, come back to us. We love you. Don't leave us...*the voice pleaded, tugging at her heart. *I was wrong...so wrong to be angry with the dragons. I wanted her to kill for me...it wasn't them that killed Bracus...I am so sorry...* And the voice that wept, softly sang...

I hear a distance drumming

Upon a distant shore...
I hear the woodlands weeping
For a soul that is no more...
The bitter wind is sighing
In the darkness of the night
For a soul that's slowly dying
Held close by candlelight
I do not want to weep
I beg of you to stay
Leave me not in the dark of the night
Or the harsh bright light of day...

Time moved on, a day, a year, a century, a millennium, a million, million years. Who could say? And then Quenelda found herself drinking in the freezing air as a bitter northerly wind blew over the retreating glacier she was standing on. It was the Sorcerers Glen, only long ago, still half buried by black volcanic ice, and thick with dragon smoke that hung like a yellow sea haar. An exhausted army gathered below with ragged banners and battered shields. Holding the higher ground were women and children and elders, huddling to keep warm. Mortally afraid. For the hobgoblins were coming.

Everywhere else, as far as the eye could see, and perched upon all the peaks of the surrounding mountains were dragons. Mostly Imperials, but where the snow met the sea loch there were seadragons: huge, magnificent, all the colours of the deep oceans. Other glimmers of gold and red, blue and green and saffron were threaded through the black, half a hundred colours of the rainbow, half a hundred different dragons.

On the top of a sculpted icy rise shot through with translucent blues and green, stood a young man, dressed in battered black armour and ragged surcoat, with four Imperials flanking him. But they were unlike any that Quenelda had seen or dreamt of.

The first Imperial blazed brightly, haloed with fire, steam rising beneath its claws. Its nearest companion was richly dark like the earthy brown crust of the One Earth. A third was scaled in pale greens and blues: delicate seaweed fronds ran along its spine and crest, and its talons were webbed. The fourth mirrored the sky in its many hues. The First Born: Earth, Fire, Wind and Water.

Suddenly aware, the young man turned towards her. Hair black as a raven's wing. His elven face fine boned. Only his oval reptilian eyes were the golden eyes of an Imperial.

'Come.' A single word of invitation in a surprisingly deep voice. He held out his hand, and in taking it, Quenelda became one with him and discovered she was his twin. When he knelt in homage to his four sisters and brothers, she knelt as one with him, for these were the First Born of the Matriarch, the first children of the One Earth, still living, as old as their world. And behind their Prince, the army knelt, and beyond them all the peoples of the Old Kingdom and their families knelt.

We are kneeling in homage to the dragons! It struck Quenelda like a blow. *Our stories all tell of the peoples of the Seven Kingdoms kneeling to their Dragon Whisperer King and his companions. We have forgotten the truth! The power is theirs and theirs alone, not ours! My brother kneels before them. The lost Dragonsdome*

Chronicles show it truly...who hid that dangerous truth so long ago, and why? We named the FirstBorn regiment after them, but we have forgotten why. Guardians beyond count have defended the HeartRock from all save the next true born Dragon Whisperer.

So, the First Born bestowed upon their brother, Son of the Morning Star, a mortal prince raised by Imperials, more dragon than man, their shared wisdom and power, so that he came to know the nature and language of all living things as they did; of earth, fire, wind and water. Together, Dancing with Dragons and Son of the Morning Star became one with all the One Earth's myriad creatures, predator and prey; knowing their languages, their songs and stories, their strengths and weaknesses, and their magic. For every creature, no matter their size, had a story to tell, had power of a kind, and together they held the One Earth in perfect balance.

All the companions withheld from their brother, Son of the Morning Star, were the Matriarch's Words of Making. For no mortal should hold the power to destroy the One Earth and the life it nurtured.

As dragonsong filled him, Son of the Morning Star's black armour and skin rippled and became scaled, and wings that swept to the ground grew between his shoulder blades. In that heartbeat a Dragon Whisperer was born of dragons and man. When the Dragon Whisperer stood in front of his peoples, so Quenelda was also standing by his side, an otherwordly crown of dragonglass about her brow as it was about his. And she turned with him as the army before them knelt in the snow to their King and the dragons.

And finally, Quenelda fully understood her purpose.

CHAPTER FORTY-EIGHT
Dire Deeds Afoot

Down in the Inn of the Furtive Lobster by the north Harbour Master's house, Knuckle had gathered all his men when the news first reached his ears.

'She's sick?' Knuckle mulled over an idea. 'How sick?

'Very sick, Boss,' Gaff asserted. 'She ain't been seen at Court or on Dragon Isle for a half-moon, since all those dragons went queer.'

'Y'know that kitchen scullion at the palace?' Dornoch put in. 'Broke his neck, slipped on the ice like you said he was going to, Boss. Me second cousin who took his place was summoned to carry apothecary's equipment when 'is apprentice tripped and knocked his head. An...'

Knuckle rolled his eyes.

'He saw her!'

'So?'

'Well, she ain't got no scales, Boss. None.'

'None? Now that *is* interesting. I thought she was supposed to be half dragon these days? It's all everybody talks about.'

'Nah, not quite half dragon, Boss. No tail,' Gaff put in. 'She ain't got no tail, leastways not when she is walking about.'

'What?' Knuckle frowned, feeling the conversations slipping away yet again.

'Well, how could she sit down if she had a tail, you eejit?' Dornoch contended.

'What?'

'Well...she couldn't sit, Boss, if she had a tail. Stands to reason. It'd get in the way...wouldn't be able to sit down with a tail. Stands to reason!'

Knuckle rolled his eyes. Their combined intelligence was that of a slug...a stupid one at that.

'If she dies well and good. If she lives...we're going to kidnap her.'

'What?' Fathrin's mouth fell open. 'We're going tae kidn...' Fathrin found Knuckle's infamous knuckles clamped round his face.

'Shut your mouth!' Knuckle cursed. 'The City Watch are everywhere. Can't trust no one. Guild are waxing clever. They got a network of children an' old folk listening out for them.'

'How we going to...do that then, Boss?'

'Yeah. We chased 'er up north for moons and never caught her.'

Knuckle groaned inwardly, eyes crossing. He hardly needed reminding of that disaster, nor his second ignominious failure which had led to being knocked out by a well swung ham and waking up in jail. Would ruin his reputation if that little fact became widely known. His master would not tolerate a third failure. This was one he could not afford to get wrong. Best not tell anyone until it succeeded. 'I don't know, yet', he snapped. 'But we'll find a way. If she's ill, no chance of us getting toasted by her is there?'

Faces nodded happily.

'Dornoch! You've got your second cousin twice removed working in the royal stables, mucking out? If the princess recovers she's bound to go there, let's see what he hears. There's gold in it for him. I've bought the loyalty of men-at-arms at the palace. Meantime...' he looked at his motley band, 'it's time to spread rumours.'

His men nodded. Rumour mongering was right up their street.

'Taverns and drink find ready ears. Here's some coin. Buy drinks and spread the word that the dragons were bewitched by the WarLock King; that's why they've flown, never to return. That their precious Dragon Whisperer is a fraud. She's not ill, she's in hiding, 'cause she can't make them come back. Without their dragons, the SDS are nothing! And without their Dragon Whisperer, the people are nothing'

CHAPTER FORTY-NINE
One Kind

The dream continued, timeless... *it must be a dream,* Quenelda thought, *but it's so real...* the chill wind on her face, slipping on the icy mud. The snap of tattered banners. The unfamiliar armour. The cry of a baby, the hot breath of the dragons. The rusty dinted mail of the ragged army that knelt in the snow; the pungent smell of dragon dung that made her eyes water.

One by one the greatest Lords knelt in turn before each of the First Born in homage, and swore to honour and to protect the One Earth and all who dwelt upon it. And in return the Four conferred their magic of Earth, Wind, Fire and Water upon them, and the Lords rose as Dragon Lords, to bond for life with a noble dragon, to become One Kind.

With their chosen dragons, led by their Dragon Whisperer King who could speak with man and dragon, the early Dragon Lords turned for the first time towards the advancing hobgoblin banners with fire in their eyes and bellies, and drove them back, back into the sea, where the mighty Seadragon Lords banished them to the darkest deeps where they had come from.

But then that vision faded to whiteness, and when it returned, Quenelda was lying on an unfamiliar bed, her face thin and deathly pale. A gaping dragon shaped hole was punched through the wood panelled wall between her mother's chambers and where she lay. Seated in a rocking chair by the fire, Drumondir dozed.

'Come.' Son of the Morning Star beckoned her, 'come,

leave them, they betrayed us. Come, Dancing with Dragons,' her twin held out his scaled hand....join your beloved dragon, Two Gulps & You're Gone, and leave fickle mankind to their deserved fate. Come, Dancing with Dragons, for all time amongst the stars.'

'Am I dying?

'Yes. Your peoples have betrayed the Covenant, turning from their Imperials long ago...they have forgotten their pledges, and the Matriarch is wrathful. But you can choose life. You can relinquish your powers and return to your family and peoples.'

'You mean, I will no longer be a Dragon Whisperer?' Her question sounded childish even to her own ears.

'Yes, you will no longer be One Kind. You will be as all other mortals. Is this not what you wished for when you sat on my throne? Not to be different? Not to bear the burden of your gift? Are you not happy?'

Quenelda bent her head in shame. It should be true. All her life she had been bullied for being different, mocked because of her ineptitude with magic, her strange affinity with dragons. But as she grew into a young woman her gift was recognised: the SDS and the people had hope for the first time. But faced with the rising power of the Abyss, the weight of their expectations had become too heavy, and she had wanted to be free of it.

'Be careful what you wish for,' Drumondir's warning rang in her head. Had she brought this down on herself by refusing to accept her responsibilities? She was the dragons' only voice in a world blind to their suffering and abuse. Who would speak for the dragons if she turned her back? Would they even survive the coming war?

Even if I am no longer a dragon whisperer I can fight. I can give dragons a voice! I have fifteen winters and am a Dragon Lord. A princess. She raised determined tawny eyes, her decision made.

'You would return to your world as a mortal? It will not be an easy path.' Son of the Morning Star warned. 'Many believe you already dead. Your SDS soldiers say you danced with the dragons and will return to lead them to victory. Others are spreading the rumour that the dragons killed you. That you are no true dragon whisperer. Your peoples are afraid. There are riots in your city. Mankind does foolish things when he is afraid, without counting the cost to others who share our One Earth.'

Quenelda bit back her fear, raised her head defiantly. 'There is no choice to make. The WarLock has betrayed everyone, man and dragon both. He and others on both sides want power at any price; they do not value those whose lives they deem lesser than their own, whose language they cannot hear or speak. They would fill our world with dominion and death, and would destroy the living One Earth. It would become barren, devoid of beauty.

'I will fight at my father's side, my family's side, honouring the dragons and all creatures on the One Earth; and if we lose, it will be because of *who* we have become, *what* we have become. Greedy and soulless. I will willingly pay the price for my people's folly. For the WarLock's sacrilege.'

'Why? Why choose to return to such a world?'

Quenelda searched her heart for the right words. 'Because although there is greed, violence and ambition, there is still also love, hope and beauty, and they are worth fighting for. Although the WarLock King cares nothing for the One Earth, there are many who have learnt from our past mistakes. After the Long Winter of the Mage Wars all dark sorcery was forbidden, as were training collars in my grandfather's time.' She took a deep breath.

'Because my family ~ my father and mother, Root, Tangnost, Drumondir and Armelia ~ they cherish their world and honour Two Gulps, Chasing the Stars, and Storm. My father...whilst I was lying here, he told me the SDS will go down fighting before they compel Imperials to fight each other. Their love calls me back. It is stronger than dominion and death.'

'You may lose this war and fall into darkness and dust under the heel of your WarLock King. You are certain of your choice?'

Quenelda nodded.

Her skin shivered as if a cold breeze brushed over her, and she was merely a young woman, who felt naked without her inner dragon. Her scales were gone save the one. She turned her palm up, and there was a single red gold scale. A tear ran down her face to be caught by a finger that brushed her cheek. She looked up into sympathetic eyes.

'You will always bear that scale. Not even the Matriarch can break such a bond as you had with Two Gulps & You're Gone; that is a love which burns so brightly in the heavens that it will endure for eternity.

You will be one with him again. Now you will forget this dream, for you are become a mortal, and such knowing is a dangerous thing in mankind's hands. Be well, Dancing with Dragons. I will wait for you, sweet sister.'

'I can't hear them anymore!' Quenelda raised anguished human eyes to her brother's reptilian ones. 'It's silent. I can't hear their song. I can't hear their song...I can't-'

Quenelda's world faded into darkness.

CHAPTER FIFTY
Dark Dragon Dreams

'I can't hear their song anymore!'

Drumondir stirred, knuckling her tired eyes, shaking her head to clear the cobwebs. Quenelda was tossing restlessly, crying out in rising panic.

'I can't hear their song.'

At last!

The BoneCaster stumbled over to the bed, more than a little wobbly herself. It had been one of the longest half-moons of her life. They were all exhausted. Too little sleep and food. Root had been granted special leave, and only just this morning had returned for a training exercise, taking Two Gulps with him. The sabretooth had been loath to go and yet sensed the need in the young gnome, a heart on the edge of breaking.

'Quenel-' Drumondir began, jerking backwards as the young woman suddenly sat up, blinking in confusion.

'I can't hear them anymore!' Tears streamed down Quenelda's face as the BoneCaster wrapped her in a hug and held her sobbing. 'Can't hear them...'

As I feared...

'Hush, child, you have come back to us. You have come home'

A short while later there were loud shouts of alarm. The room vibrated, the floorboards dipped, and there was an explosive shower of splinters. Two Gulps arrived. The door had been closed.

A helmet rolled in behind him. Leaving Root reporting

to Tangnost on Dragon Isle, the sabretooth had returned as fast as he could. Hearing Quenelda cry out, he had put his talon down, leaving a trail of seriously dented armoured toes in his wake. He came to a confused stop. He couldn't hear her anymore! Dancing with Dragons was there, but… she was silent. Gently, the sabretooth leant forwards and snuffled. Smoke trickled out and then a long tongue snaked out to lick her tears.

'I can't hear Two Gulps! Why? Why can't I hear him?' There was a panicked, frightened edge to Quenelda's voice. Then she noticed her bare arms, turned her palms. One hand went to her brow. 'What's happened to my scales? What's happened to me?'

Sabretooth and young woman gazed at each other in mutual misery as Drumondir beckoned a terrified young servant who was trying to avoid the agitated dragon's crooked tail flailing. 'Find the Queen. She will want to know immediately her daughter is awake. And find a messenger to fly to Dragon Isle to tell Root Oakley and BearHugger. They are on military exercises. Wait! The princess needs food, something light. Fruit and cheese and bread. Cranberry juice.'

'Child, wait,' she cautioned Quenelda who was throwing back the covers. 'You are weak. Let the kitchen bring you some food and drink before you try to rise. What do you remember of what happened?'

Quenelda frowned. 'I-I remember going with Root to go flying. And-'

'And anything else?' Drumondir gently prompted after a long pause.

'No, nothing…there is something I can't remember.

Why am I in bed? Did I fall? Where's Root?'

'Hush. He is out on exercises. Child,' Drumondir took Quenelda's cold hands in hers; melting snow trickled down onto the coverlets. 'You have been asleep for a half-moon.'

'A half-moon? How? Why?'

And so Drumondir told her all that had happened.

'You remember nothing of it?'

'No.' Quenelda shook her head miserably. 'Nothing. Root and I were going flying... Tears welled. 'What does it all mean? My scales are gone! I can't even hear Two Gulps, and he is beside me.'

'Sometimes,' the BoneCaster said cautiously, 'you have said you wanted to be like Armelia and Root. The same as any other young lady. Now you are, you wish it were not so?'

'Yes. But- I became frightened that so many people thought I could sort everything, that I can win this war for them. That I could defeat the WarLock. The Maelstrom. I've only fifteen winters! I... wasn't ready.'

'But now you are?'

'Every time I entered the Heart Rock and sat on the DragonBone chair, I grew somehow. I shared memories, lifetimes that weren't mine. I knew impossible things. I drew on its power as if I had put down roots and become...part of the One Earth, nurtured by its magic, its mysteries, its memories. But now, I can't even talk to dragons and those memories are gone. Like a fading dream...just beyond my reach. Now, I'm no good to anyone. I can't teach anyone anything. Who am I?'

'Child,' Drumondir reached out to cup Quenelda's

head. 'You are still the same young woman, a Princess, a Dragon Lord. You are the daughter of the King and Queen. You are a friend to Root, and Armelia and Tangnost. Beloved by Two Gulps, and his sire, who,' she turned the hand with the scale, 'who is part of you for ever. None of that has changed. Nor will it ever.'

'But I cannot fly! I cannot lead others. Everything I knew is gone. Everything that made me special.'

Drumondir shook her head and smiled. 'No! It was not just your inner dragon that was special, it was *you.* Do you think you are so diminished without your inner dragon, whom none of us could see? Do you think your family and friends will love you less because you have changed? Have lost a scale or two? A love that is rigid and unbending is no love at all. We are all unique, you are still special for half a hundred reasons. You will not have forgotten how to fly, how to be a Dragon Lord, how to love Root. Will those you trained suddenly not obey you? Two Gulps is still yours.'

Biting her lip, Quenelda nodded, reaching out to where one wing had unfurled protectively about the bed, to where a great golden eye was wistfully watching her.

There was the sound of running feet, clanking and clonking along the corridor.

'I think at least one of your friends has heard the news,' Drumondir smiled. 'I will pass you into their care.' *I must talk with the Queen and the King.* 'I -'

'Ouff!!!'

CHAPTER FIFTY-ONE
Ouff!!!

There was a huge crash outside, followed by a clang, and a helmet rolled past the broken door. Spoing...poing... oing... Laying down their pikes, the guards disappeared as Drumondir and Quenelda ran to the remains of the doorway.

Smothering their laughter, the guards were pulling a partially armoured knight to his feet. Drumondir and Quenelda ran to help. It wasn't easy. Root was wheezing and huffing and puffing, holding his side with a stitch as they set him back on his feet. The young gnome was red in the face, although whether that was embarrassment, or the fact he had run up two flights of stairs in armour and caught a pointy toe under a carpet was moot!

'Que-nelda!' Root bent over to catch his breath. 'You're – you're awake! Guy brought me the – the moment we heard the – the news.' Hands on knees, trying to catch his breath, Root was smiling through his tears. 'Oh, Quenelda,' they returned to the royal apartment. 'We thought you were never going to wake up. But you're better now?'

But the eyes that looked up into his were entirely human and in a face that held no joy, were utterly bereft. 'I can't hear them anymore, Root! I can't hear their song.'

Taking her trembling hands, trying to steady his, Root struggled for words. 'Song?'

'Dragonsong....Oh, Root, Oh Root,' her face crumpled. 'I can't hear the dragons anymore.'

'Two Gulps! Get off!' Quenelda tried to bat her

sabretooth away, but a talon caught the end of a wooden bed which had already been struggling with the weight of an armoured knight. It collapsed.

On the floor again, Root sat up. 'Quenelda. I am so sorry, it's all my f-'

A finger gently sealed his lips. 'No, it's not Root. It's not your fault.'

CHAPTER FIFTY-TWO
Armelia

'Root,' Guy had come up to chivvy his navigator. 'It is wonderful to see you are awake, Lady. Apologies, but Root, we have been asked to report back, stat.'

The young navigator nodded. 'I'll be back as soon as I can. Two Gulps will look after you till then.'

Armelia arrived as Root and Guy were leaving the royal quarters. A quick hug in passing and Root was back to operations. It was the first time Armelia had seen her friend smile since he had brought Quenelda home.

'You're awake!' Armelia flung herself around Quenelda gripping her in a fierce bear hug, nearly knocking her off her feet. Your mother is coming the moment she can leave the Guild. She let me come immediately. How are you?' They must have talked for bells before Armelia told her friend what was happening in the Glen.

'Oh, Quenelda, afterwards, lots of dragons never returned to their stables. They have flown. People have been saying terrible things. That the dragons killed you. That you aren't a Dragon Whisperer, you're a fraud. The people are afraid. The City Watch are struggling to keep order. The people need to see you.'

'They want to see me?'

'They need to see their Dragon Whisperer.'

'But I'm not one anymore, Armelia. Don't you understand? I can't talk to the dragons anymore. I *have* lost my scales. They are right. I'm not a dragon whisperer. I'm no use to anyone.'

And I don't have dark dragon dreams anymore...

CHAPTER FIFTY-THREE
Never Give Up

'Your father has landed on Dragon Isle,' the Queen kissed her daughter as she read the courier's note and waved the page away. 'Go to him.' Caitlin hid her fears for her downcast daughter, catching Armelia's worried glance. 'He flew back the moment he heard you had awoken ~ through terrible weather. And your young friend Quester has been asking for you every day. Your father kept him busy at his side.'

'Take Two Gulps,' Armelia suggested. 'He has not eaten a thing since he brought you home. Drumondir said he was pining.'

Quenelda looked dubious. 'Not eaten a thing?'

'No. He refused all food. He has destroyed half the palace, but for once he hasn't eaten it!'

But her mother clearly did not mind. 'He insisted on staying close to you and no one could persuade him otherwise!'

'And he's lost a lot of weight,' Armelia said brightly. 'Tangnost says he is almost the correct weight, and that as soon as possible you must re-join the Juveniles who are training in the Labyrinth. They need you.'

'Tangnost has been?'

'Of course. As often as he had a free heartbeat, sweet-heart. He loves you so very much. Root says he has been unbearably grumpy, like a bear with a sore tooth. He has taken command of training your young friends, but his heart is with you wherever he goes.'

'Is that where his nickname, The Bear, comes from?'

Armelia asked with interest as Quenelda left, sabretooth in tow. 'Grumpy as an old bear?'

The Queen smiled. 'I think he fought a bear once, bare handed in his clan's rituals of adulthood. Hugged it into submission but then let it go. The claw talisman he wears was dug out of his shoulder.'

'Papa?' Quester was still stripping the King's armour as she arrived in her father's quarters, and grinned a silent welcome.

'Oh, Papa!' Quenelda had moved so softly even he had barely heard his daughter's arrival at the threshold. Blind to everything others saw, Rufus DeWinter could now tell by the tread of her boots that she had lost weight, from the metallic clink that she was wearing her familiar studded jacket and breeches.

'Goose.'

'Oh, Papa!'

He held her in his damaged arms and let her cry until she ran out of tears. 'Goose,' he kissed her head. 'You are back on your feet thanks to your friends' love and care.'

'But I can't fly anymore, Papa. I tried. I am tied to the land. I'm no use to anyone.'

'Goose, you are weak and distraught. You do not yet know what you can do or cannot do. You must give yourself time to heal. As Quester knows only too well. You must talk with him.' He nodded at his esquire. 'Go, get something to eat and get your head down. We return tomorrow.'

'Come,' he sat his daughter down by the hearth and gave her some mulled cider. 'Drink, slowly now, it's hot.

And here,' he beckoned a servant over with some food. 'Eat. You must be starving. I know I am!'

'Now,' he tilted his daughter's chin, looking at her with blind eyes and the acuity of his inner dragon senses. 'Look at me. I am changed; burnt by the maelstrom. Do you love me less for it? Am I less a King or father for being blind? Are you less a daughter because you cannot fly? When you found me, you told me to never give up. That I was loved. That no matter what had happened, that would never change. And so, it is with you.

'Goose, you cannot talk to the dragons, you have lost your dragon scales. You are not alone with your confusion and loss. Many have lost their sight, or limbs, or are crippled by injuries. That is the reality of war, and if you are to fight one, then you need to learn this, no matter how hard the lesson. Tangnost lost all his sons to the war, and his wife died of grief. Root's father died saving the Howling Glen, and all but one sister died in the mines. Quester lost a leg. War turns life on its head: the young die before the old and the families of those who die bear the hardest burden, for they must live with loss for the rest of their lives. War is not glorious save to those who do not know it, and they are all too quick to judge us when they have no experience of what we do.

'War brings out the best and the worst in men. Norfolk broke my command out of fear and ignorance, and I suspect ambition, but our young Warden of the Wall has risen to the challenge and has the makings of great leader, a great man. If war itself is not great, those who fight can become so, and bonds forged in the crucible of war are stronger than any other in your life. These are all things that the heir to the Seven Kingdoms needs to learn.

'I will tell you what I tell all our men who bear injuries, hidden or seen.'

'Like Quester?'

'Yes. His scars are hidden. Don't dwell on what you cannot do, Goose, but on what you *can* do ~ for your family, your friends, your peoples. And who knows what tomorrow may bring?

'You are my daughter, a princess growing into a beautiful young woman who will succeed to the throne, but you have much to learn of statecraft and command. If you cannot fly yourself, you are no different to the rest of us mere mortals.

'I must return to the Wall on the morrow. Come with me, and bring your sabretooth. Time you both had some fresh air and exercise; you are both peely-wally[2]. It will give you time to decide what to do, but, my darling daughter, if you cannot fly, then return to the Juveniles. They are training in the Labyrinth attached to the III Brigade, and they need a talon wing leader. Tangnost needs you.'

She is lost to me? Stormcracker asked as the royal dragon pad rose as dawn was barely a pencil on the horizon. *She cannot hear or speak to me?*

No. We betrayed your trust. Her gift has been taken.

The great head descended to blow softly about the young woman. Stormcracker's tail lifted her gently up

[2] Scottish ~ pale and sickly in appearance.

beside her father. Two Gulps clambered up an offered wing as Stormcracker began to warm up and the ground crew cleared the pad. Lights winked on. T- 2 to lift off.

Dark was falling, the braziers blazed about the dragon pads. They would be staying at the fortress for five days, inspecting forts and troops and planning for the coming war games.

Quenelda hesitantly stepped down Storm's wings, Two Gulps in tow. Recognising her, someone shouted. And another and another. As she reached the ground they pressed forwards greeting her, patting her, bowing. Grooms and soldiers, smiths and Dragon Lords, healers and troopers, but all mindful of Two Gulps smoking behind her.

'Dancing with Dragons!' The call went up. 'Dancing with Dragons.' They were using her Imperial call sign. 'Dancing with Dragons!'

'Princess...'

Smiles, warmth...clapping...

'You danced with the dragons, Princess... we could see it here!'

'Like a spinning top in the sky, Princess.'

Their Dragon Whisperer was back amongst them.

'Lady,' the now familiar voice greeted her.

'Sir!' The soldiers were saluting and turning back to their tasks as the Warden of the Wall arrived to greet his guests.

'Lady...you are... well?' The perceptive eyes were quizzical.

Quenelda nodded. *Did he really want to know?*

Would he understand?

'It was truly a wondrous thing to behold,' Major Cawdor was watching her carefully. 'The gyre was so large we saw it here rising into the clouds. No one has seen a gyre in living memory.'

'Well, I still haven't.' Quenelda found herself admitting with a wry smile. 'I don't remember anything.'

Cawdor laughed. It broke the tension. 'In truth I thought them fairy tales from the nursery! They were said to be portents of change.'

'Well, that part is true.'

'The men are saying you were dancing with your dragons. Others that you had become a dragon and the princess was gone. Others still, that they were crowning you, that you would return to lead our armies to victory.'

'It's never going to happen now.' She bit her lip but raised her head defiantly. She didn't want to be pitied. 'I've lost my gift. I can't talk to them anymore. I can't fly anymore. At least, not without a dragon.'

'Lady,' he sat her down, and took her hands. 'I am sorry. Heartfelt sorry for you.'

'I feel...strange without my scales. I don't remember what I felt when they began to grow. All the other girls were disgusted. The boys envious. But now that I've lost them I want them back.'

'You feel like I do without my armour. A tortoise without its shell?'

Quenelda laughed. 'Not very glamorous.'

'But war is not glamourous, Lady, is it? It is noise and blood, injury and death as you and your young friends Quester and Root discovered when you were here last year. Funnily enough, ballad peddlers and singers are rarely to be found in the middle of a battlefield! But,' his eyes held hers. 'There are many things on this One Earth worth fighting for. Are there not?'

Quenelda let out a short breath and nodded thoughtfully, as a sense of peace settled about her shoulders like a warm cloak. 'Yes, yes there are.'

CHAPTER FIFTY-FOUR
A Secret Meeting

A secret meeting was taking place in Drumondir's quarters, which were now next to Quenelda's in the royal apartments at the palace. Wood-workers were sawing and hammering away, repairing the damage done by Two Gulps. Root and Tangnost were the last to arrive from Dragon Isle. Quester was with the King, and the object of their discussion.

'How can we help her?' Armelia was fretting. 'What can we do? She is so... quiet.'

'Well, what do people see when they see Quenelda?' Drumondir was curious as to how others saw her pupil.

'Someone who looks like a stable hand?' Root said, to an outbreak of laughter.

Drumondir sighed and tutted. 'What else? Why do the people believe she is a Dragon Whisperer? What do the people see?'

A girl with a dragon... no, a battledragon,' Tangnost answered. 'Two Gulps, and Quenelda may not be able to talk the way they once did, but you'd have to be blind not to see they can still understand each other.'

'A dragon whisperer...' Armelia mulled it over, thinking back to her own journey from lacy gowns to her flying leathers. It had been scary and exhilarating to wear flying leathers for the first time. Daring. And visible. 'I know! Find the finest armourer the Guild or SDS have.'

'Why?' Root frowned, 'what are you thinking of?

'To make her black-scale armour!' Tangnost bestowed a grateful smile on Armelia who smiled back.

'Yes! But proper armour, not just small scales stitched like my latest design. Magic armour like you wear, Root. She's still a Dragon Lord! Give her some of that magic back!'

This was greeted with a thoughtful silence.

Root nodded, the anxiety that knit his face relaxing. 'You have it, yes!'

'And... the people will see their Dragon Whisperer is back!' Armelia added. 'The longer they don't see her the more they-'

'Believe those vile rumours,' Tangnost finished grimly. 'Knuckle Quarnack, the WarLock's Dragon Master, escaped when the dragons all flew. I know he's behind this, feeding off superstition and people's fears. Fear gives words wings. We have men searching for him. I think...I am certain there are Lords hiding him. Giving him gold to go about his business, planning sedition and riots.'

'Traitors? Here on the Black Isle?' Hand over mouth in horror, Armelia couldn't believe it.

'Almost certainly. And the Guild. Even on Dragon Isle he will have spies biding their time, those in thrall to him long before he showed his hand.'

'It would have to be very light, and the scales delicate,' Drumondir was thinking out loud, bringing them back to why they had gathered. 'The scales would need to move naturally. I imagine the SDS smiths are the only ones with the skill to bind metal and magic.'

'I don't know, Tangnost said doubtfully. 'To craft something that as a living skin that binds scale to scale like hers did, will require Words of Making. There are few now who can forge spells into armour and weapons.'

'Do you not have any Mage Smiths on Dragon Isle? The BoneCaster raised her eyebrows. 'Is not your dragon lords' armour forged and bound with magic?'

Tangnost sighed. 'Bound with battlemagic, yes, of course. Ancient lore known only to the Dragon Lords. But no longer with Words of Making. We have not the skill anymore. None can forge with Words. We would need at least one to make a second skin.'

'Words of-? I know!' Root said eagerly. 'I know someone who can! My esquire, Squirrel, has a friend, a young dwarf we also rescued when we retook the mine, the name of Anvil. His friend's family come from a long line of smiths who can forge,' the young gnome frowned. 'I don't understand what it means. Words of Making? He said his father, Faldir, was the greatest smith in the Seven Kingdoms, Squirrel thought it just boasting. B-'

'Faldir?' Tangnost gripped the young gnome's arm hard. 'Are you sure? Faldir?'

'Yes,' Root nodded, confused. 'Why? What does that mean?'

'If it is the same family, then Anvil's boast rings true,' Tangnost considered, deciding to share one of Dragon Isle's secrets. 'Faldir was our Mage Smith on Dragon Isle. All armour and weapons for our Dragon Lords were forged by him and his eldest son. He was visiting kin last year to the north of the Isle of Midges when he and his family vanished. Not a word or a trace has ever been found of them.'

Root went out into the anteroom, quickly spotting his esquire still trying to knock the dent out of his helmet! 'Squirrel, can you find your friend, Anvil, and bring him here?'

Within half a bell his esquire returned with a skinny young dwarf who looked as nervous as a new born fawn, another who had not yet got over his brutal treatment in one of the WarLock King's mines.

Tangnost gently took the boy's shoulders and searched his face. 'Anvil, Root says you were rescued from the brimstone mines at midwinter. We want to hear about the rest of your family. What happened to them?'

The young gnome bit his lips. 'We...we took passage on one of the last Sea Eagle longships trading north in the autumn. They were waiting for us', Anvil looked tearful. 'As if they knew we were coming. The boats were beached on Arran and pulled up beyond the high tide and tethered. Our kin had mountain goats ready, when two Imperials decloaked. My Fa...my Fa and three brothers were taken bound onto one, which then vanished.

'My Ma, my sisters and I were bound and taken on the second to...' he faltered. 'To the mines. There were many other families there. Just the old, the ill and the young. My Ma and four sisters did not...' his young voice broke helplessly as Tangnost gathered him into a bear hug. 'They d-didn't survive down there. They were dead long before you freed us. I d-don't have a family anymore,' he wiped his nose on his jacket.

'You do now lad, you have us. Root here was no different when he first came, he too lost all his kin. We are all family here. We will look after you.' *This was dire news indeed*, Tangnost thought, as he comforted Anvil. 'Had your father taught you much of his craft?'

'I know how to make a unicorn shoe!'

'Do you now, lad?' Tangnost found a smile. 'Did he teach you any Words?' Tangnost held his breath.

'He taught me one. All eight of us were given one Word, only together could we forge. My Fa, he said it was to protect us, that Words were dangerous.'

'That they are. Well, then, Anvil, would you like to become apprenticed to one of our Master Smiths? You can teach him your Word of Making, and he can teach you his craft as your Fa would have done.'

That brought a hopeful smile. 'Yes, Dragon Master, yes!'

'Time to fight back, lad. And if you have any of your Fa's gift, we'll make a Master Smith out of you.'

CHAPTER FIFTY-FIVE
Black Scales

'Come', Drumondir held out her hand. 'Come and see.'

Quenelda hesitated before the span across to the HeartRock, full of doubts. 'Perhaps I cannot cross anymore.' She was head down, on the verge of tears, shoulders shaking.

'I do not believe it for one heartbeat! Even in her wrath the Matriarch would not kill her mortal child. She returned you to us for a reason. I believe the HeartRock will still be a place of sanctuary for you, where others may not follow.'

Quenelda sat on the bones waiting. But they remained cold and hard as stone, and the HeartRock remained dark, lit only by distant stars as it had when she first found it. There was utter silence, save for her ragged breathing. The song had gone. The magic had all gone! The Matriarch no longer spoke to her. Nor, she realised, did the dark dragon invade her dreams...

'Come,' Drumondir was full of hope. 'We have a gift for you from all those who love you. From Tangnost and Root, from Armelia and your parents. It was Armelia's idea. She is a true friend.'

Baffled, Quenelda allowed herself to be led beyond the four stones and there, starlight reflecting off it, dark against the greater blackness, hung an armour stand with a suit of scales.

It was, Drumondir admitted, a beautiful thing. Impossibly delicate.

Quenelda reached out a hand to touch the scales. *So*

light...?

'Who made this?' she husked.

'One of our Master Smiths, assisted by Anvil, youngest son of Faldir, SDS Mage Smith who was captured by the WarLock we now know, along with his three elder brothers. His sisters and mother did not survive the Brimstone mines. Each child was given one Word of Making, and Anvil's one went into the Making of your armour. It is hoped that it will allow the scales to fit you like a living skin when you put this on. Would you like to try?'

Quenelda nodded wordlessly. It was a beautiful gift.

'See, here? It is laced, here and here with black, invisible. Let me help you. It is lined with a thin layer of felt and cotton to keep you warm.'

Drumondir saw they had guessed right, as the armour shivered, seemed to shrink to fit Quenelda, to flow naturally. The face that looked up was still pale, the eyes bewildered, but you could see the change in the way Quenelda stood, stretching, testing the unfamiliar feel. 'It's so light!' she smiled. 'The scales...some are so tiny... But my face,' Quenelda realised. 'There are-'

'Here,' Drumondir smiled, thanking Armelia with her eye for fashion, and lifted a slim black circlet hung with tiny scales. 'Worn under your hair, just so, it will give the appearance of scales on your brow. And, if we apply some of this,' a small vial was produced and a sticky gum, then she offered tiny scales, 'these can glue to your face. None will know. Now, how about a visit to the Black Isle? I am to visit Winifred at the Guild. Come with me.'

It was very gusty and Drumondir felt sick. Two Gulps landed badly on the Guild dragon pads which didn't help, as Drumondir struggled to maintain her dignity and staggered off a little dishevelled after getting a foot stuck in a stirrup and knocking her head against a talon. Word passed swiftly from mouth to mouth that their Dragon Whisperer was back with her tame sabretooth, accompanied by the exotic BoneCaster from the far north, and the cheers grew louder as the crowd rapidly grew larger.

From the smoky door of the Hump-Backed EarWig across the square, Knuckle's eyes narrowed thoughtfully as he knocked back a beaker of oat beer with his men. 'You may fool them, but not me, little girl.' Hood down, scarf about his face he joined the dense throng gathered about Quenelda. It was so easy! He too called out the Princess's name, reached out as those about him were doing. As he was knocked by no one, he put his hand out seemingly to steady himself.

Once back with his men he unfurled his fist and laughed. 'So, she really is just a fraud!' He lifted the delicate scale, bored through at the top so it could be threaded and smiled. 'We have her!'

Knuckle watched as the King's daughter swiftly disappeared into the Guild, followed by her sabretooth which was considerably larger than when he had last saw it. In fact, it was big for a sabretooth, and no longer fat as a barrel. It looked lean and mean as a pedigree battledragon should. Whatever his plan was, he had to separate her from her dragon or they would be toast. She might be a fraud, but that battledragon certainly wasn't, and it walked at her heels like a lap dog! He took a pull on his pipe and thoughtfully exhaled. He needed a plan.

CHAPTER FIFTY-SIX
A Secret Uncovered

Drumondir was tired, her neck stiff as she dismounted Two Gulps Too Many and gratefully removed the unaccustomed helmet. She had been in the hospital most of the night helping surgeons and healers treat frostbite, then helping the midwife with a difficult birth.

The BoneCaster didn't mind the blizzards or the biting cold, they made her feel more at home far to the south of her clan lands. But she could not get used to flying solo on an overly affectionate sabretooth who had the alarming habit of turning around to check that she was alright, instead of looking ahead. Quenelda's generous offer of Two Gulps for a few days before they both returned to battle exercises wasn't to be missed, and a sign of the sabretooth's affection for the BoneCaster that he had been persuaded to leave Quenelda at the castle, even if Drumondir had had to bribe him with a bag of honey tablets. She made sure these ones had no dragon's bane!

After talking with her father, mother and Tangnost, Quenelda had decided to return to the Juveniles with Two Gulps, taking Root with her. Guy De Bessart on Phoenix Firestorm was to continue as her Imperial pilot, with Root now as his navigator. It was, Drumondir thought, a chance for both to begin to heal, away from prying eyes, with friends of their own age. Imperials would have to continue their training without the King's daughter, but Tangnost was confident his Dragon Masters and Mistresses and their Imperials knew what they were doing.

The BoneCaster drew in a deep breath of bracing air. Lack of proper sleep and food over the last three-quarter moon had left her thick headed and dull witted, although the chilly weather was remedying that in no time. Now that Quenelda was back on her feet, if not fully healed, the BoneCaster wanted to resume her searches for the Dragonsdome Chronicles and books on the Mage Wars and the Kingdom's first Dragon Lords. She had been exploring the damaged library at Dragonsdome as often as she was freed from other duties.

Throwing up her hood, warm cloak wrapped about her, Drumondir carefully picked her way through the heavy slanting snow, leaving Two Gulps eating a burnt spar with relish. Despite the sabretooth's confusion that he could not speak with Quenelda, his appetite had returned.

Dragonsdome was still a wreckage of charred beams and shattered tiles buried under deep snow and filigreed with frost. Part of the roof had burnt, and a weakened wall had crumbled, but the King had cast a protective ward to keep out the elements, and the Dome of Dragonsdome was also untouched. There was the slightest tingling sensation as she passed through the ward and suddenly the whine of the blizzard was muted, the air warm and still. Taking out flint and knife she struck a spark in the fireplace, gently feeding the kindling until it took. Adding broken flooring and wooden panels it was soon blazing, despite the snow drifting down the chimney.

Drumondir was up a ladder searching when she heard a rip. Turning, she could see Two Gulps had begun eating a tapestry. It was fire damaged and stained, the wool faded with age. Two Gulps was snuffling at it, smoke trickling from his nostrils.

'Two Gulps. NO!'

The sabretooth guiltily jerked his head. There was a loud crack and the heavy hanging tumbled to the ground, burying the sabretooth who flapped and squealed beneath its unexpected weight. Drumondir didn't know whether to be exasperated or laugh. Certainly, it was never quiet when Two Gulps was around. Moons ago she had asked Quenelda to tell the sabretooth he was not to touch the books, which he took as permission to eat anything else. Swiftly descending, she gripped an edge and pulled to no effect. The tapestry was far too heavy for one person to shift. The juvenile, however, was using his powerful back legs, jumping up and down. Head shaking, he soon shrugged it off. Drumondir danced backwards out of the way as a portion thudded at her feet.

'Two Gulps!' she admonished him. 'You can't just e-'. She stopped in mid-sentence to squint at the tapestry. Returning to the fire she lit a candle. Frowning, she knelt. The threads that caught the light were vibrant yellows, reds and blues, pure snow white as if they were dyed and spun that very day. The sabretooth nudged her, nearly knocking her over as he lipped at it hopefully. The BoneCaster let out a deep breath. 'What have we found, boy?'

She stood, walking carefully she examined as much as

possible. First light. A dark sky bright with stars... snow... surely those were scales? Different peoples... The BoneCaster turned her examination to the tapestry itself. No wonder it had flattened Two Gulps, it was even thicker than tapestries normally were. It must weigh an imperial or two! But that was because...it was two tapestries, not one!

'Why hide this one behind? Unless it was supposed to be hidden. Come on, boy. I think we need to get this to Dragon Isle.'

The weather was deteriorating. Thinking it might have been quicker to walk and wishing she had, Drumondir's normal calm evaporated as the gusting gale pushed the heavy sabretooth perilously close to chimney pots and roof gables. She could see the Guild Guard's mouths dropping open at the dishevelled apparition that landed on their lower pad, wrapped in washing lines. She had not had the pleasure of meeting Mistress Winifred, who in turn had never met a BoneCaster. A hawkish yellow gaze met a steely grey one, and an Imperial was requisitioned along with a half complement of BoneCrackers assigned to guard the Guild.

'Helmets on and please strap in, ladies!' The navigator wiped his visor clear of snow. 'We don't want you blowing away, ha! ha! You may feel a little unwell when we cloak and uncloak. Nothing to worry about. Ha! Ha! It gets easier every time! Barf bags are there beside your seats. Hang on to your hats!' With that cheery thought he left them to consider the privilege of flying on the greatest battledragon on the One Earth.

Drumondir's return to Dragonsdome was nowhere

near as bad. The powerful Imperial ate up the distance swiftly and was barely bothered by the howling wind or washing lines. They put down near the ruined library. It took all twenty troopers with rope and tackle to get the tapestry onto the waiting Imperial, slipping and swearing as they went.

'Careful there, man!' Winifred barked at a hapless commando who had tripped on the snow slicked rubble. 'This is priceless! Priceless!' With the unspoken inference, Drumondir thought with a smile, that the careless trooper wasn't. Winifred should be Grand Mistress! By all accounts, Rumpole Spellskin was a timid creature with a love of pomp and circumstances, and a heartfelt loathing of dragons and warlocks: unfit to lead the ancient Guild in a time of great peril... The tapestry was loaded. Time to fly!

Until now, only the SDS or those of royal blood set foot on Dragon Isle, its secrets revealed to no others, not even Grand Masters were permitted. The Guardian's purpose, and those countless who had come before him, was to keep its secrets safe. To guard the HeartRock. But these were extraordinary times, and as an authority on weaving, Drumondir was confident that Winifred could help unravel the tapestry's secrets. And they needed to do that away from prying eyes. Landing on one of the Academy's lower pads they were greeted by an armed escort and given guest quarters above the Fellows Hall of the Lower Cloud School.

'Forward!' The sergeant shouted as her BoneCrackers staggered drunkenly beneath the weight of the thing. 'Left, right, left, right...'

Drumondir rolled her eyes and exchanged glances with Winifred. *Why was it that the military had to shout everything?* In her ice-bound lands far to the north, silence was the watchword. Else you would never catch your dinner or might be caught for someone else's dinner, apart from anything else.

Dropping it heavily, the troopers were about to step forward to unroll the tapestry when...

'Boot's *off!*'

Drumondir shook her head to stop her ears popping: Goodness! Winifred was certainly getting into the spirit of things!!

The BoneCrackers fell about themselves to obey her parade ground voice. Barefooted, they rolled the heavy tapestry out. As more of the hanging was revealed, it appeared as if giant moths had eaten away at the ancient threads, nibbled away the corners, leaving random holes. Finally, it was laid out, a little unevenly. Chandeliers heavy with candles were carefully lowered down to barely three strides above head height, so that the two women could examine the detail.

Plumping down on a creaking chair, Winifred unlaced her sensible shoes. Drumondir copied her example, unbuckling her practical snow boots. Bending to their task in stockinged feet, the small BoneCaster and large Guild Mistress began carefully, oh so carefully, to brush away the dirt and soot, revealing the story beneath.

Time was passed in fascinating conversation with Mistress Winifred about spinning, dying, looms, wefts and weaves and techniques. Time was also passed with the BoneCaster describing a wondrous frozen world of crystal caves and felted tents, huge ice bears and colours that danced in a night sky thick with stars. But gradually they fell silent as the tapestry finally revealed its story.

'It's extraordinary,' Winifred said. 'The colours, after all this time, they are so vivid, they bring it almost to life!' She considered the wools and dyes and explained to the fascinated BoneCaster. 'This is dyed with grubwort, I am sure of it. Woad, and hare's foot there, all plants of the deep south, lost to us now. This looks like smirkal seaweed, gives a lovely soft lilac. Lore has been passed from generation to generation, from my Elder Mother to my Mother to myself.' She darted forwards. 'And still we are learning.' She pointed to the mountains beneath the BoneCaster's feet. 'I have never encountered this knotting technique before. This wool woven for the snow...? I think,' she rubbed a twist between her fingers and sniffed. 'I think it comes from the wild white dumble sheep which once roamed these glens. They are long gone now. Drumondir,' she looked at her new friend, 'this tapestry is old, very, very old.'

'I, too, think so,' Drumondir agreed, 'and I think it portrays the First Alliance, or what the older texts call The Covenant. This young man here is Son of Morning Star. These...dragons, his family. I believe this tapestry describes a time *before* the first Dragon Lords. And it is not what I was expecting! No...' she said thoughtfully, 'not at all.'

CHAPTER FIFTY-SEVEN
The Dragonsdome Chronicles

The King and Queen arrived and were escorted in by the Guardian, flanked by several of his Deans of Faculty and an excitement of scholars. The tapestry had been hoisted to hang from one of the hammer beams, making its examination much simpler. The King cocked his head. He could smell the charred wool, but his blindness gave him no clue which tapestry Drumondir was so excited about. The scholars quietly moved to examine it.

'Drumondir, Seamstress,' the Queen gestured. 'Speak, please.'

'Your Grace,' Winifred attempted a clumsy curtsey, but struggled to rise. Just behind, Drumondir stepped swiftly forwards to help, but was not, in the event, needed, which was probably just as well. Caitlin schooled her face to smother a smile.

'Majesties, Guardian. I have examined the weaving, weft and warp of this tapestry, the dyes, the knotting techniques, the spin of the wool. Old and skilled techniques bring this scene to life, very old. This tapestry is ancient beyond reckoning. There are plant dyes here even I do not know because the plants no longer exist.'

There was a polite nod. Magnus Fitzgerald raised his brows questioningly.

'The lost Dragonsdome Chronicles are said to hold secrets of great power,' Drumondir took up the story. 'For generations beyond count many have sought their fabled promise of immortality and dreams of power beyond imagining. All have been searching for books, grimoires, sagas or scrolls, but nothing was believed to have survived the First Age. But we,' she smiled at Winifred, drawing her into the story. 'We think the Chronicles are tapestries, woven in an age when few could read, so that all could learn the story of the First Alliance, the Covenant, and honour it across the ages.' There was a heartbeat of silence, of indrawn breath.

'You believe *this* tapestry to be one of the Dragonsdome Chronicles?' The King asked, as the Guardian stepped forward to examine the ruined hanging. 'And that there are others?'

'Yes, Your Grace,' Winifred and Drumondir answered together. 'I would suggest this is the second, though we cannot be sure. The first likely tells the story of the dragons themselves.'

'And this came from Dragonsdome? But I do not recognise it,' Caitlin said

'Yes. It was hung the other way about. Such a simple ruse to conceal it. Hidden in plain sight. Perhaps you are more familiar with this one, Caitlin?' The three women moved about to examine the more familiar scene on the other side.

'It shows the forging of the First Alliance, Rufus,' the Guardian told his friend, studying the tableau. 'Son of the Morning Star,' he glanced at one of his Deans who nodded. 'Is in the centre, bowing, arms raised to either side linking the peoples of the Seven Kingdoms and... four Imperials. But not four Imperials such as we have ever seen!'

'Why?' The King's senses tingled with anticipation. His scales felt cool against his burnt skin.

'One of them is scaled all the hues of the sea, Rufus, exactly like those you now bear. A second is wreathed in flame and a third greens and browns. The fourth ...it is hard to choose a colour...those of the sky. Earth, wind, fire and water.'

'The four elements at the heart of all sorcery?' the King was frowning, trying to understand what he could not see.

'I believe these are not just his brother and sisters,' Drumondir suggested, 'As we have been taught. I think we are looking at the First Born, the Matriarch's own children.'

'The name given to the first regiment on Dragon Isle,' Jakart DeBessart said. 'My III First Born!'

The Guardian nodded. 'Yet another thing we have forgotten! A clue right in front of us. They have guarded the HeartRock throughout the Ages. Your daughter showed me the first hall in the HeartRock, showed me the four Imperials in stone that guard the DragonBone throne that sits there.'

'If this is true,' the King said, 'if they are not ordinary Imperials as we thought, then their powers must be immense.'

'Truly,' Drumondir agreed. 'They are the creators of all life on the One Earth.'

'You have doubts?' the King turned to the Guardian, sensing subtle hesitation.

'No, not as to what it is claimed to be. But Son of the Morning Star,' the Guardian frowned. 'Here he is arrayed in armour and surcoat, sword and battered shield. Not scales as we are used to. In this tapestry, he is clearly just a young man, a prince.'

'There is more?' Caitlin asked, watching the scholars' intense murmured debate.

'Possibly,' the Guardian observed, eyes flicking to the BoneCaster and back. 'Look at Son of the Morning Star, Caitlin. The Lords, and behind them, the army and people.'

'They are all bowing.'

'So?' The King frowned. 'We know this.'

'Not quite, Rufus. At their head, Son of the Morning Star is also bowing.'

There was a thoughtful silence.

'He is bowing *to* the dragons?

'Yes!'

'Then how -?'

'The dragons' nostrils are smoking,' the Guardian observed. 'There is also a soft light about them. An aura.'

'Perhaps the cold?' Caitlin said. 'Is it not just their breath in the freezing air?'

'I think it is more than that,' the Guardian strode forwards and pointed. 'See here? There is a similar light also about Son of the Morning Star and our Lords, but it is as if a mist were blowing from dragon to man.'

The King frowned. 'Are you suggesting that ...?'

'Yes,' the Guardian nodded grimly. 'And if it is true, we are in far greater peril even than we thought. It explains why your daughter's gift has been taken from her.'

'I fear that may only be the beginning,' Drumondir warned.

'Retribution?' The Guardian suggested. 'We clearly

betrayed the Covenant during the Mage Wars, and repeat that folly now to our mortal peril.'

'Imperials,' Jakart shook his head. 'We believed ourselves to be at the very least their equal, their masters, and yet here we learn the secret at the heart of the fabled Chronicles. It is *they* who bestowed power upon us! Who willingly chose to fight with us, not at our bidding!'

The King held out his arms, turning his wrists so the light caught the scales. 'I of all people should know this, for I was dying, crippled. Now, not only do I have the senses of a dragon, but I can talk to Stormcracker, just as my daughter can – could – talk to all dragons. How could we have been so blind?'

Caitlin smiled sadly, placing a gentle hand on her husband's shoulder. 'Perhaps it has taken your blindness for us to truly see, my love.'

'Perhaps,' the King laid a burnt and scaled hand over hers. 'Perhaps, my love. In which case it has been a price worth paying. We must pray we are not too late to remedy our errors and ignorance.'

'Drumondir, Mistress Winifred, invite my daughter to see this. Say nothing, let her study this for herself and see if she has any memory of it. We have to be sure we understand.' A sudden insight came to him. 'Young Root,' he turned to Drumondir. 'His unexpected affinity with wychwood...'

'Your Grace, yes! His people honour the old ways: the land and all its creatures. To them every living thing has a story to tell, all things and creatures have a magic of their own. Gnomes, it appears can still release that magic.'

The King smiled mirthlessly. 'Hugo will not imagine for a moment that lowly gnomes, whom he despises, have a greater natural affinity with magic than he! His disdain and arrogance towards all save sorcerers is his weakness. Gnomes may yet surprise us all.'

CHAPTER FIFTY-EIGHT
Our Memories are Short

'It is no coincidence that a Dragon Whisperer has been born into our times,' Drumondir warned. 'Given this chronicle and my people's sagas, what I have learnt in the HeartRock, I now believe all life balances on a knife edge. Not just ours. A great battle is coming, beyond our imaginations. We may all yet pay for the WarLock King's betrayal. We may already be too late. The One Earth itself may fail if the WarLock wins, and may become ash and dust like our twin moons.

The Queen was distressed. 'How could so much be forgotten? Has our chance passed with our daughter's gift being taken?'

'Many Ages have passed since the First Alliance, Caitlin,' the Guardian suggested. 'History became legend, and the truth was forgotten, or was hidden? Our memories, like our lives, are short, and the ambitious ever bend the truth. Gifted with dragon magic,' Jakart continued. 'The weaving of elemental power, we rose to rule the One Earth as Dragon Lords. Noble Dragons became fewer and fewer, who knows why or when? Their magic waned as ours grew.'

'Until dragons became "just animals", beasts of burden to do as commanded,' Drumondir finished. 'Even mighty Imperials. And now-'.

'We are binding them to our will, to our wars,' the King shook his head. 'Hugo, what have you done?'

CHAPTER FIFTY-NINE
War Games & WarLocks

The Grand Master sat in the High Hall of the Royal Palace, overwhelmed by the powerful aura of the Dragon Lords about him, which was giving him a bad headache. He really had no idea why everyone got so excited over the wretched SDS war games. The Dragathon race took place every year, and yet everyone went mad, betting small fortunes upon their favourite Dragon Lord or brigade or regiment to win the coveted Dragonglass Crown, handed down countless generations from Son of the Morning Star. Had they not had enough of battle already? The cost of equipping the SDS for this winter warfare has just about bankrupted the Guild, and had blown up the Alchemists Academy down by the harbour. Whatever they were up to had been commissioned by the Queen herself, and not even he was party to their secrets. There were rumours too that the Dean and Professors of the Faculty of Fire had been constant visitors until the old Academy had been reduced to rubble. Thereafter their collaboration had been removed to Dragon Isle for safety. Or perhaps for secrecy?

Absolutely everyone had gone quite mad. The Queen and her lady-in-waiting were daily overseeing the digging of the Great Ditch! He had heard her lady-in-waiting had actually tried to help, earning the people's affection. Extraordinary. And to top it all off, Hindsight & Foresight's Exclusive Emporium were no longer as exclusive as they ought to be. It was quite outrageous! The repairs to his ceremonial hat and gown, quite ruined by his disastrous encounter with the wretched WarLock, had been delayed, whilst they employed all their craftsmen in the making of woollen unmentionables, and heavy-duty flying leathers for the SDS.

He was all for patriotic fervour, he just wished it would cost a little less. A lean year beckoned, with few of the feasts and pageants that had been so wonderful before that wretched WarLock destroyed everything.

Guild warehouses, too, had been commandeered and the SDS had begun laying in stores for their assault on Roarkinch. Canvass and rope. Timber and iron and tar. Charcoal for the forges. Oats, grain, salt, honey and flour. Potatoes and salted pork. Not of course that the Guild knew why. The certainty of spies meant that not even the Grand Master knew the true purpose behind the preparations. Gold ever bought allegiance and wagging tongues.

The Ice Bear Clan in their metal shod sledges pulled by great ice bears had arrived, laden with mountains of mammoth wool and felt, adding to the growing excitement in the City. The bears wore white armour and tinkled with great bells about their necks. Igloos were thrown about the loch side and soon the air was thick with the smell of walrus from their roasting pits. Their elderly and the very young immediately set to work with SDS armourers, to craft warm felted winter barding for the dragons, including padded sheaths, to keep their talons from cracking.

To the exasperation of dragon masters and officers, the frozen loch close to the City became crowded with admiring townsfolk watching the bears put through their paces ~ from a safe distance, of course; although some of the children dared each other to run and touch one. Other clanswomen, with their menfolk, along with seven hundred ice bears and their handlers, remained out near the Sentinels, forming part of the King's attacking army and deployed on joint exercises with marines and frost dragons.

Whenever there was a break in the weather, the wealthy took to the sky in their hot air balloons by the hundreds to watch the increasingly complex exercises between the attacking and defending regiments playing out at the Sentinels, Dragon Isle and the Black Isle. The balloons hung like bright jewels in the sky the length and breadth of the glen. Already the noble houses were judging which battalion, talon, wing or soldier stood out, which or who showed the most promise. Small fortunes were changing hands. There had been two collisions between dragon and balloon before the Guardian ordered a squadron of frost dragons to move them to a safer distance during air-to-air combat.

Soon the sound of booms and bangs and low flying Imperials made the casement windows rattle. Rumspell retreated into his inner sanctum, fortified by a roast beef dinner, a very expensive bottle of his favourite wine; and tried valiantly to ignore the noise. Mistress Winifred had told him, as if he shared her enthusiasm, that ice bears could lie unmoving for days waiting for their preferred prey to appear: hobgoblins. The Grand Master shuddered. He had never seen one of the revolting creatures, and hopefully never would. He would leave them to the warmongering SDS.

CHAPTER SIXTY
Hungry Moths

It was another quarter moon before Root, Quester and Quenelda were all back from exercises at the same time. Quenelda had told them that Drumondir had been closeted with a lady from the Guild, and wouldn't say a word of what she was up to.

'I don't recognise that rune,' Root observed interestedly as they approached the hall. 'It's a cloaking ward, a powerful one.'

Quenelda's step faltered as the runes turned red. *I can't feel its power any more. I can see it but not feel it. It's like suddenly being blind.* She had taken her gift for granted; now she would have to go back and study like everyone else had to!

The battlemage standing there nodded to the guards who raised their pikes and let the small group pass. The trio paused at the threshold, baffled by what they saw. A half dozen battlemages were in the room, their auras visible. The tapestry was still hung on heavy ropes from beams, but the rest of the room was a hive of activity. Scholars, bright as birds in their faculty robes were everywhere, perched on scaffolding, hanging from the beam! The tapestry was being drawn in careful detail by several artists at a table. Others were examining samples of wool, or deep in debate over pots of dyes. They paid no attention to the incomers who stood there in amazement.

'What is it?' Quester asked, even though he could see for himself.

'A tapestry?' Quenelda shrugged, equally baffled. 'There must be something more.'

Finally, they had been noticed, and Drumondir waved them over to where her friend from the Guild was eating her way through an impressive spread, napkins tucked under her chin. She wiped away a few crumbs and stood with a smile.

'Allow me to introduce my friend, Mistress Winifred of the Seamstresses Guild. Winifred, you may have already met the Princess?' Quenelda almost looked over her shoulder, not many called her Princess. 'This is Root, adopted son of Sir Gharad, and Sir Quester.'

'The brave young men who fought the hobgoblins and saved the King?' Winifred smiled. 'It is an honour to meet you. The Guild bards tell children stories about how you two young men saved our King. It's very popular.'

'It is?' Root's mouth fell open.

'They do?' Quester's mouth decided to join Root's.

'Indeed, yes,' Winifred's enthusiasm was unfeigned, and if she saw they had both gone red in the face with embarrassment she never mentioned it.

'It still sounds strange to be called, Sir,' Quester admitted.

'But thoroughly deserved, young man!' Winifred slapped him on the back almost lifting Quester off his feet. She turned to Root and Quenelda who took a step backwards. 'And you are both Dragon Lords. What brave young people you are!'

Root and Quester grinned at each other, punched fists. Quenelda shook her head.

'Now!' Elbowing expertly through the scholars intent

on their tasks, the BoneCaster and Guild Mistress took them over to the other side of the hall where the press was thinner, and it was easier to take in the whole tapestry. 'Now,' Drumondir asked. 'What do you see?'

The youngsters studied the tapestry carefully, looking for the catch.

'It's obviously not just an ordinary tapestry,' Root thought out loud for them all. 'There must be over a hundred scholars and mages in this room.'

'Drawn from all four Faculties,' Drumondir agreed. She was quickly learning how to distinguish scholars and their ranks from their robes.

Quester took the plunge first. 'Son of the Morning Star? But what is so special about that? There are similar tapestries and oil paintings about the Academy.'

'And in the palace and at Dragonsdome,' Quenelda put in, but she was staring at the scene intently.

'The First Alliance?' Root offered. 'But are those Imperials? That can't be right!'

'We think so,' Drumondir nodded, glancing at Quenelda who was gazing at the tableau silently. 'But, as you say, Root, not like any Imperials we have ever seen.'

'That's because those are the First Born,' Quenelda said softly. Suddenly certain. *How do I know that?* A tattered remnant of a dream fluttered in her mind...took shape. 'As old as the One Earth. They are the Matriarch's children.'

'But...' Root said, looking from the BoneCaster to his friend. 'How do you know? I've never seen Imperials like those before.'

'I'm not sure, but I know. When I was... asleep I lived

this dream,' Quenelda answered. 'I was there. I felt the cold. Smelt the fear. I saw Seadragons, their breath hot in the freezing air. It is the First Alliance, the Covenant, but...' she frowned, rubbing her forehead. 'It's not what we think. We've forgotten the truth.'

Drumondir's calm face hid her excitement. *She is remembering. Perhaps her powers have not all gone... perhaps some return?*

'Not what we think?' Root asked in confusion. 'What on Earth are you talking about?'

'We're all taught the nursery story that Son of the Morning Star was special because he was One Kind: half dragon, half man. That his power came from both lineages, even though we were also taught that the Dragon Lords were the masters. But that's not true.'

'What's not?' Root felt like an echo.

'Son of the Morning Star *was* unique ~ One Kind, like I am. But...*his* power, *our* power, my powers...Earth magic ~ it all comes from the dragons! Sorcery is how *we* are taught to conjure, control and wield it. To draw it out, mould it to our will.'

'The basis for all our sorcery,' Quester realised. 'Everything we are taught, every spell and cantrip is one or a combination of earth, wind, fire and water.'

'Yes,' the BoneCaster nodded. 'And every reagent we use, wood or metal, mineral, herb or spice. Once magic resided in every living thing, every creature, plant, stone and tree had a story to tell. Only,' Drumondir sighed, glancing at Root. 'Few of us can hear their voices, can read their stories anymore, can learn what they teach us.'

'Yes!' Drumondir agreed as Winifred beamed. 'That is what the Guardian and his scholars think also.'

'How do you know all this?' Root asked. 'What changed? Those dreams when you were dying?'

Quenelda nodded. 'Because...somehow I was there. Because Son of the Morning Star is my twin brother.'

Even Drumondir's eyes widened like an owl.

'But-' Quester stuttered. 'But that changes everything we believe about ourselves.'

'And, how we treat our dragons!' Root gasped.

Quenelda nodded. 'It's why I couldn't learn sorcery. I – *didn't* need to. Lessons just confused things. Magic is...*was* all around us. Root, your people...wychwood ...you know what I mean. The squadron trainers said you had an affinity with your navigator's chair. You were the first to graduate out of your class because you have an instinct for magic. You can call upon the wychwood's magic, it responds to your touch.'

'I know.' Root bent to his boot sheath and drew a slim dagger out. He held it out on his palm. It was rich grained and beautiful, fashioned from a single piece and lethally sharp.

'A wychwood dagger,' Quester breathed, hand unconsciously dropping to his leg. 'Where did you find that?'

'When I was out on the moor, cocooned within my chair waiting for the harriers to rescue me, I realised I had lost my flying knife. The Forsaken were approaching, and I had nothing to defend myself with. The wood just reacted to my need, my unspoken thought. I'd barely begun withdrawing my hand and it was there! It fits my palm perfectly, look.'

'It's quite beautiful,' Winifred said. 'May I?' Nodding, Root gave it to her. 'I've never seen wychwood before. It's as rich as honey, seamed with soft gold.'

'Both magical and priceless,' Drumondir added. 'The Wychwood groves did not survive the Long Winter. So,' she turned to the tapestry again as Root sheathed his dagger. 'What else do you see?'

Quenelda, Root and Quester looked at her in surprise. There was already so much to think about!

'Look at the way Son of the Morning Star is kneeling, facing the dragons? He links the dragons to the great Lords who are also kneeling. But he is not clothed in scales and they wear only battered armour. There are no Lords on dragons, instead the First Born are arrayed about him, facing our armies.'

'What was left of them,' Quenelda added, eyes looking back in time. 'Our people were starving, exhausted and frozen. Families and soldiers were dying every day in the long retreat. They were all going to die. But because Son of the Morning Star was their brother, and the hobgoblins the enemy of all living things on sea and land, the flaw in the Matriarch's design, the First Born offered mankind an alliance. The One Earth and all dragons were to be honoured for all time in return for the magic of creation. We are the custodians of the One Earth and all creatures who dwell there ~ man or beast.'

'There is more.' Drumondir turned to Winifred.

'This tapestry is ancient, truly ancient,' Winifred said, eyes still riveted on Quenelda in amazement. 'I have examined the dyes, the way it has been woven. We believe that this is one of the Dragonsdome Chronicles.'

'Tapestries? The Chronicles are tapestries?' Root was wide eyed with excitement. 'Of course! Not many can read, even now. It makes sense!' He grinned. 'A tapestry that is a story...woven so that everyone can read it!'

'Why was it hidden then?' Quester asked.

'And by whom?' Root added.

'This is very dangerous knowledge in the wrong hands,' Drumondir warned. 'There are many reasons why it may have been hidden, for good or for ill. Your father has commanded that it be kept secret until we find some of those answers.'

CHAPTER SIXTY-ONE
A Thunder of Mammoths

It sounded like midsummer thunder rolling down the glen, becoming louder and louder. Citizens on the distant Black Isle looked skywards into the wet falling snow. But it was no storm. Instead the ice itself had come alive!

Forewarned by the frost dragon outriders who had escorted the Clan of the White Mammoth for nearly a moon, the SDS battlegroups arrayed about the Sentinels and Dragon Isle in turn had stopped their ground attack exercises to watch, as a seemingly endless thunder of white woolly mammoths, near invisible in the blizzard, lumbered past at a gallop.

The ice vibrated beneath the mammoth's huge feet, and they trumpeted joyfully, trunks in the air, great curled tusks wearing spiked torques swinging side to side. Each bore two score clan warriors on their backs and archers on their flanks. Young and immature mammoths harnessed in threes pulled behind them vast sledges of felt, or elders, clansmen, women and children. The smallest of all bore two riders. Finally, the Mammoth Clan had arrived at the end of their long journey, the first from their homelands since the ending of the First Age.

Escorted by Nos 3, 6 and 11 Frost Ground Attack Squadrons, the thunder swept around the frozen base of the eastern cliffs to where mammoth caves had been prepared with huge stockpiles of fodder, and camps of felted tents erected by BoneCracker engineers to welcome their two-legged guests. After meeting the King and the Guardian, their officers and scholars, and resting for one night, the White Mammoth Chieftain, his BoneCaster and Clan Elders continued with half of their Jarls at a slower pace towards the Black Isle, escorted now by half that Isle's population.

Great herd bells rang. Pendants gaily fluttering behind, racing frost dragons ducked and dived between or daringly beneath the mammoths. Children on skates tried desperately to keep up, or fetch a stolen ride on the mammoth sledges. Thousands of raised torches and flares blazed through the snow in welcome, lighting their way until the White Woolly Mammoth Clan Chieftain finally arrived at the frozen western harbour as dusk fell. By then the ice was alive with soldiers and citizens holding torches aloft, who greeted them with cheers and small gifts of food for their huge mounts; now they finally understood what the huge ice igloos around the loch were built for!

There too, the Queen, her Constable Sir Gharad, and the Inner Council of the Sorcerers Guild in their all finery and furs greeted their visitors. Led by the II Heavy Unicorn Cavalry they were escorted to the Palace.

The White Woolly Mammoth Clan had arrived to join the war!

CHAPTER SIXTY-TWO
White Claws

The sky was brilliant cobalt blue with not a cloud in sight, the crisp snow on the loch was crisscrossed by tracks. The King was putting his newly formed White Claw Attack Brigades through their paces, watched by his Queen and Armelia, and the Guardian, and Arch-Professor Scrumbleworth and his research team, whose tactics they were putting to the test. They were airborne on Stormcracker, so that Scrumbleworth's team, and the King through his Imperial's eyes, could analyse how their theories unfolded from their vantage in the air.

A full Marine Expeditionary Force of SeaReavers, staged as hobgoblins in their new white armour, had disembarked from their troop carriers anchored at the mouth of the glen and were massed on the ice in undisciplined formation. A red flare rose and the 'hobgoblins' began to move forward towards the auroras of polar bears and five thunders of mammoths arrayed about Dragon Isle.

'We've created thirty White Claw Brigades around a core cadre of six battlemages as you suggested, Arch-Professor, each commanding six Talons of Ice Bears and mammoths, along with three squadrons of frosts and harriers for air and ground support. Watch.'

The marines continued moving forwards, seemingly unopposed. The wind whistled over the ice and hummocks of drifting snow. Then suddenly the ice appeared to explode upwards with a life of its own as the 'hobgoblins' found themselves under attack from within their own ranks by ice bears. Swiftly, pockets were isolated and 'dispatched.'

Those who escaped continued to move forwards. The ice shifted, and a dull thunder rose as massed ice bears in arrow formations, followed by mammoths, ploughed through the remaining hobgoblins who had formed defensive circles. They were swiftly surrounded by trumpeting mammoths who then swung inwards, tusks and front legs raised to strike.

'A truly wondrous sight,' the Queen and Armelia were amazed. 'Creatures out of legend have come to life, and come to aid us.'

'Congratulations, Arch-Professor,' the King was well satisfied. 'Our four legged allies are proving very apt pupils, and I have already deployed ice bears and mammoth brigades to the flanks of our Marine Expeditionary Forces, freeing Sabretooths and Bone-Crackers for tunnel clearing, which they will find more to their liking.

The Guardian nodded. 'I intend holding five brigades of White Claws in reserve to swiftly deploy where we are most in need, and Tangnost has begun training them to deploy on Imperials with combat insertion and extraction, alongside the BoneCrackers and sabretooths. The hobgoblins won't know what hit them.'

The King smiled grimly. 'Nor will Hugo!'

CHAPTER SIXTY-THREE
Training Deployment

The buzz of anticipation died away as Quenelda and Tangnost arrived in one of the larger briefing rooms. Everyone knew of the King's daughter's absence for half a moon after the gyre that had turned life in the glen upside down. No one had ever seen a gyre; but many said no one had seen a dragon whisperer before either. They were living in an age of legends springing to life, and the Academy had been buzzing with excitement. The news that she had been seen at the Old Wall raised speculation to fever pitch.

'Officer on deck!'

The Juveniles stood. They were wearing camouflage armour designed by Root, half white, half moss and earth. Ideal for winter exercises across tundra, on ice and in caves. They had been reformed as the same Juvenile Brigade that retook the Brimstones, causing great excitement. Quenelda looked about the room, reminding herself of each member of her talon, their names, their sabretooth's names, how they had deployed and performed individually in their first operation, remembering those who learnt fastest. She was going to need their help now.

'The Guardian in his wisdom has returned your command to me,' Quenelda announced to a drum of fists. 'We showed what we could do during Operation Brimstone.'

Tangnost nodded: his pupil was clearly comfortable in her scaled armour, Quenelda was regaining confidence and a sense of purpose. If she was no longer a dragon whisperer, none could tell save her family and close friends.

'BearHugger will be taking our training to another level. We are to learn how to survive in the tunnels of the Labyrinth. You are going to experience what it is like to be underground for days, how to tell night from day and how to orientate yourselves in darkness. You will learn how to deploy, supported by your BoneCrackers. Phoenix Firestorm will become your home: Imperials, talons and troops fighting as one family. You practise and practise until you don't have to think what to do next, or what your Imperial or commandos will do next. Because you will *know*! There are often no communications in the tunnels, so hand signals and coordination could be the difference between life and death.'

She paused theatrically drawing the moment out. 'In half a moon we are to begin training with twelve other talons as part of the V Reconnaissance Brigade deployed as part of the Close Ground Support Wing of the Thunderstorm Battlegroup. In other words, we will be part of the attacking force in the upcoming exercises.

'We begin at 0600 hours tomorrow in the Labyrinth. Twelve other talons will also begin survival training. I will see you in the roosts.'

'Sir, yes, Sir!'

CHAPTER SIXTY-FOUR
Measuring Tapes At the Ready, Ma'am!

The dwarves, Winifred decided, were potentially a challenge when it came to unmentionables. She had learnt from her new friend that the clans fashioned and forged their own distinctive armour and were notoriously prickly when it came to personal questions. No one was quite sure of their...dimensions; they were considerably shorter and broader than most. In any event every dwarf unit was training, until Drumondir had a word with Tangnost, who had a word with Commander Jakart's personal guard.

Unlike the Grand Master, Winifred was thoroughly enjoying herself. Life had been difficult after Renyard died on the Westering Isles, on what was supposed to have been his last operational deployment before he hung his spurs up and took up a professorial post in the Academy. They had been childhood sweethearts, and being a large clumsy woman with a rather stiff and awkward manner made making new friends difficult. But the gruff Seamstress and the flint eyed BoneCaster had found an unlooked-for friendship, and with a lifetime of being a military wife, Winifred was rising to the challenge. She and her 'gels' were needed to make unmentionables for the troops, she had a sense of purpose again, could 'do some good' in honour of Renyard's memory.

Helmet and goggles firmly strapped on, wrapped in a heavy cloak and sensible boots with three layers of socks, breathing in the cold air as the Glen spun past twice a day, was exhilarating! Winifred began to understand the Queen and the Lady Armelia's passion, although the latter's figure-hugging flying suits were a definite 'no' for those of more generous proportions. Yet, for some inexplicable reason, her gels weren't looking as though they were enjoying their flights to Dragon Isle as much as she was.

'Do buck up, Daisy!' she said, giving one unfortunate young lady clinging to a sick bag a hearty thump on the back. It didn't quite have the desired effect. Daisy's stomach capitulated. Within a heartbeat all the girls were retching miserably. Flying clearly wasn't for everyone.

Today on arrival, Winifred and her gels were greeted by Drumondir as usual and shown into a crowded and unfamiliar, long slate-flagged hall, brightly lit by branches of candles. Large cauldrons of water were being heated over four large roaring fires, along with a welcoming cauldron of spiced dwarf cider.

Once she had a steaming mug to sip, Winifred was introduced to scores of Drumondir's clanswomen, and the BoneCaster welcomed hundreds of newly arrived clanswomen from a half dozen northern clans serving in the SDS. She looked about, wondering why they were gathered here. Against the walls, in between stacked pikes, shields and other weapons, they were acquainted with mountains of mammoth wool and felt, but luckily not to their owners.

'If you would stand on the opposite side of the tables to ourselves,' Drumondir then directed, 'We'll give you a demonstration how to make the felt.'

Are you familiar with mammoth wool?' The Bone-

Caster asked. 'No? Feel it, pass it round. It's soft, warm, oiled to repel the wet...'

Winifred's girls watched as Drumondir and Elders from the Ice Bear, White Fox, Walrus, Wolf and Mammoth Clanswomen laid out tufts of wool in the same direction to cover the trestle tables that ran the length of the hall.

'Just so,' Drumondir was explaining. 'And now we lay a second layer in the opposite direction.'

A herd of stable apprentices arrived to bring over ladles, and buckets of hot water from the cauldrons. 'We apply the water just so, pressing down, flattening the wool.'

Winifred gave it a go.

'Now work the wool gently up and down and side to side,' Drumondir demonstrated. Winifred was a quick learner. Finally, the wool was turned and the same on the opposite side.

'Now,' Drumondir nodded. 'The felt is ready for measuring and stitching. Winifred? Perhaps half my women can felt, and the rest, and the children can assist you? As you can see,' she gestured. 'Large piles around the hall are already waiting for your attention!'

'Gels! Tape measures at the ready! Mildrud!' Winifred barked. 'Bring in our troops!'

The door clanged open making her young gels jump. A gruff voice, so deep the air almost vibrated, split the silence.

'Forwaaaard... Quick Maaaarchhh! Left, right, left, right! Haaaaltttt!!!!'

A score of armoured BoneCrackers arrived, scattering

snow from their boots, bringing cold air with them. Winifred shook her head. Her gels couldn't possibly measure up commandos! But the platoon had already begun to shed their armour ~ to reveal women, both young and older.

The Sergeant marched up to Drumondir. 'Ordered to report to you, Ma'am!!'

The BoneCaster tried not to wince. *Why on the One Earth did the military have to shout all the time!?* She found what passed for a smile. 'Err, thank you. Yes. Err...?'

The Sergeant removed her helmet revealing the young dwarf who had unceremoniously rounded Guild members up at the Ceremony of the Red Squirrel and smuggled them into the palace's hidden walkways to catch the WarLock.

'Sergeant Hammerstone, Ma'am! What do you need us to do, Ma'am?'

Gently removing the nonplussed BoneCaster to one side, Winifred stuck her chin and chest out in similar fashion and bellowed back. 'Unmentionables, Sergeant Hammerstone.'

Unmentionables clearly wasn't a word used by dwarves.

'We need to measure you up to fit felted undergarments, to err, go err, under your armour. To stop you from freezing to death, Sergeant!'

'Understood! Ma'am!'

Drumondir nodded. 'What we need is not just clothing to maintain body heat, but to stop armour freezing to the skin, and to prevent frostbite...' she explained to her friend. 'Hands and feet are the most vulnerable, and face masks will be needed, too.'

Winifred had never heard of frostbite. Drumondir explained it to her in dreadful detail. It sounded positively ghastly. 'Fingers and toes go black, and fall off?'

Drumondir nodded. 'Then if frostbite is not treated, everything else follows!'

There was a dull thump.

Winifred sighed as the BoneCaster knelt. 'Gels, does anyone have smelling salts? No? Do get Daisy off the floor. Perhaps some fresh air?'

'So,' Winifred turned back to Drumondir as the hapless Daisy was removed. 'Socks and gloves, hoods to fit under helmets leaving only eyes and mouth, as well as undergarments?'

'Yes. Thousands of them.... we are going to need every girl you have, and their Mas and Grandmas too!'

Winifred nodded. She was just beginning to realise the scale of the challenge. 'I'll send word to the Guild to round up anyone who can hold scissors and needles!

'Righty ho! Gels! Forward! Heather, Rosemary, Saffron, Willow...measuring tapes, scissors and pins at the ready!'

Well, Winifred mused, things were certainly a little different in the military. Divested of their armour, dwarves were scattered around the room in a diverse range of stances, each wielding a different weapon, their faces inscrutable. Flexibility seemed to be the watchword. Whatever they designed had to be as flexible as their jointed armour, allowing them to climb and jump, to hammer and stab, to cut and twist and to run up and down dragon's wings in a hurry.

'Winifred,' Drumondir beckoned her friend over to where two lines of commandos were facing each other like an eightsome reel, only these couples were sporting a wicked array of nasty looking weapons. 'The troopers are about to execute a weapons demonstration so that we understand what is needed.'

'Jolly good!'

Clang! Clang! Clang! Spark!!! Bang! Thump! Clang! Spark Clang!

Their speed was breathtaking. Winifred had seen Renyard at the lists, but had never seen a sword raised in anger. Axes arced, shields were raised, swords flashed, and maces sidestepped.

'It's almost like a deadly dance...' Winifred found her mouth hanging open like Daisy's and hastily closed it. War had not come to the Sorcerers Glen. Until now. And maybe, just maybe, it was time to stop sending others to die...dragons and men both.

'Shall I show you how, Ma'am?' the Sergeant offered Winifred her weapon.

Winifred allowed that she might. 'I have never held a battleaxe before,' she weighed it in her hands as Hammerstone adjusted her grip.

'What you do, Ma'am, is lift the-'

What Winifred lacked in accuracy she certainly made up for in strength. Luckily the sergeant was considerably shorter than the seamstress, so just had her hair parted. Even so, Hammerstone had trouble pulling her axe out of the oak table.

CHAPTER SIXTY-FIVE
Terminal Stupidity

'Boss,' Graff sat down with a pint of oat beer and looked about furtively.

Knuckle groaned inwardly.

'Good news!' Graff whispered loudly. 'We struck lucky! Last three days she's been going in them caves down the loch past the woods...with that dragon of 'ers, sometimes with one of them scouts. Crept in after her, Boss.'

Knuckle kept his face straight. For once terminal stupidity was an asset.

'Took me mate, Grubwell, yesterday. Dwarf, Boss. Did some mining once. Good in caves. He had a look around after she'd left.'

Knuckle nodded, hoping for once this was going somewhere.

'She goes into the big cave...it's huge, Boss. Mammoth Cave they call it.'

Knuckle raised his eyebrows questioningly

'Well, Grubwell, he says there's a passage leading up into it where the walls close in, just enough room for one of them orange dragons to fit through. But it can't turn for a good ways beyond. Well, one level up, there's a hole in the ceiling. Like a murder hole, Boss.'

Knuckle sat forwards. This was more like it.

'He reckons we drops a net and we'll get 'er, Boss. An' her dragon, it can't do nothing. Bang her on the head, bang her in a sack, and she's yours, Boss.'

'Well...' Knuckle thought about it. *What could go*

wrong? Plenty. But it might be the only chance they had. If her fat dragon got stuck all the better. No one would even know where to look. SDS war games were going on fifteen leagues away near Dragon Isle so no chance of being caught.

'Right! We're going for it. Graff, you get us the fastest ground dragons gold can buy...if they do find out, they'd expect us to fly. Dales or spitting adders: we'll ride to begin with till we're well clear. Meanwhile, I am going to get us an Imperial.'

Five jaws dropped.

'How'yer going to do that, Boss? Going to steal one? Har! har!'

'Never you mind. Graff, I want to meet Grubwell early tomorrow. I want to see where she goes. Meanwhile, Dornoch, get some big flour sacks and some sacks of turnips to hide her under. Gaff, steal a fisherman's net and some rope. Don't want to leave no clues behind.'

Finally, something might just go right. A Lordship and castle beckoned.

CHAPTER SIXTY-SIX
Cave Painting

'I've been deep into the Labyrinth scouting for Quenelda…' Hesitating, Root looked up at Armelia with tears in his eyes. He was still dressed in soft colours, brown and sand and rose to blend in with the tunnels and caves, with rags breaking up his outline. He had leather knee and elbow guards on. His leather helmet and rucksack lay on the floor, along with night sights. He had come over to the Royal stables to feed Chasing the Stars some of her favourite chocolate mushrooms that he had foraged on the lower slopes of the White Sorcerer Mountains. 'I haven't been scouting since Bracus and I were in the Brimstones. If he wasn't so huge he would have been a good scout himself…he learnt quickly.'

'No news?' Armelia reached out to squeeze his hand.

'No.' Root laid his head against the mare's soft muzzle, stroking her. 'Still MIA. They haven't even found Night Frost. They've just disappeared. The Brimstones, Armelia, they aren't like the mountains here. They're like jagged serrated teeth, full of deep narrow ravines. S&R had to abandon the search. They were needed elsewhere.'

'Oh, Root. I'm so sorry. I know you had become best of friends.'

Root nodded. 'His friendship was precious to me. It was hard won.'

Armelia nodded. 'How did your scouting go? Quenelda said that your objective would be to work around or ambush BoneCracker talons from the Howling Glen at the far end of the glen, and attack the Sentinels from behind?'

'It's well named, the Labyrinth. It's immense, Armelia. You could get lost and never find your way out. Compasses don't work. Communications don't either. There are dozens of galleries, stalactites, and at least two rivers race through it, carving wondrous smooth waterways through the softer stone down to the loch. Countless caves and caverns that glitter, passageways and tunnels. Many have names: the Cave of Echoes, the Shaft of the Dead Man, Coffin Canyon, the Chimney, the Mammoth Cavern.'

'Because it's so big?'

'Partly,' Root smiled. 'But also, there are cave paintings there, mostly of mammoths. And I found new ones, Armelia. Some are of sabretooths, but others are horses, bison and bears, unicorns and sabretooth cave lions. And dragons, though I think those are very, very old, and the caves are almost inaccessible.

'They're so beautiful, I know you would love them. Do you think you might want to see some paintings? We could take Two Gulps.'

Guy DeBessart arrived. 'Lady Armelia, how are you?' he grinned. 'I heard you have been busy showing them how to dig the City defences!'

Armelia blushed but smiled in return. It sounded like everyone had heard she had knocked herself out.

'Root, I thought we could go flying, run through a few manoeuvres so we could get to know each other, and you could get to know Phoenix Firestorm. She's smaller than many Imperials, but she's beautiful to fly!' He sighed. 'I know I won't be able to replace Bracus. I won't try to.

But we could become the best there is in his memory? She's waiting on the DeWinter pad.'

Root nodded. 'Armelia, Quenelda's been wanting to explore the Labyrinth herself. Could you give her these rough sketches I've done? Perhaps she can take you to see the paintings.' He kissed her on the cheek and left her in the stables grooming Chasing the Stars.

Quenelda studied Root's diagrams leading deep into the Labyrinth. 'I think I'll explore them later with Root. I've never been that deep inside. But, yes, I can take you to the Mammoth Cavern. It's one of the easiest caves to find at this end, and huge parts of the ceiling are open to the sky, so not too scary if you've never been underground before. But I'm training with the juveniles all day tomorrow. I'll collect you at first light if you're game?'

Armelia nodded. 'I can be ready by the hour of the eager beaver.'

Quenelda laughed. 'That's not first light, that's halfway through the day! No, I meant 0500 bells. The hour of the yawning dormouse,' she translated to a horrified Armelia.

CHAPTER SIXTY-SEVEN
Bound and Bagged

Armelia looked around nervously. The vast darkness was scary despite the burning torches they both carried, which barely penetrated the pressing gloom. She was glad of Two Gulps' reassuring bulk. Strange noises echoed and re-echoed. There was a bang.

'Must be some other talons in here,' Quenelda said cheerfully. 'Or the BoneCrackers. This is where they practise abseiling, combat dismounts and cave fighting. It's so vast you could lose all seven regiments in here!'

Armelia gulped.

The tunnel gradually narrowed, and the ceiling dropped down.

It's freezing in here...

Bound to come soon...

Quenelda thought she heard whispers and a clash of steel and sighed with frustration. Her dragon sixth senses would easily have heard. She tried not to think of flying or talking to dragons, tried to focus on her own natural talents. But sometimes it was hard.

Water dripped loudly.

Suddenly there was a very loud banging behind them. Two Gulps tried to turn to face the danger but couldn't...so he leapt away. Suddenly Quenelda and Armelia were jerked violently backwards out of their saddles by a net catching their necks and arms. Armelia's scream was cut off by a rope tightening about her throat.

'Get her up, lads. Gods! She weighs a lot!'

Thinking quickly, grabbing her boot knife, Quenelda

sawed at the net with her knife. The two of them tumbled out, dropping hard onto the passage floor. Quenelda leapt to her feet, but Armelia was slower. Her helmet had come off and she was grasping her head.

'Two Gulps!' Quenelda's urgent call echoed down the passageway. 'Two Gulps... Two Gulps...'

There was the sound of talons on stone as the sabretooth tried to turn back, and a distant light bloomed as he flamed his frustration. *Two Gulps I...* Quenelda closed her eyes in frustration. He couldn't hear her any more...

There were voices carrying in all directions. The sound of rushing feet. More than one assailant was heading their way.

'Come on!' Searching for a place to hide, then throwing her torch along the passageway, Quenelda dragged her friend onto her feet. 'We can hide in here; this crevasse is big enough to hide both of us.'

Barely had they squeezed into the cool darkness than torches lit up the passageway and armoured men ran past.

'What do you mean, you 'lost' her? Find her. She's in here somewhere. Quickly now, before her sabretooth finds a way back, or we'll all be toast.'

'Knuckle Quarnack,' Quenelda breathed, recognising the voice. 'The WarLock's Dragon Master.' This was bad.

'W-what? The one who chased you in the north?' Armelia was in shock.

'Yes.' Thoughts were running through Quenelda's mind. Without Two Gulps they couldn't escape or fight their way out, and she had never fought anyone hand-to-hand. Incomplete memories could not replace training. With her inner dragon gone, she was just a young woman. The sound of their hunters grew closer. She drew her flying knife.

'Quenelda, Go!' Armelia whispered. 'Run! Get out of here.'

'What? No! I'm not leaving you.'

'Go!' Armelia wiped away tears angrily. 'Go! It's you they are after, not me. They'll think I'm you! Whoever it is, they don't know about me. Go! There are too many of them for you to fight. You'll be captured or killed. *You* can save us, I can't! Once they have me they'll stop looking.' With that, ramming her helmet on to hide her face and hair, the young woman turned towards the sound of pursuit.

Quenelda hesitated, but the rattle of armour was almost upon them, and there was no help to be had. Two Gulps hadn't found a way back to her yet, though she could hear his frantic calls echoing through the tunnels.

She grabbed her friend's arm. 'I'll come for you,' she whispered fiercely. 'We'll come for you. The SDS leaves no one behind! Pretend! Pretend you still love Darcy to stay alive. He will protect you.' And then she pushed back into the crevasse as Armelia ran blindly into the tunnels.

It didn't take long. There was a scream and the sounds of a struggle then sudden silence.

'Best hope you haven't hit her too hard!'

'She's got a helmet on! How can I hit her too hard?'

'Get this bag over her.'

'Come on, let's get to the dragons before that sabretooth finds us.' And then they were gone.

Waiting for silence, Quenelda turned and ran to get help, rage in her heart. The torch from the passage floor dipped and went out. But Quenelda didn't notice, she could see in the dark.

As she leapt across a water course and wove between stalagmites, doubt grew. Would Darcy be able to protect his wife from his father's rage when they found they had captured the wrong quarry? The WarLock King would surely kill her, a distraction his son could do without. An unwelcome reminder of his past. Skidding to a halt, Quenelda changed direction. Scales began to sheath the young woman like a second skin as she ran, but Quenelda didn't notice.

As the tunnels became wider wings unfurled, but still Quenelda didn't notice. Talons struck sparks on the stone as she hurtled out the caves into open sky. *North. Where were they? What would they be flying? If they were going north, frost dragons?*

The Imperial called out…*where are you sisters, brothers? You carry a burden precious to me.* But lying close to death for so long had robbed Quenelda of her strength, and wherever they were they did not answer.

Nor could the sabretooth storming through the tunnels, hot on her trail, hear or sense her.

CHAPTER SIXTY-EIGHT
Missing

'Quenelda and Armelia are missing.' Face white, Root's eyes were wide with shock. He doubled over in the roosts, trying to catch his breath. He had been looking all over for the Dragon Master.

'Missing?' Tangnost's heart thumped. 'How do you know?'

'I told Armelia about the cave paintings in the Mammoth Cavern. And I found some new ones. I was going to take Armelia to see them, but went training with Guy, so Quenelda took her. We just got back. Two Gulps returned to the roosts without them and she never turned up for training. Nobody's been able to get near him.'

Cold shivered down Tangnost's spine as he looked towards the sabretooth, spinning on his hind legs, rearing up and flaming. *Two Gulps would defend Quenelda to the death. What had happened?* He ran to the porting stone and pressed a glyph.

'Scramble, scramble, scramble, search and rescue, the Labyrinth. Quenelda and the Lady Armelia are missing.'

Up in the SeaDragon Tower, the Officer of the Watch blinked hard. 'Repeat, BearHugger?'

'S&R scramble, scramble, scramble. The Labyrinth, repeat, the Labyrinth. Missing sabretooth riders. Ladies Quenelda and Armelia are missing. Two Gulps returned without them. Send to the King,' Tangnost ran a hand through his hair. 'His daughter is missing. Root, tell Guy to warm Phoenix Firestorm up again. We'll be flying north.'

CHAPTER SIXTY-NINE
Fire and Ice

Quenelda was struggling, exhausted; muscles and tendons slack from illness, unused to such treatment, were on fire. As the crescent moons rose, ice began forming on her wings, and she was too weak to flame to melt it. Rage gave way to exhaustion, and then finally to tears. How stupid she was…to think she could catch them. To think she could save Armelia on her own. She was no longer a naïve child, she had to stop acting like one. She should have found Two Gulps. She should have called Guy and Root, so they could fly and navigate, bring her swiftly and safely here. Alerted the Old Wall to throw up an intercept protocol. She hadn't been flying for over a moon. No one knew where she was. No one knew what had happened. Armelia was lost and so was she. And where was Two Gulps? How could she have flown without him?

Soon she was spiralling down into the swift gloom on the edge of losing control. The Imperial shivered. Scales and wings disappeared, and a young woman fell with a thin scream into the woods. Snow soon covered her unconscious body.

High above, a patrol out of the Old Wall was heading back to base when they suddenly found their wing banking as if on synchronised display manoeuvres. None would respond to their Dragon Lord's commands.

'Wall Tower,' Cawdor said calmly, 'we are putting down…' his navigator checked co-ordinates. 'Our Imperials are not responding. We are putting down.

BoneCrackers establishing perimeter.'

The Imperials landed in an outward-facing circle, forming a formidable perimeter. It was snowing heavily, thick fluffy flakes building up too much weight too quickly; they would have to de-ice wings before take-off. Smoke billowed threateningly from their mounts' nostrils.

'Scramble the RRF. We don't want to get caught on the ground. Sergeant, he turned. 'Get some boots on the ground and find out what is going on.'

'Fan out,' the BoneCrackers of Felix Company were advancing cautiously, although the depth of snow made progress difficult without snowshoes.

'Thermal imagers on...nothing, Sir,' the Sergeant reported. 'Ouff! Argh!'

Branches and twigs cracked. A heavy load of snow dropped on him from the tall conifers, followed by a body bouncing from branch to branch.

'It's a young woman,' the BoneCrackers lifted Quenelda off their Sergeant. 'In a flying suit.'

'Is she alive?' Cawdor asked.

'Barely, Sir, it's hard to tell. She's covered in frost.'

Wrapping the body in several cloaks the commandos swiftly returned. But even before the sergeant could mount, his Imperial's head swung down. Smoke blossomed in the cold air enveloping both in fog.

'Put her down gently,' Cawdor ordered as he ran down and saw who it was. 'And walk away. Good. *Move, soldier*!'

Next heartbeat, Quenelda was enveloped in flame.

CHAPTER SEVENTY
Lost and Found

'They've found Quenelda.'

Root sagged with relief. They had had to return empty handed as Guy insisted Phoenix Firestorm had to be rested, or they, too, would need rescued. 'And Armelia, is she safe?'

'No,' Tangnost shook his head. 'Just Quenelda.'

'No? Where is she? Where's Quenelda?'

'Our Warden found her three furlongs from the Wall. She was nearly dead; their thermal imagers barely registered life. She would be dead but for the Imperials. They refused orders and put down in a perimeter with her at their centre.'

'What?' Root was struggling to understand. 'But... How did she get there? Two Gulps is here!' Root's thoughts were racing in too many directions. 'She's barely alive?'

'She *was*. She is exhausted but recovering. Cawdor, thank the Gods, knew what to do. Quenelda said he had good instincts. His Imperials wrapped her in flame until she woke.'

'Flame? But that means s-'

'Yes,' Tangnost nodded. 'She can fly again, it's the only explanation.'

'But where's Armelia?'

'I don't know, lad. We'll find out soon. Cawdor is bringing her home, ETA, the hour of the creeping lynx.'

'What? What is it?' Root asked. Tangnost had gone thoughtfully still. 'What's wrong?'

Tangnost pursed his lips, remembering. 'The first time she went into a deep sleep it was after the trauma of losing Two Gulps. She woke up changed. She had become a Dragon Whisperer. Root, what if Armelia's disappearance has done the same? She has become a Dragon Whisperer again?'

The young navigator nodded slowly. 'Whenever it really counted, she could do unimaginable things.'

'Whatever happened,' Tangnost reassured the young gnome, 'she tried to save Armelia, but for some reason she couldn't. But she tried, Root. She wouldn't have let her go without a fight.'

CHAPTER SEVENTY-ONE
Armelia

'Armelia? The WarLock's men took Armelia?' Root looked stricken, joy at reuniting with Quenelda swiftly dashed. 'But why? Why would anyone kidnap her?' He coughed. Smoke still hung in the air after Two Gulps' fiery reunion with Quenelda which had lit up the roosts.

'It was Knuckle Quarnack and his thugs. T-they weren't after A-Armelia,' Quenelda was talking so fast she was tripping over her words. She looked utterly exhausted. 'They were after me. Armelia worked it out first. She knew they were after me, so she led them away from me deliberately. They went straight for her in her –'

'Flying leathers,' Root finished flatly, finally understanding. 'No one wears them but you.'

'And Armelia.'

'But why didn't you stop them?'

Quenelda looked stricken. 'How?' She raised her arms helplessly. 'I can't fight soldiers. We didn't have Two Gulps; they'd trapped him. My inner dragon only returned as I raced to rescue her. I don't know how or why it happens. By then it was too late. I had no idea where they went, so I flew north. I know it was stupid. I should have raised the alarm. Root,' she looked at her friend miserably. 'Forgive me?'

'But we have to find her!'

'She's gone, Root,' Tangnost said flatly. 'Depending on the dragon they could be half way to Roarkinch by now. We wouldn't even know where to begin. Cawdor has placed the entire Wall on full alert. They are stopping and searching everyone crossing, on the ground and in the air. Both he and the Howling Glen have Imperials and harriers out searching.'

Then to everyone's consternation, the youth broke down in tears.

'Oh, Root,' Tangnost finally understood, looking meaningfully over the gnome's head at Quenelda. 'Why don't you take Root across to Chasing the Stars,' he suggested? 'And I'll send a message to Sir Gharad?'

'Root, lad. I will talk to the King, to see if there is anything else to be done. But don't get your hopes up. I'm sure Darcy will be delighted to see her, and she's clever. She'll play him along as she did before, when we were searching up north for your father. With some pink dresses and pompoms, even the WarLock King will be fooled.'

'But, but when will I see her again?'

'I don't know, lad,' Tangnost said heavily. 'But you will. We will get her back, I promise.'

CHAPTER SEVENTY-TWO
Dark Dragon Dreams

Hunting…hunting…hungry…so hungry…

The WarLock's dragon Queen powered southwards through the crowded icebergs into the Inner Sea, her hunting calls echoing in Quenelda's mind. A killer whale pod were nearby...time to feed. But other hot-blooded morsels had been promised...those kindred who had cast her out so long ago. Since then she had grown in the ocean's cold dark depths, the ancient canyons that had once towered so high they kissed the cold depths of space, then drew the dark's power down and down into the deeps, tainting her mind.

How she hungered...for revenge. She had waited so long, nursing her hatred until the cold green power of her master filled her, sang in her veins. But first she had to break a chain to let the hobgoblins through. She could hear their gurgling calls far away. They did not taste good. When she was crippled and starving she ate them in their thousands, bony and foul. Green light angrily flickered along her length.

Hungry…so hungry…

The young Dragon Whisperer awoke with a start and shivered. Her dark dragon dreams had returned. What was this creature? What was it hunting? It felt as if it were drawing near...

CHAPTER SEVENTY-THREE
Nothing to Say for Yourself?

Nearly unconscious, Armelia nonetheless screamed as she was dropped out of the flour sack with a thud onto a hard floor that stank of the sea. She could hear the gurgle of the tide. Somehow the bitter cold had lessened; the stone was comfortably warm.

'It's the Void for you…' Knuckle sneered, as Armelia moaned and curled up to protect herself. The sound of armour and dragon spurs withdrew, and a heavy door swung shut, leaving her in the dark.

The bindings on her wrists and ankles ate into Armelia's very bones, and blood oozed from a cut where a brigandine stud had torn her cheek. Her head still hammered from where they had knocked her out. As the heat warmed her through, she began to get pins and needles in her hands and feet. The sack over her head allowed her to see a little, but dark was falling rapidly. She had no idea of the day or time, or how far they had travelled on the Imperial.

Armelia tried to quell her fear. What if the WarLock King touched her mind as Quenelda had described, and learnt of all the Queen's and King's plans? What if Darcy didn't love her anymore. What if…?

Footsteps could be heard in the passageway beyond, and muted voices. The rattle of the key turning the lock and the door rasped open. There was a silence as a figure moved about her.

'So, you are not so strong now, and where are your vaunted dragons? I hear the peasants and commoners call you a Dragon Whisperer? Why have you not turned into a dragon then, sister, and saved yourself? Because it's all a lie, isn't it? Knuckle said you wore a suit of scales. Cleverly done. But it only fools the stupid peasants.'

Armelia curled up trembling. The voice was familiar, but there was a cruel edge to it, and it had suddenly become very cold. Frost was creeping over the rocks beneath her. More footsteps. A cough. Knuckle had returned.

'Hook her.'

Armelia was hauled roughly to her feet, her tied hands looped over a hook. The tips of her boots barely touched the ground. A blow took her in the side of the head. She screamed.

'So, sister, time to put an end to your insolence. My father has plans for you. You will be returning to Dragon Isle once he has done. Another spy in the heart of the SDS to unlock its secrets. Nothing to say for yourself, little sister?' Darcy whipped off the hood and roughly grasped her chin in an ice-cold hand, to tip her face. He raised his torch. 'Let's see ho - *Armelia*? Armelia? Is it truly you?'

Husband and wife stared aghast at each other.

'Cut her down,' Darcy rasped, ripping his heavy cloak off to wrap her warmly. 'Your damn knuckle draggers have taken the wrong woman.'

'My Prince?' Knuckle was confused as he severed the rope binding Armelia's bruised and bloodied wrists.

'But...but she's wearing flying leathers.'

'Pink? Have you ever seen my sister wear pink? With pom-poms? You damned fool, did you not think to check who your men took?'

'But –' Knuckle's hopes of wealth were dashed as he protested. 'But she's in flying leathers. She was riding a sabretooth and-'

'This is my wife, dammit!' Darcy swore, as he scooped Armelia up. 'Call the physician to my chambers. And make yourself scarce.'

'Your Highness,' he could yet redeem himself. 'I have information about their Imperials...they won't f-'

But Darcy was gone.

CHAPTER SEVENTY-FOUR
Forget Everything

1900 bells and the Juveniles assembled in the lower roost briefing room. The room was abuzz.

Quenelda arrived in the company of Tangnost, Root and Guy; she was not only scaled: she was winged, and some spines swept back from her head and brow that were new, as if she wore a helmet. The room instantly quietened.

'Sit,' Quenelda told them, quashing down her fear for Armelia, focusing on the task at hand. They would take Roarkinch to find and free her friend. This was *for* Armelia.

'What we are about to do is highly classified; you can only tell your family and friends they won't be seeing you over the next two moons.'

That caused a murmur of speculation. Root willed her to hurry up. He wasn't sure why he was here. Bracus was still MIA, and his redeployment to the Juveniles had not been formally confirmed. Teasingly, Quenelda told him he would have to wait for the briefing like everyone else, now he had an inkling why.

'Once again we will continue our training deployed on Phoenix Firestorm piloted by Guy. Root will combine navigator and Talon scout.' She held her friend's gaze and was rewarded with a smile.

'You have been taught by the best,' she looked at Tangnost. 'The greatest Dragon Master in the SDS. As a result, half of you were chosen to take part in Operation Brimstone, even though you had not graduated. We saved lives. We saved families. Our family. We took part in the first counter-strike since the WarLock betrayed us.'

She looked at them, a glint in her eye, a touch of a smile. 'What do you know about sabretooths? Speak freely.'

Answers came from all corners of the briefing room.

Quenelda nodded. 'Now you are going to forget everything you've been taught. You're beginning from scratch. You are going to learn tactics that aren't in any book.'

Root smiled. That made them sit up! There were whoops and cheers.

'We're going to do the impossible: we are going to create a rapid reaction talon that can be deployed everywhere from rapid advance reconnaissance to cave and tunnel insertion. By the time Operation White Out takes place, we are going to be the best talon in the SDS, and we will win the DragonGlass Crown, for our talon, for our brigade, for our regiment, for the SDS!'

Fists drummed on benches and tables. Fatigue forgotten, they were eager to begin. You couldn't hear above the whoops and cheers. Quenelda let them celebrate. What was coming was going to be brutal: only she knew why, knew what it would cost her talon to be in the vanguard of the attack on Roarkinch. For now, this was on a strictly need to know basis.

'Training with your sabretooths begins right away. From now on you eat with your mount, you sleep with your mount. Because you are going to become One Kind with your mount.'

'Sir,' a hand went reluctantly up, followed by others.

'But Sir, that is impossible. We might...'

'Get eaten?' Tangnost commented dryly.

'Sir! Yes! Sir! You taught us, Sir, that sabretooths are notoriously highly strung and unpredictable. That the last place we wanted to be was close to anyone else's mount. To be very respectful of our own mounts!'

'Yes,' Tangnost agreed. 'I did.' *The teacher has become the pupil.* 'And everything you learnt still applies to other talons. But we have a Dragon Whisperer, and we are going to rewrite the rule book. By the time we deploy, we will be ready for everything. And the WarLock's army and his hobgoblins aren't going to know what hit them.'

Quenelda nodded, eyes alight. 'We begin training at 0600 hours tomorrow in the Labyrinth. I will see you in the roosts at 2100 hours tonight. Dismiss!'

'Sir! Yes, Sir!'

'Root,' Quenelda turned to her friend as her talon dispersed. 'While I begin training, I want you to scout the Labyrinth for a different objective: to see if you can find a way through from one end to the other for our dragons. We are going to do the unexpected: we are going to take the Sentinels from behind. The Cave Bear V Brigade will never expect it, and that will be their weakness.'

'They won't expect it with good reason,' Root cautioned. 'No one has ever found a route through that maze of caverns and caves and passageways ~ let alone with sabretooths!'

'If we are going to beat the WarLock then we have to rethink everything we know. We must think the impossible. If anyone can find a way through the Labyrinth, Root, it's you. You're the best scout in the regiment!'

(*Drawing kindly supplied by Phoenix Wilson*)

CHAPTER SEVENTY-FIVE
My Princess

Armelia was resting in bed still shaking like a leaf when a familiar face from the Queen's Court entered her chamber.

'Child,' the apothecary gently took her hands, scrutinising her face as if he, too, sought a face from home. Armelia wiped away an errant tear. She was still afraid. Confused.

'Where am I?'

'Hush, child, don't fret. You are still in shock. You are in the Dark Citadel of the WarLock King's Court on Roarkinch.' The old face was concerned as he examined her chaffed wrists, took her pulse and felt her forehead. 'Tsk, who hurt you, child?'

Armelia shook her head, then turned to retch, Darcy's blow still aching. 'I feel sick.'

He nodded, tutting. 'The way they treated you I am not surprised. Those are nasty bruises on your brow. They were rough with you.'

'Well,' he completed his examination. 'No broken bones, but severe bruising. I will give you unguent for the torn skin on wrist and ankles and some poppy milk to ease the pain. But you need to rest. I will prepare you a drink; it will help you sleep, allow your body time to heal. And you must try and eat to gain your strength. I will send to the kitchens.' He looked at her sadly. 'I will return on the morrow, but should you take ill, send for me immediately.'

Armelia soaked up the heat in the sunk obsidian bath in her chambers, slowly relaxing. Finally, the ache and tension began to unknot as a maid gently tended to her. Why, this was better than Dragonsdome or the royal palace, where maids had to struggle with buckets of heated water that was already cooling by the time she slipped into the copper bath tub. But here! Her palatial chambers were made of the same polished black stone, hung with rich tapestries and rugs, and lit by dozens of chandeliers. Despite their vast size, they were comfortably warm, warmer than the huge fires could account for. *How was the citadel so cosy and warm in this freezing land? Where does all this heat come from?*

Wrapped warmly in a bed cloak, Darcy arrived as she was nibbling on oatcakes, a salty cheese and pears. He sat down on the bed, careful not to disturb her tray.

'My Princess, you are still too pale. Are you better?'

'Tired. I am still tired,' she sipped her hot chocolate; the temperature had suddenly dropped. 'And I have a terrible headache.'

'Forgive me, sweeting.' Darcy turned his emerald gaze on his wife. 'Why were you wearing flying leathers?'

'My Prince?' Armelia pulled the eiderdown about her for comfort, and fluttered her eyelids, exaggerating her exhaustion while her mind raced for a plausible answer.

'You were wearing flying leathers,' Darcy gently brushed a strand of hair from her eyes, touched the bruised forehead. 'That is why Knuckle's men mistook you for...' Darcy's handsome face hardened into a snarl at an opportunity missed. 'Quenelda.'

Her husband's frown was curious, as yet not suspicious. 'Your sist- Quenelda and the Queen, they decided that all the ladies of court should wear them, should learn to fly.' she pouted. 'I had no choice!'

Darcy's frown softened. It was the right answer. 'But the Labyrinth? What were you doing there?'

'Now Qu-she is a princess, she demanded ladies-in-waiting of her own, and chose me. 'I was on her awful dragon, the err,' she flapped her hands about as if she was still clueless. 'Red and gold.... the fat dragon. It...it can't fly so...'

'Her fat sabretooth?' Darcy laughed. 'She still has that runt? Why do people think she knows anything about dragons?'

'So,' Armelia continued, 'Quenelda was going to show me some cave paintings. We went into a cave, and then, and then we got lost,' she lied. 'It's like a maze and dark. And then something snagged me. I fell off. She didn't even notice, and then....' she shuddered...'and then there were shouts and....I was captured...oh, Darcy!'

Her face crumpled and she began sobbing. 'It was terrible, I was so frightened. So c-cold.' The tears and fear were unmistakably real as fear and pain finally overwhelmed her.

'My darling,' Darcy swept her up in a strong embrace. 'How you have suffered. No matter. Forget her and the Queen. Forget flying leathers. Here you are a princess. Here you can have anything you wish for. I – I had these chambers prepared for you next to mine,' he admitted. 'Should you choose to join me. When you are rested, I will show you.'

Princess! Armelia's face lit up, not entirely feigned; delighted he had been hoping she would change her mind and come to him. What young lady had not dreamt of this? *Quenelda* her inner thoughts inconveniently answered. *Quenelda... and you. Now I want to fly...not dress like a doll...well not all the time...*

'I can make you happy here, I swear it,' Darcy was earnest now.

He, too, is looking for comfort, Armelia realised. *So far from home.*

'And it will not be so long before we are back in the Sorcerers Glen, back in the palace. We will rebuild Dragonsdome! You may design it as you will! You will have as many balls and banquets and races as you wish. One day, you will be Queen!'

Armelia hid her shock and found a wide-eyed smile. 'Truly? Back in the Glen?' She took Darcy's hands in hers. 'Tell me, my darling. *What are you planning?*'

CHAPTER SEVENTY-SIX
FireBall

Quenelda spent five nights with the Juvenile's dragons in the roost. Beginning by talking to each rider, she then spoke with their dragons themselves, one by one, taking Two Gulps with her. As night fell in the roosts you could see their eyes and Quenelda's glowing in the darkness. One by one the Juveniles began sleeping with their mounts in a hammock strung across the roosts. Within days they were sleeping at the centre of their curled sabretooths protected by tooth and claw. It was unheard of, and the steady stream of visitors did not believe it until they had seen for themselves highly strung sabre-tooths curled about their riders as if they were nursing fledglings! In the field that one action might well save their lives if they were taken by surprise. Who could have imagined such a thing? Only their Dragon Whisperer.

'Well? Tangnost asked as Quenelda led her talon out into the paddocks to begin field exercises. Phoenix Firestorm was warming up on a pad due to take off to the Labyrinth. 'Can you do it?'

'They are going to try not to kill each other.' She grinned happily.

He smiled with relief. He had feared for her recovery, but the resurgent dragon whisperer was shining as if lit by an inner radiance. And, as once before when Two Gulps & You're Gone had died, she had clearly grown as she lay in a coma: there was a confidence and quiet gravity he had not seen in her before. A young woman had emerged who was growing into both a princess and

SDS commander.

Nodding with approval, he took his leave for a half moon. 'I have to train the ice bears, mammoth, Bone-Crackers and Marines to fight as one Ice Claw. Call if you need me. Or,' his eye twinkled, 'I may call you!' He kissed her forehead, quietly noting that the tiny scales had increased about her shining eyes.

Out in the churned up slushy paddocks, riders in heavy training leathers began by leading their mounts knee to knee from end to end. There was some bucking and the odd snap of bad temper. Ruraigh Mclachlan was carted off to the infirmary with a broken shin where a talon caught him unprepared, and several sabretooths were nipped, but, incredibly, that was all.

'Mount up,' Quenelda instructed, Two Gulps at her heels. 'Now ride them knee to knee.'

As the morning progressed, this evolved into a measured charge. Drumondir briefly arrived to watch before returning to her duties in the hospital, treating training casualties. When she wasn't there, she was with Winifred making garments for the troops or at Dragonsdome or the Guild Libraries. Dragon training did not appeal, and her pupil was clearly in her element.

By lunch the Juveniles were riding full tilt into an army of turnip scarecrows, mowing them ruthlessly down, except for Two Gulps who stopped to eat several before Quenelda reprimanded him. Old habits died hard; but his antics made the talon laugh.

Quenelda nodded with satisfaction as she congratulated riders and dragons. Soon every morning was spent studying and arguing and debating tactics, every afternoon trying to execute them, and every evening after debriefing in the roost with their mounts, bonding with them, becoming one with them just as she and Two Gulps were one. It was a punishing routine, but Tangnost nodded as he inspected them one afternoon, the Juveniles of the III Heavy Brigade were turning into one of the best disciplined, most talented talons in the SDS. Provided they could hold the line in combat of course, for that was a *very* different thing.

The Juveniles also practised again and again traditional sabretooth formations such as Arrow and Whirlwind, and rescuing downed troopers at a gallop. But before long they were adding unheard of manoeuvres: FireBall, StarBurst, Circle, SunBurst. Complex, difficult and *very* exciting! Some attack, some defence. Off duty dragon masters and mistresses, Dragon Lords, Faculty scholars, Professors and Deans were to be seen in growing numbers at the paddocks, or out on the ice, and even in the depths of the Labyrinth.

The King sat watching the Juveniles through his dragon's eyes, accompanied by the Queen who wanted to watch her daughter, the Guardian, Tangnost and Major Cawdor, Warden of the Wall, taking a break from the weight of command, and training with the ThunderStorm Battle Group with two of his squadrons. It was impressive as the massed closed ranks of sabretooths thundered over the ice, stirrup to stirrup. As they stormed past they suddenly broke right and left of Phoenix Firestorm and swiftly surrounded her; flaming, they moved inwards. Half flamed about her, but every second sabretooth pivoted to face outwards so that there were two rings of fire, inwards *and* outwards. Claps floated across the ice. Spotting their audience, Quenelda walked over to gather feedback, and to show her talon off.

'Two Gulps is going to show you a new tactic to support attacks on the rear of a column.' She was bubbling with confidence.

Sometimes it was the wonky tail; it meant Two Gulps accidently went in a completely unpredictable direction. But it wasn't the tail this time, it was a big toe. Jumping over a company of BoneCrackers to support the rear of a marine unit trapped in a gully by hobgoblins, Two Gulps was distracted by low flying barnacle geese taking off from the loch and carelessly snagged a talon throwing him forwards. An armoured ball of flaming sabretooth took off down the gully while the goose thanked its lucky stars and put some air between itself and the departing battledragon.

'My word,' the Guardian observed, taking his pipe out his mouth as Two Gulps bounced out of control down the hillock, scattering terrified marine units; flooring several-dozen unfortunate marines who weren't quick enough to move aside, before gradually coming to rest. At this point the by now bad-tempered, thwarted sabretooth uncurled and flamed in one smooth circular movement, destroying a veritable army of wooden hobgoblins out of pique.

'Look at the damage just one sabretooth has done to our Heavy Marine Corps!' the King commented. 'Imagine the devastation in tunnels packed with hobgoblins! That manoeuvre will wipe them off tunnel ceilings too!'

'That was jolly brave of them to volunteer for that demonstration!' the Queen said innocently.

'I wouldn't have thought of it, tactics *without* riders. We must get used to having a Dragon Whisperer,' Magnus Fitzgerald smiled at Quenelda. 'But even so it's impressive ...if a whole talon could do that without their riders...' The Guardian shook his head. 'It would radically reduce casualties.'

'Yes, err, yes, indeed,' Quenelda agreed, avoiding Tangnost's sceptical gaze. 'It's called, err, the Hedgehog...yes, the Hedgehog,' Quenelda said, thinking on her feet. 'Also for umm...breaking up massed enemy.'

'Well,' the Guardian's raised eyebrow took in his Heads of Tactical Research and the Head of Defensive & Offensive Tactics in their golden robes, 'I think this is one to research; see if it can't be rolled out...' a rare flash of humour, 'across all our Brigades. Yes?' It was an order.

Tangnost grunted in Quenelda's direction. She had the good grace to blush, but already she had thought of a way of building on what they had just seen. It would be risky, very, very, risky but if the Juveniles could manage it...

CHAPTER SEVENTY-SEVEN
Dark Dragon Dreams

Hungry…so hungry…

The water was inky black and freezing as she sped forwards; icebergs shot with aquamarine, hung like ethereal stalactites, their size above sea only hinting at their great depth below. Sound was amplified but there was nothing left save her in these empty seas now, as she approached the Chain. She had eaten the last pod of killer whales she had encountered, enough to sate her hunger. A few had fought together, but they stood no chance against the greatest predator in the deep sea. But she was hungry, oh so hungry…for revenge.

Hunting…hunting…

CHAPTER SEVENTY-EIGHT
Findibar

'My lady,' a slim girl in dark blue dress bowed, something about her face, her blond hair was familiar. 'I am your hand maiden if it please you.'

Armelia smiled. She would have to win her over. 'What is your name?'

'Findibar, Princess.'

'Have we met?'

'No, Princess,' the young girl looked cautiously about. 'But you have met my brother. My twin. Quester. Can you give news of him? Our parents were wroth he chose not to come north, and never speak of him.'

'I never knew Quester had a twin! Many families are sundered as yours is,' Armelia said sadly. 'They fight on both sides. It is bitter when family fight family. But I have wonderful news of your brother. Quenelda gifted him a wychwood leg after he saved the King, and so he has mended and walks as if he were never wounded. And he is a knight now, esquire to the King, in place of...' she gave an odd laugh, 'of my husband. His Imperial is called Wychwood Warrior, to honour Quenelda and the magic of trees.'

Findibar smothered a sob.

'Hush, my dear,' Armelia reached out. 'I did not mean to distress you with my news.'

Findibar shook her head, wiping her tears. 'Pardon, Princess, I am happy for my brother. I just miss him so. And the Sorcerers Glen. This hateful place will never be home; it is a cold and cruel place.'

'You are right,' Armelia agreed. 'This place will never be home. We must find a way to return to ours,' she squeezed her maid's hand. 'To those we both love.'

CHAPTER SEVENTY-NINE
Know your Enemy

'You've trained in tunnels. Many of you saw action in the Brimstones. You and your sabretooths are at home underground. But,' Quenelda looked about her troop. 'Fighting hobgoblins is different to anything you have encountered. They are fast. They are huge. They can leap as far as your sabretooth. But the thing nothing can prepare you for are their sheer numbers. They come in their hundreds of thousands. They don't just come at you on the floor of a tunnel; like spiders they can move just as well upside down on the ceiling.'

That caused a collective indrawn breath.

'I think it's time to take another look at your enemy. I believe if we meet in battle, the WarLock will use his hobgoblin banners to wear us down; to overwhelm us, before his army and dragons even lift a finger. If I were him that is what I would do.

'You have had a brief glimpse of Galtekerion but most in the Sorcerers Glen have not seen the face of their enemy in ages beyond count. Do you know why?'

'Because of the Sentinels,' one youth piped up. 'I've been out fishing with my Da. They're the muckle stone dragons who guard the entrance to the glen.'

'They're supposed to be very old, my Granda told me,' another girl answered. 'He was a fisherman. Said that a great net was hanging under the water to catch hobgoblins like he was catching fish, only you couldn't see it because it was woven with wards.'

Quenelda smiled. 'Your Granda was right. The

Sentinels were built at the time of the First Alliance between dragons and men, and a great chain bearing a net was strung between them. The SeaDragon Lords then cast powerful spells to ward against hobgoblins. Since then, until we were betrayed, only the SDS and those outwith the sanctuary of the glen had confronted the banners. Your families don't know the face of their enemy, but you must; because when they come, and they will come in their tens of thousands,' her eyes roved over her talon. 'That is when we must stand fast and hold the line,' she finished softly.

'I requested his prison be changed. Since we cannot swim underwater and would not last a heartbeat if we could, a second ward has been cast so that he can come out of the sea if he chooses, and his armour returned to him. This way you will begin to understand the enemy we will face in battle. Follow me.'

Down and down they went again as they had once before, but this time there was a collective indrawn breath of trepidation as they looked through a ward.

Galtekerion was in full view, crouched like a frog on a rock, huge thighs bunched ready to spring. The hobgoblin WarLord wore dragon-bone armour and bangles as he moved about. His weaponry had not been returned. The pale luminous eyes looked straight back at them. He bared his teeth making the Juveniles stare in disbelief at the three ragged inward curved incisors.

'You can speak,' Quenelda reassured the Juveniles. 'He cannot see us or hear us like we can him.'

There was a long sober silence.

'What is your first impression?' she encouraged them.

'The size,' they were all answering at once.

'The suckers...Sort of pops and squelches at the same time.'

'The smell! It's horrible! Like rotting fish.'

'Yes, it is, but that could save your life. You remember this smell and you'll always know if hobgoblins are close.'

'They're just huge,' someone repeated. 'How can we beat them?'

'Their teeth,' someone shuddered. 'Rows of them!'

Suddenly there was a thump and a blur of movement causing shouts of consternation. A huge chunk of meat had been dropped through a grill above, and in the same breath, Galtekerion was gone, over at the other side of his prison effortlessly ripping his meal apart.

The entire class had jumped backwards, hands over mouths in horror.

'*That* is your enemy,' Quenelda warned. 'But remember, the more you know, the less you have to be afraid of. Root felled him with a frying pan. Expect the unexpected!'

'Expect the unexpected!' they shouted, hands lifted together inwardly. Quenelda's new motto had become the Juveniles' motto.

CHAPTER EIGHTY
DragonGlass

Armelia was back on her feet, but weak, and horribly stiff and sore. Dressed in exquisite black, lined with furs, hand-sewn with emeralds, Lords and Ladies bowed low before their Black Prince and his Princess. Glances caught Armelia's eyes then looked swiftly away. Was there sympathy here? A winter raven had been sent to her parent's castle commanding them to attend Court, as the future Queen's family. Would they come north? In mid-winter when flying was so dangerous? Armelia doubted it; they would plead age and ill health. She was lonely, aching for her home far to the south. For her true friends. All the fawning courtiers and professed friendships rang hollow, spoke only of ambition. And she was certain both husband and his father had spies amongst her ladies in waiting. She and Findibar had to tread softly.

Once the sight of Darcy would have sent her into a swoon. She would have been quite giddy with joy. She was the envy of Court when he had proposed, dashing the dreams of every hopeful young lady in the Seven Kingdoms. But that seemed a lifetime ago. Darcy was now the Black Prince, or she had heard servants softly call him the Prince of Darkness. Now he and his Knights of Chaos were notorious throughout the Seven Kingdoms for their wanton cruelty and for shackling prisoners for his father. But there was also some new alchemy at work.

There was something about Darcy now, a dark aura like a shadow. Something akin to what hung about the WarLock King. Like his father, Darcy was now unnaturally pale, and he always seemed cold to the touch. His green eyes were flecked with black. Armelia tried to rid herself of the image of a striking viper ~ scaled, swift and deadly, the badge of the WarLock.

Pretend. Quenelda's words rang in her head. *Pretend you still love him. My brother will protect you.* But how about the watchful eyes of the WarLock King? He would not be easy to fool. And so she focused all her attention on making Darcy happy, binding him to her.

'Sweeting, I want to show you Roarkinch, so you can know your realm before we leave for war. It is a...strange world of ice and fire. I have never seen its like before. Father's scholars say the whole world was like this once...' Darcy stood behind Armelia with his arms wrapped about his wife looking down from the Citadel Tower. The weather was so cold it made Armelia's cheeks ache despite the fur lined hood and silk lined mask which covered all her face save her eyes. 'Not the barracks or the frost roosts,' Darcy hastened to add. 'Or the parade grounds, but the island itself.'

Armelia smiled and swept a gloved hand at the alien and wondrous world far below. 'It is strangely beautiful,' she found herself admitting. 'But I would like to see it all, Darcy. Everything, roosts, barracks and all!'

'Will you ride a frost dragon then, sweeting? Now that you can fly? I have chosen a mare for you. She has a gentle nature and is not trained for war. I have had a special saddle made for you.'

The frost dragon Armelia was introduced to was both gentle and beautiful, reminding her of Chasing the Stars.

She swiftly blinked tears away. She had to be strong. Had to believe that somehow, she could return home; but she didn't want to return as part of a conquering army! There must be a way to escape to give the SDS a warning of the traitor in their midst. Seeing the WarLock King watching, she gave all her attention to White Wilderness, pressing her forehead against the mare's muzzle. The blue veined white dragon was harnessed all in white, with furs and saddle set with dark jewels.

'What are these?' Small stones were like diamonds, glittering, beautiful, but black.

'DragonGlass, sweeting. Rare and priceless, more valuable than gold or diamonds. They are said to be relics of the First Age, some even say the Sky Citadel was built of dragonglass. Let me help you mount up.'

The sun already rode the horizon, the winter shadows long. Armelia's frost skittered backwards with a flap of its wings as a column of boiling water and steam shot up into the air. Instantly freezing, water drops rattled like hail on the ground.

'You were right! It is a realm of ice and fire.... Such a wild landscape. It's beautiful, Darcy!' Armelia looked at a bubbling hot spring. 'This is what keeps the citadel warm?'

He nodded. 'Yes. It is funnelled through volcanic rock aqueducts my father created.' He had been unsure how his wife would react to the bubbling fumaroles, mud pools and geysers that lay cradled within Roarkinch's world. But Armelia had changed. Was...stronger...had grown from the thoughtless girl she once was into a blossoming young woman. In a burst of affection he dismounted and reached up to kiss her.

'My household knights will care for you should you wish to ride or fly when I am away. I am leaving a dozen behind for your care and protection.'

'It's lovely, Darcy,' she repeated as they both dismounted. 'Show me all of it, underground too. I want to see those frost dragon caves, the lava pools, everything.'

And so, at the beginning of each day they went out riding and flying the island. And Armelia carefully remembered it all. The barracks and training grounds, the roosts, the armouries and nursery roosts, and started to nurture the beginnings of a plan.

CHAPTER EIGHTY-ONE
Heritage

The DragonBone Chair warmed to her touch, wrapping Quenelda in its soft golden glow. Eyes closed in gratitude, Quenelda took a deep breath and opened herself wholeheartedly to the HeartRock, for the first time truly welcoming her gift and embracing all that it would bring. The young woman realised that a part of her had always fought the responsibilities of her heritage, that she had wished to remain a child forever, denying her birth right and the burden that carried. Now, she had passed a test, she had chosen of her own free will. She was a true daughter of the Matriarch.

Cold air and the sound of calling dragons told Quenelda she was no longer in the HeartRock, rather standing on the crags of the White Wizard mountain beside a young man scaled like her in black, with wings like hers that swept gracefully down to the ground.

'Dancing with Dragons,' he kissed her hand. 'Sister, I rejoice to see you again.'

'Why? Why have my gifts been returned to me? I failed you.'

He denied her assertion with a shake of his head and a smile. 'No, you didn't. You could have chosen to keep your powers, shackle dragonkind, and win this war to your eternal glory amongst your peoples. In time you could have wrested power from your WarLock King and taken all for yourself, binding both your peoples and mine to your will. The light to the dark. Fire to ice. Dominion over the One Earth and beyond; for this is what your WarLock seeks.

'You chose not to, knowing then that without dragons you may have fallen into eternal darkness, losing all those you love. You have taught us that not all mankind has become corrupted by greed and power. Those who love you swore to uphold and protect the One Earth and Dragonkind: your parents, your companions. That for some, love is the truest treasure in our lives, the greatest gift we can bestow.'

She looked at her brother, so like and so unlike Darcy. 'Can I call on you in times of need?'

A wind was already blowing as Son of the Morning Star held his hand out to gently cup her face. 'My time on this world has passed, but do not fear, my mantle shall pass to you.'

She opened her mouth to protest, to call him back.

He shook his head. 'Many have already flown ~ I go to join them. But the First Born chose long ago to remain here, should the One Earth have great need. They await your summons for the war that is to come.' He was fading fast now, stardust in the wind... 'I will await amongst the stars for you, sweet sister...look for me, look for those you love.'

And then Son of the Morning Star was gone.

CHAPTER EIGHTY-THREE
Weigh Anchor

Darcy took his leave of Armelia as first light tickled the horizon and the crescent moons were beginning to wane. Serpents of torches glowing like fireflies wended between the hot pools, barracks and drilling grounds, about the skirts of the volcano and down the cliff steps to embark. Bell upon bell the holds were slowly being filled with dragons and men and provisions.

'Darcy!' Simon called. 'Come on! We're in The Bitter Wind. We sail with your father.' For once he was full of joy, swept up by sheer wonder, by the prospect of glory and home.

'Sweeting, I shall send Imperials for you as soon as I can. Or...my father has swifter ways...' Darcy was fully armoured beneath a heavy hooded cloak. The black armour flecked with green made Armelia nauseous, and she was shaking with tension and fear, for she too was embarking with the Armada, bearing precious news. She swayed. Her husband mistook her concern.

'Armelia, don't fret for me,' he held her gently. 'My armour is imbued with sorcery, with words of Making. No sword or spear can penetrate it. I will be safe. And their Imperials will not fight ours. It will be a killing field.'

They knew! Armelia felt faint. *So, Knuckle knew. How?*

'H-how long will the v-voyage take?' Armelia tried to keep the tremor from her voice, dreading the answer.

'Two moons, mayhap less if the winds and fortune

favour us. We don't know how fast the current flows that carries us south, or what icebergs and pack ice may block our way. Father says his dark dragon Queen will break a passage, but even it must tire.'

'His dark dragon Queen?' Armelia's chest fluttered. Darcy had never mentioned it before. 'What d-dark dragon Queen?'

Her husband's lip curled at the thought of that fell creature. 'You need not worry your head about it, sweeting. He set it loose to hunt before you arrived. The Abyss birthed it eons ago in the ocean depths,' he shivered.

He's afraid of it, truly afraid. The Black Prince is afraid... 'Darcy? What's wrong? It frightens you?'

Darcy swallowed, nodding. 'It's an ancient sea creature, part dragon once, father says. Like the hobgoblins it can come out of the sea. A predator whose very breath freezes. She will overpower their Imperials and destroy Dragon Isle.'

'Darcy! Where are you?' Simon was back, impatient. Come on!'

'Sweeting, I must leave you. He kissed her. 'My father takes the blizzards with us to hide us from discovery. He wants me by his side. He means to teach me.'

He can conjure winter storms?

Sweeting, yes, his power grows...winter is his weapon. Armelia froze. Her husband did not appear aware of that sudden invasive thought, but Armelia was. She tried to blanket her thoughts, fill them full of pink ball gowns and pom-poms, but Darcy was full of the coming adventure.

'Our spies and scouts will tell us when they begin their foolish Dragathon...' Darcy would never admit that he had dreamed of winning the greatest endurance race in the Seven Kingdoms, of lifting the coveted dragonglass crown for himself and his regiment. 'We will bide our time until the third or fourth day when they are spread out across the Highlands, and then strike. They will not even be aware we are amongst them until it is too late. Our hobgoblins will be sacrificed to breach Dragon Isle, the dark dragon will destroy it. It will be over swiftly. SAS ranks are swelled with children, veterans and peasants!

'I will win Dragonsdome, the Queen, and the Black Isle. My father will take the Queen and Kingdoms both. But for misfortune they already would be his. He will not fail again, nor I you,' he kissed her hand with a courtly bow. 'Wait for my word!' and he was finally gone.

Daylight came late to this dark land, but for once the sky was flawless blue, and a fresh northerly wind had risen, making Darcy wonder anew at his father's power as he flew over Roarkinch. If he could command the elements at will, it made the Battle Academy scholars' petty magic irrelevant.

The old and young, constables, wives, cooks, children and sweethearts, grooms and smiths, commoners, all those left behind on Roarkinch were gathered on the cliffs to see their Dread Lord and his Dark Armada sail. No one had seen such a thing. White from keel to the tip of their sky scraper masts the Armada was breath-taking, stretching away, lost in the glaring white expanse where ice merged seamlessly with sky. Black gorrangochs, invisible against the basalt rock, launched from the cliff roosts into the white sky. The vanguard of frost dragons had already flown to guard their passage from prying eyes.

Darcy carefully put down on the pads on the aft castle of his father's immense iron-shod flagship, Bitter Wind, well apart from his father's gorrangoch. Dismounting, throwing reins to the dragon master, he stepped down the curving balustrade to thread his way forward past the seven masts, the dragon roosts, the hundreds of labouring sailors trimming rope and sail, to climb up to join his father on the forecastle with its great catapults, its iron spikes.

The WarLock King raised his arms. His outline shimmered, became insubstantial as ink swirling in water. A concussion of thunder rolled in the clear sky. Beside him, Darcy could feel his father's power ripple out to encompass the entire fleet. Closing his eyes, the WarLock wove a web of sea haar and smoke ~ all blues and greys and green ~ and cast it like a net onto the ocean.

He smiled at his son; a predatory, feral smile. 'They will not see us coming until we are upon the Sorcerers Glen.' He turned to his Captain. 'Set sail, you have the deck.'

'Weigh anchor!' The Captain's call was carried to where scores of sailors manned great horizontal wheels. They began to push, slowly at first, and four massive chains rattled through the lug. The huge anchors began to rise through the icy water as curious hobgoblins beneath darted in about them. Unfurled sails caught the rising wind like plump pillows. As cold currents caught her, Bitter Wind began to slowly move. It would take four days before the final ship left harbour.

CHAPTER EIGHTY-FOUR
Dressing Down

Dark fell, and still more troops and dragons and provisions made their way onto the departing ships and boats and galleons. From the Citadel, Armelia could see the tiny pinpoints of light converging into streams of fire flowing like lava towards the harbours. It was time finally to put her own plan into action. It was the hour of the dozy bat before she stepped from her chambers, dressed as a servant wench in clothes Findibar had been leaving behind each day. It was the bleakest hour before dawn and the sentries were also dozing. The wall torches had burnt low. Here in the heart of the Black Citadel there was no threat, and their Dread Lord and Master had already set off to wage war in the south.

Heart pounding, quiet as a mouse, she took the back stairs, past the servant's quarters and then down to the kitchen. Men-at-arms come off duty were there, breaking their fast, their talk soft. They smelt of wet wool and leather and brimstone. The WarLock King and his creatures were clearly feared.

'Don't envy them, not with those suckers swimming about the boats.'

'Aye, hobgoblins make my skin crawl.'

'But at least that fell creature o' his has long gone.' The tall guard looked about before touching the amulet about his neck. 'Twas huge. A deadly twisted thing. Made me retch it did even to look at it. T'aint natural.'

'You scared?'

'Odin's Hammer! Aren't you? Any sane man would

be. I was up on cliff when it left. Never seen nothing that big. Black with unearthly green wisps about it...taint no dragon, leastways none I ever saw.'

'T'ain't natural what he did to them Imperials neither. Harrock still has nightmares. Many roost hands who care for them died since of the black death.'

'How can he take Dragon Isle? No one has taken the Isle, never!'

'That dark dragon Queen'll devour their precious island.'

'Word is he has a traitor at the heart who'll let him in if his creature fails.'

A mug of water dropped from Armelia's lifeless hand. So even the soldiers knew of a traitor. Heads all turned towards her as she bent to lift the leather mug.

'You!' one called. Armelia's heart slammed into her chest. She kept her head down, hair hiding her face.

'Sir?'

'Sir!' The man's friends guffawed. 'He's just a fisher-son like you're just a maid. Come over,' the guard slapped his knees. 'I'm cold...don't be shy. Serve me some porridge!'

Armelia gulped. 'My Princess bade me return once my errand was done here.'

That instantly silenced them. 'He don't mean nothing by it,' one of them anxiously nodded as they returned to their meal. No one wanted to get on the wrong side of the Black Prince. 'You go on your way, lass.'

Armelia slipped two loaves of bread, sausage and a truckle of cheese beneath her shawl and tried to calm herself, whilst studying the kitchen. There, the third door, she was just rising to leave when Findibar appeared.

'Lend me a hand, Gwen. How're you doing, lads?'

'All the warmer for seeing you, lass!'

Findibar laughed lightly. 'In your dreams, frognose! Come on, Gwen.'

Nodding, Armelia followed her maid through corridors and pantries carrying bundles of blankets. Down another level to where barrels of beer were stacked, and smoked hams and fish hung, and down again.

'They store armour needing repair here, Princess. And training gear for the young 'uns. We might find something to fit us.' Shielding the lantern, she opened the door.

'Lady,' Findibar put her bundle down as Armelia shivered uncontrollably. The rooms weren't heated down here. 'These are the warmest undergarments I could find in the laundry room. They are all wool and silk. Put on as many layers as you can, else we will freeze to death out there. Let me help you, Lady.'

Armelia nearly fell as she clumsily pulled on the stiff dirty breeches Findibar had chosen for her, and the loose grey hooded shirt stank of sweat and was stained with who knew what. Her long hair lay sheared on the floor.

'Help me!' She couldn't believe the weight of the chain mail that fell to her knees. Her legs buckled, and she fell.

'That won't do,' Findibar cast around.

'Shh!' They froze suddenly as a group of soldiers passed by talking loudly. '-oing to catch them in the middle of their precious war games. We'll give them a war game they won't forget…time the north rose – '

'This one, my Lady,' Findibar offered. 'It's more holes than mail; it may be lighter. Try walking.'

Armelia waddled clumsily forwards.

'Perfect, Lady. They all walk funny once they've been kissed. They fall over. And everyone is wrapped up, else they die. None will notice us.'

Finally, two hoods and a scarf swathed about her face, Armelia selected a light leather-padded helmet with a slitted half visor. Heavy leather gauntlets over three woollen pairs and cold uncomfortable boots several sizes too large went over four layers of socks and padded with yet more. Memories of frostbite and blackened fingers as described by Drumondir almost froze her to the spot, and she wavered. Could a pampered young woman cope with a dreadful journey amongst the forsaken in the dark dank hold of a troop carrier? Armelia's heart raced as panic took hold. She began shaking violently.

'Lady?' A hand reached out to hers. 'Lady,' Findibar whispered. 'You are not alone. You are young and brave like my brother.' Findibar hugged Armelia awkwardly, both held apart by layers of clothing until the shaking stopped.

Armelia nodded. She had to forewarn her friends that there was a traitor, and she had to go home or die in the attempt. For all its beauty, Roarkinch was an alien world. And she knew every part of the island fortress now, priceless information for the SDS. Lifting her head, she smiled weakly. 'Thank you,' she whispered, breath clouding the air.

Two heavy felted servant's cloaks completed their disguise as they made their way out into the corridor in darkness. Both carried a rough sling which served as a bag around their shoulders under cloaks packed with food. Findibar had added oatcakes, smoked fish and pickles to their hoard, as much as she could carry.

'Come, lady...' she held Armelia's hand as she led her down the back stairs and out into the night. 'Everyone's down loading the ships, there aren't any guards.' There was no need after all, not here on this frozen island. Not here after the kiss of the Abyss.

'Where would any run to on an island surrounded by ravenous hobgoblins? Our only chance of surviving is to stay at the heart of the holds. Those on the edges will freeze, but they don't know it anymore.' Snow crunched under their feet as they slipped through the dark and down out past the outer walls down to the holding pens, and just in time. Half of them were already empty, more on the move.

'Move out!' A voice barked in the darkness. 'Get moving. We sail at midnight.'

Shuffling slowly, they pushed deep into the heart of the moaning, shuffling rocking crowd. A few were chewing on dried strips of dragon meat. Countless dragons had died here; now they fed the WarLock's armies. Some had limbs bared to the bone or other horrible injuries. Many had frostbite. Armelia tried not to be sick and failed. Shivering on the icy ground, they leant against each other for comfort and waited until it was their turn to embark. Ship after ship set sail. The blood red sun was going down by the time they were rowed out to board a huge, heavy-bellied transport galleon which would carry them home.

CHAPTER EIGHTY-FIVE
Snowmen

A quarter moon of intensive training followed for the Juveniles, out on the ice as well as in the depths of the Labyrinth. For there was going to be a lot of ice when they attacked Roarkinch, they needed somewhere to practise with a lot of space to minimise injuries, and the frozen loch was perfect. Once they had mastered a manoeuvre to Quenelda and Tangnost's satisfaction, they then perfected it in the dark tunnels and caves of the Labyrinth.

'Today I'm going to show you a new tactic for breaking through, or out if we are surrounded. This same FireBall will also clear tunnels.' This was the idea she had nurtured since Two Gulps smashed through the ranks of marines curled up in a ball. If a riderless manoeuvre was unheard of, then no one would have dreamt of this one in their wildest imagination! She considered her talon and nodded. It was very dangerous, but the Juveniles were good enough, confident enough, to try it now.

'You've had a look at our new saddle design.' The talon nodded. They had been curiously studying it since Two Gulps arrived. 'The leather workers are at this moment making the same saddle adjustments for you. So, there are more grabbing loops and handles, but you might not understand this new reverse stirrup design. Can anyone tell me what it's for?'

Heads were shaken.

'It's for hanging on,' Root had been peering beneath Two Gulp's tummy, where he had spotted two stiff leather grips and two shallow pouches. He frowned, wrinkling his nose, took a guess. 'Upside down?'

Quenelda nodded. Root had been practising mount and dismount with her for several bells a day, until the young gnome could ride Two Gulps at a charge, arm out, picking up Quenelda as the pair thundered past, or she had ridden Two Gulps with him jumping up behind her; a standard cavalry battlefield technique for picking up riders whose mounts had been killed. They had been taught this before deployment to Operation Brimstone. But now he knew it was part of something more.

'This circle of snowmen you've just been building ....' she caught all their eyes ~ it had degenerated into a snowball fight until one hit Tangnost and went down his neck. 'And these ones there, are hostile troops. We are going in to rescue our troops being held prisoner in their centre. Rapid insertion and extraction. Watch.'

Phoenix was coming in slow and low gliding, one wing now just about touching the ice. Two Gulps pounded down the wing and then Quenelda disappeared out of sight round his belly and Two Gulps...curled up and rolled! The entire talon blinked, eyes wide. Somersaulting, the young sabretooth pulverised the 'soldiers' in his path until he hit the ring of snowmen when his huge talons lashed out to arrest his momentum. As he unravelled, Quenelda pulled herself up using the straps, then with one arm round the pommel, she grabbed Root, who leapt up behind her.

Flame!

Kicking out in front and behind, Two Gulps jumped in a circle. A lethal combination of talon and fire vapourised the snowmen still standing, before the pair leapt forwards to where Phoenix Firestorm was once again decloaking. Sabretooth and rider leapt onto the rising wing and were away. Phoenix cloaked and was gone.

Drumondir, who had taken a break from her studies and search for more tapestries, yet again found her mouth hanging open, like all those of the Juveniles, who were speechless.

'Now I see why you might need someone who can set arms and treat burns attached to the Juveniles!' she said dryly to Tangnost, who was looking like the cat that had got the cream. 'I didn't know such a thing was possible.'

'Neither did I,' he met her level gaze, then allowed a smile as cheers and whoops broke out and Phoenix Firestorm uncloaked as she put down. 'Neither will the WarLock.'

CHAPTER EIGHTY-SIX
Cold

It was so cold it burned! Dark and damp. Despite clinging to Findibar, Armelia had never been this cold, had never imagined it could be this cold; and the relentless crack of ice and the deep sucking swell and roll of the heavy-bellied galleon made her sick. The boom of the drum for galley rowing slaves was an unrelenting heartbeat that sounded out night and day and made her head ache. Sometimes there was a horrible groan as they steered too close to an iceberg and the galleon's hull planks creaked and threatened to split; at least four boats had sunk following a collision, drowning all hands. Indifferent, the Forsaken lay shivering beneath thread-bare cloaks and moth-eaten furs as if consumed by fever. Barrels of water froze with the ladles embedded in the ice. Hot porridge or thin soup was shared at dawn and dusk, and twice a day they were herded up on deck for exercise. Overnight, dozens died, and their stiff bodies tossed overboard to feed the hobgoblins. Juvenile warriors took to circling the ships that bore the WarLock's enslaved army, waiting for food.

Out on deck with Findibar, Armelia closed her eyes. It was so bright her head hurt, even within the shadow of her hood and helmet. Fourteen days' sailing had brought the Armada to a halt, hemmed in by a huge ice shelf. Even the WarLock's razorbacks and gorrangochs harnessed to the lead ships could make no progress. The two young women had heard a bugle calling through the hull but had no idea what it meant. As days passed everyone appeared to be waiting for something. They were surely going to die here; frozen to the bone and aching with hunger, their own stolen rations all but gone and the thin rations not enough to keep skin on bone. The hobgoblins, too, were dying in their droves. She could see bodies in the water being eaten by their ravenous fellows.

Then, as they walked on deck to keep warm, out of the endless expanse of ice there came a grinding thump that vibrated through the ice and the ships' hulls. A sudden unnatural silence fell. No one moved. No voices called. An ear splintering crack rent the ice. Then hobgoblins were leaping out of the sea, croaking frantically with fear. The air was full of their shrieks. Desperate fights broke out on decks as the crews fought them back over the railings. Frost dragons and gorrangochs took off in their thousands from galleons and the ice, filling the skies with their calls of alarm.

Thick chunks of ice opened outwards like petals. Another thump, and a third. A bestial stench wafted over the Armada, bringing sailors and soldiers to their knees. A glimpse of black, a fountain of water like a whale breaching, and then another thump. Armelia felt faint with terror and choked back a scream as Findibar held her hand tightly, no less petrified. Ice cracked and snapped, ragged gaps spread outwards, and still the darkness rose. Great flows were tossed aside like flotsam. A troopship overturned, thin screams whispering across the ice field. And then a multifaceted eye and vast bulbous maw broke the surface.

Armelia stared in disbelief as insectoid appendages clicked on the ice. Whispers leapt from mouth to mouth, deck to deck. 'The knokongoroch...' A sailor's ancient fear given form and name. Truly the WarLock's dark dragon Queen was the stuff of darkest nightmares. Never had Armelia seen a fearsome dragon such as this, or so huge. It dwarfed the WarLock's flagship! To think she had once been afraid of her small, gentle Chasing the Stars; how Armelia wished she could throw her arms about her beloved dragon, feel that reassuring hot breath on her cheek, the curl of a wing about her. Tears poured down her face freezing her eyelashes together. Would she live to ever see her precious girl again? Armelia willed herself not to move, not to betray her presence amongst the indifferent Forsaken.

Disappearing back into the ocean, creating a swell that rocked the Armada, with a surge upwards and forwards, aided by four great pectoral fins, the creature breached, thumping down on the ice again and again. The drumbeats began again.

'Make sail,' the order boomed out as, obligingly, the wind rose. 'Make sail.'

CHAPTER EIGHTY-SEVEN
Thistles and Leaves

Root staggered drunkenly upright, brittle thistles and icy leaves attached to him. A disgruntled hibernating hedgehog dropped to the ground. There was the sound of muffled mirth. It didn't last long.

'Ha... ha... ha...' Fergus set them all off. Tangnost, thank goodness, Quenelda thought, as the Juveniles dissolved into merriment, was elsewhere. Two Gulps carried on happily scoffing the gorse bushes where he had put the brakes on to see if there were any rabbits, unceremoniously dumping Root.

'Well,' Quenelda pursed her lips as Root tried to recover his dignity. 'You just about got the hang of that.'

*Two Gulps? **Two Gulps!!***

The sabretooth looked guiltily up. *You are supposed to curl about your kin riders. Not leap into bushes. You might have injured Root.*

Watching Drumondir pulling some gorse thorns, Quenelda winced in sympathy at Root's muffled, unmanly squeals. Perhaps she was pushing the Juveniles too hard, what they were practising had never been done before. But time was pressing. FireBall was ~ nearly ~ perfected out on the ice and the tunnels. It was time to take it one talon further.

'We are now going to deploy our FireBall manoeuvre for clearing infested tunnels,' she had told her talon three days earlier after demonstrating what she and Two Gulps wanted. 'This can be done with you or without you: but in the second case I've shown you, it can be followed by

SunBurst. If we are cut off from our BoneCrackers, if we are on our own, or in the vanguard, then this manoeuvre will be vital. Our sabretooths will keep us alive until help arrives.'

And so, training had begun in earnest with their new saddles. Initially, the entire talon were paired one by one with Two Gulps, so that by the time the Juveniles were reunited with their own mounts, they had mastered the tricky exercise of slipping beneath and between those huge muscled, scaled rear legs. While they continued to practise, watched over by Tangnost's steely eye, Quenelda worked with all their individual mounts, teaching them what she wanted, practising endlessly with them from dawn to dusk and beyond, so that by the time rider and mount were paired again, the sabretooths knew what was needed. By then their daily audience had swelled to the point the paddocks were becoming unsafe, and Quenelda moved them out onto the ice. The crowds followed them and grew larger by the day.

No one had seen this temperamental, argumentative breed work so closely together, without biting, flaming and attempting to disembowel each other or their riders, let alone allowing the Juveniles to curl between four lethal sets of talons and emerge unscathed, like a magic trick. Their Dragon Whisperer was achieving the impossible! How, many soldiers asked, could they lose?

'No, not that way,' Quenelda quietly instructed. 'Place your hand *here*, left hand on the pommel, swing down with your mount between you and the hobgoblins. Now, slowly, yes, move this hand and grip here, yes, and grip here ~ ah! If you don't grip with both you're going to fall,' she helped Fergus to his feet. In less than a half moon, as Operation White Out drew near, the Juveniles were ready to test how their training could be deployed underground.

'Line up...watch.' Quenelda leapt onto Two Gulps and climbed up one of the crumbling scree slopes leading into the Mammoth Cavern. Torches barely lit its vast outer darkness. Swiftly, she swung down beneath him and then the sabretooth jumped and curled. Gathering speed, he bounced off boulders, the sides and even the top of the passageway down into the cave where he bounced sideways off another boulder before unravelling to disembowel and injure as he spun in an arc of fire.

'Well?' She asked, a little puzzled after a long silence. 'What do you think?'

'I'm... thinking you're joking! Surely you're not asking us to do that?' Root spoke for them all.

CHAPTER EIGHTY-EIGHT
Dark Dragon Dreams

Hunting... hunting....

She was so hungry it ached as she sped through the freezing darkness...now hobgoblins were zipping through the water around her. Thousands, tens of thousands, hundreds of thousands ...

Crying out, Quenelda sat up. Drumondir, a light sleeper, instantly came awake

'Child,' putting down a branch of candles Drumondir looked at the bruises under Quenelda's eyes with concern. The young woman was clearly exhausted. And it clearly wasn't just the training; it was Quenelda's dreams, her nightmares, which were becoming more frequent and more frightening, that concerned the BoneCaster. Now, even during waking hours, unease was growing in Quenelda's mind as the dark Queen drew nearer; the thoughts of a nameless dread, a hungry predatory mind, full of malice were invading her thoughts.

And Drumondir for once was at a loss how to help her pupil.

CHAPTER EIGHTY-NINE
The Chain

The rip tide was going out swiftly, the deep cold current flowing between the links of sky-metal guarded by the Sentinels. The dark dragon Queen could sense the heat from the wards that bound the links, melting icebergs that had made it this far south on the same cold current that had brought her here. Powerful waves demanding she turn back; but she was a primordial creature of the Abyss, born of the dark matter between stars, ice to fire. And these ancient wards were crumbling. She arrowed swiftly forwards on her four paddle-like fins, her power rippling through the sluggish frozen darkness. The links shattered at her approach; the sound boomed underwater, heard by the hobgoblin and razorback banners approaching the Inner Sea beneath the Armada.

'The wards are broken.' The Warlock King raised a glass to his war captains and son seated about the great oak table in the stateroom of Bitter Wind. 'To my dark dragon Queen.'

The WarLock arrived in the Inner Sea at the witching hour, bringing winter with his Armada. The temperature dropped brutally. Night gave way to an unnatural heavy twilight beneath heavy snow-laden skies as they dropped anchor. The Sentinels reported that a thick yellow fog was rolling towards the glen, eating up familiar contours, swallowing everything in its path. Then it stopped, sitting out to sea. No one noticed that the icebergs that drifted in never came out. And Quenelda? The only person who could penetrate the WarLock's cloak of deception? Who had recognised Roarkinch for what it truly was? Her mind was elsewhere.

CHAPTER NINETY
Expect the Unexpected

The Juveniles were in the briefing room. for a final briefing under Tangnost's watchful eye before Operation White Out began the following day. He was quietly impressed. These young riders under Quenelda's command had exceeded his expectations and already he was mulling over the implications for the attack on Roarkinch. Despite their youth they were disciplined and focused, many with the potential to become officers. But first things first: time to see how they deployed in action. Hundreds of Faculty scholars, researchers, stewards and Dragon Masters and Mistresses were going to be evaluating the success or otherwise of their training and tactics, and so he was going with the Juveniles to assess the potential of this intended Rapid Insertion Talon. Root and Guy were down in the east flight cavern with ground crew, harnessing Phoenix Firestorm in her winter armour, going over final painstaking minute preparations for an early morning take off. Their BoneCrackers had been finalising their kit for a moon in the field and were now getting some shut eye.

However, Quenelda arrived in full battlegame armour. She looked up and smiled with satisfaction. 'We go in tonight before the exercise begins.'

Tangnost's eye didn't blink. If you were watching closely and you knew him, you might have seen the tiny smile that kicked the side of his mouth. He coughed to smother his amusement. *So, again the pupil becomes the teacher. A lesson well learnt.*

'Sir?' There was a confused babble.

'Expect the unexpected,' Quenelda told them while smiling at her teacher. 'That is rule number one we were taught last year.'

'Isn't that cheating?'

'No,' Quenelda asserted vehemently, 'it's initiative! War isn't a game where you play by the rules. The WarLock isn't going to play by the rules. He's not going to give us warning if he attacks. His treachery nearly destroyed us because we were fighting by the rules, the way we always had. We must do the unexpected, and that means you are ready to deploy with your mounts and your equipment on the Shard upper cliff dragon pads at 2300 hours. Do any of you have a problem with that?'

'No! Sir! No!'

'You are ready to go?'

'Sir! Yes, Sir!'

'2300 bells it is, then. Dismiss.'

There was an undignified scramble to the door. Field packs had to be ready. Sabretooths had to be harnessed.

'Root estimates it will take us at least three, maybe four days to navigate the route he's discovered,' Quenelda explained as Tangnost studied the map. 'We put down here at Echo Cave, cloaked, with our full BoneCracker Brigade, you move forwards every day to our agreed positions in case we require back up or combat extraction before we reach our main objective.

Tangnost nodded. Whilst Quenelda had been training, Guy, Phoenix Firestorm and their BoneCrackers had been practising rapid insertion and rescue from their pre-agreed rendezvous co-ordinates, and diversionary attack options in support of their talon.

'There will be five defending talons from the Howling Glen holding the position behind the Sentinels. They'll be expecting a frontal attack.'

'And if their Talon Leader is like you, and is expecting the unexpected?'

Quenelda grinned. 'They won't be expecting us to arrive before the end of the quarter moon, will they? Not if the exercise doesn't begin until 1200 tomorrow. We go in behind them, you and Guy drop them here and our BoneCrackers abseil down from the Trolls Tongue and hit them at the same time in a diversionary pincer movement.

'This is our chance, Tangnost, to take them by surprise and test our new tactics. To show that we are ready to be part of the attack on Roarkinch! That a Rapid Insertion sabretooth talon can be rolled out across the regiment!'

CHAPTER NINETY-ONE
Operation White Out

Stormcracker sat cloaked on a granite outcrop of the White Sorcerer mountain, along with fifty attacking squadrons drawn from four regiments. The King, accompanied by the Warden of the Wall, strode along his Imperial's back between ranked battlemages arrayed in their battlespheres.

According to the Joint Air Delivery Test and Evaluation Unit, the deployment of the Academy's new battlespheres had been operationally flawless since their introduction. Their impact would be immense; might even tip the scales in the battle for Roarkinch: Hugo had nothing to match the brilliant minds in the Academy's military researchers. Time for his CAC on Storm to test their co-ordination capabilities in the air in a live-fire exercise against the kind of defences, traps and challenges they would face at Roarkinch. Listening as they counted down, the King nodded, satisfied with the deployment of his cloaked regiments and Ice Brigades.

Quenelda's father was also intrigued by the classified collaboration between the Faculty of Water and the Pyromancer's Guild. He had attended the talk by Professor Diphthong on their new dragonfire anti-hobgoblin mines; barrels that blew up at varying depths, triggered by hobgoblins, or in training, by a sonic pulse. Modified Ice Bear, Narwhal and Walrus swift iron-shod longboats had proved perfect for sowing mines in coordinated pattern sweeps. He had seen Diphthong's scholars in their bright robes out day after day in appalling weather, testing the volatile barrels and their safe dispersal. Four boats had been blown up along with nearly one score casualties, including five academics. But for the first time since the demise of seadragons, the SDS were going to take the fight to the hobgoblins underwater, removing one of the WarLock's huge tactical advantages. Two days into the exercise, his regiments would withdraw overnight to allow Magnus's research team to test them: coloured powder paint revealing the different depths they were weighted for, so they could assess their impact. The King took his pilot's chair: bonding with Stormcracker, he looked out on the glen through his Imperial battledragon's eyes.

'Cloak.'

'Cloaking,' his navigator confirmed. 'Storm Command is cloaked.'

'Let it begin.'

Quester signalled the marshals.

The flares rose red, red, red to explode, their boom ricocheting around the glen to loud cheers and celebrations on the Black Isle. Battlemages spun in their battle spheres along Stormcracker's twin spines and bent their minds and magic towards taking Dragon Isle. Operation White Out had begun, only to end when Dragon Isle triumphed or fell, however long that took.

Out to sea the WarLock King smiled and waited as his gorrangochs were harnessed and armoured, his troops readied to go, his high mage Lords ready to strike. Let the SDS begin their petty endurance race. Once they were committed and their regiments spread over the western

Highlands and the length of the glen, his hobgoblins would begin their hidden assault on Dragon Isle's inner wards. If the wards held, then he would unleash his dark dragon Queen and the maelstrom. One way or the other he would annihilate the SDS in their heartlands, just as he had at the Westering Isles.

Under cover of night and the cloying haar now swirling about the Sentinels, a banner entered an underwater cavern into the Labyrinth, searching for a mountain watercourse which would carry them through the maze of caverns and caves past Dragon Isle's loch defences towards the unsuspecting Black Isle, where Darcy and his Knights of Chaos would be waiting for them to assault the city. Hostages and the Queen taken, and the Guild and Palace secured by his son, the hobgoblins would finish their task and the Black Isle would fall. Once they knew their families were taken or dead, Dragon Isle's resolve would waver. Then it would only be a matter of time before the Queen, the crown and the Kingdoms would be his.

CHAPTER NINETY-TWO
Heads Down

There was no night or day deep in the bowels of the Labyrinth to mark the passing of the days.

'Mogri, Fergus, take the first watch on point; Jamie and Connor, the rear,' Quenelda ordered. 'The rest of you get some hot food and heads down.'

'Sir, Yes, Sir!'

The Juveniles positioned their sabretooths in circles of nine, facing outwards in the small caverns where the passage widened. Safe within that perimeter, their riders laid down their bedrolls and set a fire to eat, and torches to see by. The hour glass was turned; Quenelda would let them all rest for a full eight bells. 'The Funnel' as Root had named it, had been so difficult with its stepped elevation and narrow ceiling they were all exhausted. Down here in perpetual darkness, despite their training, the talon was finding it disorientating. All, save Root and some of the younger cave dwarves. By his count, tomorrow would be the fourth day of the exercise, and they would reach their objective. Tangnost would be preparing for their BoneCracker's diversionary assault. Having checked troopers and dragons, Quenelda lay back against Two Gulps and closed her eyes. Exhausted she fell asleep instantly. Opposite her, Root opened his eyes. He was worried, and so was Drumondir, who had taken the young man into her confidence. He had promised to watch over his friend until Operation White Out was completed.

Quenelda began to twitch. It was dark, and the water

was beautifully cold. She exploded forwards, bubbles echoing underwater, over the large links that had fallen to the seabed, into the forbidden Sorcerers Glen for the first time.

*Hungry....so hungry...so close...*like a leviathan she waited there amongst the rocky kelp beds...waiting...she pounced, and the hobgoblins were gone...mere morsels...snapped up to stick between her great teeth. Slime and bone. Quenelda's face wrinkled in distaste. Slowing, she sank down to the rocky sea bed... waiting...waiting...for her master to call.

Hungry...so hungry...

'What?' Quenelda started, swallowing, before sticking out her tongue and wiping her mouth to rid herself of the fishy taste.

Root hid his worry and smiled. He hadn't said anything. 'What did you hear?'

'Didn't you say you were hungry?'

'No. No one did. Your dream again? You were... swaying in your sleep.'

She nodded. 'It's becoming more and more real...I'm swimming...'

'Swimming?'

'Underwater.' She shivered again as goosebumps raised her clammy skin. 'It's cold and dark...I'm waiting...I've been waiting for so long...'

'What for?'

'Revenge.'

CHAPTER NINETY-THREE
The Forsaken

The Armada rode at anchor cocooned by the yellow haar. Silence was absolute. Woe betide any who betrayed their presence. Several sailors who erred were thrown overboard, freezing in heartbeats or eaten by the starving hobgoblins. Frozen, sick, the Forsaken's number dwindled by the bell in the dark freezing hold. Hunger gnawed at Armelia and Findibar, but the Forsaken felt no hunger, so they could not beg for food. They could hear the muffled boom and crack of SDS battlegames. Then, as light began to fade on the eve of the third day, the hatches were raised.

'On deck.' The towering ships about them were barely visible. All around, troops and the Forsaken were disembarking onto flat-bottomed boats.

'Down those nets,' a whip licked out. 'The Black Prince wants you for the Black Isle. He's going to take you back to your families and friends. Har... har... They'll be reluctant to kill you...reluctant to kill us until it's too late!' The guard laughed cruelly.

'The Black Isle!' Armelia felt hope leap in her chest as Findibar managed a squeeze of her hand. Perhaps they could escape to the Guild, or the Palace?

Barely able to hold on, trembling all the time, weak with hunger, the two young women began the perilous climb down icy nets on the side of their rocking galleon into a shallow troop landing craft. The sun was barely penetrating the bellying snow cloud, but it grew steadily lighter. It took a long time to row through the porridge ice and clog of rowing boats to the WarLock's huge battle galleon, the climb up the nets even longer onto the deck of Bitter Wind. Wobbling like drunks, hands unfeeling due to starvation, many fell, to disappear into the black water.

'Get them mounted in the hold,' Darcy ordered. 'I want to be ready to fly at dawn tomorrow.'

Stupid really, Armelia's heart was battering at her chest. There was no way her husband would see through her disguise, would imagine the vain, empty-headed young woman he married could possibly be amongst the bowed prisoners who shuffled past him. She had to survive. She had to find someone, someone she could trust. She had to pass on that the WarLock had a spy at the heart of the Kingdoms, a dark thread at the heart of the tapestry. Climbing up Night Mare's tail, the Forsaken sat mindlessly on Darcy's Imperial in the hold and waited for the call to battle.

CHAPTER NINETY-FOUR
Hobgoblins

A horn sounded through the deeps. A single blast.

Ten banners of hobgoblins approached the Sorcerers Loch and the deep sea came alive with their calls. The rip currents were deep and cold and swift. They passed beneath the metalled hulls of the attacking SDS battlefleet at the neck of the sea loch and sped towards Dragon Isle, where they had been promised a feast, to where weighted barrels hung suspended like strands of kelp in the sea.

CHAPTER NINETY-FIVE
Hostages

Darcy was going over his plans for the Black Isle one last time in his stateroom on Bitter Wind. His knights were rowdy, dicing and drinking, bored after a moon and a half at sea, eager for the attack to begin. Tomorrow they would take back what was theirs.

The WarLock's son straightened out the crumpled map. Throwing down a tankard of ale he belched with satisfaction, then turned to his newly arrived Dragon Master. 'Our task is to take the Black Isle: to secure the Guild, the Palace and the Queen.' *How he was looking forward to that!! He had warned them when he fled from Court they would all pay for denying him what was rightfully his. For humiliating him. He would wipe the smug smiles from their faces!*

'You take the Guild,' he pointed, 'and hold it securely. I will take the Palace. Do not let the Guild be plundered, nor their warehouses. Use men and dragons to guard them. Once the hobgoblins swarm it will be chaos, and the rest of the city will be swiftly overrun.

'We begin at first light before my father attacks, when you take the noble and guild galleons anchored on the loch to watch the exercises. No one will be paying them any attention, they will be asleep with barely a watch posted. Scouts confirm they are anchored half way between Dragon Isle and the Black Isle. We capture them and their families. Richard and Gareth's cloaked Imperials will fly you and your Knucklebones at the hour of the Yawning Dormouse, and I have given you four fists of my father's troll BoneBreakers in support. The Guild are fat and pampered. They won't put up much of a fight. Those Lords that do, make the point quickly and the rest will surrender. Hang them from the yardarm if you must.'

'Families?' Knuckle frowned. 'Why? What good are families?'

'Hostages.' Darcy said bluntly. 'All will be noble houses or high-ranking guild families. With hostages, the Guild and Palace will surrender without a fight. When Dragon Isle discovers we have their loved ones, their children, many will lay down their arms. If they refuse us, we shall return their loved ones one by one from our catapults.'

'And the SDS Imperials stationed to guard the Guild and Palace, my Prince?'

'I will send a score of gorrangochs to kill them. The SDS Imperials will not fight, so we will be able to despatch them swiftly.

'As we speak a banner of hobgoblins should have flanked Dragon Isle through the Labyrinth and be looking for a way back into the loch. They will destroy the City Watch and Guild Guards you are so worried about. I will capture the Queen; my father *will* marry her. Capture my sister should you find her and bring her immediately to me.'

'And then?'

'And then we kill the hobgoblins and take our hostages to my father. And Knuckle?' Darcy's emerald eyes flared with an uncanny fire. 'Don't disappoint me a third time.'

'My Lord Prince,' Knuckle bowed out and returned to his men in one of the smaller ships, in a filthy mood. *Surely the information that the SDS Imperials would not fight was worth a lordship?*

CHAPTER NINETY-SIX
Dragon Isle ~ Battle Dome

The Guardian had been roused. It was nearly dawn. A lull in the fighting and a withdrawal of all galleons and heavily armed dreadnoughts to the neck of the sea loch was allowing the underwater mines to be safely tested. He was getting his first proper sleep in three days of fighting. Muted pops and booms carried through the still air as he was roused from his bed, but that didn't worry him. The Officer of the Watch in the Battle Dome below the SeaDragon Tower, Major Gisborn, and two senior Mages from the Pyromancers Guild were in debate when he arrived.

'SitRep?'

'Lord Guardian. The mines are exploding.' Gisborn was an excellent officer. Injuries at the battle of the Line had lost him a leg, a hand and his field command, but he had an eye for detail with great intuition. He had worked with his commanding officer to spin a matrix of inner wards about Dragon Isle that Rufus was finding hard to penetrate.

'They were supposed to be fired tonight were they not?'

'Yes, Sir. But the Faculty Mages have not triggered them.'

'How many?'

'Thousands, sir, tens of thousands.'

'Pattern?'

'Concentric, Lord Guardian,' the Pyromancer said.

'Faulty?'

The Pyromancer shook his head. 'No, Sir.'

'Why? How are you so certain? There were mistakes during testing. Would one failing not trigger the rest? Why not now?'

'The pattern is not natural. They were triggered sequentially, as if a tide were coming in and sweeping about Dragon Isle. They are exploding at all points of the compass.'

'Which are being triggered first?' Intuition was whispering at the back of the Guardian's mind.

'The outer rings.' The Major threw up a bright transparent display of the Glen, swiftly homing in on Dragon Isle, changing the perspective to look from above. It was now alive with clustered explosions radiating inwards. The outward circles were gradually dying to darkness.

The Guardian stepped out onto the gantry. It was as if the stars had fallen into the loch. 'Scramble the Rapid Reaction Wing.'

'What are they looking for, Sir?

'Anything that is out of place. No matter how insignificant. And signal the longships. I want them ready to drop everything they still have on board on my mark, once these have all exploded.'

'Sir?' one of his Mages in the array of battle spheres swivelled about. 'The third ward is being drained ~ infinitesimally. I didn't report it because there is no sign of magic, Sir, let alone battlemagic.'

'The Core is mine.' Walking along the smooth jutting plinth of stone, the Guardian stepped into the Core: the inner battle sphere at the centre of the battledome ~

about him up to four hundred individual battlespheres orbited and spun, each controlled by battlemages defending individual wards, the deployment of marines and BoneCrackers, airwings and battlegalleons. Here in the Core, he could draw the world into one sphere.

Now… Blue eyes narrowed. *Is it possible?* From the centre of Dragon Isle, its contours and tunnels and flight caverns all picked out in soft light, his gaze roved over the battlefield from the Black Isle back to the Sentinels, homing in, turning, a detail here. Swiftly drawing in, moving spheres about him in and out. Nothing yet to explain the infinitesimal drain of power. And yet, and yet, his intuition told him something was very wrong. Something was cloaked…

Then the Guardian saw what he had feared, moving forward and forward again, increasing resolution: tiny sparks in the dark all about the island under water, a flicker and gone, faster than the blink of an eye. Thousands. Tens of thousands. With each impact the ward was draining, the runes growing dimmer and dimmer.

'It's not battlemagic,' he said flatly. 'It's hobgoblins. Thousands, tens of thousands.' He focused inwards, but resolution was deteriorating.

'The third ward is losing integrity, Lord Guardian.'

'Set condition one, Major. Dragon Isle *is* under attack. Alert Storm Command and the First SeaLord. We need them in immediate support. Battlegames are over. This is real. We are under attack.'

'Sir?' No one could believe what they were hearing.

'Hobgoblins, Major. They are overwhelming our

wards with sheer numbers.'

'Set Condition One, Set Condition One. Dragon Isle is under attack,' Gisborn's voice rang calmly throughout the island. 'This is no longer a battle game. Dragon Isle and the Sorcerers Glen are under attack. Scramble... scramble...scramble...'

Wwwwwwwwwwwwoooooooooooooooooooo

Wwwwwwwwwwwwoooooooooooooooooooo

The unthinkable was happening.

'Lord Guardian,' Gisborn reported. 'The Third Ward is failing. The third ward is down.'

'Guardian,' a second Mage reported. 'The Sentinel's scouts reported unidentified troops deploying over the last few bells. They assumed they were part of ThunderStorm Command's newly created Strike units who hadn't turned their runes on.'

The Guardian's head snapped up. 'This isn't just a hobgoblin attack. It's Hugo. This is the WarLock.' The Guardian nodded as disparate pieces of the puzzle fell into place.

He's using hobgoblins to overload the wards. These are just the shock troops to be sacrificed before he unleashes the maelstrom.

'Make reply to all field commanders: any unidentified units to be treated as hostile. All senior officers not deployed, to the Situation Room. We've been training for this for three moons. Initiate DefCon One. And Captain. Get eyes in the air, stat.'

'Guardian, Strike Commander Cawdor scrambled his Ground Attack Squadrons a quarter bell ago. He reported he was taking them into that haar to have a look. Several galleons have disappeared. We haven't heard from him since.'

'StormCommand report the King is inward bound. ETA a quarter bell.'

'You'll want to hear this,' Gisborn hit a rune.

'-a fleet. StormCom, repeat, there is a hostile fleet shrouded by the haar. Thousands - battlegalleons and troop ships. The WarLock's standard. We've caught th-napping. Wall Strike, follow me down. Fire as many a-you can. Weapons free. Weapons free!'

Below the ice in the deepest part of the loch, close to Dragon Isle, the WarLock's dark Queen thrashed and snapped at her tail as new explosions pulsed through the water, hurting her, deafening her, confusing her. She turned tail and fled for the calmer sanctuary of the Inner Sea.

CHAPTER NINETY-SEVEN
The Armada

The WarLock's head had lifted sharply from the map on the table in his stateroom as muted pops had reverberated through the hull, eyes narrowed, senses questing outwards: the SDS had resumed their fight. His son and Captains had left for their assigned tasks as he contemplated the day ahead. When the inner wards were about to fall they would unleash their full attack. Ten hobgoblin banners were in the loch deep underwater, dying in their droves, softly draining the wards.

His gorrangochs would take off at first light, cloaked, to surround targets from Dragon Isle to the Black Isle, waiting to pounce in a synchronised attack that would obliterate Imperials and win open sky. Fire and brimstone would rain down on Dragon Isle and the Black Isle. Remaining banners would be released to overwhelm both and the glen. His dark dragon Queen would then destroy the SDS's ancient lair. There were hurried footsteps on the stairs.

'Father!' Darcy burst in. He was already fully armoured. They were mounting troops on the dragon pads. 'Scouts report explosions all around Dragon Isle!' He looked stunned. 'They say it was as if the sea under the ice was on fire.'

'What?' The WarLock's mind raced. 'They can't have discovered them yet.' It didn't make sense. *Even if they were discovered how can the sea be on fire?*

'I – What's that?' Darcy frowned as the faint sound of bells grew to a crescendo. 'The fools. They'll betray our presence! S-'

The sound of flaming dragons was upon them like a roaring wind as the Warden's squadrons of cloaked Imperials sped low over the anchored Armada, leaving mayhem in their wake. Unquenchable dragonfire leapt from ship to closely anchored ship.

The WarLock's cold eyes met his son's. 'Go! Launch your attack now. Take the Black Isle and the Queen and hold them for me. We are discovered.'

'Father,' and Darcy was gone.

Whump! The blast of battlemagic struck again and again. Whump! Air Wings of swift frosts and vampires joined battle with those rising from the stricken Armada. Coruscating magic fizzled over the huge galleons, deflected by wards onto the unprotected flat-bottomed boats packed with soldiers and the Forsaken who disappeared in a midnight flash. Hulls exploded as spells ripped through weakened wards and five levels of decking. Ships and galleons began to list and sink.

'Dread King,' Lord Jamie Hepburn appeared, hard eyes grim. 'The Dragon Lords are upon us! My men are moving onto the ice as we speak to form up. My knights are taking to the air to engage them. Your commands?'

'Signal our Armada, get every gorrangoch in the air now! Take their Imperials down!'

'Dread King, I and my sons will lead the attack on Dragon Isle. I will target their ground troops on the ice. That should draw them out.'

The WarLock turned to one of his knights. 'Perigrin, signal the hobgoblins to an all-out attack. The time for subterfuge is past.'

'Dread Lord.' His knight bowed and was gone.

The dark aura of the WarLock flared as he strode up the spiral staircase and through passages to where his gorrangoch was being readied for take-off, followed by his Household Guard, standard bearer and knights. 'To battle, my Lords. We shall command from the Sorcerers Knoll overlooking Dragon Isle. Join me there. Get your men onto the lower slopes on either side. The Army of the North will take up positions on the loch below. Hold your forces until we have won in the air.'

'The Armada, Dread King?'

'Abandon it, we have no need of ships anymore. They have served their purpose. We are here to stay.'

CHAPTER NINETY-EIGHT
Dark Dragon Dreams

'Quenelda? Quenelda?' Root shook his friend roughly. He couldn't wake her. She would wake the entire talon soon. 'Quenelda?' He gently slapped her face. Dazed, Quenelda came awake, shaking her head like a dog. She put hands to her ringing ears as the terrible magnified sounds faded. 'What? What's wrong? My head hurts!'

'You were thrashing about wildly in your sleep.' She looked awfully sick, faintly green.

'It's here, Root.'

He didn't need to ask what. He swallowed. 'Here? Where?'

'Here. In the loch. But there are explosions in the water. It's confused.'

'*In* the loch?' he said softly. 'How can that be? What is it? Aren't they testing the dragonfire mines?' Root lifted his head to listen to the silence. 'But how can you possibly hear them?'

'I don't know how, but I can hear its thoughts...No that's not right. It's as if I am it! It slips into my head. It must be part dragon. Root, something's very wrong. Can you find a way through to the glen from here?'

'I can try,' he was frightened now. 'What am I looking for?'

'I think the WarLock's here,' she replied softly. 'And this creature is his.'

Root's eyes opened wide, but he didn't argue.

'Go as swiftly as you can and report back. I will let them sleep until you return. They are going to need it.'

Nodding, Root retrieved his helmet, night sights and water bottle, and was gone into the darkness. Quenelda sat leaning against the reassuring bulk of Two Gulps and was afraid.

CHAPTER NINETY-NINE
The Battle Begins

Directed by the Guardian, Cawdor had withdrawn his squadrons to pursue and engage a hundred and fifty hostile Imperials flying east under cover of the snow storm towards the Black Isle. In the Core, along the cliffs and throughout the coombs the Guardian gathered and directed his Faculty Guard to defend Dragon Isle. The King's stealth battlegroup took up offensive and defensive positions about the Isle and the Glen.

Dense black clouds, barely visible through the snow, were rising from the doomed Armada; advancing like night, Imperials filled the sky. On the cliffs of Dragon Isle Jakart DeBessart, in command of the combined Imperials from the III, XX, IV, V and the King's Own battlegroup, realised there were tens of thousands of Imperials, perhaps hundreds of thousands, and knew that Dragon Isle would fall. Maybe not today, or this moon, but without the might and magic of their Imperials, it would surely fall.

He addressed his squadrons. 'We know we are in the fight of our lives. Our Imperials will not injure theirs, so they are confident we cannot hurt them, that they will take us down. Target their mages and troops. We have trained for this. Our Imperials have trained for this. We'll give them the fight of their lives. Our loved ones' fates are in our hands. Lift off. Weapons free! Weapons free! Let's take as many of them down as possible. On Wings of Vengeance!'

'On Wings of Vengeance!' Forty thousand throats

roared their defiance.

On the high cliffs of the glen looking down on the SDS fortress, the WarLock raised his cloaked arms and the blizzard died in a breath. Blackness spat and cracked between his hands as a virulent black wave gathered and was cast. Rising higher and higher at breath-taking speed, merging loch to the sky, it swept like a tidal wave across the ice, devouring everything in its path with a midnight flash, before smashing against Dragon Isle in an explosion of spume and smoke.

'Ward integrity will fail in moments,' Gisborn warned. As if to emphasise his words, the glyph flared with a final pulse of magic and fell into darkness. All heads turned towards the Core. On the star cartouche, all wards had turned to dark, save for the last.

Already the Guardian was drawing upon his battlemages' power, chaining glyphs, spinning them into a ward, casting it about the Isle. Others were lending their strength to the King and his cabals of battlemages arrayed on cliffs and coombs, battlements and dragon pads who responded. Fire balls struck the cliffs above and below the WarLock's army, raining chunks of stone on his unprotected troops, and tumbling others to their deaths. Lances of gold seared through stone like a hot knife through butter. Earth fountained skyward. Shrapnel broke bones. Ice splintered. At the base of the cliffs the trolls of 43 Royal Marine Commando Regiment, protected by fifty battlemages of the Faculty Guard and the WinterKnights, dealt death and ruin on the hobgoblins emerging onto the ice, pursuing them amongst the countless dead. The Isle became a whirling inferno as carnage and magic and death erupted in a fiery halo. SDS sorcery arced upwards as the WarLock and his Lords rained down fire and brimstone. The battle for Dragon Isle had begun.

Then gorrangochs began falling from the sky like black snow.

CHAPTER ONE-HUNDRED
Drop Dead! Drop Dead!

'Three thousand strides,' Jakart reported. 'Engaging the enemy.'

But then the unexpected happened. As wing after wing of SDS Imperials peeled away, their Imperials folded their wings and dropped.

'Drop dead! Drop dead! Drop Dead!' The baffled cries overlaid each other as the Guardian watched the battle unfold.

Seemingly enraged, the Imperials were striking out with a ferocity that was frightening. Breaking backs or snapping necks, plucking enemy pilots and mages, ripping them from their seats and throwing them into the air where they fell screaming. Flaming, they destroyed all the troops on the gorrangochs' backs, slashing out with unbridled rage, before killing their mounts by snapping necks; a swift clean death. The creatures they fought radiated pain and made no attempt at defence, despite desperate orders to cloak. The thump of their deaths vibrated through the ice and the mountains.

Quenelda looked up in shock. Anguished and tormented minds were being snuffed out like sparks in a gale; a heartbeat of peace, of joy, and then oblivion. Soon their bodies falling to earth were like the beating of a drum, a rising tattoo of death.

What has he done? What has he done to my kin?

CHAPTER ONE-HUNDRED-AND-ONE
Rage and Retribution

The King swept low over the battlefield through the roiling smoke-filled clouds and rising fumes of battle-magic. Choking debris and blood misted his helmet and armour. Banking, Stormcracker tilted his head so that the King could survey the battlefield. The hobgoblin banners had been slow to react to the mines, and so two more banners had annihilated themselves before reaching Dragon Isle. The ice looked like the surface of the moons, pocked with craters. Mounds of hobgoblin dead sprawled everywhere about Dragon Isle, and the black sea was awash with pale bodies. Nonetheless, the second ward had fallen as survivors swarmed, driven by a malevolent mind that cared nothing for their deaths.

Watching through his dragon's eyes as gorrangochs tumbled from the skies, feeling the rising rage that filled the Imperials around him, a suspicion was growing. *Why do you kill with such rage? What are these creatures that the WarLock has created?* The King asked his battledragons: *Why do you honour them with a swift death?*

They are our kin. Their pain is unbearable...

The King faltered. *These were our brothers and sisters?*

These are our kin, Stormcracker agreed. *It is a kindness to kill them...they are screaming inside. They are compelled by the darkness...our power has waned, and he has enslaved us...but we cannot live bound to any will other than our own...we will not live this way...*

The King's voice cracked. 'StormCom to all squadrons.

These creatures are Imperials kissed by the Abyss. These creatures were once our Imperials, as the Forsaken were once our kin. To kill them is a mercy.'

'Acknowledged,' Cawdor responded grimly.

The Guardian swivelled in his Core as the message was sent to all units. Throughout the Glen, the SDS and their Imperials fell with rage and retribution from the skies onto those who had tortured their loved ones.

CHAPTER ONE-HUNDRED-AND-TWO
Twisted and Tears

Another impact vibrated through the mountain as Root saw daylight. What was happening out there? Root crept forward to look out through the crevice. There was a sudden urgent sense of impending darkness. The youth turned instinctively away when an enormous impact blew him off his feet. How long he lay there he didn't know, but when he came to, he was covered in rubble. It was freezing, his head was aching, and it was growing dark. As he carefully sat up, debris fell to the floor. He scrubbed a hand over his dust crusted eyes and blinked. His ears had been numbed by the percussion and he could hardly hear a thing. Gradually, he saw a chink of light and crawled towards it. It wasn't dark. Something was blocking the crevasse. He crawled beneath it, frost crunching beneath his hands, and stood.

The clatter of falling scree behind him made him jump backwards. Into something huge and horrible. With a gasp he stumbled off the wing he had stood on and scrabbled backwards on all fours in horror. The mangled creature was a mass of torn flesh and broken bone, but the blood that soaked the snowy ground was green, and a faint green phosphorescent aura hung about the body. This was no dragon, this mangled twisted creature, that he had ever seen before. The wrongness of it hurt his head. *Only.... only, Root realised with dawning horror, it was an Imperial, at least it had been an Imperial, once.*

With a choking scream Root scrabbled back into the safety of the rock coombs where he retched miserably.

CHAPTER ONE-HUNDRED-AND-THREE
The Black Prince

Ten leagues eastwards of Root, at five thousand strides above the loch in a white out, Major Cawdor looked at his HUD thermal split display, the contours from his navigator's HUD guidance on the other half. The snow was thinning, but not enough to get visual confirmation.

'Strike Leader to CoreCom. Intercept ETA in five. Target flying low and slow.'

'CoreCom to Strike Leader,' the Guardian's high mages had been busy. 'Fifty of your hostiles are identified as Imperials,' Gisborn informed him. 'The Black Prince is one. Multiple targets, sending to your navigator, *were* Imperials...'

'*Were* Imperials?' The young Warden's voice hardened with sudden intuition. 'The kiss of the Abyss?'

The slightest of hesitations checked Gisborn's reply

'Affirmative. Our Imperials are killing them. Drop dead is a go. Take them down, Major!'

'Strike Leader to all squadrons.' Voice hard with barely contained rage, Cawdor passed the intelligence on. 'Red squadron with me. Target the Imperial's mages and soldiers. Let's take the so-called Knights of Chaos this time. Blue and White, your Imperials will target their Forsaken. Give your Imperials free rein: this is as much their war as ours.

'Strike Leader, confirm? We give our Imperials free rein?'

'Affirmative. They are dropping dead.'

'Red Squadron, follow me down. We kill or capture as

many of the Knights of Chaos as we can.'

Escorted by over a hundred of his lords, joking with his Knights of Chaos, the first Darcy knew of Cawdor's attack was when the lifeless body of a gorrangoch ripped through the air, striking one of his companions. And then they were gone from sight in the blink of an eye.

'Richard?' he screamed, reining Night Mare in, turning, not understanding until hot bolts seared through the snow, smashing against his shields. Then gorrangochs, driven down by Imperials, began falling all about, crashing into others. In heartbeats it was bloody mayhem as the bodies of mages and men ripped from their gorrangochs' backs fell out of the sky.

'The SDS!' Simon screamed as a huge Imperial decloaked in the middle of Darcy's knights, scattering them, his dragon flaming. Simon peeled away as golden bolts seared through the snow. Another of Darcy's knights screamed as white hot lances struck him, punching through his shields and his dragon sheered away.

Darcy saw the distinctive banners of the 21st and 41st Royal Attack Squadrons about him and remembered their last bruising encounter. An Imperial was battling its way through the firefight towards him.

The Warden of the Wall...

Cawdor's reputation was spreading; the son they said, the King should have had. They would pay for that folly.

As a Dragon Lord passed beneath, Darcy compelled his Imperial to attack. Great talons ripped across the SDS battledragon's spine, ripping BoneCrackers from where they sat, tearing through the spinal plates, baring to the bone. The Imperial tumbled away.

Rage rising, Cawdor struck, bringing his battle staff down in a blaze of fire. Laughing, invulnerable in his spelled armour, feeling the dread power of the elixir and the dark energy it drew upon, Darcy attacked. Black magic rolled along the oncoming Imperial's spine devouring everything until Cawdor deflected it in its path with a backhand gesture, the impact throwing him into the back of his chair. Five gorrangochs and their mages and troops disappeared.

Darcy dropped.

Through the aerial battle, through misted clouds, through bolts crisscrossing the sky, through explosions, Cawdor and Dawn Bringer kept on Darcy's tail. No matter what Darcy tried, how he drove his Imperial ever more recklessly, he was no match for the driven young man, determined not to let the notorious WarLock's son get away a second time. Having to stall to avoid a fight, Cawdor began to swing his imperial round but then he...let the reins go.

Trusting his Imperial, he let her fly, feeling their souls sing in unison as they pursued Darcy. His new HUD meant he could see, despite Darcy cloaking, and Dawn Bringer was calling to her kin. Heartbeat slowing, cold air streaming past, Cawdor lifted his spelled sword as they rose up cloaked beneath the Black Prince. Astride his Imperial's head as the great maw struck sideways at Night Mare's hated collar, Cawdor leapt to confront Darcy. With a single back stroke he cleaved Darcy's armour full across the chest. Agony shot up his arm, wrenching the sword out of his grip. He jumped, arms flung wide, trusting Dawn Bringer, and his Imperial was there, rising up gently as he landed on her back, running to his seat.

'CoreCom, the Black Prince is down. The Black Prince is down.' No one could survive that killing blow. *Now for the rest of them.*

The Knights of Chaos were scattering under the assault, their young lords fleeing in all directions, pursued ruthlessly by the Royal Attack Squadrons. Those that survived the impact of crash landing clambered to their feet, only to face the wrath of the Ice Brigades.

CHAPTER ONE-HUNDRED-AND-FOUR
Headaches and Hysteria

Despite the heavy shutters, closed to keep the winter out, the distant boom and crack of magic made the Grand Master jump. Ever since that appalling evening when he and senior fellows were taken hostage to witness what turned out to be a WarLock hell bent on murder, any bang, any unaccustomed noise made him jump. After three sleepless nights he was not at his best, baggy eyed and bad tempered. A yellow haze had been drifting steadily inland for days bringing a stench with it and the bitter cold froze him to his bones.

He never understood the excitement caused by the Dragathon, 'except this year it's called Operation White or something or other...' he muttered pensively into his gold beaded beard. But still the same hysteria, the gambling of small fortunes on the outcome; Guilds and Lords and their entire families packed into their galleons to watch their heroic Dragon Lords. Three days or three-quarter moons of battle across the Highlands, pitching regiments, brigades, talons and wings against each other through mind blowing obstacles and tests. Anyone could win, soldier or Lord Sorcerer, dwarf or Dragon Lord: whoever was the bravest and boldest.

Whoever raised that antique crown of spun dragon-glass would garner fame and fortune everlasting, and glory for their regiment. Oh, how the commoners and peasants loved a good show! Worse, the Guild had to provide free food and drink for the City at the Dragonglass Ceremony at the end. Outside, he knew there would be long queues to use the Guild Observatory's telescopes, the only time the rabble were allowed. A noise penetrated his self-pity. People were screaming.

Bang!

The casements rattled, and a goblet fell, splashing bright red wine across the rug.

Blood! Spellskin nearly fainted.

Bang!

'What on earth is happening?' Mistress Winifred was back from whatever she had been doing on Dragon Isle, all very hush hush, and was making his life difficult again. She had been going around the Guild peering at and behind paintings and tapestries! Asking if any were in his Lodges, as if he had inappropriately appropriated them! Flinging open the casement, taking a lungful of air, she stepped out onto the balcony to an extraordinary sight. From all over the city, Imperials were taking off, and ignoring normal protocol, immediately speeding west towards Dragon Isle, leaving havoc in their wake.

'I think,' Winifred judged, 'you might want to see this Grand Master.'

Whoomph.... whoomph...

'What's happening?' Rumspell quavered plaintively, quite certain that he wouldn't want to see it whatever it was.

Whoomph.... whoomph...

'Come out and see...'

The balcony was shaking, and it wasn't Winifred's

weight. The Grand Master fearfully turned towards their dragon pads and flinched as an Imperial's talons gouged out chunks from one of the enamelled onion domes as it leapt from the middle dragon pads...its vast black belly going on forever overhead as it strove for height, before the down stroke knocked them all off their feet. Towers tumbled beneath talons. Dust and downforce swept down the wynds and closes. Carts were overturned. Citizens tumbled head over heels. Roofs were blown off.

In the distance, the familiar barrage had become more urgent, and contrails were crisscrossing the freezing air. A blizzard was blowing in from the sea, rolling down the loch at an alarming rate.

Rumpole Spellskin stared. Behind him he heard a gasp of horror. '*What* is *that*?'

He looked upwards to where two falling Imperials were locked in combat overhead. Even to his jaundiced eye it almost looked like it was for real. Sorcery flashed. *No! an Imperial and...* 'What in the Abyss is it fighting with?'

Dragonfire blazed brightly, their aerial battle leaving a twisted smoke trail that spiralled down towards his city. Another Imperial joined the fight; a snapped neck and then one of the creatures was dropping. They watched horrified as the great beast clipped a tower and then disappeared. The impact was huge, destroying surrounding houses and mansions, sending debris high into the air. A choking dust cloud billowed outwards. The window casements shattered, showering them with glass. Flimsy wooden houses exploded into matchsticks and their wreckage spewed up bodies before oily smoke obscured their view. Screams and cries carried thinly on the cold air.

'Poor souls,' the Grand Master husked, fervently hoping the creature had not landed on his newly rebuilt Guild Palace. The City was barely getting back to business, and now the SDS and their wretched games were out of control! 'Wh...wh...what on the One E-earth is that dreadful smell?'

Matron Winifred took a deep breath, bringing her several inches closer to the Grand Master. 'Notify the City Watch and call out the Guild Guards! Rumpole? Rumpole?' She took in the Grand Master's glakit expression and delivered a well-judged slap.

'You must summon all able-bodied citizens to our defence. Move, man! We are under attack!'

'N-no, it's just the w-wargames.' How his jaw still hurt!

'Open your eyes, man! That was no dragon! He's here! The WarLock has returned!'

Finally, the Guild bell began ringing. Out on the square panicking crowds streaming away from the impact turned towards the balcony, looking for guidance. Shoving the Grand Master kindly but firmly behind her, Matron Winifred pushed forwards, an unstoppable force.

Her voice boomed out across the square.

'To Arms! To Arms!' Winifred boomed, voice carrying clearly over the distant percussion roll of thunder.

'Fire the beacons! We are under attack. This is not a war game. The WarLock has returned. Bring your loved ones to the Guild and Palace for sanctuary. Men, woman and children who can lift a weapon, arm yourselves with anything you can find. Muster here or at the four Watch Towers! Go!'

She stepped into the hall. 'Open the armoury! We must arm ourselves and ride out to muster our defence!'

CHAPTER ONE-HUNDRED-AND-FIVE
Confusion Reigns

Tying his scarf about his face to shut out the smell, Root crawled out again.

Whump!

Earth and ice fountained up, the concussion blowing him off his feet for a second time as three uncloaked Imperials swept past in pursuit of another dark dragon like the carcass at his feet. Deafened, dazed as dirt and pebbles rained down on him, Root struggled to his feet. For a moment, he just stood there confused, trying to make sense of what he was seeing: it was raining dragons.

Dragon Isle had all but disappeared inside a swirling inferno as the maelstrom rained down death and destruction. Carnage filled the air: as far as the eye could see, open sky was a confusion of battling dragons leaving crisscrossed trails of smoke as they fought across the length and breadth of the glen.

As he looked east towards the Black Isle, hidden by mountains, black oily smoke was rising. He swung his sights westwards to where turbulent wind gusted and blew, revealing the largest Armada of ships Root had ever imagined. Half were alight, many sinking.

And then sound and understanding came together, driving him back against the mountains, covering his ears. This was no wargame. This was a battle, and people and dragons were dying in thousands. And he had no idea who was winning.

He had to warn Quenelda!

CHAPTER ONE-HUNDRED-AND-SIX
Hospital

The WarLock's position on high mountain ridgetops overlooking Dragon Isle was scorched and battered. Enormous cliffs below had fallen into the loch, as waves of sorcery sought the WarLock. Five of his battle captains arrayed in groups about him unleashed their own power.

Far below, taking heavy casualties the Army of the North had engaged with SDS Ice Brigades on the broken ice. In the sky his airwings were being decimated by the SDS.

Time to summon his dark dragon Queen and breach that final ward.

Waves of necrotic sorcery were slamming into Dragon Isle, breaking through its weakening defences. The whole island shook as huge sheered slabs wreathed in flame fell into the sea. The crown was scorched and cratered, the Academy's west wall had fallen. Cabals of battle mages were arrayed around the top of the cliffs and the Shard, but their numbers were steadily diminishing.

Deep within the Isle, in the hospital, Drumondir stood and took a deep breath, wiping her forehead with the back of her arm. It sounded like a hurricane had hit the Isle, the relentless assault had become a pounding heartbeat like her migraine. The hospital wing of Dragon Isle was crammed with the dead and dying. Casualties were coming in faster than the healers and surgeons could treat them, and many lay untended on pallets on the floor.

Some, tainted by the maelstrom, were beyond help. They had set up adjoining rooms, isolated by bubbles, to where healers, knowing they too may die, gave the dying what comfort they could.

CHAPTER ONE-HUNDRED-AND-SEVEN
The Labyrinth

Root was cautiously scouting well ahead of his talon, no longer certain if there would be BoneCrackers or any SDS left alive at the Sentinels.

'Our position is here?' Quenelda had pointed, golden eyes gleaming in the dark, lighting the map.

Root nodded.

Quenelda took a deep breath, drawing on her other self for guidance; the lives of the Juveniles rested on her decision.

'Root, scout ahead. If the SDS still hold the heights, we take refuge there and join the fight. Otherwise, we withdraw and retreat towards the Black Isle and our nearest rendezvous with Guy and Tangnost.'

Sssssssssssssssssssssss...

There was a strange ghostly whispering, the faintest glow in the dark ahead. Root instinctively dropped to the ground. And then the smell hit him. If anyone knew what a real hobgoblin smelt like it was Root. He had seen them at close quarters as a child. Smelt them at close quarters as an esquire.

His heart leapt in his throat, memories of his father flashing through his mind. The King, then SDS commander, had told him how his father, a scout for the Howling Glen had saved the regiment; how Bark and his mount had given their lives to warn the regiment that hobgoblins had found a way through the mountains. It was happening all over again! The hobgoblins were trying to flank the SDS so that they could fall on the unsuspecting Black Isle.

'Fa, watch over me...' he whispered.

He flicked down his special night sights and swung his head then froze. He arrowed in then out again as the crawling mass continued their inexorable approach. Softly, silently, he worked his way backwards and ran, his soft soled boots not making a sound.

CHAPTER ONE-HUNDRED-AND-EIGHT
Hold the Line!

'SitRep?'

'Hobgoblins in the Mammoth Cave,' Root reported for Quenelda's ears only. 'Real hobgoblins, not Bone-Crackers.'

Quenelda did not doubt him. 'How many?' She called Fergus over.

'Tens and tens of thousands,' Root shook his head. 'They covered every handspan of the sides and roof. Thick as maggots on a carcass.'

'How long till they get here? '

'At least a quarter bell...I came down a chimney. I think they may be trying to flank Dragon Isle. But Quenelda,' Root raised his night sights, his gaze intent with meaning. 'How?' He said softly. 'How could they know there was a way through? I only discovered it two moons ago.'

'I know, but not now. Now we must stop them. We can ask questions later. Right. Where? Where can we hold them?'

They struck a precious flare, scanning through Root's maps and notes, discarding them until... 'Here,' Root pointed. 'This is what you are looking for. It's perfect. It doesn't matter how many ways they come from the west, they have to come through this cave into this bottle-neck...The Hangman's Noose...'

'Go now! Find Tangnost and Guy and get our BoneCrackers in here in support!'

'I can't leave you!'

'Root, it must be you. No one else has the instinct you have. We'd get lost and die. We can hold the line,' she said confidently, nodding at Fergus who was looking frightened. 'If they break through they'll fall on the Black Isle and it will be carnage.'

'But we've taken three days to get this far!' Fergus argued, panic tinging his voice. 'At least three days. How can you get back in time?'

'Yes,' Root agreed quietly, 'but that was with sabre-tooths. I will be far swifter alone. And you're forgetting. Tangnost and Guy were moving forwards each day to support us. Expect the unexpected? Remember? We'll be back in no time at all.'

'What if you get lost?'

'Fergus,' Root put a hand on his friend's shoulder. 'I won't fail. I promise I will bring Tangnost. You must help Quenelda now. You have to hold on till we arrive.' Quenelda and Root hugged.

'Be safe!'

'Stay alive.'

Root turned and disappeared back into the darkness.

Quenelda turned to her talon. They weren't ready for this: she had to give them confidence. Leadership. 'Listen up,' she said quietly, leaping onto Two Gulps' back. 'There are hobgoblins coming our way. Root has rushed to rendezvous with Phoenix and will return with our BoneCrackers.'

There was a rustle of anticipation: they did not know their danger yet. To them it was still a battlegame.

'Marines? The Ice Bears?' someone asked. 'We're

ready for them.'

That garnered a cheer.

'No,' Quenelda shook her head. 'These *are* real hobgoblins.'

'What?'

'In the glen?

'How can they be in the glen?

'We'll be overrun in a heartbeat.'

'We can't fight hobgoblins yet!'

'We don't have any supporting troops.'

Fear was infectious. Panic was taking the talon. They were all talking at once, raw terror overwhelming their training.

'Slow down,' Quenelda's calm voice cut through the babble effortlessly, her eyes aglow in the dark as wings shivered down her back. She felt alive. Strong. Alight. For the first time, everything in her life was drawing together in this one moment to save her talon, her home, her people. This was why she was a Dragon Whisperer. And she had freely chosen it. There was sudden breathless silence as they saw her wings unfurl and spread...gold and white motes sparkling about her like an aura. Her joy calmed them, her Dragon Whisperer's strength held them silent.

'The WarLock King is here. He has attacked the Sorcerers Glen.' She frowned, uncertain. Root had made no mention of aerial battles when he reported back to her. She let it go, she had to remain focused. 'We have no idea how the battle is going, all we can do is deal with the challenge in front of us. I believe this banner heading our way is intended to attack the Black Isle. And that,' she paused, 'is why we must hold the line here and now. Prevent as many of them as we can from encircling Dragon Isle and reaching our homes.'

'My family's there!'

'Mine too.'

'Which,' Quenelda said calmly. 'Is why we must hold them, until Root returns with help. We have the best scout in the SDS. Guy and Tangnost are waiting for our call, they will be here in no time at all.

They were nodding.

'This is what we trained for,' Two Gulps reared up, talons flailing the air, he could smell hated hobgoblins. Quenelda grinned and nodded towards her sabretooth. 'This is what *he* trained for! This is what *you* trained for! Half of you saw action in the Brimstones. This is no different. Not if we put all our training into practice.'

'How? How can a talon hold a banner?' Dougal asked.

'We are falling back to Hangman's Noose. Every tunnel for leagues up and down feeds into this one point. They cannot get past us if we hold this passageway.' She picked up the flare. 'Calmly, one at a time, see what I mean then mount up stat!' She reached out to their dragons.

Two Gulps, brothers and sisters. Follow me. Our enemy is here. We must stop them...

A battle? You could fear their eagerness. *The slimy soft skins?*

A battle. Your two-leg mates, they are young and afraid. You must protect them...and all that we have learnt together, all those exercises we learnt together. We are going to need them now…

'Your dragons know what is needed of them. Put your trust in your bond…. Form ranks and move out. Silent as we go.'

CHAPTER ONE-HUNDRED-AND-NINE
The Sentinels have Fallen

Guy de Bessart turned to BearHugger as they banked over the Sentinels, shock on his young face. A red viper flag was flying amidst the rubble of the western Sentinel. Corpses of dragons and men lay on the churned bloody snow, thick as autumn leaves. Beyond, the pebbled shore was crammed with shallow troop carriers, and beyond that the masts and prows of burnt battlegalleons stuck out above the low tide. The fighting here had moved on, leaving no living thing behind, unlike the raging firestorm they had witnessed about Dragon Isle on their brief cloaked reconnaissance into the Glen, following the shocking message to all units from the Guardian. Worse, they had witnessed Dragon Isle's inner defences falling to the WarLock mounted on some fell creature from the Abyss.

'They've fallen! We must retreat to Dra-'

'No, Sir,' Tangnost's hand was firm on the young man's shoulder. 'One more Imperial won't matter to Dragon Isle either way. We look after our own: and the Juveniles are our own. They're our family and they are down there without our support: no Imperials no Bone-Crackers. We go in. We find them, and then we bring them home. We fight as one, Sir, and we die as one.'

Guy nodded, ashamed. 'Sorry. I wasn't thinking clearly, I just can't believe the Warlock is here. But the Labyrinth is huge. How do we find them without a scout?'

Tangnost glared at Root's maps scattered on the

navigator's empty seat, unwilling to admit he had never been comfortable reading them. He turned one about, that was better. Taking a deep breath he took a decision. 'We look here, Sir. We put half in here, and half here.'

'How can you be so certain?'

'Because Root said three days, and like his father before him, he is a natural scout. So, it's day four and they must be in this sector here. We approach them from both sides. To warn them, or if they've engaged, to support them. We forget everything else. Be prepared for a vector take off if we hit trouble.'

'Lift off, lift off, lift off...cloaking. Low and slow.'

'Gather round. We're going in...to find our Juveniles,' Tangnost briefed his BoneCrackers, grateful that he had insisted on ten fists of battle hardened veterans to back up the youngsters. 'Rapid insertion, cloaked, here and here to converge here. Fast roping, boys, no time to rappel. We need boots on the ground, stat. Our objective is to find and support or extract our missing troopers. Given what we saw at the Sentinels, we must assume there may be hostiles in the Labyrinth so be prepared for a fight. Search and rescue and retreat.'

Phoenix Firestorm swept low towards their insertion coordinates. At Guy's side Tangnost was frantic with worry, he should have insisted on their BoneCrackers going in as support.

A red flare burst against the whiteness.

'There, Bearhugger, there!' Guy's HUD vectored in and he gave Phoenix her head. Sweeping in, the mare stalled, raising a flurry of snow...Tangnost was running down her wing as she uncloaked...running to where broken cave entrances pocked the mountain's skirts.

'Root? Root?'

'Tangnost,' it was Root, dizzy with fatigue, stumbling up the scree, anxiety and relief on his face.

*Expect the unexpected...*a laugh... Tangnost shivered.

'Root? SitRep.'

'Hobgoblins, in the Labyrinth. A-at least a banner. The Juveniles are holding them at Hangman's Noose.' He pulled out a map, cursing as it ripped, then cast his eyes about trying to get his bearings. 'We're...here. They're holding here, where it's a bottleneck.'

'We have to find another way in... it's taken me three bells to reach you. Here,' Root pointed, 'we can rappel down here. The Chimney.'

Carabiners were locked onto studs that lined their Imperial's wing as Phoenix Firestorm swiftly lifted to the dark gash in the middle of the snow that was the Chimney. Armed and shielded, balanced against their Imperial's flanks, BoneCrackers let out their ropes ready to drop as the Imperial reached the right spot.

'Uncloaking.'

'Go! Go! Go!' Targe and axe slung across his back, gloves on to stop his hands taking rope burn, ignoring the pain of the old leg injury, Tangnost swiftly followed his men down onto the mountainside.

Phoenix Firestorm cloaked. Guy stood, staff in hand, gazing after them, desperately wanting to follow, but he had to be prepared for emergency extraction should they encounter hostiles.. He did not see another Imperial put down stealthily below him, nor a rune flare on Root's wychwood runes.

CHAPTER ONE-HUNDRED-AND-TEN
The Harbour ~ Aim at the Ships!

Turning her thistle dragon, eyes squinting into the white glare, Winifred looked at the brightly painted merchant galleons flying guild banners, bearing down at full sail towards the harbours, fleeing from the battle further up the glen. The thickening, sludgy porridge ice about the Isle was slowing them down.

'Lower the boom!' the Harbour Master ordered. Down at the harbour entrance the great chain winches were already being lowered as dale dragons were harnessed in reverse.

Friend or foe? Winifred scanned the sails. There was the sigil of the Apothecaries Guild, and there the golden boots of the Cobblers, the crossed spades over a coffin of the Surreptitious GraveDiggers Guild. Master Wright was there, she scrutinised another galleon. And that was Mistress Treadwell.

But... Winifred suspiciously narrowed her eyes. There was something wrong. No shouts. No children running all over the deck. No dragon kites and balloons. The sails were whipping all over the place to begin with, as if those who climbed the netting had no idea what they were doing. In fact, where were the crew?

'Your telescope' she demanded, hand out without looking, in a voice used to being obeyed instantly.

'Lady Mountjoy.' The Captain of the Watch meekly handed it over. No one could argue with that patrician tone.

The snow gusted. Winifred sucked in her breath and

blinked to clear her eyes, wiping the lens with a lacy handkerchief. The sails were rent in places and arrows pricked them and the prow. That was a body hanging off the ropes near the mizzen mast. Grappling irons were trailing from broken railings. These ships had already been in a battle; had they broken free or...

'Belay that order!' Winifred boomed. Their decks had been thronged with merchants and their families when they sailed. Now, apart from a handful of Guild Masters or Lords, the few men visible were wearing armour hidden under their cloaks.

'Fire on those ships!' she bellowed in a voice heard at the other side of the harbour. 'Raise the boom, raise the boom.'

'Lady?' The Captain of the Watch looked askance. 'Have you lost your mind?'

'Fire on them. Dragonfire! Can't you see, man? They've been captured by the enemy. Those are armed knights and men, not families.'

Hastily the order was given to a runner who sped off around the harbour walls. Glancing towards Winifred in armour, astride her hapless puffing dragon, the captain couldn't decide who he was more scared of.

The only hobgoblins Knuckle had seen so far were dead ones; mountains of them lying amidst churned ice turned green with their blood, as they swept past Dragon Isle at barely five hundred strides to avoid the battlemagic arcing above them. Those that had made it up onto the ice were being ruthlessly hunted down by animals that Knuckle had never seen: the armoured muckle hairy creatures with long curving tusks he had only heard stories of; they looked like long extinct cave paintings. Only...obviously, an awful lot of them weren't extinct, indeed were thriving thank you very much! Supported by frost dragons in the air and ice bears on their flanks, walls of marines were annihilating the hobgoblins. It did not bode well for the Black Prince's plan. Nonetheless, the first part had passed without a hitch. His heavy armoured dwarves had rappelled down and taken over fifty galleons with barely a fight. There was sporadic fighting, but once the Knucklebones captured their wives and children, most had capitulated without a fight.

Dropping anchor outside the harbour, Knuckle had waited for too long for the promised banners to arrive, by which time the air battle had reached the Black Isle. Even the dunderheads in the City Watch were alerted that something was wrong when a gorrangoch crashed to earth in the Boulevard Circle. He had given orders that prominent Lords and Guildsmen and women were to stand at the prow of each ship, so that the City let down its guard. But some interfering old baggage in antique armour on a thistle dragon had seen through his deception somehow, and was prancing about yelling orders, rallying the City Watch. Now they were being fired upon by catapults ranged about the battlements, and clearly, for a ragtag bunch of children and old folk, they had been practising.

The time for subterfuge was past, as an ampoule exploded on the prow of Knuckle's lead galleon, spraying some of his archers who ran for the gunwale and the sea. Once dragonfire took hold there was no putting it out.

They'd have to abandon ship and their hostages, leaving an armed guard, and take the city by storm instead.

'Fire!' Knuckle lowered his arm. A hail of arrows arced up from the forecastles towards the harbour walls. Winifred cringed as her inexperienced teams began to fumble ratcheting the catapult to reload as arrows fell amongst them. Their second ampoule missed, landing on the harbour wall, setting fire to bales of sugar and wool. There was an explosion as the Whisky Distillery warehouse to the west got hit. Next second the flames were reaching skyward and you could taste the malt on your tongue.

'Dragons teeth, man!' Winifred was unrelenting. 'Aim at the ships! They're big enough. 'You're way off beam, left! Left!'

'We're *trying*!' The Captain muttered well out of her hearing, as the petrified catapult crews fumbled to obey her imperious command. Already the boom chain was being frantically raised, as the next volley of arrows fell amongst the dale dragons and their handlers pulling it up.

Thunk, the catapult hit the cross beam. Fire blossomed as the ampoule smashed into a second galleon's mizzen mast and set the sails on fire. Winifred and the City Watch cheered. The galleons were within easy range now and crowded together. Soldiers were abandoning ship, leaping for the harbour wall. Fighting broke out as families seized their chance to escape. The enemy obviously had not expected any organised opposition...soon three galleons were ablaze as fire leapt from ship to ship, fanned by the hot gusting wind of battle magic.

Knuckle swore. 'Where are these damned hobgoblins?' As his soldiers jumped onto the broken ice, some fell into the water, and the surface broke into a frenzy of eating. The hobgoblins had arrived.

CHAPTER ONE-HUNDRED-AND-ELEVEN
Fire the Hole

'*Razorbacks...*' the trembling whisper was taken up. No one had ever seen one, but there was nothing else the horrifying spined creatures could be. Black rocks stuck with sea urchin spikes, infested with hobgoblins, began emerging out from the high tide to climb up the harbour ramp...

'There's a moat, Boss,' Gaff held a torch. Hobgoblins didn't like fire.

Knuckle's eyes crossed. 'Course there's a moat, you dunderhead! I helped dig it.'

'They're hiding behind the moat, Boss!'

'Well, of course they are, we're about to ram the harbour wall.' They had better hit that harbour wall before they sank, or they would be dinner. Flames were licking up the sails and burning patches falling to the deck. The dragons were getting skittish. In an explosion of breaking timber and boarding planks, troops were leaping off the commandeered galleons and racing around the harbour walls towards the City gates being shut in their faces. A portcullis crashed down with satisfying finality and the ramp was being raised.

Massed hobgoblins were leaping out of the water as Winifred and the City Guard abandoned the outer catapults and fell back behind the moat, leaving their dead behind them. Their enemies were rapidly approaching the Big Dig.

'Wait, wait!' the call was passed...'wait till they're in the moat. Pretend to flee.'

An elderly man fainted. If her breast plate had not held her upright, Mistress Winifred might have joined him, but she was made of sterner stuff. She snatched at a brand in the brazier and held it high.

Knuckle frowned as he raced along the wall. 'What does that old baggage think she's doing?'

'Trying to call for help, Boss.'

'Stand back! Stand back!' the Watch Captain warned. 'Hold, hold a little longer...' Hobgoblin warriors were now leaping into the ditch. A few were leaping at the wall, their suckers slipping on the icy stone. Winifred gulped.

'Hold, ready now.'

It seemed like a bell had passed before the ditches were full of armed men and dwarves and hobgoblins, and the order was finally given.

'Fire in the hole!'

Mistress Winifred wasn't familiar with the military term, but the word 'fire' was used. She swung her arm, almost throwing the brand backwards before seeing it arc over the outer city wall. All along the lower circle battlements flaming brands were cast. There was a massive *whoomph* that blew them off their feet as a fiery wall of flame rose, sucking in the air.

Hair smoking, brows and moustache gone, a sooty Winifred struggled to her feet, hand raised against the intense heat. Her thistle dragon had bolted. Thick tarry smoke was enveloping the Black Isle. It stank. The very stones were glowing, the air sucked of oxygen. Beyond, their attackers were trying to rally, trying to lead their panicked dragons from the wreckage of their ships. They'd stopped the hobgoblins, but it was the WarLock's men they now had to fear. She turned. Cheering died as the close packed crowds stood uncertainly. Then Winifred had an idea.

'Right,' she said grimly, dusting her sticky hands off, 'that's sorted those thugs and their hobgoblins for now. Let's turn our attention to rest of them.

'Come,' she beckoned. 'Quickly now.' As the unwashed masses crowded about her, Winifred laid out her plan. Toothless faces grinned and nodded. They could do that!

'Back to the Guild, boys!' she shouted at the City Guard. 'You! Give me your dragon!'

CHAPTER ONE-HUNDRED-AND-TWELVE
They Are Coming

Quenelda smiled, her eyes flaring gold in the dark, as she held up a flare and jumped onto a boulder. 'We are going to hold the line here!' The light danced over the rocky passage, letting them all see why she had chosen this place. 'Don't be afraid. You *are* ready for this. All your training has led to this moment. To being in the vanguard, unsupported. Your sabretooths are the best trained in the SDS. And you have a Dragon Whisperer!'

Her talon cheered loudly.

Quenelda's experienced inner memories assessed their tactical situation. 'So, tactical deployment: in the van, Arrow formation with me at the fore, supported by five lines of Shields at twenty strides, and behind, as the cavern widens, fifteen Starbursts of eight, in turn forming a larger starburst. Injured are to be taken within their protection. As we fall back you join those starbursts.

'Only those of you in the starburst and in reserve are mounted, and bowmen you are providing an inner circle of defence. Your mounts are going to protect their bond mates, should you need them: you all practised tactical mount and dismount at full stretch. Twenty of you will be held in reserve. Fergus, Calder, Ruraigh, Dufta, Guy, Jamie, Elliot, Grimbald, you command the starbursts. Healers into the centre of starbursts to treat the wounded, along with emergency survival packs.

'Use the flash bangs in dire need. They will kill hobgoblins, but you too could be injured or disorient-ated. Your mount's armour and scales can withstand them. They must not get out of this bottleneck until Tangnost and support arrives.'

Removing her call sign from Two Gulps' saddle, Quenelda planted it as her standard in the centre of the eight starbursts, themselves forming a defensive ring. 'If you are overrun, rally to my standard. If we fall, then use FireBall to break out, and retreat. Trust your sabretooth to find a way out. Deploy.'

'Sir! Yes, Sir!'

Quenelda supervised as the sabretooths were rapidly drawn up halfway down the tunnel, five ranks deep. Behind them at twenty strides a second and then a third, fourth and fifth. Without their riders. 'I will command them. This deployment will allow us to cover the roof and sides of the passageway without risking you. They are not expecting us,' she grinned then raised her voice.

'Expect the unexpected!'

'Expect the Unexpected!' They roared back with one voice.

Sssssssssssss
Sssssssssssssssssssssssssss
Sssssssssssssssssssssssssssssssssssssss

It was an unnerving sound as it echoed through the tunnels from every direction, growing louder by the heartbeat. A faint luminescence began to light up multiple tunnels and caverns.

At the apex of her talon Quenelda shivered as she fully became a dragon. An Imperial who was outstripping the juvenile of her youth, who had grown and now filled the greater part of the tunnel.

Quenelda stretched her wings to fill the passageway. Talons chinked on stone. Golden eyes watched as hobgoblins poured from tunnels and caves, and waited, and waited, and waited, and then white hot dragonfire blazed like a furnace.

It had begun.

CHAPTER ONE-HUNDRED-AND-THIRTEEN
Priceless Pointless Portraits

Winifred urged her thistle dragon up the winding streets of the Black Isle, as whispers spread from mouth to mouth, from circle to circle, rising from the Gutters to the Boulevard Circle ahead of her. When the press of cheering crowds slowed her down, she anxiously took to the air. It wouldn't do to let Knuckle Quarnack reach the Guild before her.

The Grand Master blinked at the amazing vision beating down through the roiling, spark-filled smoke suffocating the city. Mounted on a sooty dragon, in tartan plaid and a... generous... breast plate with a very big sword, someone put down on the empty lower Guild pads. He blinked again.

'Is that...Mistress Winifred down there? Surely not?'

He peered at the blackened face, half hidden by a ceremonial helmet. Equally sooty soldiers were putting down all about the Guild. Avoiding the rubble from the damaged dome, they formed an outer perimeter. Winifred was addressing the crowd, gesticulating towards the harbour and then the Guild. Commoners were nodding their heads, raising bricks and stones and rolling pins.

'W-Winifred? Where have you been?' He asked plaintively, as her dragon reached the broken balcony. 'What on Earth is happening? What have you been doing?'

'Dispatching hobgoblins and traitors!' Winifred

bellowed, as her thistle dragon staggered under her weight. 'We fired the moat, but it won't hold them back for long. Whittled down their numbers, though.' She dismounted, swinging a pair of sensible size eight winter boots through the air. The Grand Master ducked, slipped, and sat down in the slush with a squeal of dismay.

'Oh, do get up, man! The WarLock's thugs are heading our way. You there, get the Grand Master a dragon and a sword. We'll go down fighting.'

'A d-d-dragon? Err...my carriage?' he ventured hopefully... If we have to flee I'd-'

'Can't lead a battle from a carriage, man!'

'L-l-lead? B-battle? M-me?' He had had quite enough of those.

The great Guild bells were finally tolling. Summoning the citizens of the Black Isle to rally to their nearest City Watch tower. War... Fire... Foes....

'Stewards,' the sword was unsheathed with gusto, making those about her duck or lose their heads. The Grand Master wasn't quick enough. He screamed.

'My hat!'

'Oh, do get a grip Rumspell! It's only the tip! Round up all who can fight, every man, woman and child here in the Guild! The WarLock King has returned, and he is coming for us. Open the armoury! Go!' She clapped her hands. 'Go! We have to prepare our defence!'

'Come on, man,' she chided Rumspell as she stepped into the huge hall, 'don't just stand there!'

The Guild Guard and defenders stood to attention in a line, the latter arrayed in an odd assortment of mail and helmets and plate armour.

'We have no more shields, Mistress.'

Winifred looked thoughtfully at the countless oil paintings of past Grand Masters decorating the Squirrel Hall and the corkscrew staircase, and the gloomy corridor beyond, reaching back into the mists of time. All stoutly framed in oak. 'Well,' she looked them up and down, hands on hips. 'These might stop an arrow.' She summoned the butler who had arrived armed with boxes of wine to drop on heads. 'Rip them off the walls. Get them ready at every window.'

'B-b-but You can't use them,' Rumspell was horrified. 'they're priceless!'

'And they'll be pointless if we are all dead!' So saying, Winifred ripped the largest and most recent off the wall, bringing down a shower of plaster with it. Let's build some barricades, troops. She took the life-size oil painting and planted it firmly on the balcony. Then she poked the eyes out, peered down. Yes, that gave her a good view!

'And poke the eyes out so you can see what is happening,' she added.

'P-poke! Bu-ut! But t-that's mine! In my n-new robes!'

'Use this one to bar the entrance! Choose your weapon and take your positions.'

'W-w-weapons?'

'Well, you can throw a bottle, can't you?' Winifred heaved over a box and thrust a bottle in the Grand Master's hand.

Rumspell inspected the label. 'But b-b-but,' he blustered. 'You can't waste this! It's a Castle Wilderness.' A sly expression briefly lit his face. 'O-on the other h-hand. Yes. Give me the box. I'll take the alcove w-window.'

There was the pop of a cork and the sound of furtive glugging, followed by an appreciative belch.

'Would you like a goblet, Grand Master?', the butler enquired as he offered a pike from the walls.

CHAPTER ONE-HUNDRED-AND-FOURTEEN
The Knights of Chaos

'Let's have some fun boys!' Darcy's Knights of Chaos swept up over the city walls and through the smoke. As they decloaked they were greeted by wild celebrations below.

'The fools think we're here to save them,' Arthur DeCressy laughed wildly, waving back as he banked over the steeply rising city streets and markets.

The first the Black Islanders knew of their mistake was when spells exploded in their midst, raising thundering columns of dirt, stone, cobbles and bodies. Thickly crowded, fragile wooden-framed houses, stables, towers and bridges collapsed under their thunderous assault. Earth rose skyward in great pillars. Stones ripped through flesh and bone.

The air stank of burnt stone and magic. Dragon flame devoured entire streets, leaving runnels of flame in the dark below. Fires raged in half a hundred streets, thickening the air with swirling sparks and smoke. The crowds ebbed and flowed like the tide, seeking a way to safety. But there were none. Soon the screams of the wounded and dying filled the thunderous air. Revenge was sweet. Bright dragonfire engulfed the city.

CHAPTER ONE-HUNDRED-AND-FIFTEEN
Battle for the Battlements

Darcy put down with his standard bearer and twelve of his friends inside the third battlement, well away from the heat and smoke that still gusted around the moat of the spark filled City.

'Darcy? Darcy?' Simon ran over. His imperial had guided Darcy's down.

Darcy was slumped back. The fearsome helmet was gone, the young man's face drained of colour. A great sword cleaved the seat and rent his armour and chest, pinning the body to the spiked black seat.

'Gods! Darcy!' Simon reached forwards, then snatched his hand away. The uncanny armour was fluid. Green runes moved reforming, knitting. Tiny emerald motes sparked.

Darcy took a sudden breath, making them all jump back. He groaned. The armour, reformed, became hard. Darcy's eyes opened.

Simon stared. 'Darcy?'

His ribs were on fire, and yet the rise and fall of his chest had not faltered. Searing pain had swiftly died too. The hilt of a sword was still embedded in his seat. He pulled it out and stood. 'Gods, my ribs hurt.' Darcy looked up at the circle of horrified faces. 'Where in the abyss is Knuckle.'

Simon scanned the City with concern. Cloying smoke stank. The Royal Standard still flew above the Palace, and the Guild Standard above the Guild. The outer moat they had flown over was full of charred razorbacks and shrivelled hobgoblins, and galleons burnt to the water line clogged the harbour entrance. Even here the cleaved bodies of gorrangochs lay everywhere, but not a single Imperial.

'Darcy, look!'

Disquiet rippled through the WarLock's son. Taking the City should have been easy, and yet they were being denied. His father needed the Queen and hostages to show the soldiers and Dragon Lords of Dragon Isle. Without that threat to their Queen, their families, the SDS would surely fight to the last.

The streets were packed with citizens armed to the teeth with anything from rolling pins to homemade spears and black smith's hammers. They had fallen back when the Imperials put down, but an ugly murmur swept through the crowds at the sight of the infamous banner. Now they were just watching. There would be a reckoning with the peasants, but he had a Queen to capture first. If his father had not demanded hostages, they could torch them all and be done with it.

Knuckle knew he was not doing well, but he had been busy elsewhere and now had a priceless golden nugget of information for the Black Prince which would mitigate his failure. He reined in and dismounted, full of rage at that old baggage in her armour who had denied him the harbour, and now the Guild. Half his men had stormed the Palace drawbridge, hoping to trick them, pretending to be fleeing citizens, only to find themselves overwhelmed. But he wasn't going to tell that to Darcy. He would take the Guild first, then turn his attention to the

Queen.

'Well?'

'Lord Prince', Knuckle bowed. 'We have both Guild and Palace under siege.'

'Under siege? Whose army are defending them?'

Knuckle swore inwardly. 'The Guild and City Watches have defied us. The noble houses are rallying to them.'

'What? You have failed to take the Guild *or* the Palace? You have been held by a ragtag army of women, children and old men?'

'Sir Gharad and the Queen hold out in the castle.'

Darcy sneered. 'That old fossil? His day has long gone.'

Swallowing his rage at the injustice of it, Knuckle attempted to explain. 'The moat was filled with dragonfire, my Prince. Not water. Most of my men died crossing it as did a few hundred of the hobgoblins and razorbacks who attacked. The promised banner of hob-goblins has vanished. Only hundreds, mayhaps a few thousand arrived.'

Darcy paused, hand touching his armour. 'How can a banner vanish?' He glanced towards the Labyrinth. In this at least he could see for himself his Dragon Master was telling the truth. Surely not? A thread of fear uncoiled. Surely all his father's hobgoblin banners could not have died around Dragon Isle?

Seeing the hesitation, Knuckle decided it was time to reveal his intelligence. 'Your sister...' he groaned, inwardly kicking himself, 'the *King's* daughter, she is in the Labyrinth with a talon of sabretooths, the Juveniles. Perhaps that is why the hobgoblins have failed to break through.'

Darcy rose to the bait in a fury as his Dragon Master had intended.

'Quenelda? And a bunch of jumped up peasants?' It would take a regiment to hold a banner. Take the Guild and as many hostages as you can. If you can manage even that.'

Darcy turned to go, summoning his friends. Only twenty had survived Cawdor's attack. 'I have some prey to hunt in the Labyrinth.' He could not resist. 'Simon, take the Palace, the Court and the Queen before the SDS realise their families are in danger.'

Heads all turned to the west where the cacophony of battlemagic rose higher.

'When I return with my sister, we fly for my father with our hostages.'

CHAPTER ONE-HUNDRED-AND-SIXTEEN
Glory, Gold and Guild

Chastened by his stinging encounter with an ungrateful Darcy, Knuckle was in a filthy mood as he recklessly spurred his spitting adder into the burning City with his KnuckleBones, ahead of his foot soldiers, riding roughshod through the narrow winding streets, cursing the crowds who clogged them. He'd lost more of Darcy's men than he had owned up to at the harbour; over three hundred dead, with fifty badly injured, including Darcy's BoneBreakers scaling the walls.

That interfering old baggage was going to pay for humiliating him; she'd learn to her cost how he earned his nickname. But she and her City Guards had melted away into the dense crowds. The same crowds he gradually realised, who were now sullenly watching him and his men, barely moving aside as he beat them back with curses and the flat of his sword, cruelly spurring his armoured dragon forwards up the hill, careless of the injured left behind them.

A thread of unease uncoiled in his mind. The mere sight of the WarLock's and Darcy's banners usually cowed their enemies, let alone peasants. Only these crowds were pressing close: too damn close. Instead of being intimidated by armoured men, a threatening growl was growing louder about them. He regretted sending his vampires and harriers on ahead to begin attacking the Guild before they organised their defences. Ground dragons had their limitations, and being in the middle of a hostile crowd was one of them.

There was a crash behind. Reining in, Knuckle swore as a filled chamber pot broke on his helmet to shatter on the cobbles, splattering him and making his spitting adder rear up. Chamber pots began raining down from the overhanging houses, breaking limbs and heads, spooking the dragons. Bricks and hammers, pans and pots sang out a merry tune as they dinged helmets and armour. Unseating their riders, several dragons bolted. The crowds opened around them and then closed again.

Far behind and below in the City, Knuckle's four hundred foot soldiers slogged their way through the barrows and midden heaps, swearing when chamber pots were emptied out on their heads, or lumps of ice and mouldy vegetables were thrown; but whenever they turned, sword or pike in hand, there was no sign of their attackers. Then, at the rear of the column they began to disappear.

A vampire inexplicably flew into a suddenly raised clothes line. A soldier bringing up the rear was knocked out by a thrown turnip. A raised broom made one of the spitting adders rear up, dumping its rider in the midden heap where the rooting pigs delightedly tried to see if he was edible. One by one, Knuckle's troops were isolated and dragged down by the people, tied and dumped underfoot, to be tormented by the children. Others were less fortunate. Those that fought, died. Their numbers were few and the hostile crowd of tens of thousands, many driven from their homes far to the north, were restless for revenge.

Ropes suddenly pulled taut brought down dozens of dragons on the greasy cobbles and their riders were set upon. Commoners had never been allowed to ride dragons, but now young men and women vaulted onto their backs, and hanging on gamely, galloped towards the Guild, the crowds cheering them on their way.

Expecting to see the Guild under siege and his men rounding up prisoners, Knuckle and his remaining men finally broke through the Boulevard Circle into the square in front of the onion-domed Guild Halls, to be greeted by an uncanny silence. Churned snow, blood and bodies lay everywhere. Several burning brands giving off a sickly sweet cloying smoke lay abandoned on the ice. He looked up. The crowd was ominously silent. Unmoving.

A half dozen vampires were running loose, reins trailing, one dragging a body by the stirrup. Every attempt to capture them failed as the dragons bucked and kicked wildly.

'Boss?' Cider pointed.

There were vampires in the air, circling, chasing their tails, bucking, somersaulting!

'Boss, they ain't got no riders!'

'I can see that,' Knuckle replied through gritted teeth. 'Where in the abyss are they all?' he snapped. *You couldn't just lose fifty vampires and harriers.* 'Find them!'

A vampire landed on wobbly legs and rolled over on its back slobbering.

'What in the name of the Abyss is wrong with the vampires?'

Wheeling his dragon about he looked at the corpses heaped about the Guild and realised most of his missing men were in fact dead, but it looked like the extravagantly armoured Guild Guard had died with them. Well that should make things much easier.

'Righty ho, troops!' Winifred rallied the guildsmen and women, the merchants and bankers, the servants and remaining Guild and City soldiers to her. 'They're here, and the WarLock's Dragon Master is a killer. Into your defensive positions, weapons at the ready.'

Servants and scullions from the kitchens moved to the barred front doors, holding sheaves of dragon's bane at the ready. Braziers smouldered. They were mostly children, wide eyed, eager, thinking this was all a game.

Their Guard had done them proud in a short fierce battle, defying a wing of vampires and harriers. When one very young soldier had been thrown to his death from a vampire, the crowd had snapped.

Outraged, fearful, suddenly aware there weren't that many enemy dragons, the mob had turned on their attackers, overwhelming them by sheer numbers, pulling dragons and men to their death. In the end it was murder. Nonetheless, hundreds of Black Islanders also now lay injured and dying, the lucky ones safe inside, being tended by those members of the Honourable Healer's Guild, trapped when the attack began.

Winifred took a deep breath to steady herself, check the buckles of her breastplate and donned her husband's helmet, ramming it down firmly, wishing he were by her side. Hefting a heavy war mallet from the armoury wall, she went to mount her dragon, stabled in the Squirrel Hall on the Grand Master's floor, along with those vampires captured from the enemy.

'Mount up! Be ready to charge!' The Guild wouldn't be able to hold out for much longer, but every heartbeat they could deny the WarLock's men surely counted. They had one last surprise for Darcy's detested Dragon Master, and, by jingo, they would go down fighting!!

'Cider, Gaff, begin the attack.'

'Without air cover, Boss?' Dornoch asked.

'Yes, damn you. The SDS have long gone and their vaunted Guards are dead. They're a bunch of overfed, pampered merchants and tradesmen. How much trouble can they possibly give us? And the Black Prince wants his high-ranking hostages, including the Grand Master, just as soon as we can get them to Dragon Isle!'

'Right, Bo-' Cider's eyes crossed as he slid unconscious from his dragon with a bottle shaped imprint on his forehead.

'Oh, I say,' Winifred, slapped Rumspell heartily on the back. 'Jolly well aimed, Grand Master!'

Rumspell hiccupped happily and slithered off the window seat, still clutching his remaining bottle very tightly indeed. He wouldn't let go of this last one without a fight.

Knuckle lifted a broken shard to read the label ~ Castle Wilderness. Darcy's favourite at ten thousand golden guineas a bottle. Distractedly he read the label.

An elixir of magical proportions, it boasts a delectable dense ruby colour as well as an extraordinarily flamboyant bouquet of black fruits, brimstone, crushed diamonds, subtle oak and a hint of bad tempered steel. It smacks the palate with a thundering concoction of fizzy, juicy blue and black fruits, graphite shavings and a hint of spices. Minerality. Full-bodied, but very light with a finish that lasts many heartbeats, this is one of the most remarkable vintage wines conjured in the Seven Kingdoms.

'What utter twaddle!' Disgusted, Knuckle threw it away and kicked Cider bad temperedly to see if he was awake yet. To hell with Darcy's instructions, he'd take the weak Grand Master and masters of guilds and leagues as hostages, then loot their opulent halls before firing them. Lording it over everyone, time those overfed gaudy tradesmen learnt their true place: rebuilding their wretched City in chains like he had had to do.

'Bowmen to the fore,' he shouted. Darcy's short bow men were the best in the Kingdoms. Their crude bows were fashioned of rare wych elm and could pierce even heavy armour at close range.

'The rest of you get ready to ram the doors.'

Winifred stood back hastily from the casement.

'Portraits up!' she hollered. 'Move away from the windows. Snuff the lights.'

Footmen and scullions, maids and butlers heaved the huge portraits up behind the glass and hammered them firmly in place using priceless agar wood floor planks they had ripped up. The Grand Master had tried to stop them, but had been rounded on by everyone within hearing, and politely told to be quiet in no uncertain terms. Candelabra were lowered and put out.

'Boss, they've still got a lot of defenders,' Graff looked worried, and sure enough, as Knuckle looked up there were pale faces at every dark window and balcony, many arrayed in old fashioned armour with lifted swords and spears. Stupid!

'Fire!' Arrows sped towards their targets. Most swiftly found their mark, but the defenders didn't fall. They didn't even move!! Confused, the archers rapidly let fly again. Knuckle stared. These arrows could penetrate a handspan of oak. The defenders were thickly feathered. Taking a risk for a closer look he shouted.

'Stop, stop! You blithering idiots! Can't you see they're not real people! They're paintings!'

'Sorry, Boss. They looks right lifelike to me!'

Knuckle groaned. They had spent most of their arrows, some of which were now being returned. One of his men fell with an arrow in the thigh. This was rapidly degenerating into a farce. Knuckle willed his foot soldiers to catch up, so he could mount a full attack. Shouts and curses heralded the arrival of barely fifty...out of over four hundred! Then he noticed Cider had disappeared.

Furious, the Dragon Master turned on the crowds. Swearing, he drew his sword threateningly. The crowd were like a rising tide swallowing his army, and he and his men were relentlessly being pushed forward within range of the defender's missiles.

'Drive them back,' he ordered. Arrows whipped into the crowd as soldiers lay about them with their swords. There were screams and cries then a low hiss began growing in volume. There was a whisper of air and a thud and one of his soldiers fell. There was a muffled squawk. Spinning on his mailed boots Knuckle couldn't see Grit now, and the Black Islanders were closer still.

Time to end this.

If only Darcy had given him one Imperial, the rabble and Guild would already have been brought to heel...

'Break the doors down.'

Men were on the steps and mallets were raised when the doors swung viciously open, smashing his men between door and stone. Smoke billowed out as children rushed down the steps with torches of burning grass. What were they doing? He turned back, wrinkling his nose at the sickly herbal smell. Snorting at the top of the steps was an apparition from the Abyss itself.

Then one of the dragons at his side somersaulted, its rider screaming as he fell.... Disbelieving, Knuckle saw two crash into each other, whilst a third rolled on its back killing its rider. The sabretooths were all over the place.

A wonky bugle rang out. 'Chaaaaarge!'

The elderly thistle dragon did its best under the circumstances, but it tripped down the steps and once it had gained momentum on the icy cobbles it simply couldn't stop. With a sinking feeling, Knuckle tried to rein backwards as half a ton of dragon, armour, and an enraged Guild Mistress ploughed through his men towards him. He was lifted into the air and was scrabbling to his feet when a mailed fist attached to sixteen stone caught him on the jaw and lifted him off his feet again. Then it was stars and darkness to the fading sound of cheers.

'How dare you!' Winifred disentangled the stirrups and shakily stood, before helping the wobbly thistle dragon to its claws, and giving it a slap on its rump which knocked it over again. It landed on Knuckle who was just coming around.

'Righty ho!' Winifred turned towards the five Imperials circling the Palace. Smoke was rising but the royal standard still flew. 'Follow me, troops! We're needed at the Palace by the looks of things.'

CHAPTER ONE-HUNDRED-AND-SEVENTEEN
The Hangman's Noose

The Hangman's Noose was a furnace. Light flared and died back to darkness as nine defensive starburst circles flamed sunburst again and again and again. The croaks and undulating hobgoblin war cries were a rising crescendo of noise. The oily fishy stench of charred warriors clogged nostrils and clung to scales and skin, coating sabretooths and juveniles in grease. The weight of warriors falling from the sides and ceiling caused havoc as the Juveniles struggle to stay mounted, and on their feet. Within a bell hobgoblin dead almost blocked the full length of the passageway, but they were still coming through on the ceiling, relentlessly forcing Quenelda and her talon back into the wider cave. Darts and spears pricked the dead, smashed off stone and bone. Within two bells, the Juvenile starbursts were encircled.

Quenelda in Imperial form was everywhere, fiercely protecting her talon, her jaws, claws and tail dealing death, her incandescent flame keeping the full onslaught of their enemy at bay. Dwarfed by her Imperial, Two Gulps spun and flamed. When a sabretooth was too badly injured or died, he took their place until the starburst reformed. If a juvenile was isolated or surrounded, he was there to be mounted; curled within his protective armour he returned them to the safety of a circle.

By three bells the starbursts were still holding, but the number of wounded at their centre was growing, and nine had become six, falling back blow by blow. One by one as they retreated, they curled up within their sabretooths and rolled away from the press of hobgoblins into the safety of the starbursts. But it was exhausting. Quenelda, with scores of minor wounds was tiring, diminishing, despite her inner anxiety. Two Gulps had taken a dozen wounds. Fergus wiped the sweat running into his eyes as he used the last of the field dressings to bandage an ugly wound. They were still holding the line. How proud Quenelda was of them. But for how much longer?

'They're breaking through!'

'Plug that gap!'

'Lachlan's injured. Badly injured.'

'Whirlwind! Whirlwind!' A sabretooth pirouetted, driving the hobgoblins back as a besieged starburst held. *How much longer?* A fifth starburst collapsed as Fergus and three sabretooths joined another, fighting every finger of the way.

'SunBurst, SunBurst!'

Crack, crack! Crack, crack! Explosions bloomed outward in the roiling phosphorescent darkness. The hobgoblins screamed, scuttling and leaping away.

Deafened, exhausted, covered in soot and blood, soaked to the bone under their damaged armour, it took the Juveniles time to realise that help had arrived. There was the thunk of axes, the clash of shields, the growl of battle cries as the line of BoneCrackers began to steadily push their enemy back, shield wall and swords dealing death. And then the young troopers were surrounded by their commandos, weeping, embracing, shouting with sorrow and joy.

'Did we hold them?' In a breath Quenelda had changed back to a scaled young woman, blood riling from countless cuts soaking into her clothes.

Tangnost nodded, grinning, lifting her off her feet in a bear hug. 'You did! The Black Isle is holding! Without the hobgoblins, the WarLock's men are struggling.'

Then, as the medics and scale smiths arrived, so did Root, rappelling down, scanning for his friends. Quenelda ran to him, to where the wounded were being helped. 'We did it!' they hugged. 'We did it. The Juveniles held the line!'

'Fire in the hole!'

Boom...boom...

'Tunnel Rats.' Tangnost reassured them. 'They're collapsing the Labyrinth so there will be no route through ~ ever.'

Quenelda was crying with exhaustion, elation and anxiety, tears tracking down her dirty face. 'What's happening out there? I can feel the maelstrom and death, so many deaths.'

Tangnost's face instantly sobered, became guarded. 'The WarLock attacked...he unleashed his hobgoblin banners to take Dragon Isle by stealth, to bring the wards down before we realised what was happening. But you remember those new dragonfire mines the Guardian's pyromancers were so proud of? They were triggered and most of the hobgoblins were wiped out before they could even reach Dragon Isle. Those that escaped onto the ice are being wiped out by our Ice Brigades. He had a cloaked Armada in the Inner Sea, but our young Warden ambushed them instead, and his ships are burning.'

Root joined them, as the last hobgoblins were driven from the cavern.

'He then unleashed his Imperials, thinking to destroy us in the air and ice so he could let his armies besiege Dragon isle; so many it was like night coming down.'

'Our Imperials will not fight each other, so how can we stop them?'

'Because,' the Dragon Master hesitated, knowing the anguish his words would bring. 'They aren't Imperials anymore.' Tangnost's relief mingled with pity confused the exhausted and emotional young dragon whisperer.

'What?' she turned to Root. 'What do you mean they aren't Imperials anymore?'

'Oh, Quenelda,' Root shook his head at the memory of what he had seen. 'I'm so sorry,' he swallowed. 'I-I couldn't bear to tell you,' he took her bloodied trembling hands in his. 'His Imperials have been kissed, just like the Forsaken.'

'They can't cloak,' Tangnost added. 'By tormenting them, breaking them, the WarLock broke their magic too. Our Imperials, recognising their pain, killed their crew first out of revenge, then gave their kin a quick clean death.'

'Quenelda,' Root choked, couldn't speak for grief. 'They're, oh Quenelda, they were falling like rain out the sky.'

'Those strange thuds?'

Root nodded wordlessly. He was crying.

'Your father said we should look for the WarLock's mistake, and we found it,' Tangnost said grimly. 'The

Warlock thinks he can twist everything to darkness, but he is wrong.'

Quenelda's golden eyes dimmed almost to darkness. Rage crackled about her, sparks in the dark.

Boom... boom...

Quenelda's head whipped around towards the west. *Something isn't right...why do I feel a threat closing...is it the dark creature of my dreams?*

The clash of armour echoed down the passages.

Ignoring the sounds Tangnost paused, choosing his words. He put his hands on her shoulders, there was so much for the young woman to take in, but she was needed. 'Quenelda. Dragon Isle is under attack, not just by the WarLock, but by some fell sea creature he rides. It brings death to all. It dwarfs our Imperials.'

*Feeding.... feeding...*images of terror flashed through her mind...*feeding...* its song sang in her head. Its joy. 'A dark dragon Queen,' she shivered.

He frowned. 'You know? How?'

'I've felt its approach for moons...I think it's part dragon, so I heard its thoughts...but I didn't know what it was, where it was. It's been raised from the Abyss'

'She's been having nightmares about it,' Root was worried by his friend's deathly pallor, the grief. He turned to Two Gulps who restlessly snorted and reared up. 'What is it?' he tried to gentle the sabretooth. 'What's wrong, boy?'

Tangnost was still shocked. 'It's broken through the final ward and is destroying Dragon Isle. The Dragon Lords have combined under your father. Jakart is collapsing the coombs to prevent it going any further. The Guardian directs defence from the Core. But we are losing. The east flight cavern has already fallen into the sea, the harbours and forges collapsed. Much of the Academy and the north of the island was destroyed in the battle to breach our defences. The last ward fell. We are being driven back.' He shook his head. 'I never thought to see this day. I-'

'This foe is beyond them, I must fly to Dragon Isle and summon aid.' *I am not strong enough... Two Gulps come...*

'*But,*' Root ran after her, '*Quenelda, stop! Y-*'
There was a cold laugh and a flash of green lightning lashed across the cavern. The violence of the explosion threw them off their feet.

CHAPTER ONE-HUNDRED-AND-EIGHTEEN
A Fight is Coming

'Dragons teeth!' Tangnost grunted, spitting dust he found his feet, almost falling again over scorched rubble. It stank of battlemagic. He felt his head; blood was pouring from a wound above his ear, and he had an injury to his right shoulder.

'Quenelda? Root? Quenelda? Grimbold? Quick! Light me a torch!' Snatching it from the BoneCracker, he held it up and searched for them. The tunnels they had entered from were blocked. No sign of Quenelda or Root…or Two Gulps. *What happened?*

'SitRep? Casualties? Call in.'

Darcy, he'd swear that laugh was Darcy. Tangnost's thoughts raced. *If he captures Quenelda, he'll take her to his father.* He had to get back to Guy; Phoenix Firestorm had to intercept Darcy. *But how had Darcy got past the sentries when gorrangochs could not cloak?*

'Sir,' Grimbold reported in. 'Five dead and two with broken legs or arms. Two missing. Several with burns.'

Darcy must have Imperials. And at least one was out there waiting for the Black Prince, maybe all the Knights of Chaos were cloaked out there. He had to call Guy for a combat extraction. Let other brigades arriving clear the tunnels.

'Grimbold! I think that was the Black Prince. He is trying to capture Quenelda. Summon the men. We must find our way back to Phoenix and prevent her being taken to the WarLock King. Silent now. There is at least one hostile Imperial out there, perhaps all the Knights of

Chaos.' He paused. 'A fight is coming...' he smiled grimly, hefting his axe. 'Move out, sergeant, swiftly now.'

CHAPTER ONE-HUNDRED-AND-NINETEEN
Run Like the Wind

Quenelda lay on the ground, head ringing. Boulders rattled down. Sounds were muted. She coughed, choking on the dust. It was pitch black. 'Tangnost? Anyone?'

'Quenelda? Quenelda?'

'Root? What's happened?' She touched her head, blood came away. Her ears hurt.

Root pulled down his night sights to light the absolute darkness. More boulders shifted from the huge pile beside them. They scrabbled backwards as a head appeared, boulder sitting on top of it. A pair of confused gold eyes blinked open.

'It's Two Gulps!' Root laughed weakly, with relief.

'What happened?'

'I don't know…'

'Here, Two Gulps. Root, we need to find a way out. I *must* return to Dragon Isle. My talon's safe in Tangnost's hands.'

'Leave it to the Guardian and his battlemages. You're exhausted. Your father will know what to do.'

'No, he won't. This is a foe beyond them! They don't know what they are fighting, or how to fight it! It was spawned in the Abyss!'

They jumped as dust rained down from the cavern ceiling.

'Quenelda, you don't have to go,' Root laid a retraining hand on the stirrup as she mounted. 'Please. You're not ready for this. If battlemages can't stop this creature, what chance do you have?'

'It's what I am here for, isn't it?' she smiled oddly, torn between bitterness and pride. 'What I was born to do? I was given back my gift for a purpose.'

'But not yet! Not today!'

'Root, if he gets into the HeartRock, nothing will be able to stop him. Don't you understand. There will be no tomorrow. Can you get us out of here?'

Sadly, he nodded. 'Yes,' he scanned the cave with his night sights. 'I've scouted many passages, but Quenelda, I've never been through them with a sabretooth yet. I don't know if Two Gulps can do it.'

'We have no choice.'

Suddenly she flinched backwards as an arrow shattered on the rock. At the same time, light flared at the distant side of the tumbled cave. An armoured knight had entered, troops crowding about him.

'So, sister,' the cruel voice mocked. He had her trapped this time. 'Shall we leave BearHugger to his hobgoblins? So easy, cloaked, following him; too busy looking for you to look behind! Careless.

'Take her alive. Kill the dragon and him.'

Men-at-arms were pouring into the cave, lighting it up with burning brands. Spitting adders, light on their feet, were not far behind. And sabretooths. She could sense them.

There was a groan...

'Well, well, well, what do we have here? One of your friends? Pull him out.'

Fergus screamed as he was dragged out, struggling all the way. 'My arm's broken.'

'Fergus? They've got Fergus!'

Root met Quenelda's horrified gaze.

'You can't, Quenelda. You can't. We must leave him. Fly, Quenelda!'

'Come and get him, little sister. The SDS don't leave anyone behind. Little sister? He's squealing now. Wait till my father has him!'

Vaulting on Two Gulps, tears were streaking down Quenelda's face.

'Quenelda!' Fergus cried. 'Root! Don't leave me!'

How could he possibly know where I was? She was already on Two Gulps. *How could he know?* 'Root!'

Thanking his lucky stars that the talon had been training basic cavalry mount and dismount at full gallop, Root leapt up in one swift practised movement as two Gulp's hind legs bunched, and the powerful young sabretooth leapt forward and away from the hail of arrows. 'Go! Go! I'll guide you!'

'Run, Two Gulps, run like the wind!'

'You can't escape, sister,' Darcy shouted, voice magnified. 'There is nowhere for you to run. My father takes Dragon Isle as we speak,' Darcy laughed, turning to his companions. 'My men and the Knights of Chaos take the Black Isle. You have nowhere to go. Hunt her down bring her to me. Bring my sabretooth! My father wants her by the time he reaches the HeartRock.'

Two Gulps leapt away into darkness as more arrows ricocheted off boulders, one grazing his flank and breaking a scale. There were cries of anger and a scream as a pursuing sabretooth behind them slipped backwards on the treacherous scree, cannoning into Darcy's foot soldiers, crushing them. Highly trained, Two Gulps swiftly outstretched those in pursuit, his long powerful hind legs propelling them effortlessly forwards.

'Straight ahead!' Root's night sights were slipping. 'One hundred strides! Rising up over the river!'

Root caught a glimpse of a knot of sabretooths off to their left through glittering stalactites and arches...but they were struggling in the dark, their torches creating caves of light that gave no warning of danger. Darcy obviously didn't believe his sister was a dragon whisperer, or he would have known she could see as well in the dark as Two Gulps.

'Ouff!' The chasing sabretooth's riders smacked into a stalactite that plucked them both from the saddle as their sabretooth continued without them, before veering down a side passageway, followed by several close behind despite their riders trying to turn them.

'Turn right, head down...' Leaning flat over their mount, they clattered through a narrow passage, Root's helmet sparking as it scraped along.

'Huge drop twelve paces ahead,' and they were already there as two Gulps spread his wings to cushion their fall. Shouts echoed through the tunnels behind them. Light flickered behind followed by a crash, consternation and curses. A tendril of green reached out then faded.

'Tunnel on the left, twenty strides,' Root shouted, searching the darkness up ahead... 'immediately downhill, rough terrain,' as Quenelda reined Two Gulps in to negotiate the boulder-strewn floor. It was painfully slow work, they could not afford broken bones. No sign of Darcy's troops yet, but you could hear their shouts as they advanced.

'It's a dead end!'

Two Gulps pivoted. Cursing, Root pulled his map from his navigator's thigh pocket, then thrust it back and closed his eyes. *Fa, guide me!* Trusting to instinct he swiftly took his bearings.

'Back up, back up…to the last fork and take the right.' There was a glint of steel ahead. 'FireBall, FireBall!' she warned Root.

Smoothly slipping about the saddle, next second the pair were curled within a flaming furious sabretooth. There were screams, two or three massive jolts that were swiftly cut off as they regained the fork. Swinging back into the saddle, Two Gulps swiftly rose up, and was away. But even the young sabretooth was beginning to tire. He too had fought a long battle today and a wound in his leg was beginning to burn.

'Left! Left, Left! Slow!' Root shouted as he lowered his helmet night eye. They raced for the league long portal that led to the longest river cave system in the Labyrinth, and one of the most hazardous. Part of Quenelda was aware the dragons behind were struggling to keep up. *Slow down, my brothers and sisters…*

'Hole in the ground. Jump!' Root shouted. 'Heads down, side saddle,' he commanded. He needn't have worried. Two Gulps was leaping over the dark gulf. Already airborne as Root flung himself to one side, narrowly missing a stalactite himself.

He flinched as an arrow thunked into the saddle and

two more broke against the rock face, and they were pulling away again. They plunged through a freezing flat riverbed and into the Spirit Bear Mountain where the immensity of the Mountain River Cave swallowed the light, so that it was like a starless night overhead. Eight hundred strides at its widest, the distant roof three hundred strides, even Root's night eye could not penetrate its depths. 'One thousand strides until ground rises... Nearly there!' The watercourse was becoming increasingly hazardous. Twisted and gnarled as tree roots, it led them down and down.

There was a chink and a curse to their left as a rider clipped a stalagmite, and the click of talon on stone. Then the thundering subterranean snowmelt river from the unseen peaks high above vibrated through the rock, carving channels as they sought a way down to the loch. The thunder of their passage made it impossible to hear anything as Two Gulps dodged boulders left and right and left again. Now they were in a tributary of the old watercourse. The passage ceiling was low and smoothed by eons of water rushing through it, so low Quenelda reined Two Gulps in to a walk. Leaning forwards, their helmets almost brushed its surface, and then a drop.

'We've made it!'

Traversing a steep upwards slope, they could see faint light up ahead, and as they bumped and jostled icicles hung about the edges of the huge skylight, the pale light of the rising moons guided them.

Two Gulps, I must fly with all haste...

Somersaulting off Two Gulps, even as she stepped forwards the young woman was changing into a dragon.

With one of the largest leaps Root had ever seen, Two Gulps jumped, carrying them both high onto her wings as the Imperial that was Quenelda was on the rise and cloaking.

CHAPTER ONE-HUNDRED-AND-TWENTY
She's Not Ready

Quenelda, Root and Two Gulps swept up and over the mountains into the Sorcerers Glen, and into a raging firestorm. Without saddle or bridle to hang onto, it was a frightening bumpy ride, bringing back unwelcome memories for Root of when he first learnt to fly. Quenelda was thrown about by sorcerous explosions and pockets of hot air rising from countless fires. Flashes lit up Dragon Isle through the smoke, what was left of it. Huge parts of the island had fallen away into the sea as the dragon that was Quenelda banked, aghast at the destruction. Bursts of battlemagic lit up the cliffs. But the chill of the Abyss held every living thing in its frozen grip as the maelstrom burrowed into Dragon Isle.

I'm going to land on the top of the Isle. It's too dangerous anywhere else...

The scene about the Academy was confusing: a whirl storm of tumbling towers, explosions, and magic that arced through the approaching night. Dragon pads lay shattered and broken, the ground pocked with craters. Fires raged unchecked. The air was thick with smoke and cinders. Dead gorrangochs lay everywhere. Circling what remained of the crown of Dragon Isle, Quenelda banked between broken towers and put down on the rubble strewn Cauldron, where scores of wounded dragons and troops were being tended at field stations.

Feeding...feeding.... the joy...

Ragged survivors covered in dirt and blood lay or sat, whilst healers and friends tried to save their lives; the wreckage of brigades and talons still fighting below on the ice. There was a flash of light and a dull boom, followed within moments by a second and a third as AirWings of the Faculty Guard retook the upper battlements.

The dragon that was Quenelda shivered.

Quenelda what's wrong? Root missed nothing.

It's below. It makes me sick.

Your dark dragon?

Yes...she brings the black death...the dark dragon of my dreams...

Feeding...oh so sweet....

When the Imperial that was Quenelda turned into the King's daughter, the soldiers and knights nearby cheered. Soon they were surrounded by wounded soldiers and academics, commandos and rangers and marines, all talking, all reaching out, all believing they were saved.

'Dancing with Dragons, where have you been?' one called out joyously.

'Dancing with Dragons, the WarLock's creature is killing everyone. My sons are dead. They froze...' the soldier wept.

'Lady, they've been searching for you since the attack began!'

But other faces were not so kind, and neither were their words.

'Why haven't you joined the fighting?'

'My friend died because you weren't here!'

Another tremor ran through the island. Another section of the cliffs broke away to crash down into the loch, taking its defenders with it.

'Dancing with Dragons, you must fly, or we're all dead. The SDS will fall.'

'Save us, Lady.'

'Why won't you fight? You're not a real dragon whisperer, are you?'

'Fool, you just saw with your own eyes!'

'He rides a fell creature from the deeps. It freezes everything. Why aren't you fighting it?'

The mood was turning ugly. Two Gulps smoked and turned, driving them back.

'She's not ready,' Root protested again as Quenelda shivered: she looked sick. 'We need to retreat. She's already fought one battle. She isn't ready for another! She's injured. He's a WarLock. The Guardian and his Faculty will beat him. The King and his Dragon Lords will bring him down.'

But desperation made them deaf. Dragon Isle had never fallen, not since it was raised by Son of the Morning Star. Yet their island was breached. If Dancing with Dragons would but rise and fight, they could still win.

I'm leaving Two Gulps with you, so you can look after each other...

But Quenelda... Root looked at the circle of exhausted, accusing and expectant faces. 'No!' *If you must go, let us go with you!*

I won't be on my own. Storm and Papa are down there, and the Guardian... I will seek help from the HeartRock... from my brothers and sisters.... I will not go into battle alone... I promise... Look...

More and more Imperials were putting down, Dragon Lords dismounting. *More help is arriving, arriving every heartbeat...battlemages are joining the fight all over Dragon Isle...*

Earth gouted up as flaming balls tore through a field hospital. To a chorus of screams, the growing crowd about them pushed and trampled in their haste to get away.

But then why go?

I must - and you can't help... she added gently. *No one can. Stay here. I will fight better knowing you are safe...*

They hugged. 'Stay safe,' he whispered. 'Promise me you'll stay safe?'

I promise... and then with a running leap as soldiers scattered out of her way, a young Imperial took off over the cliffs and disappeared.

Root pressed his head to Two Gulps and whispered. *'We can't let her fight on her own, boy. Come on.'*

CHAPTER ONE-HUNDRED-AND-TWENTY-ONE
Defend the Queen

'Defenders to the walls! Man your posts!'

Watching from the top of the Winter Tower in the castle, as sorcery rained down indiscriminately, devastating his city, Sir Gharad Mowbray's face was grim as he identified the standards fluttering from the approaching Imperials.

'The Knights of Chaos!' Never had he dreamt they would attack the City that had nurtured them. Where was Darcy? Then the outer battlements lit up as spells hit the wards cast by the Guardian and the King.

'Captain, see to our defences and get our vampires in the air. Fire the braziers. You, Sir Jamie,' he turned to the Captain of the Queen's Guard. Take Her Majesty to the White Tower. You know what to do if the castle falls.'

'Sirs, my Lords,' he addressed the elderly knights and Lords, mages or battlemages one and all about the table in the Great Hall. 'Defend the Castle and the Queen. Dragon Isle cannot help us. We are on our own.'

'Lord Constable, Your Grace.' Sir Jamie had turned. 'Look! An Imperial flying the royal standard is attacking the others!'

The Queen smiled. 'We are not entirely without our shining knights!'

CHAPTER ONE-HUNDRED-AND-TWENTY-TWO
The Forsaken

'Kill,' the dreaded command finally came as Imperials put down on the crowded pentangle in front of the palace, crushing countless people beneath their massive claws. Armelia struggled to remain conscious, was feeling drowsy, warm; wanted only to sink into the snow and sleep.

'Kill all who oppose you. Take the castle. Only the Queen must not be harmed.'

Weak with hunger, cold and cramp, Armelia and Findibar fearfully stood on numbed legs, staggering, stumbling, starved, and took in her surroundings. The smoke. The rubble. The thump of catapults. The flashes of sorcery. It was the Royal Palace! The place she had dreamt of returning to these past moons. What a stupid plan! Trembling, dazed, Armelia tripped and Findibar clumsily grabbed her as the Forsaken shambled forwards. She had helped no one with her foolishness, rewarding Findibar's loyalty with certain death on a battlefield at the hands of the very ones who loved them. She had no strength even to shout, no tears left to shed. They truly were forsaken.

Herded forward by whips, taking whatever weapon was thrust into their hands, the half dead stumbled down the Imperial's wings and into the trampled bloodied snow of the Outer Bailey, coughing and dying in a whirlwind of smoke and arrows.

CHAPTER ONE-HUNDRED-AND-TWENTY-THREE
The Queen!

'Combat extraction! Combat extraction…hostiles nearby.

The runes on his vambrace counted down…Phoenix Firsstorm was at the exact same coordinates.

Tangnost emerged with five score BoneCrackers and was running up Phoenix Firestorm's cloaked wing when he saw an Imperial in the distance, bearing a sabretooth and a young scout swiftly rising up and away over the lowest pass of the mountains towards Dragon Isle. *Thank the Gods*, Quenelda had escaped her brother, to his great relief.

Wings already warmed up, recloaking, Guy was gently lifting Phoenix Firestorm into the air when Tangnost's spyglass found Darcy's Imperial on the ground ~ uncloaked! ~ three thousand strides to the west of their position. Wherever his friends were, they weren't waiting for their Black Prince. With sinking heart, Tangnost knew where they would be, where Darcy would go the moment he returned, furious without his sister. Quenelda was lost to both brother and mentor for now; the Dragon Master could no longer protect her. But he could protect her mother or die trying.

'The Palace, Guy,' he ordered. 'Vertical ascent, free rein!'

'Acknowledged,' Guy urged the mare into a vertical climb, only deployed in gravest need.

CHAPTER ONE-HUNDRED-AND-TWENTY-FOUR
The Time and Hour Are Upon Us

Sir Gharad deflected a wave of sorcery, throwing up a shield to protect his troops. Wildly undisciplined, the Knights of Chaos had failed to breach the sophisticated wards, but the castle and its elderly defenders could not hold off over twenty Imperials. Two had been downed by the unidentified Imperial flying the royal standard which had fought with reckless bravery, trying to protect the citizens, but they were being overwhelmed. The outer curtain walls were badly damaged as four Imperials had put down, crushing stone and men to mangled dust and rubble, and the enemy had poured through the gaps. Pulses and fireballs rained down, thudding into stone, lighting up the wards in the growing twilight.

The Forsaken, driven forwards by Darcy's brutal men-at-arms and archers into the arms of their loved ones, battled the royal garrison, forcing them back towards the moat. The vampires of the Queen's Flight had been valiantly brave in their defence, but one by one had swiftly fallen to the Imperials' might. With an ominous rumble one of the Gate Towers fell. Putting down, bringing the inner bailey wall down, the Knights of Chaos themselves mounted on sabretooths, supported by their veteran troops, were streaming down their Imperials' wings for the final assault, when many things happened at once.

A second Imperial flying the royal standard and the golden dragon banner of their Dragon Whisperer decloaked directly overhead, immediately engaging with the Knights of Chaos who were attacking the crowds. Battlemagic coruscated overhead like a lightning storm, diverting attention from the crowds.

The Queen, refusing her Constable's pleas, abandoned the beleaguered Keep and flew out on gentle Chasing the Stars, surrounded by Sir Gharad and her remaining Lords and knights, to rally the people, just as Winifred, at the head of her victorious Guild 'army' arrived to swell their numbers. Cheers of loud affection greeted their arrival. Standing in her stirrups so all could hear her, taking her helmet off so they could see her face, Caitlin appealed to her peoples, to the Black Islanders and all those refugees from the north whose loved ones had been taken for the mines, as galley slaves, or who were kissed by the Abyss.

'My loving peoples! We see the endless night of the WarLock approaching. We hear his assault over the loch. Soon now, we will meet him face-to-face. He thinks to divide us, but he will never do so again, for we are one people and one Realm. I am resolved, in the midst and heat of the battle, to live or die amongst you all. While we stand together, the WarLock shall not win. Let him come with the armies of the Abyss; they will not pass! And when this day of battle is ended, we shall meet again across the bridge, or on the field of victory.'

Men, women and children, dwarves, sorcerers, trolls, goblins and gnomes cheered her loudly. Brandishing any weapon they could find, or none at all save fist and boot, the citizens rose up against their enemy as one people. The crowds surged about the castle, across the outer defences and broken battlements, to fight the Knights of Chaos. Seeing their danger, the young knights unleashed a fiery death, driving them back as buglers recalled their troops from the Palace. Snapping up hundreds in their lethal maws, flaming to scour the ground about them, two Imperials managed to get airborne. Swooping low they unleashed battlemagic into the crowds when the two royal Imperials engaged them, forcing them skywards.

But it was not until eight Imperials of the Royal Attack Squadron uncloaked above the castle and fell on their enemies that the tide of the battle turned. Hostile surviving Imperials were forced to land. Dragging the soldiers down, the crowds turned on Darcy's hated and reviled knights. Dying in their droves, sacrificing themselves as battle magic was wielded with reckless abandon against their pots and knives and hammers, they washed over the Imperials on the ground like an incoming spring tide breaking over the rocks. One by one the peoples of the Black Isle brought Darcy's young Knights of Chaos down.

CHAPTER ONE-HUNDRED-AND-TWENTY-FIVE
Lost Her!

'Lost her!' The two words pounded like a heartbeat in his head. In a fury Darcy spurred his Imperial towards the palace on the peak of the Black Isle, oblivious to the battles raging the length of the glen. Oblivious as to who was winning...or losing, focused only on his father's need for a Queen when he came to claim the throne of the Seven Kingdoms. It never entered his thinking once that, despite the decimation of the hobgoblins and the gorrangochs, his father could possibly lose. The WarLock King and his dark dragon Queen would claim all, and his Knights of Chaos would be rewarded with titles and lands, gold and dragons, glory beyond imagining. He rose up above the outer city wall following the trail of wreckage left by his companions, up and up. But first they must take the Palace, and the WarLock King did not want it spoilt. The outer walls and towers mattered not. But he wanted the trappings of power, the historic royal palace and fortress built about the huge White Tower that dominated the City. The vast curtain walls and forts could fall but the symbolic ancient Keep would declare his power and right to rule.

CHAPTER ONE-HUNDRED-AND-TWENTY-SIX
My Mantle Shall Pass to You

Quenelda might have known Drumondir would be waiting for her at the span to the HeartRock.

'Child,' the BoneCaster hugged her fiercely. 'I have been waiting for you since word came from Tangnost that you fought the hobgoblins! No,' she put a finger to Quenelda's lips. 'Tell me later, once we have won. You have work to do here. But let me bind those wounds properly.'

Quenelda smiled gratefully, although the bindings would not survive her transformation to a dragon. But she allowed it, knowing Drumondir was doing it out of love, was desperate to help in any way she could. Exhaustion was a heartbeat away, and no one could take that away.

As they entered the HeartRock, the din of battle faded, although you could still feel the violence of the assault throughout the island. In its stead the familiar thread of a melody rose, the joyous chime of a flute beckoning, welcoming Quenelda as she sat. But a discordant note now disturbed the rhythm, a dark thread ran through it as it had once before. Something uncoiled in answer to a summons, but then its notes were drowned out.

Drumondir blinked as the throne shone in a radiant flare of wild magic. Was it the throne growing smaller or Quenelda growing larger? It was as if the great bones were rearranging themselves, assuming their original form and overlaying those of the young Dragon

Whisperer at their heart. As the inner radiance grew almost unbearably bright, Drumondir saw the ghostly bones shrink and begin to knit into their true pattern as the girl within became a dragon without.

Never fear, my mantle shall pass to you, sweet sister…

It was no more than a whisper, but now Drumondir heard it.

'My brothers,' Quenelda's voice rang out, underlain by another. 'My sisters. Dragon Isle calls for aid. A creature born of eternal darkness breaches our sanctuary, so that another may enter here and plunder our heritage. May take our One Earth from us and all that we hold dear.

'Will you answer my summons?'

CHAPTER ONE-HUNDRED-AND-TWENTY-SEVEN
Fell and Deadly

'Majesty,' Simon deMontfort laid his sword at the Queen's feet, blood riling from a deep wound. He could hear the feral growl of the crowd outside the castle baying for blood, furious that the Black Prince had eluded them. Darcy had not been found amongst the living or the dead.

The Queen's expression was glacial, Simon looked at Sir Gharad, once Strike Commander and now the Queen's Champion. Would the old soldier understand?

'Tell us why we should not execute you,' the Queen's voice was cold. 'For your many crimes.'

'Majesty, I have purposely placed myself in your power. I have fought my friends today.'

'It was you, the lone Imperial who attacked them? Who flew the royal standard?'

'My Lord Constable, yes.'

'You seek only to save your skin.'

'Majesty, no.' The young knight unbluckled his breastplate to reveal a hidden surcoat in the colours of the royal house. 'I have hidden and protected villagers many times. If Darcy knew of it, he would have killed me without hesitation. He has grown fell and deadly like his Sire. I let prisoners go when I could. I do not wish to be part of what he has become. But no man can kill him; he should have died today at the hands of your brave Warden. His ensorcelled armour is forged with words of Making, of sky metal. But I can help you capture him.'

'How?'

'My standard, Majesty,' he held out the hated green banner. 'Raise it above the castle. He is eager to capture you for his father. He will fall for the ruse. He was ever reckless. Once he is on the ground you can take him. I can welcome him, stand at the inner gate. He trusts me. He will dismount.'

'If his armour is woven of the Abyss, how may we capture him without losing more brave knights? Too many have died this day already.'

Sir Gharad laid a hand on her arm. 'We have just the means, Caitlin. Captain?'

CHAPTER ONE-HUNDRED-AND-TWENTY-EIGHT
Invincible

The smoking, shattered summit of the island was pocked with craters and hillocks of the dead as Darcy circled, heart suddenly catching in his chest. Had so few of his friends survived their encounter with the Warden of the Wall? The Knights of Chaos Imperials were grounded about the broken battle ground and the ruined inner bailey of the castle, with mounds of dead about them. The falling snow was turning them into featureless hillocks. But finally, the royal standard was no longer flying from the White Tower; his own flew there.

Huge crowds were gathered in ugly mood. He could see their raised fists as they cursed him, but they were held at bay by sabretooths and vampires. It was clearly over, there was no one left to fight. He laughed. Nothing could withstand him.

Darcy banked over the courtyard, the thunder of wings flattening everyone with its back draft. Simon! His childhood friend stood in front of the inner portcullis waving. Braziers were burning in the courtyard and beside the drawbridge. Smoke hung thickly on the ground. He reined Night Mare in. Sabretooths raced down spread wings as troops poured down the tail to form a guard. Where were the rest of his friends? Celebrating in the great hall? Darcy mounted his magnificent pedigree sabretooth already harnessed in royal trappings. Escorted by his standard bearer, his retinue passed through the tumbled outer gate tower.

A half dozen of his knights, supported by men-at-arms, had just reached the inner portcullis when cauldrons were emptied down the murder holes. Boiling oil! Screaming, troops leapt to the side to find they were perfectly well. With a triumphant shout they ran on. Darcy sneered. Whatever it was, it wasn't stopping anyone. Killing a wounded man-at-arms who rose threateningly with a flash of black, he spurred his pedigree sabretooth forwards and under the arch. The young prince was elated. Nothing could stop him now. He would take the Queen to his father in triumph.

It was almost like the patter of rain on armour that fell on his head. Darcy looked down, confused, at the dark rusty specks. Only, drops of rain normally ran downwards whereas these were spreading in all directions. He shook his arm greaves as he reined the dragon in. They didn't fall off the smooth metal. What in the Abyss? With irrational rising panic, he shook again, then grabbed his gorget. *Scale mites?* Gods, they were everywhere, digging their little teeth in!

Then his sabretooth began bucking violently, and he was unseated and kicked as he fell. He landed heavily, head spinning. All about, sabretooths were throwing their riders, rolling on their backs, and drooling. Darcy's sword slipped from his grasp. Discarded armour was flying all over the inner bailey as he lay clawing at his buckles. One of his knights was hopping around in his long johns, and about to abandon even them when a large lady in dusty apron felled him with a rolling pin! All over the drawbridge his knights were meeting a similar fate.

Even so, he was still frantically trying to discard his

ensorcelled armour when the tip of a sword grazed his throat and a pointed boot pressed down on his breastplate. 'Yield,' the Queen said, grey eyes hard as flint. 'Or die. I care not which you choose.'

CHAPTER ONE-HUNDRED-AND-TWENTY-NINE
Earth, Fire, Wind and Water

The chamber was suddenly gone, its boundaries pushed back as power bloomed, the weight of it pressing Drumondir to her knees. The music fell silent. The four stone dragons were kindling with a soft inner light, growing rapidly in size. Drumondir moved away from Quenelda's side as the nearest statue combusted, and a beautiful fiery Imperial, wreathed in **fire,** rose up and up. Stretching her wings, she moved towards Quenelda and melted into her, so that the young Dragon Whisperer became slightly more substantial with scales of gold and red and orange.

Aware of the immense privilege, Drumondir watched with bated breath as a second dragon began to move, becoming fluid; a restless tide of hues, all the colours of the **sea** from storm to sunset. Shaking out its wings, showering Drumondir with water, it too approached Quenelda only to melt within her, and more of her scales coloured, became visible. The third was **earthy** hues of ochre, russet, glorious browns and green. Filling the HeartRock fleetingly with the scent of loam and spring it too was gone. More of Quenelda's scales took on hue and colour and substance. The fourth was almost transparent; fleeting clouds, rose sunsets, the **wind** over a field of barley. Then Quenelda and Drumondir were alone in the HeartRock. Her scales were no longer black, they shone and shifted with every colour imaginable. The colours of living magic, of the One Earth.

When Quenelda lifted her head, Drumondir saw the

dragon in the girl for the first time. Quenelda was the same, and yet she was different. It was as if a girl had taken the throne, but now a young woman sat in her place. She stood with the certainty of a Dragon Whisperer, her molten eyes as bright as the sun, and just as dangerous. Drumondir raised a hand lest she was blinded. The ground was beginning to tremble like a fluttering heart. Dragon Isle was coming *alive*!

'I have to kill this creature...this dark dragon will never stop. Our kindred are dying in the testing of it, and the Isle will fall. HE is coming.' As another thud shook the bones of Dragon Isle, Quenelda spread her wings and vanished.

Standing on shaking legs, Drumondir staggered and sat down again on the steps. *Earth, Wind, Fire and Water: she has shed her juvenile scales, she has come of age...perhaps there is hope!* And then, as Drumondir stood with jerking steps to return to the Infirmary, where she was badly needed, she remembered the last lines from the One Earth Saga and finally understood them: they meant Son of the Morning Star and Dancing with Dragons:

Earth, wind, fire and water,
Earth's own son,
Earth's own daughter.

CHAPTER ONE-HUNDRED-AND-THIRTY
Armelia

The silence rang loudly in Armelia's head as she searched the cratered battlefield for Findibar. She found herself in the moat, almost filled with the dead or dying. Friends were searching for loved ones. A surgeon and apothecaries were helping soldiers lift the wounded. Fumbling and falling, she was utterly spent. Numb from the horror and shock, head aching, bleary eyed, she tripped and fell heavily over a body. Ochre dust encrusted her from boot to hood, her ragged cloak about her as she crunched over broken bodies at the ruins of the palace Gate Tower, what was left of it, seeking sanctuary. Her mail was rust mixed with blood. She had not even felt the wounds she had taken in her fight to stay alive ~ she was numbed in body and soul. A dead soldier had fallen over her, protecting her from the mob who had run rampage, taking no prisoners. She had seen one of Darcy's friends pulled down and torn apart by the mob.

Their rage still throbbed in the air, but she had heard a familiar voice calling citizens back to the pentangle where their wounds would be tended. It was that voice Armelia now sought as the Queen walked the battlefield, with Winifred by her side, searching for and tending the injured. She pulled the silk standard she had hidden next to her heart, cherishing this one reminder of home.

'Your Grace?' Winifred's eyes were narrowed.

'What is it?'

'There, Your Grace.'

Caitlin looked up from tending the wounded at the

figure staggering across the wreckage of the castle bailey, trailing a royal standard in the ash, its bright gold and russet a gleam of colour against the pale ash and snow. Its chain mail was too long, hair ragged as thistledown. And yet... And yet...eyes locked, one in horror, the other in dulled recognition.

'Caitlin?' Armelia's voice was rough and thick with smoke, ragged with grief as she staggered towards her Queen and friend.

'Armelia?' Caitlin threw her helmet off and stepped forwards, joy on her face, arms wide to gather up the broken figure. Powdered snow and ash was falling softly. Sound was muffled as Armelia slid on the rubble. She opened her mouth. 'Caitlin! There's a traitor in-'

Thunk! The arrow embedded itself in her right side, slamming Armelia to the ground where she tumbled over bodies and rocks into the tarry slush and blood.

'Noooooooooo!' the Queen screamed at the man-at-arms. 'Nooooooooooooo!'

'Your – your Grace?' The man's triumphant smile died. 'I-I thought it one of the Forsaken.'

But the Queen didn't hear him, didn't see anything but the body slumped in the puddle of filthy snow. She half fell into the crater as Winifred rushed to assist, stumbling as she cracked a shin. She never noticed the sharp ice take the skin from her hands as she effortlessly lifted the slight body of a young woman she looked upon as a second daughter.

'Armelia? No!' Resting in the inner courtyard, Chasing the Stars heard the cry of despair, and spreading her wings, sprang into the air.

CHAPTER ONE-HUNDRED-AND-THIRTY-ONE
Dragon Isle is Falling

Dragon Isle was shaking under the WarLock's assault. Dark sorcery had been unleashed: old as antiquity and cold as death. Where rock met sea, ice was racing inwards filling every crack, every crevice, splitting the island from within. Basalt exploded into lethal shards. Enormous cliffs, sheering from the Isle, fell into the sea, falling through dark columns of smoke, wreaking havoc and ruin upon the soldiers who still fought on the ice. Jakart's retreating battlemages of the III FirstBorn were collapsing the inner coombs to stay the WarLock's passage, casting wards as he pulled his own men through traps to safety. Quenelda could feel the shining aura of the Guardian, gathering his battlemage's power into the Core, chaining it with spells and channelling their conjoined strength to her father. But it was not enough. Dragon Lords were dying, the distant grief of their Imperials a rising lament as they fell.

*Father...Storm...I am coming...I am bringing my brothers and sisters with me...wait for me...*Quenelda was a thought, a shadow as she blew through the broken tunnels, caverns and coombs to where the dark dragon Queen drove its defenders back.

The west flight cavern was rubble and bone. Men lay scattered like grains of sand. Frozen in black ice, dead dragons and their Lords were clustered in great mounds where they had held the WarLock and his creature for a while. Hundreds, perhaps thousands of Imperials had died here, before her father and the Guardian forbade them and withdrew them, cloaked with all their other dragons to the safety of the glen, far from this nightmare. Only Stormcracker had refused his Dragon Lord, his twin soul who needed his eyes, his voice. There was nothing Quenelda could do here. The black death had claimed the living, would claim any who lingered in this blighted place. Quenelda turned inwards.

Through the trail of carnage left by the WarLock and his army, through the retreating brigades and talons of battling sabretooths and BoneCrackers under Cawdor's command, who denied the WarLock King's Lords and soldiers every stride of the way, through the explosions and tumbling rocks, through the screams of the dead and dying, Quenelda passed, seeking only one quarry.

The battlefield at the centre of Dragon Isle reeked of fear and chaos as spell and counter spell spat death and destruction throughout its halls and galleries. Waves of black, writhing necrotic sorcery crashed in spumes of smoke against Dragon Lords' shields, rebounded and scythed down their unshielded troops like summer barley. Balls of fire shattered bones and rock with equal ease.

Hillocks of splintered bones and smoking armour lay thickly where Quenelda's father stood astride Stormcracker, Quester at his side, casting high battlemagic in an unrelenting blaze of white hot fury that held the WarLock's advance. About the King, without their dragons, cabals of BattleMages and Dragon Lords joined their own coruscating power to his to strike at the WarLock's black Queen: but they were exhausted, wounded, many struggling simply to stay alive as the cauldron of war raged about them. Although most of the WarLock King's Lords had fallen, unequal to the SDS's training and battlemagic, the dark dragon was death itself, and soon Dragon Isle would fall.

*She is coming...*Storm whispered as Dragon Isle trembled. *They are coming...*

The air cracked and snapped, heralding the young Dragon Whisperer's arrival between her father and her foe. Power burst about Quenelda in a blinding flash as she took dragon form and saw her enemy for the first time, the creature from her *dark dragon dreams.* A wave of charged air exploded outwards, stunning everyone. The WarLock blinked and shook his head as the blinding light faded, leaving images at the back of his eyes. By then an otherworldly dragon towered over him with an aura so hot it blazed like a star in the firmament. Its raw power sang joyfully in his mind, overlaying his dark dragon's triumph. He recognised that this creature was as ancient as his, as powerful as his.

How? What is it? Was this their vaunted Dragon Whisperer come to life? Doubt and fear whispered in his mind. Spinning in his Core, the Guardian was asking the same question as battlerunes blazed like molten gold. Dragon Isle had come alive: the HeartRock sang in defiance, and everyone in the Glen ~ friend or foe ~ could hear its terrible song.

Wings stretched to fill the cavern, the unearthly dragon's neck coiled back to strike the WarLock's dark Queen with fearsome fangs and white-hot dragon fire. The dark dragon Queen retaliated with a blast of frozen death. Unearthly screams cut through the air as they battled: dark against light, frost to flame. Then, as the WarLock began to beat back the exhausted young Dragon Whisperer, the one dragon at the nebula's epicentre become five ethereal dragons with blazing colourful auras.

What? What are these? Their primal elemental songs of creation filled the WarLock's head... Coloured threads were spinning, spinning about his Queen like a cocoon. He shrieked his rage as death erupted about them: earth, wind, fire and water had come alive.

It was as if jagged black shards of the Isle itself rose to engulf its enemies, crushing his dark dragon in a closing crippling fist. Ribs snapped and broke, blood that froze all it touched sprayed. In the same breath, the water dragon dissolved into icy seawater surging through the coombs to become an onrushing river of death sweeping away his troops and razorbacks, washing Dragon Isle clean of enemies, leaving its defenders whole, before hunting those hobgoblins who remained in the loch. Flame hot as a furnace roared in a wash of potent crackling breath that killed his dragon's bitter burning kiss. Screaming, the Queen began futilely snapping at her tormentors, just as a wind howled through the broken Isle, plucking the WarLock from her back before sweeping over the ice to drive the remnants of his Armada onto the rocks and ruin.

Armour smoking, beset on all sides, recognising with disbelief the doom of his ambition in the thrashing death throes of his chaotic dark dragon Queen, the WarLock unleashed a necrotic spell. Toxic sorcery lashed out across the chamber, venomous green tendrils snaking and snapping on a hundred thousand hungry fingers: the darting fangs of snakes bringing death to all the Dragon Lords and troops who had defied him, to all on Dragon Isle within his reach.

With a calm inner peace that had eluded him since he fought Galtekerion, Quester embraced his death and flung himself to stand as a living shield in front of his King. The maelstrom took the young knight full on his chest and he was thrown across the crumbling chamber to slam into the far wall, where he slid brokenly down onto the bones below, bloodied royal standard beneath him.

Raging, under cover of his deep cold spell's chaos, the WarLock abandoned his mortally wounded Queen and his body, and swept upwards like dark dust through cracks and crevices towards the beating heart of Dragon Isle, following a fine black thread that sang to him. *Where was his son? His hostages? Why had his son failed him?*

CHAPTER ONE-HUNDRED-AND-THIRTY-TWO
Heart Attack

The dark air was alive with icy winds that thrummed through the deserted broken coombs, searching for a way into the hidden heart. Dragon Isle's battlemages and Dragon Lords were engaged elsewhere, unaware yet he had slipped their grasp. But Jakart DeBessart had not been idle, and every passageway and path was sown with cunning and powerful wards and traps, throwing up webs to ensnare him, sounding the alarm. Even as the Strike Commander and his battlemages raced to confront him, guided by the Guardian, he eluded them, floating through their nets like smoke. Yet everywhere he was thwarted in his attempt to reach the HeartRock.

Battlemages were returning to Dragon Isle every few heartbeats, knowing now where the true threat lay. He could feel them adding their strength to the Core, their conjoined power channelled to the King, now driving his mortally wounded Queen back. Time was no longer on his side; the Guardian would surely turn all his power towards him the moment his dark dragon Queen died. But he was within heartbeats of gaining his prize, and then even Dragon Isle's collective might could not thwart him.

WarLock King flowed through the maze towards its centre, like smoke blown by the wind, using deception to cloak himself, so that those eyes that saw him did not know it, and slid onwards, did not raise a hue and cry. Questing, hunting, following the dark thread of power that led to the HeartRock. Finally, he found it.

CHAPTER ONE-HUNDRED-AND-THIRTY-THREE
The Queen is Dead

The dark dragon was dying but still deadly, lashing out with her dying throes she could yet bring the SDS to their knees, Dragon Isle to ruin. Sensing the WarLock had fled, summoning the First Born to return to her father's and Dragon Isle's aid, Quenelda was gone, wind rushing through coombs striking a chord like a harp's silver notes that resonated through the island. Fear turned to sudden joy: Root and Two Gulps were waiting for her at the HeartRock, understanding where she would finally come, where she had to come.

'Quenelda!' Root hugged her fiercely as she became his friend once more, aghast at her dull eyes, her broken scales, the multiple injuries she had taken, the injured arm.

'Quenelda, you can't face him alone, not after fighting his dark dragon! Wait. I'll go and fetch the Guardian or your father...Tangnost. I-'

The ground cracked as ice raced inwards, embracing all that stood in its path. The Dragon Guards froze in a single breath, falling to shatter into crystals as Quenelda threw up a shield about her friend.

'Go! Go!' Quenelda screamed as her eyes blazed in the onrushing darkness. 'It's too late. You are no good here. **He** is coming! Flee!'

Calling Two Gulps, Root fled.

Infinite coldness closed about Quenelda, cutting her off from Dragon Isle, from breath, from thought. The blazing rune at the heart of the Guardian's Core that was Quenelda, winked out. The Guardian stopped breathing. Had their young Dragon Whisperer just fallen?

A wounded young woman, armoured in scales, barred the WarLock's way across the narrow bridge that arced the dark span to the HeartRock. Somehow, she had arrived before him. Briefly puzzled the WarLock smiled inwardly. Now he had the living key to open this greatest of mysteries. Yet he felt no aura, only exhaustion and fear.

A child in a suit of armour! She surely could not be the creature he had just fought! Whose wrath had crushed his Queen?

And yet... The WarLock King hesitated. The Heart-Rock itself thrummed with power. He could feel the threat of its wards as if it were a living creature.

What lies in this place?

You dare? Quenelda's hollow words rang in his mind as she sought to hide her weakness, to delay him, to await the return of her brothers and sisters should the dark Queen die. A surge of invisible power filled her; the slumbering Matriarch had heard her child's need.

You dare to seek the power and knowledge of the Elders? It is beyond you! The voice, suddenly cold and ancient as the stars, vibrated through the air. It was no longer Quenelda's...*you have enslaved the Elders, there will be a blood price to pay...*

Startled, the WarLock hesitated, recognising the unfettered magic now behind her words, but not understanding them; he dismissed the frisson of doubt, the single heartbeat of fear. His Armada might be shattered, his gorrangochs dead, his hobgoblins lost, but the true prize was almost his. A smoking man-like creature infused with chaotic power took form, veined in green with eyes of utter darkness. Radiating malice and madness he moved forwards hungrily to the edge of the bridge, drinking up the darkness. Whatever had attacked his dark Queen, they were not here. The King's daughter stood alone. Foolish. Futile.

He released a spell of screaming bitter cold to test her. Quenelda rebuffed it. *I will deny you... I am One Kind born of the One Earth, and I deny you this place...*her aura bloomed brightly woven of many colours.

One Kind? What childish nonsense was this?

Laughing, the WarLock struck again. Spells and counter spells coruscated between them, shattering rock, burning the very air, collapsing the coombs. Only the HeartRock behind her took no damage, but Quenelda's aura was dimming with each strike. The WarLock was gradually driving her back across the span, as virulent power spat and sparked from his hands. He hurled freezing fireballs, struck with daggers of green lightning. She was jerking backwards like a puppet with broken strings, retreating across the yawning span that nurtured the HeartRock. Spells crashed against the basalt pulverising huge chunks. The roof cracked and crashed about them.

Falling to her knees, eyes closed, exhausted, the King's daughter raised her head, arms outstretched as if embracing her approaching death.

Brothers... sisters... I need you...answer me, else we will fall to the bottomless Abyss...

Hearing her silent plea, the WarLock misunderstood and laughed.

Your brothers and sisters are chained... They serve the maelstrom... Smoke roiled as the WarLock raised his arms to gleefully gather the injured young Dragon Whisperer into the swirling dark dust that was him.

Tripping, slipping on the ice, out of breath, Root ran to stand in front of his kneeling friend, to block the bitter cold that reached out to her.

'Q-q-quenelda! Y-your father is on his way, and the G-guardian too. Flee, Q-q-quenelda.' He felt the WarLock's cold malice shift from her to him.

This peasant! This gnome who had denied him last year by capturing Galtekerion. 'You,' the WarLock's scorn burnt the air between them, 'who will not lift a hand; you think to deny me the HeartRock. Will she still be able to fight when I throw your body at her feet? She loves you. A weakness- I will cripple you.'

'L-love is not a weakness. It is a s-strength that

outmatches your hate.' Courage hanging by a thread, breathing hard and fast, knowing he was going to die, Root stood his ground, buying Quenelda precious time. As the smoking apparition moved, ice cracked beneath its darkness and the basalt coomb about the HeartRock fractured and exploded outwards. Dragon Isle rocked to its roots. Screaming in pain as shards pierced his leather armour, Root became unbearably cold. Smoking bones reached out towards Quenelda's inert slumped form, ignoring the gnome ~ the WarLock would deal with him later. Gnomes were nothing. The boy had no weapon.

'NOOOO!' With all his supressed rage and grief for his lost family, for his enslaved people, for Bracus his friend, for Armelia whom he loved so much, for his friend, Quenelda, Root struck with all his might with his wychwood dagger, thrusting it into the WarLock. There was a shriek as it avidly burrowed into the darkness, roots spreading, constricting the writhing figure within. Darkness spat and hissed. As Root collapsed to the ground, as his frozen hand and wrist shattered in an explosion of pain, the young gnome screamed a name.

Scales sparked as an avenging golden fireball hurtled into the fractured chamber from a coomb. In a heartbeat, an enraged flaming Two Gulps had locked talons into the basalt and unfurled in the same space as the WarLock King, who imploded.

The WarLock was trying to pull himself back together when the air combusted. A whirlwind of flame in dragon form drove him back across the span and then was gone as Quenelda's dull scales took on the vibrant colours of fire. Water foamed and frothed as a dragon washed through the WarLock and disappeared. Scales of greens and blues now clothed the young Dragon Whisperer. Wind sang avenging through the coombs, dispersing the WarLock's smoking form and died away. As the WarLock gathered himself for a final strike the wrecked chamber shook, as an earth and green dragon shredded the darkness, only to vanish.

What is this? What are they?

In their place, a fearsome dragon raised its head where the young woman had knelt, its aura and wings blazed in a rainbow of colours. *A Dragon Whisperer? It is true?* Glowing molten eyes were raised towards the WarLock, alive with an inner rage, alive with the power of a sun. He averted his eyes. It was as if the very Earth was defying him. The Dragon Whisperer struck: fire to ice, life to death.

The WarLock screamed, knowing he was beaten. Taut violence filled the chamber as the void was summoned. A concussion of thunder shook the Isle as the King, led by Quester, raced for the HeartRock with a score of battlemages, stumbled and fell as rubble blocked their path. The Guardian in the Core, seeing the shield that had hidden the battle fall, summoned Dragon Lords on Imperials to fly to the Cauldron to drop into the shattered heart of the Isle. For the dark dragon Queen was finally destroyed, her cold song silenced, and the Dragon Whisperer's bright golden song was fading too.

There was a rupture in the fabric of creation. A black hole was forming about the WarLock King, its ragged edges sucking in everything about it. Dragon Isle began to collapse inwards, dense gravity pulling in huge slabs of rock. Light itself dimmed. Emerald tendrils licked out towards Quenelda trying to pull her in. As the black hole closed about the WarLock, he loosed his final blow. The maelstrom took the Imperial full in the chest as he vanished. With a grunt, the great horned head went down; one dragon fractured into five, and then back into a young woman. Quenelda fell.

As she died, the flaming sabretooths clearing the coombs became dust in the wind. Seadragons hunting the last hobgoblins swirled like ink and were gone. The storm blasting the wrecked Armada died, and with it the blizzard, and the air became still. Granite-hued Imperials defending the cliffs crumbled and fell to the ocean. Silence and snow fell softly over the battlefield.

Root sat up and swayed, eyes coming back into focus; blood pouring from nose and ears. Scorched and glowing molten magma lay everywhere. Green motes sparked and snapped but otherwise it was eerily silent, as if Dragon Isle held its breath. The chamber was torn open to the sky; but the HeartRock still stood. Ash drifted down. Two Gulps was curled about Quenelda's smoking body. His scales were cracked and burnt, his talons split, his eyes weeping.

'Quenelda?' Shattered wrist against his chest, Root scrabbled to her side. 'Oh, no...no...no...'

Rage and grief filled the air as Root cradled his friend within Two Gulp's protective wing, clumsily wiping the blood that trickled from her nose and ears. Her chest was a mangled ruin: girl and dragon were clearly dead. Two Gulps lifted his head and roared his agony. Words whispered through the ruins.

Can I survive now you are gone?
Can I survive the silence of your song?
Can my heart beat whilst yours is still?
Can my heart beat long years until
I am with you again?

CHAPTER ONE-HUNDRED-AND-THIRTY-FOUR
You're too Late

'You're too late.' Covered in thick ash and blood, barely recognisable, Root was sitting in a crater amongst the fractured rock, cradling Quenelda's head when Jakart DeBessart arrived with a dozen battle mages, at the same time as an Imperial dropped through the shattered coombs to land with a resonant thump. More rock fell as the BoneCrackers fanned out.

'Secure the Isle,' the Strike Commander ordered, as he knelt beside Quenelda's body. 'Then the Black Isle and the glen. Hunt them down,' his voice was cold. 'Destroy them.'

'You're too late.' Root's bitterness stung Jakart. 'Why didn't you come to her aid? She's fought three battles today. She saved the Black Isle, held the line against a banner in the Labyrinth; yet when we landed she was attacked for not fighting the dark dragon. She wasn't ready. She wasn't strong enough yet. She summoned the First Born to help you drive the dark dragon back, and yet she ended up fighting the WarLock alone. Alone! Where were you? Where was the Guardian? It's all been for nothing,' and he began to hopelessly cry.

The shattered bones of his frozen arm gleamed white against necrotic black as death crept up his arm, reaching out to claim one final life. Only one person was able to turn back the black death, and she lay dead in his arms. Root would soon follow her across the bridge leaving loss and pain behind. Ghosts of his family whispered, beckoning him to cross.

Hearing of the battle between the WarLock King and their Dragon Whisperer at the heart of Dragon Isle, soldiers began to gather; taking their helmets off, they placed fist over heart. Some knelt, knowing they had sent her to her death to save themselves, unable to face Root's accusing gaze. Night was falling.

'She wasn't ready for this yet, Root repeated, rocking back and forwards. 'Not yet. Not today.'

Drumondir arrived. Summoned urgently from the hospital by Jakart, she saw for herself the un-survivable wounds and shook her head. Root would not let Quenelda's burnt and broken body go, and Two Gulps threatened any who came near the pair. Her heart breaking, Drumondir laid a gentle hand on Root's shoulder as the youth flinched from her touch.

'Root,' Drumondir's voice was soft, appealing, aghast at his injury. 'Root, you're badly hurt. You'll die if you don't let me tend to you.'

CHAPTER ONE-HUNDRED-AND-THIRTY-FIVE
An Age of Wonders

The first Imperials were putting down from the Labyrinth with the surviving Juveniles on board, along with their sabretooths. BoneCrackers were still pushing back the hobgoblins, hunting them through the Labyrinth while the Tunnel Rats were blowing up the maze of caverns and passages. The injured were being carried to the hospital, though some refused to leave their sabretooths. The dead were laid gently down at the end of the long lines forming on the broken crown of Dragon Isle. Thousands had died, tens of thousands: the true number would never be known.

Drumondir, desperate, unable to help Root or Quenelda, was there to greet their talon, along with cauldrons of soup, and warm blankets. They were filthy, eyes blinking white in blackened faces, stumbling, most carrying injuries, some severe. Swiftly, efficiently, she roughly bound and treated the worst of their injuries, binding them with rags torn from cloaks.

Overhead an Imperial of the Queen's flight, escorted by a dozen Faculty Guard, put down on the remaining Academy pads bearing Caitlin and Winifred; along with news that the Black Isle had been attacked but had held against the Black Prince and his Knights of Chaos ~ at great cost. The news leapt from mouth to mouth as all those who had family there were left in an agony of suspense.

The King sent a harrier for Drumondir. Root had seemingly died from his injuries and she was needed. The

King had carried his daughter's broken body to her mother's chambers. Two Gulps refused any but Tangnost to gather up Root's body. Still, as she slowly made her tearful way up through broken halls, between exhausted and injured troops, to the royal chambers in the Academy, Drumondir saw desperate hope in everyone's eyes, as if the Ice Bear BoneCaster could raise their Dragon Whisperer from the dead.

A shuffling figure, limping, bandaged roughly, head bowed, nearly collided with her outside the royal apartments.

'Tangnost?'

The one-eyed dwarf raised a ravaged face, streaked with blood. Drumondir was aghast at the defeat she read there. Opening her arms, she clasped the Dragon Master to her. He allowed it for a moment then stepped backward as the Queen passed them at a run, armed guards trying to keep up, but he held her hand to his chest. Tangnost took a deep breath.

'Thank you. I am needed, as you are.'

She nodded. 'I will look for you later.'

'Noooooo! Nooo!' The cry was heart-breaking.

Now the King gathered his wife up, pressing her head to his shoulder. 'Hush…hush, my love,' he rocked her in his arms. But Caitlin knew it was one grief too many to bear. Armelia fought for her life, and now her daughter and Root were dead. Laid out, pale and broken.

Drumondir and Winifred's joyous reunion was muted by grief. Drumondir looked at her friend in dinted armour as black as her pinched exhausted face, and knew there was a glorious story to tell ~ only later. Winifred looked into the BoneCaster's grieving eyes and knew there was a magical story and terrible grief to share, but not yet. Now they were both needed to tend to the injured ~ and the grieving.

Sir Gharad arrived from the Palace on a second Imperial that had broken the sound barrier to bring one of the greatest soldiers in the Kingdoms to his dying son. He was too late. Armour, surcoat and face covered with blood, it couldn't hide his raw grief. 'My son?' Head bowed, shoulders shaking, he could barely speak as hot tears ran down his face.

We only just found each other…he is all I have…

Drumondir barely held back tears of her own as she held out a hand to the trembling man, and holding it tightly, she led him through to the royal apartments, tears flowing down her face.

We love in moments…we grieve for a lifetime…

She stopped in her tracks. The grievous injuries that had claimed Root's life were gone. The missing hand that had held the wychwood dagger had regrown: the young man's arm and shoulder, where the green tendrils of the black death had claimed him, were now sheathed in warm glowing wychwood. Swiftly crossing the room, she held fingers to the young gnome's neck.

'He's alive!'

Sir Gharad's head snapped up. His face lit and in one joyous bound he was by his son's side, holding Root's other hand to his heart. Tears ran down his strong face as he kissed Root's forehead.

'Root, my son, my heart,' he whispered. 'Rest and

grow strong. You are loved, my son. Come back to us.'

The face raised to Drumondir was suffused with joy; alive again with hope and energy. Leaving the old soldier, she quietly entered the Queen's chamber to where Caitlin sat with her daughter, comforted by Winifred.

'Your Grace? Caitlin. Do not give up hope yet. Wonders may yet happen. Come,' she beckoned. Face knit with grief, the Queen stood, puzzled.

'Have they found Quester?'

Drumondir shook her head sadly. 'I have no news, but Root...'

'Gharad,' the Queen whispered as her Champion's eyes met hers. 'Old friend, my heart sings for you. Truly, it is a time of wonder, as it is of grief.'

'He is bound in a healing cocoon of wychwood,' Drumondir said. 'He is safe now. I am needed elsewhere.'

She bowed and left as Sir Gharad took Caitlin in his arms and lent her his strength and hope.

CHAPTER ONE-HUNDRED-AND-THIRTY-SIX
The Guardian

The Guardian arrived in the Cauldron, along with the dawn. He walked amongst the Juveniles, one by one, by one. Talking softly to them, squeezing a shoulder, holding those that needed someone to hold on to, listening to their stories, making sure the quartermaster provided food and fodder for their mounts, that a healer tended them, he moved on. It would be nightfall before he returned to Dragon Isle.

The day brightened. As the Juveniles finally stood with their sabretooths, to be taken to the hospital and the roosts or barracks, weary blooded troops, healers, Faculty Guard and Dragon Lords formed a line on either side, fists on chests, to honour the youngsters who had saved the Black Isle, who had held the line unaided; whose talon leader and scout now lay dead. Celebration was muted by grief.

CHAPTER ONE-HUNDRED-AND-THIRTY-SEVEN
From the Ashes a Life shall be Kindled

'What are you saying?' The King's voice was broken like his heart. His daughter was dead, and nothing could change that. There was no time for private grief. He was needed elsewhere to rally the SDS and the Kingdoms. A great battle had been won but the cost had yet to be counted. Casualties and field hospitals were overwhelmed. He had to be seen, to talk to his troops, to co-ordinate the shattered aftermath, to restore government. Lords had been taken hostage, troops had surrendered, but the SDS and the Black Isle were in no mood for forgiveness towards those who had brought war to their heart and homes.

The situation room, still intact, was crowded as strike commanders, Dragon Lords, squadron leaders and talon leaders and Brigades were slowly reporting in, as Jakart took charge of hunting down the remnants of the War-Lock's army. Medical supplies, food and fodder were now being distributed by the 6th, 9th and 12th Heavy Logistics Brigades, and the mammoths of the Ice Brigades.

'Your Grace,' Dare she offer hope, after the gift of Root's life being returned?

'The bones of the DragonBone Chair are your daughter's twin's bones: before she came to your aid with the First Born, I saw them become one for the first time,' Drumondir explained. 'There is great power there still. I think we should build a pyre from those bones. Son of the Morning Star has waited a long time for his twin to be born, to pass his mantle to her. It is now her throne: it is fitting.'

The King nodded. Storm had told him to lay Dancing with Dragons on the bones of Son of the Morning Star, that she must return to the stars. He had not understood.

'Rufus?' Tangnost was grey with fatigue and injuries and loss. He was Quenelda's sworn Shield, yet she had died because he was not there to protect her. 'With your permission?'

The King agreed.

Tangnost followed Drumondir through the devastated island to where the HeartRock stood untouched. He summoned apprentices and engineers, those that could be spared. With block and tackle, with every spare, able-bodied volunteer who flocked to the HeartRock when they heard word, they managed to clear a path through the rubble, then to harness sabretooths. Even so the size and weight of the bones nearly defeated them. It took ten sabretooths to drag each bone to the porting stone, then from the Academy out into the Cauldron. It took all day.

Aided by thousands of returning soldiers, they built a pyre from the wreckage of the east side of the Academy. The bones glowed with a soft inner radiance as the witching hour approached. There, amidst the still smoking fires from battle, each was set upon the pyre by Stormcracker Thundercloud and Phoenix Firestorm. Two Gulps, badly injured, never left her side; his raw cries wrenching the hearts of all who heard.

As the sky darkened to indigo, Quenelda's body was carried out. Stormcracker's great mouth gently lifted her from her father's arms and laid it atop the bones. Somewhere a lone voice began to sing the lay of the Dragon Whisperer, a sound so sweet and pure, so full of longing and loss as it hung in the crisp air, that it made all those who heard catch their breath. A soldier with a pipe took up the tune, and then a second rougher voice joined the first, and another and another. The soldiers took up the refrain until all of Dragon Isle was alive with music in defiance of the WarLock. The beauty of it made Drumondir shiver.

As the lay ended, dragon song whispered through the glen, growing lounder and louder as wild dragons alighted on the Academy towers and turrets, on the Shard, on the cliffs.

Snowflakes gently brushed the Queen's eyelashes and cheeks like cold kisses, as she reached to kiss her daughter's cold lips one final farewell. Drumondir had dressed Quenelda in her suit of scales, so her dreadful wounds were hidden. She had washed the young woman's face and combed her hair. Her mother had placed a simple silver circlet about her brow, for she was also a Princess. The loss felt unbearable as the King and Queen stepped down.

In war the young die and the old are left to grieve... No parent should have to bury their child...

The ground vibrated. Imperials were converging on the pyre, moving softly and slowly, allowing the gathered to move back to safety. Long necks stretched forwards, blowing softly, breath steaming, they nudged and sniffed the body. Two Gulp's song ended. Then as one the Imperials and Two Gulps flamed. Incandescent dragon-fire licked the mound, setting those ancient bones alight and Quenelda was hidden from them. A torch was raised in the crowds, a lantern, and then another and another, pushing back the darkness. Out on the loch, seeing it, the ice clans raised burning brands from their fires. It was as if the stars had fallen to the Sorcerers Glen to bear their Dragon Whisperer home.

Flanked by those Juveniles who could still stand, Root was held by the strong arms of his father, an aching pain where the Abyss had touched him and a deeper ache in his heart. His father had revealed Armelia was fighting for her life, and only his son's dreadful wound held Root from flying to her side. Root realised that soldiers were pressing forwards, throwing small tokens into the flames, murmuring, some openly asking for forgiveness. Swords and arrows, leather belts, gilded helmets, coins. Many were openly weeping. The ashes of the pyre collapsed in on itself sending a fountain of sparks skywards. He was her esquire. He was supposed to keep her safe.

*Sweet sister...*just a whisper...*my mantle shall pass to you...I shall wait for you amongst the stars...*

The fire folded in on itself and the DragonBone Throne collapsed in a flurry of ash. The flames died away almost to darkness. Root hung his head. It was over. He turned into his father's arms.

'Look,' Sir Gharad said softly.

Root raised his head.

Ethereal interstellar dust of rose and gold, green and blue swirled above the pyre; only there was no wind. Wreathed in swirling star dust, spidery filaments were rising, joining, taking shape. A dragon towered above them all…stars blazing from within.

'The cauldron of creation,' Drumondir whispered to Tangnost, gripping his hand, '…the cycle of life…' She bowed her head in homage. The soldiers behind Drumondir knelt. Rippling outwards, the armies ringing the pyre knelt.

Can you hear the drum beats drumming?
For the one who will be coming
From fire comes rebirth
New life from mother Earth
From grief comes hope
From flame comes smoke
After darkness comes the light
Day always follows night
Twin worlds may spin as one
About the distant sun
Now new Life has begun…

The dragons weren't weeping, Tangnost realised, as he bowed his head. They knew Quenelda had shed her juvenile scales: finally, Dancing with Dragons was becoming a true dragon, a juvenile no longer. The flames died.

Spreading her wings, Dancing with Dragons lifted her great head and called, her hot breath smoking in the freezing air so that water ran in torrents from the steep gable roofs of the Academy. The sound carried out across the water to bounce off the far mountains. High above, a storm of dragons danced, so many they blocked the stars: answering a summons to war for the heart and soul of the One Earth itself.

Far to the north, bodiless in the Void, the WarLock King sensed her distant awakening and was afraid.

Fear makes the heart fragile
death can shatter it
love can mend it
memory can cherish it.

oooOooo

If you want to help our armed forces veterans suffering from post-traumatic stress disorder (PTSD) ~ Quester, life changing injuries; Quenelda, disabled; Tangnost who lost an eye and cannot walk without pain; or blindness ~ the King Rufus DeWinter who learns to see with the help of his battledragon, Stormcracker ~ here are some UK armed forces charities:

https://www.rafbf.org/
https://www.helpforheroes.org.uk/
https://www.blindveterans.org.uk/
https://www.combatstress.org.uk/
http://www.ptsdresolution.org/
http://houndsforheroes.com/
https://www.ssafa.org.uk/about-us

Printed in Great Britain
by Amazon